ALSO AVAILABLE BY DANIEL KIRK

NOVELS

The *ELF REALM* TRILOGY

The Low Road

The High Road

The Road's End (forthcoming)

PICTURE BOOKS

Library Mouse

Library Mouse: A Friend's Tale

ELF REALM

THE HIGH ROAD

DANIEL KIRK

AMULET BOOKS

NEW YORK

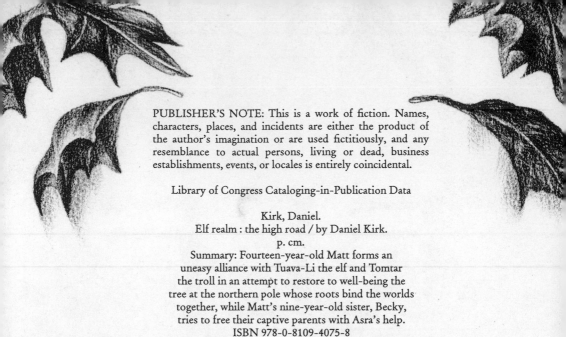

Library of Congress Cataloging-in-Publication Data

Kirk, Daniel.
Elf realm : the high road / by Daniel Kirk.
p. cm.
Summary: Fourteen-year-old Matt forms an
uneasy alliance with Tuava-Li the elf and Tomtar
the troll in an attempt to restore to well-being the
tree at the northern pole whose roots bind the worlds
together, while Matt's nine-year-old sister, Becky,
tries to free their captive parents with Asra's help.
ISBN 978-0-8109-4075-8
[1. Elves—Fiction. 2. Trolls—Fiction. 3. Magic—Fiction.]
I. Title. II. Title: High road.

PZ7.K6339Elh 2009
[Fic]—dc22
2009015494

Text and illustrations © 2009 Daniel Kirk

Book design by Chad W. Beckerman

Printed and bound in U.S.A.
10 9 8 7 6 5 4 3 2

ABRAMS
THE ART OF BOOKS SINCE 1949
115 West 18th Street
New York, NY 10011
www.abramsbooks.com

TO RALEIGH

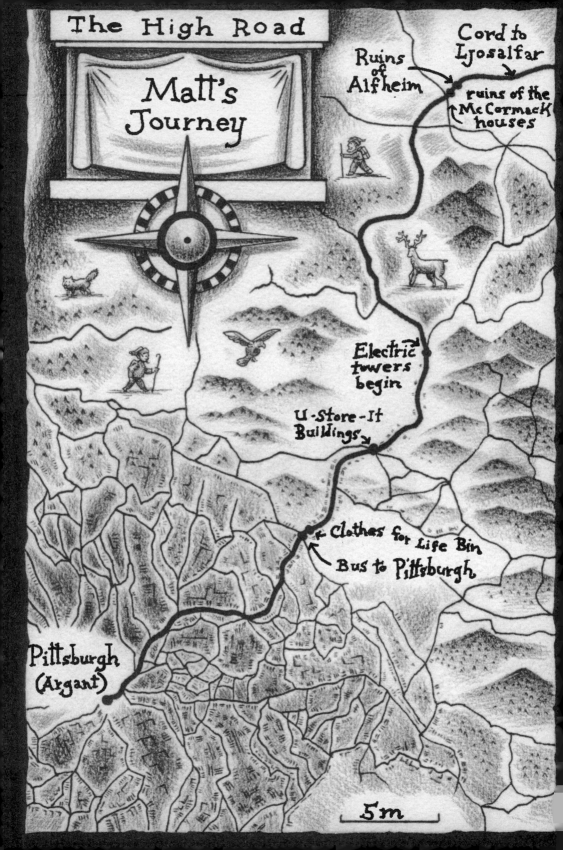

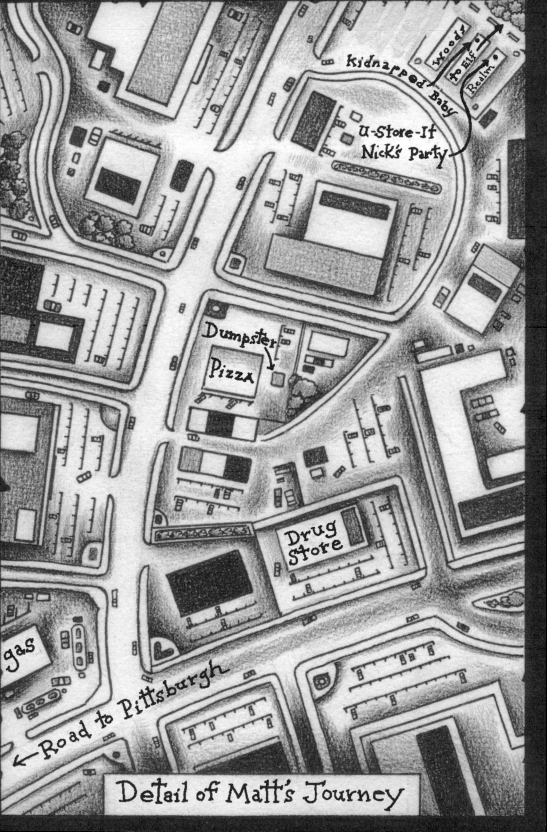

Detail of Matt's Journey

Detail of Matt's Journey

The High Road

1

MATT WAS FALLING. The ground had opened up beneath him, and as he plummeted headlong through a narrow tunnel, arms and legs flailing, there was no ending, just falling, falling, falling. When he tried to scream the roaring wind filled his throat, and only a sob escaped his lips. His mind was a blur. His panic was so intense that he couldn't concentrate on anything but the certainty that he was going to die. A heartbeat later he heard someone screaming. She plunged past him, bouncing off the milk-white walls of the tunnel. "Becky!" Matt cried.

"Matt!" she shrieked, tumbling head over heels, her voice raw with fear. "Matt, Matt!"

Suddenly the boy and his sister hurtled around a curve, and a ragged figure brushed past them, followed by another, and another, and another. Pale faces with huge gleaming eyes and pointed ears stared, then shot out of sight. With a sudden burst of shock and relief Matt realized that he wasn't falling, after all. It wasn't gravity pulling him down; it was something else, some unknown force, pulling him and his sister forward, in a vast tunnel, parallel to the ground but beneath it. They were in the Cord. They were traveling the Low Road, the Faerie passage hidden in the earth, and Matt and his sister weren't falling; they were *flying*. "Becky!" Matt cried. "Hold your hands out in front of you, keep your body straight and your eyes ahead. Look where you're going!"

"I can't," Becky sobbed, and bounced off another wall.

"Yes, you can! If I can do it, so can you!"

"I can't," Becky insisted, as Matt drew alongside her and took her hand in his.

"Then stay with me," he said, trying to keep his sister steady as they hurtled together through the tunnel. Even though Matt's heart was pounding, confidence welled up inside him; he felt a crazy certainty that he could do this, that he could navigate the Faerie passage, that he could lead himself and his sister to safety somewhere up ahead. "We're flying!" The words burst from him, fragile and explosive. "Becky, we're flying!"

Then in the distance he saw a dark line spread along the wall of the Cord, like an ink mark drawn by an invisible hand. There was a ripping sound. Dozens of tiny, filthy fingers reached into the tunnel and grabbed Becky by her hair. They yanked her from the Cord as Matt hurtled forward, unable to turn back.

In despair he clutched at the walls with his fingernails, trying to slow the insane velocity. His grip gave way. Then his perspective shifted again, and in horror he saw that he wasn't flying, after all. He was falling, down, down, down.

Silence. Matt opened his eyes and sat up in the darkness. He was breathing so hard that he felt dizzy. In the seconds it took to orient himself a glimmer of hope welled up inside, then vanished, leaving him in a place blacker than he could ever have imagined in his brief fourteen years of life. As he left the realm of dreams behind and entered the waking world, Matt had no doubt that this was the real nightmare. He wasn't at home in bed. He was in a cramped, moldy space beneath the roots of some enormous tree in the woods, where he had spent the night sleeping fitfully next to his sister on a pile of damp leaves. He brushed a leaf from his face, and peered into the darkness to see if Becky was still lying asleep beside him. He heard her quiet breath, regular and calm, and he decided to leave her alone. She was only nine. It wasn't fair to subject her to this insanity. Daytime would come too soon.

Matt crawled out from under the tree roots into the dark forest. His jeans and T-shirt were filthy, caked with dirt, even though he had turned his clothes inside out, like the Elves asked him to. Evil spirits, they said, would be less able to recognize someone with their clothes turned inside out. Around his neck hung a tangle of beads, amulets, and charms, designed to protect him from spells; or at least that's what the Elves told him. *All superstitious garbage, all of it*, Matt thought. There was a soggy lump of herbs tucked between his teeth and gums. He spit it out into the foliage. All night long he had kept the bitter herbs in his mouth, just like they had instructed. This was supposed to dull the pain from the markings they had tattooed on his chest, which they'd guaranteed would hurt. *They were right,* he thought. This was madness, all madness. And it was all his fault. Matt slipped his fingers beneath his T-shirt and felt the place where his skin had been marked. *To protect and help you,* the Elves had said. The tattoos were necessary to protect him from the dangers that lay ahead. *What dangers?* Matt thought. And how would they help? Was he crazy to agree to this? What was he thinking?

It had started with the shoe. It seemed like a lifetime ago, so much had changed since then. Matt's dad and mom had moved the family from their apartment in Pittsburgh to the hilly countryside north of town, to start a new life. Dad had inherited a big piece of property, and it was there that he built the houses on the edge of the rural highway. He was going to be a developer. He was going to transform the forest into a place where people could live. But Matt, running barefoot through the construction site, stepped on a little jeweled shoe, only two inches long, and everything changed. Matt hid the infection that began to fester in his foot. Then the Elves came to him in the night and demanded that he return it to them.

Elf, Matt pondered, was a funny word. When people thought of Elves they'd picture cartoon characters baking cookies in wood-fired ovens; they'd think of fairy tales, and silly stories meant

4

to entertain and amuse children. And yet, here were Matt and his sister, cowering in fear, obeying the commands of humanoid creatures who called themselves Elves. Because of the shoe, the little jeweled shoe, Matt had discovered a realm unknown to humans. It lay somehow parallel to his own world, though the bonds that kept these two worlds apart were coming undone. The Elves were at war, both with each other and with people; though there were few who knew that yet. The houses Matt's dad had built were all burned to the ground by some hideous, flying, fire-breathing things, and there was nowhere in the human world for Matt and his sister to go. Their parents and baby sister had been taken, abducted by a group of renegade Elves.

Matt peered into the darkness. Over the tops of the trees a streak of purple appeared; dawn was near. He heard what sounded like footsteps in the distance, clomping over the leaves on the forest floor. Elves, no doubt soldiers on guard, were patrolling the outskirts of the Elfin city of Ljosalfar. Matt moved carefully among the trees. His fingers touched carved wood; it was one of the totem poles sculpted by Neaca. She was an old friend of the Mage. The Mage had ruled Alfheim, the community of Elves that was destroyed in the firestorm that took Matt's own home. Now the Mage and her apprentice, Tuava-Li, were homeless, too, and they, along with Matt, Becky, and Tomtar, were all Neaca's guests. Neaca's forest home was surrounded by totem poles like the one Matt stood behind. She called them her *Klumma*.

"Matt, is that you?" a voice whispered from the gloom.

"Tomtar?" Matt replied.

Matt and Becky had gotten to know the Troll in the weeks after Matt had stepped on the jeweled shoe. Before the failed Elfin wedding, and the battle that followed. Before the fire. Before the black-robed Elfin monks took his parents and his baby sister in the flying machines. Before Prince Macta and the monk Jardaine entered his house with the ghost-girl, Anna, before the guns, and the fear, the running and the screaming, back when the world Matt knew was simple, and peaceful, and good. If Matt had a friend in this bleak place, it was Tomtar.

"What are you doing up so early?" Tomtar asked.

"I had a bad dream. I couldn't sleep. And these . . . these tattoos hurt. I think the elves are trying to kill me!"

Tomtar squatted in the brush between two *Klumma*. He glanced up at the boy through a mop of curls, wondering if he was making some kind of joke. "'Tisn't funny, Matt. I know you don't trust 'em, but you've got to try. The Mage knows better than us what's at stake."

Matt saw movement in the shadows ahead and ducked down. Lights, like torches, appeared. *Fire Sprites*. Matt mouthed the words. He'd seen them before, in the battle in the woods. A moment later a squadron of perhaps a hundred Elfin soldiers marched past. Matt was sure they would hear his beating heart, and the throb of blood pulsing in his veins. He squeezed his eyes shut. Soon the soldiers passed by, oblivious to the boy and the Troll. When their footsteps faded in the distance Tomtar grinned up at Matt. He rapped his knuckles on the *Klumma* and stood up to his full height of twenty-seven inches. "We've got to trust 'em, see? Old Neaca's lived here for ten thousand moons without bein' noticed, right here on the edge of Ljosalfar. These things she's carved, they keep the world away. We're as good as invisible as long as we stay inside their perimeter."

Matt stood back and gazed at the *Klumma*. It looked like a stack of grotesque heads piled one on top of the other, each face more ugly and threatening than the one below it. How could he and the Troll be invisible to other Elves, just because they were standing behind these terrifying wood carvings? "Where are the elves?" he asked.

Tomtar lifted his chin, pointing to the treetops. "Tuava-Li and the Mage are up there with Neaca in the high branches. They're getting ready for the sun to rise."

Just then Matt heard a faint sound. "It's Becky," he said, and he hurried through the undergrowth toward the gnarled old tree. Scraping his forehead on the tangle of branches, he tumbled into the leaf-dense pit and found his sister sitting up in the darkness, rubbing her eyes. "I'm here," Matt said, kneeling. "Don't worry."

"I felt a bug on my face," Becky whimpered. "Where did you go, Matt? I called for you!"

Matt could just see her thin lips quivering, a streak of dirt on her high cheekbones. "I was outside," he said, "talking to Tomtar."

"I'm starved," Becky whimpered. "I want to go home!"

Matt didn't know what to say. There was nothing he could do about a bug; surely there must be thousands of them in this hole in the ground, surrounded by tree roots, rotting twigs, leaves, and dirt. There was nothing he could do about his sister's hunger, either. Matt felt his own stomach rumbling. If they were lucky, they'd breakfast on some berries and dried twigs, or a few nuts. And home? Home was gone forever. "Come on out, Becky," he said, hoping to distract her. "The sun's coming up, and the sky looks pretty over the hill!"

Tomtar was waiting outside the tree trunk, and when he saw Becky he squeezed her around the waist. It was a heartfelt hug, and Becky squeezed him back. She stroked the Troll's hair and blinked as she watched a splinter of sunlight filter through the trees. "Is that the way home?" she asked.

"Yeah," Matt replied, "that's east. I think that's where the houses are—I mean, were. But . . . I'm not sure."

"I guess it doesn't really matter which direction it is," she murmured. "We don't have anywhere to live anymore. Everything's burned up and ruined, and Mom and Dad and Emily are gone."

Matt stared at the ground. A breeze drifted through the trees, and the forest was filled with the whispering of leaves. "Don't worry," Tomtar said, "everything will be all right. The Mage says there are maps in Ljosalfar, and I know there are maps back in Argant, where I come from, too. One way or another, you'll find your family and get them back."

"I know," Becky said, her face brightening. "Do you think the Mage and Tuava-Li will let us leave today, Matt?"

"I'm not sure," Matt said, fighting the despair that clawed at his heart. "Probably soon."

The sound of singing came from overhead and the brother and sister glanced up to see the source of the eerie, warbling voices. Three Elves sat along a wide branch, bowing to the rising sun. "What are they doing?" Becky asked. She was unaccustomed to waking so early.

"Welcomin' the day," Tomtar whispered. "'Tis one of their rituals. You know Neaca was a Mage, too, a long time ago. She was the leader of a place like Alfheim."

"What happened?"

Tomtar shrugged. "I don't know. Anyway, she was left alone, with no reason for livin' and nothin' to do, so she came to these woods and began carvin' her *Klumma*."

"They're ugly," Becky said, and Matt couldn't help but agree. In fact, the Faerie Folk themselves seemed uglier to him every day—their tiny fingers, their pointy little teeth, pale skin, and dark, wet eyes—it was all weird and strange and ugly to Matt. It was hard not to judge them by their appearance, but the feeling of revulsion welled up in him again as he watched the Elves going through their ritual on the tree branch. If he didn't need their help to find and rescue his parents, Matt would never be able to stand them for long. *It's probably the same for them as it is for me,* he thought, remembering how the Elves had covered their mouths when they first saw him, afraid that he'd contaminate them with germs. *It's only natural. We're not meant to live together.*

"Did you wash your hands yet?" Tomtar asked, his bright eyes darting from Matt to Becky. "The Mage says 'tis important."

"Oh, yeah," Matt snorted. The Elfin rituals were quickly getting under his skin, and he threw up his hands in mock alarm. "Because the dead touch us in our sleep, and we have to clean it off or they'll give us some kind of cooties, right?"

Becky's eyes widened. "What?"

"You shouldn't mock our beliefs," Tomtar said, frowning. "You said you had a bad dream, Matt."

"But a bad dream isn't the same as being touched by somebody or something dead. If I have to follow all the little rules and restrictions that the elves want me to follow, I'll go crazy. Half the things they say sound crazy to begin with."

"I'll wash mine," Becky said, holding her hands away from her body.

Matt sighed. He knew it wasn't worth making an issue of everything. Going along with the Elves' superstitions wasn't going to hurt them, even if he found it annoying. He sighed and got up. "Then let's all do it together."

"I'll lead you to the stream," Tomtar chirped. "After that we'll find somethin' to eat. You know what they say: You can't argue when your belly's full!"

2

YOUR RIGHT FOOT, FIRST," the Mage called from the crevice under the tree. Matt hesitated as he leaned into the dark space. His fingers were still stained with the juice of raspberries from the bushes where he'd eaten with Tomtar and Becky. The fresh, cold water of the stream where they drank and washed their hands had been invigorating; the pine-laden air had been sweet. But the smell of onions and garlic wafted out of the darkness where the Elves waited for him. Matt's eyes burned. The air around here always stank; the Elves believed that cutting onions and garlic would protect them from contamination, and from the influence of evil spirits that may have followed Matt and Becky from the Human realm. He shifted his right foot into the opening, but the toe of his sneaker caught on a tangle of roots and he stumbled into the small enclosure. "Noooo!" the Mage cried.

Tuava-Li and Neaca leapt up, and Tuava-Li banged her head on a branch along the ceiling. "Owwww!" she moaned.

The Mage rushed at Matt, arms outstretched. "Get out!"

She chased Matt into the open air. Becky and Tomtar stood back as the Mage took Matt by the belt loops on his jeans and spun him around, clockwise, three times. "Stumbling foretells disaster," she said, wrinkling up her face. Her white hair was a tangle of knots, full of bits of leaf and twigs. "A bad omen. Princess Asra stumbled coming out of the Cord to her wedding in the Sacred Grove, and look what happened to her!"

Matt shook his head. "This is a complete waste of time. The elves that ruined that wedding had been making plans for what happened long before your little princess stumbled. Look, I know we need your help, but you believe things that . . . that aren't true. If I stumble, or if I walk into your hole with my left foot first instead of my right, nothing's going to happen. It's all superstition."

"Good spirits on the right side, bad spirits on the left," said the Mage, shaking her head in disapproval.

Matt gritted his teeth. The Mage's commands were absurd, but mixed with Matt's rebellion was a touch of fear, too, and fear was something he'd refuse to admit as long as he possibly could. Neaca, standing behind the Mage, wore a faint smile. Nothing seemed to rattle her. It seemed she had seen too much, heard too much to be surprised or angered by anything. She turned to go back to the pots of ink she'd been stirring. Tuava-Li, though, glowered at Matt. "You insist on making us your enemies, when all we want to do is help you. You have no idea of the trouble that's ahead. If you refuse to show us respect, then show respect to yourself by behaving appropriately when the Mage speaks."

Matt sighed. "Go on back into your little hole, if you want, and I'll follow you, right foot first. I promise."

Becky and Tomtar began to follow the others into the little earthen chamber. "No," said Tuava-Li, blocking the entrance with a tattooed arm. "You stay outside."

She gestured to Matt, and he lowered himself onto a stool. The reek of onions was overpowering. He peeled off his shirt and removed the amulets, feeling naked, and vulnerable, and embarrassed. The Mage handed him a little bundle of roots and herbs. Matt knew to place it in his cheek while the work was being done. "A tattoo is a talisman," she began. "'Tis a sign of the invisible made visible, so that you know who you are. 'Tis not for the sake of others that we mark your skin. 'Tis for you, and you alone. The marks will protect you from your own bad emotions. They'll ward off evil spirits. They'll protect you, and guide you, too. They're to remind you that you cannot go back, only forward. You will never be the same, once you are marked."

Matt squirmed on his seat. "How long before we go and try to find my parents?"

"Hold your tongue," the Mage replied. "Readiness manifests in its own time."

"Then when will we be ready?"

"The first task before you," the Mage said, "is to pluck the Seed of the Holy Adri. After you plant the Seed at the center of the Earth, you may travel to Helfratheim and go about freeing your parents."

"Look," said Matt, "I really have to know how long this seed business is going to take. Are you talking weeks? Months? It's not like my parents are off at some resort, sipping drinks by the pool, waiting for me to show up. They're in danger. We don't have any idea what those elves are doing to them. Becky and I want to get this thing going, because time is everything. Don't you understand?"

"Don't talk to me of wasting time," said the Mage. "Place the pouch in your cheek, while I attempt to teach you what you must know for the journey ahead."

Neaca stirred the little pots of color on a wooden tray. The ink was made of vegetable fat, ash, and dammar resin from the trees. Matt didn't know what the source of the ash was, but the thought of what might have been burnt on his behalf left him feeling squeamish. He knew what kinds of strange things these beings put in their potions. Soon their ink would seep between the layers of his flesh, a permanent reminder of this terrible time in his life. Already there was a series of bright leaves, thorny vines, and insects on his chest, shoulders, and arm. Neaca scooted her stool into place and took up a stick with a hollow bone needle attached. She began tapping on the needle with a small mallet, piercing the skin of Matt's shoulder over and over. She rubbed ink into the tiny wounds, then wiped them clean with crushed leaves.

"The tattoos are meant to protect you, to disguise you, to allow you to pass unnoticed through the world where danger waits," said the Mage. "There are those who will wish to prevent you from accomplishing your quest. There are those who will wish to harm you. The tattoos will help prevent evil from blocking your way."

"If I'm going to rescue my parents and my baby sister from Helfratheim, I'm going to stand out no matter what I do."

The Elves exchanged uneasy glances. "We've already discussed this," said the Mage. "Tuava-Li will help you rescue your loved ones, *after* you've traveled to the Pole to harvest the Seed, and then planted it."

"And I already told you," Matt said, his muscles tensing, "that my parents are more important to me than your stupid seed. How do I know that you'll help me find my family if I do what you want first? How do I know you won't just abandon me, like you did when that . . . that bomb went off in the woods, and those fire-breathing things tried to barbecue my father and me?"

"We did everything we could to help you then," said the Mage. "Our actions saved your lives, but at the same time they turned the Elves of Ljosalfar against us. Once we were seen helping

Humans, their trust in us was destroyed. For three hundred and sixty moons I've lived as a welcome guest in Ljosalfar. Now the King and Queen won't even allow me within their walls. Tuava-Li and I must hide in the woods, and I must beg for another chance to show my loyalty."

"That's not my fault," said Matt.

"Let me ask you a question," said the Mage. "What reason would we have to believe that if we first helped to reunite your family, you'd risk your safety to help plant the Seed that will save us?"

"I guess it's a matter of trust," Matt said. "But that works both ways." He lifted his arm. "Like how can I trust that these tattoos you're putting on me won't get infected? When I stepped on the wedding shoe, it had some kind of bacteria, or germs, or something, that made me get sick. You told me then that I would die if I didn't take your elf medicine. Why aren't you giving me something like that to protect me now?"

The Mage narrowed her eyes. "Why do you think you are here, talking to me?"

"Why can't you just give me a simple answer?" Matt snapped. "In case you hadn't noticed, I'm letting you do this to me. I didn't ask to be covered with tattoos. I didn't ask to spend my nights hiding under the roots of a tree, waiting for you to decide when I'm ready and worthy for what you want. I'm cooperating with you even though everything inside me tells me to run away and not look back!"

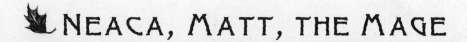

NEACA, MATT, THE MAGE

"Mistress," said Tuava-Li, edging forward.

The Mage nodded. Tuava-Li awkwardly touched Matt's arm, then drew her fingers back. It was strange, and frightening, touching a Human, but she had watched Tomtar do it without fear of contamination. "You're afraid," she said. "We understand, because we're afraid, too. Alfheim was our ancestral home. Now it's gone forever. Once, each of us had a role, a purpose to fulfill. Now we're afraid, because we're not certain what our purpose is. But if we can take the Seed from the fruit of the Holy Adri, and plant it at the center of the world, the Elf realm and the Human realm, too, will be restored. Alfheim will be reborn from the ashes, and we'll have lived for something truly important. You want to live for something, too. Without purpose, our lives are meaningless."

"I have a purpose," said Matt. "My purpose is to save my parents. I'm responsible for what happened to them, and I'm going to make things right again, if it's the last thing I do."

"Why would you choose to take the blame for your parents' abduction?" the Mage asked. "You confuse your self with your experiences, but *who you are* is not what has happened to you. You're not bad, or good, based upon what you've done, or not done. You bear no blame."

"I don't know what you're talking about," Matt said, "and I don't know why you think I would ever trust anything you say."

The Mage tensed. "You must learn trust, because we do not have the luxury of time to shape you for survival. If you cannot trust us, then you must at least learn to trust yourself in our presence. And if you do what Tuava-Li and Neaca and I tell you to do, you may live to see this task to its completion."

I may live? Matt thought, remembering his dream of falling. He held the herbal pouch tightly in his cheek and realized he had been holding his breath. His tattoos were aching.

"That is right," said the Mage. "Breathe."

"You ask about the wedding shoe, and the infection it caused," Tuava-Li said. "Because of the med'cine we gave you, your body was able to fight off the infection, and now you have the strength to resist sickness that could be caused by exposure to Elfin things. But we're not protected from *you* in the same way. Aside from the incantations, the prayers, and the rituals passed down to us, we have few tools that we can rely upon. Humans and Elves have not shared such close quarters in thousands of moons. We risk everything, absolutely everything to achieve our goal. And we cannot do it without you. Therefore, we *must* trust."

"If you're going to use that logic," Matt said, "then Becky's endangered by hanging out near you, too. You and your elfin stuff might make her sick, just like you're worried about getting sick around us."

Neaca placed her needle once more against Matt's arm, and tapped it with her mallet. "Your sister is not getting tattoos."

"This is all stupid, anyway," Matt said, wincing in pain. "Every minute I spend here, I could be looking for my parents."

"I've told you, the ones who have taken your family members

will not allow them to come to harm," said the Mage. "I know Jardaine. She does nothing unless it serves her purposes. Those you love are worth far more to her alive than dead. Tonight in Ljosalfar there will be an emergency meeting of the Synod. Fortunately for us, I have a long friendship with Tacita, the Secretary, who was willing to speak up on my behalf. Tuava-Li's been granted permission to go in my place. If she convinces the Synod to give her the maps you'll need for your journey, you may leave tomorrow. Will that be soon enough?"

Neaca spread a few drops of green ink on Matt's shoulder, and then rubbed a crumpled leaf back and forth until the ink filled the tiny puncture wounds she had made there. "Yeah," Matt said with a grimace. "That'll be great."

3

HURRIED FOOTSTEPS ECHOED along the hallways of the infirmary. The air was thick with the scent of sweet herbs, meant to cover darker smells. The siege of Alfheim had left Ljosalfar overwhelmed with the injured and dying. Over the cries of the wounded, a voice rang out from a narrow alcove. *"Go away!"*

The Queen of Alfheim would not let her daughter see her face. "Please," Asra whispered, leaning into the recess where her mother lay. "Please, won't you talk to me?"

"Who are you?" Shorya moaned. "What do you want? Are you a ghost? Are you one of the spirits that's been trying to take me?"

Asra gently drew the blanket back from her mother's face, so that she might stroke her unkempt, graying hair, and bring her some comfort. The smell of scorched wood smoke was overpowering; Shorya's hair and clothing still reeked from the fire that had destroyed Alfheim. Asra forced a smile. "I'm not a ghost, I'm your daughter, and I need you."

"Why must you torture me like this?" Shorya moaned. "Haven't you done enough? This is all your fault, everything that's happened, 'tis all your fault!"

Asra felt like she'd been slapped. Her fault? How was any of this her fault? She had felt like a victim for years, trapped in the role of princess, trapped by obligation and responsibility, trapped into preparing for a marriage with someone she loathed. It had all taken its toll on her spirit. But now, in the aftermath of what had taken place in the Sacred Grove of Alfheim, an odd feeling of liberation stirred inside her. In more ways than she could begin to fathom, she was *free*. What is a princess without a kingdom? *Free*. What is a bride without a groom? *Free*. But there was no reason to rejoice, Asra knew only too well. Her father was dead, shot by Macta Dockalfar, Prince of Helfratheim. Macta, too, was listed among the dead, along with his father, King Valdis, and most of his court. Asra's best friend was dead, and her own mother lay depressed, deranged, and helpless, blaming her for what had happened and refusing her comfort. Her freedom, in the end, was worth little, compared to what it had cost. Perhaps her mother would never get out of bed again, and Asra would stay here by her side, trapped once more in a role she must play. "Mother," she pleaded, ignoring the sound of footsteps approaching from behind. "Won't you just look at me, won't—"

"Excuse me," said the guard. "I must ask you to come with me, Princess. The Queen of Ljosalfar wishes to see you in her chambers."

Asra turned around, her eyes darting to the guard's face. His eyes were a pale blue, and his lashes were long and black. His fine nose and long ears made him handsome. He gave her a gentle smile as he waited for her reply. "Aye," Asra said. "Aye, of course."

She cast a glance at the wretched figure in the alcove, her mother, the Queen of Alfheim. Then she followed the guard out of the infirmary.

"Greetings, in the name of the Mother and her Cord," said Queen Metis, standing behind her desk in the library. "Please sit down."

She was dressed in military attire, with golden braids hanging from the shoulders of her cape and a profusion of charms and amulets around her neck. This was obviously an informal meeting, Asra thought, or the Queen would have had her come to the throne room. But why was Metis dressed like this? Was Ljosalfar preparing for war? Her Clan represented the element of Earth, the love of art and beauty. It was impossible to imagine the Queen leading troops into battle. Asra bowed slightly before setting herself uncomfortably on the edge of her seat. She averted her eyes, as was the custom, and waited for Metis to speak. "King Adon and I are deeply sorry for what transpired in Alfheim. I grieve for your loss, Asra. Your father was a friend of our Clan, and we shall miss him. How does your mother fare?"

"Your Highness, my mother is not well. I'm afraid she's . . ." Asra's words caught in her throat.

"It must be a shock. Her loss was great. Yet healing takes time, you know. I'm certain that if you continue your devotion, she'll recover."

"Thank you, ma'am," Asra said, knowing in her heart that devotion was futile. "I hope so."

"I'm also saddened by the way you were treated in this affair with Macta Dockalfar, and his father, the King of Helfratheim. All of us were pawns in his game, a game we never chose to play. The Synod is preparing a committee to investigate the events leading up to the destruction of Alfheim. We would like to take your testimony at the earliest convenience, to add to the history."

"Of course," Asra answered, wondering where the Queen was headed.

"In the meantime," Metis said, "I've decided to assign guards to accompany you while you remain in Ljosalfar. This is for your protection as well as ours, Asra, for there are many who blame you, or at least hold you partially responsible, for what transpired in Alfheim. Until your family is cleared of guilt in these matters, we—"

"Guilt?" Asra said, rising out of her seat. She knew it was rude to interrupt the Queen, but she couldn't help herself. "You

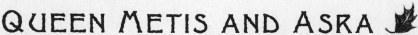

QUEEN METIS AND ASRA

know I'm guilty of nothing! My family and I had nothing to do with Valdis and Macta's deceit. Are you saying I represent some kind of threat to Ljosalfar? You have no right!"

The Queen's face darkened. "*I* have no right?"

Asra wondered if it might have been better for her to exercise a little restraint.

"You foolish child, sit down and listen to me," Metis ordered. "Don't you understand that your presence here makes my life more difficult? There are many who think I invite bad luck by allowing you and your mother to live among us after all that's happened. The King and I were gracious to extend our hospitality to your Clan for over three hundred moons. Find it in yourself to show a little gratitude, and try to see things from my point of view. From now on you won't have the freedom of movement you previously enjoyed in Ljosalfar, but at least you'll be safe."

Asra let her gaze drift along the floor. She understood that she would never be free. "You're the Queen," she said, her lips drawn into a thin line. "Whatever you say shall be so."

"So it shall," Metis confirmed, and a group of guards appeared at the door.

"For those of you who have never met the Princess of Alfheim, this is Asra. Don't let her out of your sight."

4

THE ROCKS HAD BEEN heating in the outdoor pit for hours. Surrounded by her *Klumma*, Neaca's hideaway was invisible to those outside; the smoke from the fire would not be seen. "Now what?" Matt asked the Mage, expecting no real answer to his question. The Mage seemed to say what she wanted to say, only when she was ready to say it. But to Matt's surprise she grunted and said, "Carry rocks," and gestured to the cave in the rock wall along the steep hillside.

Matt looked over at Tomtar, who sat next to him on a fallen log. Tuava-Li sat awkwardly on the other side and watched the Mage scatter dried herbs along the path. "How?" Matt asked. "They're too hot!"

The Mage pointed. Next to the entrance to the cave lay a woven rush pad, nearly hidden in leaves. Matt went to get it.

"Give me a hand," he said to Tomtar, and the two of them began lifting the hot stones from the fire.

Once the rocks were moved into a shallow pit in the cave, the Mage instructed Matt to block the opening with a heavy burlap curtain. Then she stepped inside. "Tuava-Li, Tomtar, Matthew, take off your clothing and follow me," she ordered.

Matt reluctantly stripped down to his boxers, keeping his eyes on the ground.

When the four of them were seated in semidarkness around the circle of hot stones, the Mage lifted a clay pitcher and slowly poured water over the rocks. Steam hissed up, making it hard to see, and even harder to breathe. "The prayers of three warriors, united in purpose, can move mountains," she said. "Each of you, in turn, will pray, each of you will speak the truth of who you are, and what your intentions are. This is sacred space, here in this cave. Your inner spirits will soar as you pray, and the three of you will become as one. A prayer is a journey, and when you reach your destination, all will know it, all will feel it in the crimson chalice of the heart. You must close your eyes and listen. Let your bodies be dissolved in the truth of your words, let your breath carry you to the limit of your Spirit Bodies. Tuava-Li, you will begin."

The Mage fixed her owl-like gaze on her apprentice, and Tuava-Li began to speak. "In the name of the Mother and her Cord," she said nervously, "may I be worthy of the tasks for which I have been chosen. May I find the courage within myself to do your will . . ."

Matt listened, sucking in the steam, and tried to concentrate on the words the Elves spoke. *Crimson chalice? Spirit bodies?* What had the Mage been talking about? He felt his chest constrict as he struggled for breath; he wanted to get out of the cave, he wanted to get away from the discomfort and the fear. He knew that the Mage was there, listening, judging, and weighing the worth of all the words that were spoken. He knew that when it was his turn to speak, or pray, or whatever he was supposed to do, he would come up short by the Elf's standards. He was already judged. What was he supposed to say? When would this all be over? Suddenly he felt something slap his cheek. "Owwww!" Matt cried, and opened his eyes to see the Mage, just inches from his face.

"You're not listening," she hissed.

Matt recoiled. If the Mage wanted him to open up and say what he was feeling, this definitely wasn't the way to get him to do it. Tuava-Li fell silent. Matt glanced over at Tomtar. In the gloom he could see that the Troll sat with his legs crossed and his head lowered, almost like he was dozing. His hair hung in damp ringlets around his face, and a bead of liquid formed at the tip of his long nose. *Is he paying attention?* Matt wondered. Tuava-Li, on his other side, stole a look at Matt, and then turned her face away. She was probably no happier about all of this than Matt was. He closed his eyes, and in a moment Tuava-Li began to pray again.

The air in the forest was cool and damp as Neaca led Becky through a grove of pines. The old Elf wore a simple green tunic and her snowy hair was pulled back from her face with a length of vine. Though her skin, like that of all the Elves, was pale and translucent, the deep wrinkles on her face invited shadows and gave her features a darker cast. Becky thought that Neaca was well camouflaged for a life in the woods. As she followed along behind the squat, shambling figure, she marveled at the way the old Elf's footsteps made no sound on the forest floor. If not for Neaca's constant mumbling, Becky might have lost track of the Elf and found herself alone in this strange place. The thought of being alone made her feel anxious. Sometimes, for a moment, she would forget that her parents were gone, that her home had been burned to the ground, that all of her beloved dolls, everything she had ever known and cared about, had vanished overnight. It was too much to grasp, too much to bear. She brought a finger to her mouth and began to chew on the end of a ragged fingernail. "Don't chew your nails," Neaca said, "you'll stop growing. You don't want to be short, do you?"

Becky tucked her fingers into her fist and frowned. The Elf was in front of her; she hadn't even turned her head around. How could she have seen what Becky was doing? And what did she mean about being short—Neaca was no taller than a human toddler. Was she teasing her, or did she really think that if somebody chewed her nails it would stunt her growth? "Come," Neaca ordered, bending by the trunk of a tree and digging with her fingers in a bed of pine needles. "Look here."

Becky took a few steps forward, and saw that the Elf was

cupping something in her hand. "King Boletus," Neaca said. "You know it by its cap, somewhere between yellow and green. Do you remember the bright orange and green caps I showed you?"

"I—I think so. You called them . . . Sulfur Caps?"

"And where do they grow?" coaxed the Elf.

"On rotting wood, on fallen trunks."

"And what other fungi grow on fallen trunks?"

"Oyster mushrooms," Becky said, taking a deep breath. "But I don't like mushrooms, and I'm not going to eat any, so if that—"

Neaca shook her head. "This forest is our Mother, and Mother provides. It would be impolite to reject what she offers us."

Becky had come a long way from the days when she was afraid to walk on the grass for fear that bugs would bite her. She still didn't like mushrooms, though. "Mushrooms are poisonous! At least some of them are, and if Mother Nature wanted us to eat them, we'd all be dead!"

"Mother teaches us to use our eyes and ears, our sense of smell and our taste buds, too," Neaca said. "With Her help, we become wise in Her ways. Come, child, let us sample something else from Mother's great bounty."

Becky followed the Elf and helped her gather wild asparagus, burdock roots, chicory, dandelion, cranberries, and pine cones for her basket. All the while Neaca went on and on about the nature of the plants, how they should be harvested, which ones could be eaten raw, and which should be cooked. She described which plants could be used to help heal burns and infections, which ones were good to fight fever, and headache, and indigestion. There were bitter herbs and sweet ones, hot ones and cool ones. There were even plants that could help ward off spells and curses. Becky listened, trying to remember the details, and trying to ignore the gnawing hunger in her belly. Finally she asked a question she'd been thinking about all morning. "Neaca, are you a mage, like the elf that's teaching Matt?"

Neaca stopped and put down her basket. "Aye," she said, "I am."

"I thought . . . I thought a mage was powerful, a magician, I mean, not the kind that does tricks, but that you could make magic things happen. You could use magic words, and cast spells, and curse people, and things like that. I know you carved those *Klumma* things, but you spend most of your time gathering herbs and cooking."

"The greatest magick is to bring yourself into being," Neaca said.

Becky looked blank. "What?"

Neaca gave a gentle chuckle. "You're very young. At this moment, you're bringing yourself into being; you're becoming who you will be. You create what's real with every breath you take. You call down magick; you invoke it, from the core of your being. You're making magick. You *are* magick. I do nothing more than what you do in every moment you're alive, except that I do it with greater control, and greater knowledge of what's possible to accomplish. That's part of being a Mage. But the other part is about leading a community, giving guidance, direction, teaching the ways of spirit. If I had apprentices, I'd tend to their knowledge like a gardener tends to her plants, nurturing them so they would grow stronger and healthier. But I have no plants, I have no garden, I have no students, no disciples, no monks, or followers, or apprentices. I had them, once, a long time ago, but they're gone. Now the realm I rule is my own solitude, except that I'm never truly alone, because my Mother keeps me company. She wakes me in the morning with Her golden rays, She feeds me when I'm hungry, and She takes me to the Gates of Vattar in the light of the moon."

"I don't know what you're talking about," Becky said.

"Then I shall explain," Neaca said, happy for an audience to hear the ancient wisdom.

With his eyes squeezed shut, Matt felt a strange, velvety darkness close in around him. It was tight around his skin. It seemed to lift him off the ground and hold him there, hovering. When he opened his eyes and looked down he could see that he was still sitting cross-legged on the dirt, but as soon as he closed them the strange, weightless feeling returned. He had already had several turns at praying out loud. The first time was excruciating. He felt dumb, embarrassed, and angry. His words meant nothing and he knew that the others would hear the falseness, the insincerity in his voice. But he listened as Tomtar and Tuava-Li prayed, and after a while he got lost in the flow of their words. When it was his turn to pray again the words came on their own. Matt hardly knew that he was speaking them, and a kind of vision began to form in his mind. Each word that he spoke appeared behind his closed eyelids like a jewel. As long as he kept his eyes closed, he saw jewels fall into a glittering pile before him, flaring in the darkness like falling stars. The more he prayed, the bigger the pile of jewels became. He prayed for forgiveness, because of what he'd brought into his family's lives. He prayed for courage, for strength, and for hope. He prayed for the help of the Faerie Folk. And finally every word he spoke he meant, with every fiber of his being. The pile of jewels was now enormous. As he prayed, diamonds began to float up from the pile, defying gravity. They arranged themselves in the shape of a human figure—a shining diamond man, with a head that glowed a faint, pale green. In his vision Matt felt compelled to embrace the diamond man, and when he did, the diamonds cut him. He bled, and bled, until there was nothing left of him but a wounded heart beating in the darkness, a thumping, rhythmic pulse. He heard his own voice uttering prayer after prayer, and he was amazed that he had so much to pray for. Finally his voice fell silent. The diamond man came apart, and the jewels scattered like distant stars. Matt sensed the blood throbbing in his veins, and the cloud of hot steam around his body, and he knew that in all of his life he had never felt so alive.

When the Mage drew back the curtain, Matt was the first to stumble out into the daylight. The sensation of fresh air on his skin was exhilarating. The Mage led him, along with Tuava-Li and Tomtar, to the stream that ran down the cliff side and curled through the woodlands. "There," said the Mage, pointing to a mossy pool within a circle of stones. "Cool yourselves in the water. You must be completely silent until the sun has reached its highest point in the sky."

"Cold water's going to hurt my tattoos," Matt protested, his voice sounding strange to him in the open air.

"Silence!" hissed the Mage, as she sat down on the edge of the pool.

Matt watched the Elf and the Troll slip into the water, their movements as stiff and brittle as dried twigs. *It must be freezing,* he thought, and tested the water with his toe. Once again Matt felt overwhelmed. *Why am I doing this? What is this all for?* But then he realized that if an Elf and a Troll could get into a pool of cold water, with their thin arms and small, frail bodies, so could he. He let himself sink up to his chest. The water was frigid. Matt squeezed his eyes shut and tried to get control over his quivering body. But in an instant the velvety, lighter-than-air feeling came over him again, and he saw the diamond man, coming toward him with open arms. His eyes snapped open. There were Tuava-Li and Tomtar, shivering miserably across the pool. Matt held his feelings in check as long as it was possible. Then, with his teeth chattering so hard he thought they might break, he cried out, "I can't do this anymore. Please, stop this! I've got to get out!"

The Mage glanced up. "Do what you will," she muttered.

Matt scrabbled out of the icy water and raced for his clothes, which hung from a tree branch near the cave. He tugged his filthy shirt over his head, and glanced up to see Tomtar and Tuava-Li dressing on the other side of the pool. Soon the four of them sat down to eat on the ground by Neaca's hut. Matt realized he was ravenous. Lunch was a kind of salad, with hazelnuts, pine nuts, and some little flowers on top of a bed of dark, bitter greens. There was no dressing, and everyone ate with his or her fingers. When they were finished the Mage stood up and turned her gaze on Matt. "Come with me," she said.

Tuava-Li and Tomtar got up, too, expecting that they were meant to follow. "No," the Mage said, shaking her head, "the Human, alone."

Matt followed the Elf to the trunk of another enormous tree, and slipped into a dark cavity in the ground beneath a tangle of roots. "Remove your shoes," said the Mage.

"Oh, no, I don't have to take off my clothes again, do I?" Matt complained, but complied with her command.

"Stand here, with your feet apart, and do what I tell you. Now you will breathe through your feet."

"What?" Matt cried. "That's impossible!"

"Do you think that just because you must imagine something, it means that it is not real?"

"I don't know."

"When you were in the cave, did you see anything out of the ordinary?"

"Just a pair of elves and a troll," Matt answered. "Most people would say that's kind of weird."

"When you were praying aloud, what did you see in the darkness behind your eyes?"

Matt wasn't sure he wanted to tell the Mage what he'd seen, but he had a feeling she knew it, anyway. "There was a man made out of diamonds, with a greenish head, and for some reason I felt like hugging him, but when I did, his body was so sharp that it cut me to ribbons. I bled and bled until there was nothing left but my heart."

"Very good," said the Mage. "The being you encountered was Khidr. Your kind calls him the Green Man. He's the caretaker of the living Earth. Once there were many Green Men who walked amongst the realms, as many as there were trees. Now there are just a few. The one you saw resides not on Earth, but in the sky. You can see him at night sometimes, hovering over his enemies."

"Okay," Matt said.

The Mage stared at him. "Now, I asked you to breathe up through your feet."

Matt stared back, and he wondered if she could see the contempt behind his eyes.

5

NEACA SQUATTED by the fire, stirring the stew in a shallow stone pot. There wasn't much to do before suppertime. To pass the time, Tomtar took his flute from his pack and blew into it lightly. "Music!" Becky cried. "Do you remember how you used to play for Matt and me on the hillside near our house? We'd lie in the grass and look at the clouds roll by and you'd play your flute for us. Can you do *the song*?"

"What song is that?" Tomtar asked.

"You know," Becky said, grinning.

Tomtar did know. His fingers searched the holes on the flute, finding the right key, and he began to play. When he came to the end of the tune he started over, and this time Becky sang along. "You take the high road, and I'll take the low road, and I'll get to Scotland before you, for me and my true love will never meet again, on the bonnie, bonnie banks of Loch

Lomond!" Becky smiled wistfully. "That's a song my daddy taught me!"

By the fire pit Neaca put down her ladle, listening as Tomtar played the song again. Tuava-Li looked up at Tomtar. "I once learned another verse or two of that, a long, long time ago."

"Then sing it for us," Becky demanded cheerfully.

Tuava-Li's cheeks flushed. "Nooo, I couldn't. I haven't sung a song like that in many, many moons. Not since I became the Mage's apprentice."

"All the more reason to sing now," said Neaca, leaving her place by the fire and ambling over to the others.

Tuava-Li got to her feet, feeling clumsy and nervous. She did not like to sing, unless it was a hymn to the Goddess, but this was for the sake of the girl. "O, weel may I weep for yestre'en in my sleep," she warbled, "we lay bride and bridegroom together. But his touch and his breath were cold as the death, and his hairtsblood ran red in the heather."

When the chorus came around, Becky happily joined in, trying to match the language and strange inflection in Tuava-Li's voice. "O, ye'll tak' the high road and I'll tak' the low road, an' I'll be in Alfheim afore ye."

Becky ran and grabbed Tomtar by the sleeve. "Come on," she said, "come on and dance with me!"

Tomtar nodded, happy to oblige his friend. He joined Becky in a strange, high-stepping dance, kicking his feet in the air as he played the melody over and over again on his flute. Tuava-Li

stood alongside the pair and sang another verse. "As dauntless in battle as tender in love, he'd yield ne'er a foot tae the foeman. But never again frae the fields o' the slain, tae his Moira will he come by New Lomond."

This time Neaca joined in on the chorus as well, and Becky happily spun and twirled, all the while high-stepping like she'd seen Celtic dancers do on television. But her dance was reckless and wild, so she stumbled and fell into Tomtar, and the two of them tumbled to the ground, laughing. Becky jumped up and grabbed the Troll by his string belt. "Get up!" she cried, mocking the scene she'd witnessed earlier between Matt and the Mage. "Get up, 'tis a bad omen to stumble! Now I must spin you around three times, or you'll be sorry you ever took the low road, laddie!"

As Becky giggled and nudged her friend to turn around, Tuava-Li and Neaca looked toward the entrance of the hut, not more than twenty feet away. Slowly the Mage stepped into the dappled light and shielded her eyes with her hand. "Tomtar and Tuava-Li," she said, "you would do better to preserve your energy for the task that lies ahead of you."

"What about me?" Becky challenged. "Aren't you going to tell me to stop, too?"

"You're a child," said the Mage, shrugging, "and children will play. Dance, if it pleases you, until these two return from their journey with your brother."

It took a few seconds for the Mage's remark, and what it meant, to sink in. "What?" Becky cried. "You don't think

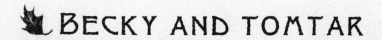

BECKY AND TOMTAR

I'm staying here, do you? I'm going with Matt to rescue my parents, too!"

The Mage raised her eyebrows and stared. Becky tightened her fists. "Are you telling me I'm not allowed to go with them?"

"'Tis for your own good."

"I'm going with Matt," Becky cried, "and you're not going to stop me!"

Tomtar reached up and touched Becky's arm. "The journey will be too dangerous," he said gently. "You'll be safer here with Neaca and the Mage until we return. Don't worry, Becky, 'twill be all right."

"When were you planning to tell me?" Becky cried. "When did you think you were going to tell Matt? He's not going to like this any more than I do!"

"Your brother already knows. The journey is to be undertaken by three alone, as it was in ancient times."

"I don't care about ancient times," Becky said, pointing a finger at the Mage. "And I don't care about you! I hate you, I hate you!"

"Don't point at me, girl," warned the Mage. "That's how a sorceress curses her enemies. Don't you *ever* point at another living being!"

With a cry of despair Becky ran to the edge of the clearing. Then she fell to her knees and began to sob. She felt betrayed by her brother for not telling her that she wasn't going to be allowed to go with him. She was frightened of being left alone with the

Elves, and terrified that she might never see her family again. When Tomtar crept up behind Becky and stroked her hair, she pulled away. "Leave me alone," she whimpered. "Just leave me alone."

Matt climbed out from the hollow below the tree where he had been resting, and saw his sister crying. He looked from face to face, and no one met his gaze. He knew instantly what the problem was. He also knew there was nothing he could do to fix it.

6

THE CORNERS OF JENSINE HALL were strung with tiny lanterns, so that in the darkness the building appeared to be outlined in gold. Moonlight shone down on the guests that arrived for the emergency meeting of the Synod at Ljosalfar. Since the Cord was now compromised to a degree that no one would have ever thought possible, most Synod members traveled to Ljosalfar in animal-drawn carriages. Along the vast marble apron in front of the hall the deer rattled their antlers and snorted. Badgers, rabbits, raccoons, and foxes were also arriving, with Faerie Folk in tow. Servants tied carriages to stakes while others greeted the guests, which included Elves, Trolls, Pixies, Brownies, Dwarves, and many others from the far-flung reaches of the realm. No one noticed the kestrel that swooped down from the night sky and perched on a gate outside the hall.

Indoors, the crowd was mystified by the new seating

arrangement. In a typical Synod meeting, chairs were arranged in a circular fashion so that all members felt that they were regarded with equal importance. Tonight, however, rows of benches faced a platform at the front of the hall, and guards led the guests to predetermined seats. Those with the better seats near the stage looked very pleased. Behind them, however, grumbles and sighs of discontent floated on the air. On the center of the platform sat a puppet stage, ornately carved, with windows draped in moss-green curtains. At the back of the hall stood a row of monks, their arms folded across their chests. These were among the ever-growing ranks that had come to serve their Mage, Brahja-Chi.

Lights flickered in the darkness outside. Tuava-Li walked nervously up the steps, as the last of the kestrel feathers faded from her cheeks, and approached the doors to the hall. "Identify yourself," ordered a guard.

"I am Tuava-Li, from Alfheim."

A Fire Sprite circled her face so that the guard could see. "The Mage's apprentice has arrived," shouted the guard. "Call the captain!"

Tuava-Li felt a tinge of shame and embarrassment. Once, at her Mage's side, she would have been an honored guest at Synod meetings. Now her presence aroused suspicion. The guards, meanwhile, stood awkwardly, uncertain if the captain would come at all. None of the Elves were professional soldiers. Until the veil that separated the Human and Faerie worlds began to come apart, Ljosalfar was a community of artists, potters, and poets. But now everything had changed. The King and Queen, faced with uncertain threats, needed soldiers, so they dressed their artisans in uniform. They needed weapons, so out came all the old bows and arrows that had been used for sport and target practice. They needed a chain of command that would obey orders without question. The new guards were barely up to the task, and they performed their functions reluctantly.

"Very well," the guard said with a sigh. "Go on in. The captain must be busy elsewhere."

Tuava-Li was seated in a row at the back of the hall. She slid onto a bench next to a poorly dressed Troll, who glanced up at her and grinned. "I'm Nicholas," he said, showing a row of crooked teeth. "Call me Nick, if you like. Have you heard the good word about Brahja-Chi?"

Tuava-Li looked away, her lips pressed shut. She knew there were no good words that she, or anyone else, could honestly say about the Mage of Storehoj. "I'm here to honor her tonight," the Troll continued, "to stand up and be counted among her disciples. She allows few male followers in her ranks, you know. Many of us are planning to act in her behalf on a project meant—well, I can't tell you, 'tis a secret for only her chosen ones to share!"

Tuava-Li knew the Troll was trying to lure her into conversation. If she rewarded him with a single glance he'd undoubtedly do his best to bore her with more of his *good news* about Brahja-Chi. She gazed about the room and noted that between a pair of hulking figures, several rows in front of her, sat a familiar figure. It was Princess Asra, slumped sullenly on the bench. Tuava-Li hadn't seen the Princess since the disaster at the wedding. Asra looked as if she had suffered greatly. *Where's her mother, the Queen?* she wondered. She decided that it would be kind to offer her sympathies to Asra for the losses of her father and Alfheim. She got to her feet and attempted to slip past a pair of Brownies at the end of the row, but a guard was there to block her exit. "Where do you think you're going?" he demanded. "All guests must stay in their assigned seats."

"Of course," Tuava-Li said, and turned back to her bench. "Forgive me!"

Copies of the evening's agenda were passed along the rows. "Invocations and Special Presentations," the program read. Tuava-Li examined the text on the parchment, searching in the dim light for her own name among those who would make official statements during the course of the night. Just then the strains of a cricket orchestra swelled, and trumpets blared with the sound of the Elfin fanfare. A moment later the stage was emblazoned with the lights of a hundred Fire Sprites. The Queen and King of Ljosalfar appeared from behind the platform, and the crowd bowed their heads as the royal couple slipped into their seats. The Poet Laureate of Ljosalfar stepped quickly to the front of the stage. "My dear friends from throughout the Faerie realm," he cried, "welcome to this meeting of the Synod of Ljosalfar. Let us honor Queen Metis, King Adon, and the many royal personages here tonight. We are called to this beautiful hall

47

under extraordinary circumstances, and though a few may be tempted to succumb to fear and despair over recent events, let us remember that we are Faeries, one and all, and the Gods smile on us despite the storm clouds that have gathered o'er our realm. In honor of this meeting, I have composed a special poem."

The Poet adjusted his spectacles and peered down at the parchment in his trembling hands.

> Pity the leaf at autumn time, abandoned by the tree,
> Who finds, upon the ground, that fate has changed her destiny.
> In summer's crown she joined the chorus praising Heaven's name;
> Oh, Beauty, it was not the tree, but Life which bears the blame.
> Although in rage your colors flare, how gently you descend,
> Your spirit draws into itself, and cannot comprehend
> That you were not a single leaf, whose hour was too soon done,
> But part of something truly vast, whose time has just begun.
> Now go back to your mother, 'tis your body she shall claim.
> Eternity is in your soul, Forever is your name.
> You are not lost, but changed, dear one, so play your part in full,
> And do not cling onto the branch, or fight the breeze's pull,
> For you were meant for freedom, in this we all are one,
> As children of the moon and stars, and pilgrims of the sun.

Silence met the Poet Laureate as he rolled his parchment and peered out over the audience. "'Tis our children who bring us hope for the future," he said, "so let us welcome these representatives from the Jensine Hall Academy, as they perform their version of the traditional Ghost Ceremony."

48

A group of Elfin children, each dressed in an oak-leaf cape and carrying a lantern, filed into the cavernous chamber. They gathered in a row and faced the crowd.

Tuava-Li glanced at the Troll sitting next to her, the one who called himself Nick. With his knit cap pulled low over his forehead he grunted, rocking back and forth, as the children at the front of the hall waved their lanterns. The Ghost Ceremony was an old folk dance meant to call upon the Gods and to raise helpful spirits from the underworld, to shield the living from the work of the Evil Ones. There were many in the audience whose faith in tradition was no more than a faded relic. For others, the Ceremony was an act of magick, full of promise and hope. For all, however, it was an uncomfortable reminder of how helpless the Faerie Folk had become, and how little control they held over their own future. The children swung their glowing lanterns and sang. When they were finished, the puppet stage curtains parted. A golden light flickered on and a shadow puppet appeared, wiggling its paper arms.

Suddenly a loud crash came from the left side of the hall. All eyes turned to see a gigantic figure bursting through the wall, in a rain of dust and plaster. "Look," someone cried from the crowd. "'Tis a Human. He has a weapon—the Dragon Thunderbus!"

'Tis Matthew, thought Tuava-Li, *but how?*

All across the hall Faerie Folk scrambled from their seats and shoved their way to the doors, many covering their faces with handkerchiefs or pressing their hands over their mouths in mortal fear of contamination. "Let us past!" shrieked a group of Pixies in the row just in front of Tuava-Li.

Faerie Folk were leaping over fallen benches, jostling for escape as the intruder let out a terrible roar. Nick the Troll, however, sat still beside Tuava-Li, beaming with a deep, almost spiritual satisfaction. King Adon cowered behind the throne at the other end of the chamber. His guards and advisors deliberated on the quickest exit. Queen Metis, meanwhile, crept behind a curtain. "You will die," shouted the Human, and a blast of smoke and sulfur exploded from the barrel of his gun. A hole in the opposite wall exploded, sending a cascade of dust and rubble on the Faeries below. The guards struggled to fire their bows and arrows. But though they leveled volley after volley at the boy, he was unstoppable.

Something's wrong, thought Tuava-Li. She pushed through the crowd and toward the stage, moving slowly against the tide. *He seems too big, bigger than I remember. It looks like Matthew, but it isn't.*

At the doorways the swarming crowd shrieked in alarm. Brahja-Chi's monks were stationed there, jamming the exits. The giant boy fired his terrible weapon again, this time at the ceiling. Once more an enormous chunk of debris tumbled on the crowd.

"You will die," shouted the boy, "you will die! You will die! You will die!"

Tuava-Li heard someone call her name, and she turned to see the face of Princess Asra. "You've got to do something,"

50

Asra cried. "Our Mage could have stopped the Human. Can't you?"

"Let me try!" Closing her eyes, Tuava-Li began her transformation to a kestrel. Her nose and mouth flowed into the surface of her face. They were replaced by a hard, black beak, as her eyes grew to immense proportions and feathers sprouted over her scalp. When the monk's robe dropped away Asra snatched it from the floor. Tuava-Li flapped over the heads of the crowd, her wings fanning the air. Other Mages in the room were using magick to try to stop the boy, uttering spells, and oaths, and curses, but nothing worked. The Human fired his weapon again and again, and his huge, heavy feet came crashing down. Tuava-Li swept past the boy's head. She opened her senses, feeling for that subtle energy given off by living beings—and her suspicions were right. *Gossana di scialla,* the words formed in her mind, the words the Mage had taught her. *Sa liniga mal farma, so liniga mor tuarro.*

It was not a spell to stop a living being, but a spell to stop an illusion. As Tuava-Li swooped across the room and came to rest at the top of the puppet stage, the figure of the Human boy began to dissolve. Everyone peered upward to see the holes in the walls and roof closing up, sealing themselves as if they had never been damaged at all. Elves and Pixies, Trolls and Brownies and Dwarves stood back from the door and watched in wonder as the figure of the boy became nothing more than a gray shadow, and then was gone.

Tuava-Li turned her kestrel head and saw the Mage Brahja-Chi, surrounded by a group of fearsome bodyguards, hurrying onto the stage. Brahja-Chi looked furious. She was obviously livid that someone had destroyed her illusion before she was ready for it to end. "Rest easy, my friends," Brahja-Chi shouted to the crowd in a booming voice, as she tried to disguise her rage. "The Goddess has spared us from the disaster you have just witnessed. And if we give thanks with our obedience, we will be spared again, for our Goddess is good, and our Goddess is loyal to those who serve Her, bless those who serve the Canon."

All of Brahja-Chi's monks repeated the blessing in unison: "Bless those who serve the Canon."

Brahja-Chi's eyes sparkled as she spoke, regaining her composure. Her voice bellowed with a power so raw, so fervent, that every soul in the hall could not help but be touched by it. "Now let it be known that the great and mighty Goddess spoke to me, and in my vision She commanded me to create the illusion you have just had the privilege to witness. She spoke to me, and told me that we have been weak in our hearts, and slow in our minds, and that we have disappointed and angered Her to the core of Her sacred being. The Great Goddess wanted to let this disaster take place. She was ready to taste the Blood of our defeat at the hands of the Human, because we have not taken Her into our bosoms, we have failed to love Her and serve Her as was our charge, and now we taste the bitter fruit of our failure!"

"Verily," the monks cried, "verily!"

"But because of me," Brahja-Chi bellowed, "and my devotion to Her and to the holy book, the Canon, the Goddess has relented, and allowed me to share with you the vision I had of our destruction at the Human's filthy hands. She has offered us another chance to rally at Her precious feet, to submit ourselves to Her Holy Will, and to stand by Her side and fight for Her as long as breath remains in our weak, corrupt bodies. Join with me, Faerie Folk, in singing her praises."

"Verily!" the monks cried again, and, joining hands around the room, they began to sing.

Praise be Your mercy, great One, how humbly we beseech
That You forgive our failures; our grasp exceeds our reach.
In darkness, how we tremble, we gnash our teeth and wail,
Alone and cut off from Your love, we are but bound to fail.
Your truth brings order to our lives, so we might walk Your Path,
And live a life of righteousness, while shielded from Your wrath.
To praise Your each and every word shall be our purpose true,
Both loyal to the Canon and the teacher serving You.
We kneel unto Brahja-Chi, in her You manifest,
We beg that You receive us, as You cast aside the rest.
Oh Goddess, hear our wretched voices, justify our pain,
And when all others perish, let their loss be our own gain.
We praise You, as Your enemies cry, roasting on the coals;
Oh Goddess, we beseech Thee, have no mercy on their souls.

When the song was finished King Adon crept from behind his throne, squinting into the chamber to see if his senses might be deceiving him once again. Queen Metis pushed past him and stalked angrily onto the stage. "Nooo," the King called, stretching out an arm, "you mustn't interfere!"

But she ignored his warning. "Brahja-Chi," the Queen said in a hoarse whisper, "you will stand down immediately or risk arrest by my guards. What you have done here this night is inexcusable. It violates every law of civility and respect—"

"Do not talk to me of respect," Brahja-Chi hissed, "when it is you who has no respect for the real Authority of our world, the great Goddess who created Heaven and Earth, and through whose generosity you take your next breath. I have been blessed to share with you the vision I had of our impending destruction, so that you could see the error of your ways and change, before it is too late. I will defer to you and your authority, because the Goddess wishes that it be so. But not, ma'am, because you demand it."

"Then—then we shall all take our places again," King Adon nervously ordered the crowd. "Metis, I command you, too, to take your seat. This emergency meeting must go on, according to the agenda that we prepared. But I trust that we will suffer no further interruptions. Am I correct, Brahja-Chi?"

"If the Goddess wishes," said the Mage of Storehoj. She turned, with the long train of her robe trailing behind her, and disappeared into the cluster of bodyguards and monks that awaited her. The King and Queen glared at one another as the kestrel sailed back into the crowd. She found Princess

Asra sitting near the doors, holding the monk's robe in her lap. *Thank you,* Tuava-Li said in thought-speak. Then, clutching the robe in her talons, she found a private place in the shadows to make her transformation from a fierce little bird into a thin, undistinguished monk.

The rest of the meeting unfolded in as orderly a fashion as could be expected under the circumstances. No one dared to speak about Brahja-Chi's stunt. Who could argue that a direct command from the Goddess might be challenged? And who would dare claim that Brahja-Chi's vision had been false? As order and custom were slowly restored, the Faerie Folk listened to the speakers on the agenda, heard their fears and their demands, and the council of Synod members noted every contribution. Many were distraught over the loss of Alfheim. Residents of Ljosalfar wondered how long they were expected to host the Alfheim Elves, who would be living amongst them once more. Some were worried about what would happen to the leadership of Helfratheim, now that King Valdis and his son Macta were dead. Everyone was worried about the failing health of the Cord, and the safety of the borders with the Human world. Everyone wanted solutions, and everyone's patience was frayed. Finally it was Tuava-Li's turn to speak. "Our next remarks come from Tuava-Li," said Tacita, the Secretary of the Synod and one of the Mage's oldest friends. "She is a young monk from Alfheim, and she is here to make a special request. Come, Tuava-Li."

"Greetings to the members of the Synod," Tuava-Li said,

swallowing dryly. She stood with her trembling hands held behind her back. "For many years I was apprentice to the Mage of Alfheim, though Alfheim is no more. Because of the Humans, and the actions of King Valdis of Helfratheim, my blessed homeland was destroyed. The charred ground is scarred and cursed by contamination now and for many moons to come." She glanced around the room, looking for the face of Brahja-Chi, and knowing that she must phrase her next point very carefully.

"Like the Mage of Storehoj, I, too, have been graced with a vision from the Goddess. The secrets of our fate are clear to me, and I know what must be done to save us from disaster. Aye, the Humans are crossing our borders, and many of them will be happy to kill us if they can. But in ancient days, it was the Human King Volsung, the Troll Mage Desir, and Fada the Elfin Prince and Warrior who traveled together to the hidden city at the North Pole in order to plant the Seed of the Holy Adri. Fada returned to tell the tale, and it was he who taught us that Volsung's life was sacrificed at the center of the holy Earth. It is he who taught us that Human Blood must be spilled, to feed the roots of the Tree and the Cords encircling our world. The Cords are ill; they are dying as we speak. 'Tis no longer safe to travel to the far corners of the Faerie realm, or even to the village just beyond the next hill. We must plant a new Seed, to nourish a new Tree, to close the boundary between our world and that of the Humans. To do this, to relive the myth that's the foundation of our world, we need the help of a Human."

Grumbling and angry murmurs spread through the audience. Tuava-Li could feel resistance sweep over her like a wave. "My Mage has arranged for me, a Troll named Tomtar, and a Human boy to go on a quest to save our realm, to relive the journey of Volsung, Desir, and Fada. I am here to make a very special request. Since the Cord isn't safe to travel, we're in need of maps to lead us overground, so that we may journey north to the Pole."

"Does the boy know what is at stake?" asked one of the Synod members. "Does he know what it will cost him?"

Tuava-Li hesitated. "He's been informed that there's great danger to be faced along the way. He's been told that the consequence of not cooperating with us will mean the deaths of many of his kind, including his immediate family, who are held captive in Helfratheim. He is willing to accompany us."

"But you have not yet told him that he will die?"

"Nooo," Tuava-Li breathed. "Until now, no one knew but me, and my Mage. These are troubled times. Though we're forced to make uneasy alliances, we know which of our secrets must be kept."

"Where is this Human now?" asked one of the Synod.

"There's no need to fear," said Tuava-Li, hoping that no one would detect the lie she was about to tell. "He's far from here, in the woods near Alfheim."

The voice of Brahja-Chi boomed from the corner of the chamber. "What this monk says is a sacrilege! She and her Mage will bring ruin to the rest of us, as ruin has befallen her own land. If they couldn't protect Alfheim, what reason do we have to think they could protect all of the Elf realm? In the name of the Canon and those who serve the Word, let us answer this request with a resounding NO!"

"Verily, verily," the monks of Brahja-Chi cried, in their hollow, mechanical way.

"Perhaps it would be wise to consider this matter in a more civil tone," said Tacita. She had been Secretary for thousands of moons, and commanded respect. "If the Mage's vision is true, then those she has assembled for her quest truly need our help. What harm could there be in providing this monk with maps to the North Pole?"

"I would also request the maps that show the route overland to Helfratheim," Tuava-Li said. "The Human boy believes his parents are likely being held there. And for his help in planting the Seed, we have promised him our aid in rescuing them. Of course, once the Seed is planted, the boy will live no more."

The agitated crowd whispered in disapproval. "Nooo," King Adon cried, getting to his feet. "This monk asks too much. Unless she can prove that her vision is true and that this quest is justified, we cannot agree to help her. Her and her Mage's associations with Humans are suspicious, at best. This is not the time for trust."

"Verily, verily!" shouted Brahja-Chi's monks, as Tuava-Li turned awkwardly and returned to her seat. It was then that a voice appeared in her mind, the quiet, frail voice of Tacita. The old Elf had once studied with a Holy Order and she was fluent in the art of thought-speak. *Stay tonight,* she said. *It is late, and many will not venture home until the morrow. Linger in the shadows behind the rhododendrons at the chapel, and I will bring you to my chambers when the moon has reached its zenith. Perhaps I can yet find a way to help you.*

7

A NIGHT BREEZE CRAWLED over the hillside, rattling branches and shaking boughs, shuffling leaves along the ground. Just outside the gates of Ljosalfar a gaunt figure arrived. He was bent with pain and weary from walking. The traveler, with only one good arm, could not help but smile bitterly. He had been here many times before, under very different circumstances. On his most recent visit he had never been happier, and his future had seemed assured. With the stolen Jewels of Alfheim, he had been fabulously rich and was about to marry the Elfmaid he had loved his entire life. But how things had changed!

Now his friends, even his beloved pet Goblin, Powcca, were dead. The Jewels were gone forever, his wedding had ended in disaster, and he'd been nearly killed when he stumbled onto a Human roadway and was struck by an oncoming truck. Now he needed help like he had never needed any single thing before.

MACTA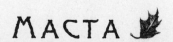

"Open the gates," he demanded, and banged on the wooden planks with his one good fist. "Let me in!"

There was a scrabbling sound behind the timber door, and a large, luminous eye peered out through a peephole at the bedraggled visitor. "Open the gates, soldier, for I am Macta, rightful King of Helfratheim, and fiancé to Asra of Alfheim. I'm wounded. Badly wounded. I've lost a lot of Blood and my right arm is—I'm afraid to even look at what's left of it. It's taken me days to find Ljosalfar. I command you to let me in!"

"Macta died in Alfheim, along with his father," the voice came from inside the gate, "and if I were you, I wouldn't align myself with Princess Asra and her stock. They've got problems of their own! I don't know what your game is, friend, but you'd best get away from here, before my soldiers take their pikes to you!"

Macta knew he must look like a shadow of his old self. Exhausted and weak, and ashamed of his weakness, he hung his head. "My father is dead," he cried through gritted teeth, "but I live, so I'm the new King of Helfratheim. You must believe me! Once I'm home again, I'll see that you're handsomely rewarded for your help. I've got to get to your infirmary. I know your monks have access to herbs and spells, med'cine and magick that can save me."

"No one can save you, stranger," said the voice on the other side of the gate. "You're deluded. Now get lost."

The Elfin guard turned and sauntered back to the game of

chance he'd been playing with his fellow soldiers. Macta heard muffled laughter, and the sound filled him with rage. He banged on the planks again and cursed, then stumbled away, feeling faint. He clutched the makeshift bandages that held his ruined arm against his torso. Greenish ooze stained Macta's shoulder, and the arm underneath the silken shirt, crushed and blackened, was dying. He knew the old Mage of Alfheim was probably in Ljosalfar. If anyone were able to save his arm, it would be she. But there was nothing Macta could say that would make her take pity on him. He suspected that his beloved Asra was inside the gates, as well. He had no doubt he'd never be allowed to see her again, after he accidentally shot her father, after her precious Alfheim burned to the ground.

"Luck," Macta mumbled, stumbling down the darkened path. "My luck has to change before long. I'm the King of Helfratheim, after all." With his good hand he reached into his trouser pocket and withdrew a small notebook, then knelt in the damp grass. With a twig of charcoal he etched a series of figures on one of the pages. He was making a bet with himself that he'd find a way into Ljosalfar in the morning. He grunted, slipped the notebook back into his pocket, and then trudged toward the darkness of the forest. He'd sleep there, huddled under a tree, and see if he couldn't enter the Gates of Vattar, like so many Faerie Folk did while they slept. Though directing one's dreams was not a habit indulged in by the Dockalfars, Macta knew that many claimed to find healing energies there.

He hadn't wandered far when he stumbled upon a carved wooden pole. It was a stack of scowling, grotesque heads, rising up out of the ground, and Macta smiled grimly as he lay down at the base of the carving. What better place, he thought, to lay his own weary head.

8

Tuava-Li met Tacita in the shadows by the chapel when the moon was high. The two Elves trod on silent feet to Tacita's rooms in an old stone dormitory building, where ivy vines crept along the outer walls and birds nested in the eaves. They'd barely begun to talk when there came a knock at the door. *Tap tap tap.* Tuava-Li's heart pounded, and her eyes darted about, searching for a place to hide. *No one must know I'm here,* she thought.

I'm expecting no one, Tacita said in thought-speak. *Do you have the Mage's eyes to see who stands on the other side of the door?*

Tuava-Li shut her eyes. *I will try.* In the darkness of her mind she brought her awareness into sharp focus, then moved it slowly, like an orb of living thought, into the hallway. A black shadow hung there. Nothing more. She tried to extend her awareness further, into the heart of the shadow. Nothing.

Can you read the visitor's mind, Tuava-Li? For all intents and purposes you are a Mage. You have the gift of sight, I know it. Who is there? Does someone mean us harm?

Tuava-Li's face tightened. *But Mistress, 'tis a violation to enter another's mind unbidden. The Mage taught me that.*

Not if there is danger, Tuava-Li. 'Tis only self-defense.

Tuava-Li reluctantly probed deeper into the shadow, and in a sudden burst of color and light, all the resistance disappeared. She could see through the eyes that waited outside the door, she could see the tray in the hands of the young Elfmaid who stood there, dressed in monk's robes. She breathed a sigh of relief. *'Tis only a servant, with a tea tray. There's no danger.*

Silently she hurried to conceal herself behind a painted screen; it was still important that her presence in Tacita's chambers be a secret. The Synod, if they knew, would be suspicious that she remained so long in Ljosalfar. Tacita cleared her throat and made her way toward the door. "Who's there?"

"In the name of the Canon and the Mistress who serves the Word," came the voice from beyond the door. "I've brought you some tea, ma'am."

Tacita turned the lock and opened the door to see a smiling young face gazing up at her. "Allow me to offer a special gift from Brahja-Chi, in thanks for your work on behalf of our Mage. 'Tis a special blend, brought with us from Storehoj. Shall I bring it inside, ma'am?"

"Nooo," answered Tacita. "I'll take it. Thank you for your kindness."

Tacita took the tray and placed it on a table by the lamp. She returned to the door to turn the silver key in the lock, as the Elfmaid's footsteps echoed down the hall and disappeared.

"Do you care to join me, Tuava-Li?" whispered Tacita, as she lifted the lid of the pot and sniffed. "It has the aroma of bergamot and honey, I think. My nose isn't what it used to be in the art of detection."

Tuava-Li shook her head. "Thank you, ma'am, but no. I feel sick with worry, hidden away in your quarters, ready to run like a scared rabbit at the slightest sound."

Bells sounded from the tower in the town square. Tacita poured herself a cup, took a sip, and smiled. "Soon most of the Realm will be passing through the Gates of Vattar, deep in slumber. Then we'll slip out of here and go to the map room. The Synod may not be willing to *give* you the maps, but no one said you couldn't *see* them. We'll copy the routes from the original maps, and before sunrise you can return to the forest with the information you need. Should we chance to see any guards in the corridors, none will question me as long as I appear to be alone. You know the spell for invisibility, don't you, Tuava-Li?"

"I—I'm not sure, ma'am," she answered. "There were many things the Mage had yet to teach me when Alfheim . . ."

"It takes time to recognize what we're capable of doing,"

Tacita said, "and some come to confidence more readily than others. Look at you—you can change into a kestrel and fly through the air! Believe in yourself, Tuava-Li. If you had a place to settle and followers of your own, you'd already be a Mage. You can accomplish more than you know."

Tacita went to her bookshelf and withdrew a small wooden box. Inside were row upon row of small pieces of tree bark, each piece inscribed with a spell. "Place one of these in your cheek," Tacita said, offering the box to Tuava-Li. "'Twill have the same effect as a Mage's magick, and it will help you until you're ready to admit to your own powers."

Within the hour Tacita stood in the corridor, locking her chamber door. Tuava-Li followed, silent as a breath, as the pair left the building and entered the square. The moon cast a silver glow over the walkway where only one shadow fell. They hurried to the Synod headquarters and entered through a side door. *I'll light a candle,* Tacita whispered. As she felt for the desk in the corner of the room, she tripped and stumbled, and cried out in the darkness. Tuava-Li helped her to her feet. *Are you all right?* she whispered. *'Tis a bad omen to stumble like that!*

The darkness makes me dizzy, the old Elf replied. *I'll be fine.*

She opened a drawer and took out a candle and a small, glowing cask in which a Fire Sprite lay sleeping. When the candle was lit, illuminating the wizened face from below, Tuava-Li thought the old Elf's face looked strained. *She's too old for these times*, Tuava-Li said to herself, as Tacita turned and opened another door.

Down several long corridors they crept until they came, finally, to the map room. "I believe I brought you here once before," Tacita said, "after you delivered the Alfheim wedding shoe to me!"

Inside, an enormous globe hovered in midair. Marked with all the major Cords of the Faerie world, each of the realms was carefully rendered on the globe's surface. But the Human highways, cities, and nations were not to be seen. "The maps of the Human realm are stored inside these cabinets," Tacita whispered. "I believe I—"

The old Elf dropped the candle. It rolled on the floor, its fire extinguished. Tacita stood with one withered hand against the wall. Her head throbbed, and out of the corners of her eyes black shapes appeared, like thousands of spiders dancing on threads. As she moaned and slumped to the floor, her fingernails scraped against the wood.

"What is it?" cried Tuava-Li. "What's wrong?"

She rushed to the figure that lay in a heap in the darkness, and took Tacita in her arms. With her face so close to the old Elf, she could smell the telltale odor on her breath. "It wasn't bergamot in your tea," she said. "It was Deathwort. You've been poisoned."

Tacita moaned again, her breath rattling in her throat. Tuava-Li searched her memory for something to counteract the poison. There were herbal remedies, and there were spells, some magick, some words that would invoke balance, and healing . . . she needed to get Tacita to the infirmary.

Tuava-Li thought of the Elfmaid in the corridor, the one who had brought the tea. At first she'd resisted Tuava-Li's efforts to enter her mind, but somehow the wall had fallen away, revealing an open, innocent soul, as far as Tuava-Li dared to see. This deception was Brahja-Chi's doing, it had to be. "Help!" Tuava-Li cried, but there was no one in the building to hear her. Perhaps she could reach out to the Mage, back in the woods, and get her to come. Tuava-Li made an effort to send a mental picture, to contact her Master. But it was as if a brick wall had been erected around her mind. A powerful force was stopping her. "Help!" she cried again. "Help me!"

Tuava-Li tried to rein in her emotions. She tried to focus her energies, to concentrate. But she knew that trying was not enough. In her mind she formed the image of a blue sphere, an orb of healing. It was a technique designed to stop time inside a shimmering bubble of energy. It was Tacita's only hope. The orb began to materialize in the room, moving like a fog over the old Elf. It glowed faintly in the darkness and floated above the floor. With the force of her will Tuava-Li moved the orb, with Tacita inside, slowly through the air. She directed the orb down the corridors they had walked just minutes before, through doorways and finally into the open courtyard. "Help me," she cried, as the blue bubble gleamed in the moonlight. But in the moment her voice rang out, echoing off the stone walls and treetop homes of

Ljosalfar, the orb faltered, sank to the ground and disappeared. "Please!" she cried. "Someone, help!"

Footsteps clattered far away. Two guards, wiping sleep from their eyes, rounded a corner and hurried into sight. "'Tis Tacita, Secretary to the Synod," Tuava-Li called. "She's ill. She needs treatment, immediately, or she'll die!"

The infirmary was dark and quiet. All were sleeping, lost within the Gates of Vattar, deep in the well of myth where Faerie Folk spent the night hours. The doors banged open as the guards dragged Tacita into the hive-like chamber. Asra, sleeping at the foot of the mat where her mother lay, stirred at the sound. She stood up, peered into the darkness, and saw two shadowy figures approaching. They were carrying something. Asra's guards got to their feet and rushed after the others, anxious to know what was going on. Asra blinked and rubbed her eyes as Tuava-Li hurried through the infirmary door. "Tuava-Li, what's happened?"

"I need your help," Tuava-Li whispered. "Tacita's been poisoned. Can you find an amulet with a flaming sun and a six-pointed star? It must have these words upon it—*Dei Omnes Me servant*. And I must have another amulet with the sun encircled by dock leaves, and these words on the back of it, *Sic esse Salubris*. But the most important amulet has to have a blazing sun enclosing a Death's Head. *Cras Mors Hodie Sol* must be inscribed on the back. Find them, and drape them around her neck. I need wormwood, to cleanse the stomach; thyme blossoms, violet root, and vinegar to force out evil spirits. I need—"

"Tuava-Li," Asra whispered, "I can't remember all of that. There are monks here who know better than I where to locate the things you ask for!"

The response appeared in Asra's mind, spreading like ripples on a pool. *Listen carefully. Tacita was poisoned by one of Brahja-Chi's monks, after she promised to get me copies of the maps I need. There's no one here but you I can trust. All infirmaries have the things I asked for, stored away in cabinets behind the wall. I'll write them down for you.*

"But they'll never let me rummage around back there," Asra whispered.

We need a distraction, Tuava-Li said, as she compiled a list for Asra, *like the one Brahja-Chi staged during the meeting. Without our help Tacita won't live through the night.*

Asra glanced at the monks and guards gathered around the fallen Elf. "Then I'll create a distraction. Have you been able to contact the Mage?"

I tried, but something's stopping me. I must return to the forest and tell her what's going on. Listen . . . Talk to Queen Metis, tell her what's happened; Brahja-Chi's disciples won't dare to cause any more harm. If the guards allow it, I'll return here with the Mage.

"Then go," said Asra. "I'll look after Tacita. I know where the map room is, too, for that matter. I can get everything you need."

Tuava-Li shook her head, and handed Asra the list she had made. *There's no need to put yourself in danger, Princess. If you help*

Tacita, that will be enough. You have my gratitude. By your actions you honor the memory of Alfheim.

Asra shrugged helplessly. *No, I don't,* she said to herself. *I dishonor it completely, but I don't know what else to do.*

Tuava-Li hurried to an open window and began her transformation into a kestrel. No one noticed as her face melted into feathers and a hard, black beak, and her arms and legs changed into wings and feathered talons. Soon she flexed her wings and dropped out of the window. Asra turned to her mother's sleeping form, hesitated for just a moment, then hissed into her mother's ear. "They're here! The spirits have returned from the dead, to take you with them!"

A tear rolled down Asra's cheek. What she was doing was cruel, terribly cruel, but for the sake of Tuava-Li and Tacita she would create a distraction, the only way she knew how. As the days passed she'd come to understand that the mother she'd known was already gone. All that remained was a ruined husk, an empty shell. What Asra was about to do would cause no permanent damage to her mother, for the damage was already done. "Get up, get up, they're coming! The spirits are coming, get up now!"

Something stirred, buzzing in Shorya's mind as her broken spirit rose from sleep. Her eyes snapped open and stared in blank horror.

"They're coming," Asra cried. "They're coming from the Land of the Dead! They say it's your fault that they died. *Your* fault!"

Asra leapt up and stood back from her mother. Now that she had set this scene into motion, there would be no stopping it. "They're here!" Shorya shrieked. "The dead have come for their revenge!"

As Shorya's screams woke others in the infirmary, the shrieking, wailing, and moaning quickly rose to a fever pitch. "The dead, the dead"—the other sick Elves took up the cry. They leapt from their mats, climbed down from the compartments in the hive, and shambled for the doors. "What's happening?" the guards cried in alarm.

Scores of Elves banged against each other, a jostling, shoving crowd on the verge of madness. Their fear had grown too large to control, and the inexperienced guards fell back before them. Patients whose fragile minds had been wounded in the escape from Alfheim stumbled through the infirmary, crying, pleading, screaming in anger and fear.

Monks did their best to soothe them; even Brahja-Chi's followers appeared and made an effort to use magick to control the Elves. And as they did so, Princess Asra hurried to the cabinets, collecting the things that Tacita needed, and returned to kneel by the Secretary's side. She draped the amulets around the old Elf's neck, and forced tinctures of wormwood, thyme, violet, and vinegar between her thin, dry lips. Once done, Asra watched as the Secretary's labored breathing became normal and quiet. The Princess choked back a sob, realizing how bad it felt to create damage and destruction for the sake of some greater good. Her mother was alive, but in a place from which she'd not likely return. There was nothing else for Asra here. No one paid the slightest bit of attention as she slipped out the doors of the infirmary and disappeared into the night. The past was truly behind her, and there was no going back.

9

THE MAGE LAY ON A BED of straw in a hollow beneath the roots of an enormous tree. Tuava-Li changed to her Elfin form as she crouched in the entryway, staring into the darkness. She was reluctant to rouse her Master from the Gates of Vattar, but the situation was too urgent for her to wait. "My Mage," she whispered.

The old Elf blinked open her eyes and got up on one elbow. She could sense from the troubled aura around her apprentice that something was wrong. "Tell me," she said.

"Tacita's been poisoned. She's in the infirmary, and Princess Asra is doing her best to care for her. I tried to reach you from afar, to tell you what was going on, but something—or someone— blocked me. That's why I had to return in the midst of all the chaos. There's much tension between the King and Queen, and Brahja-Chi struts about like she's in charge. I think she's responsible for poisoning Tacita, and she may have been trying to poison me, as well. She doesn't want me to have the maps that would help us reach the Pole. The monk that brought the tea, I thought she was an innocent soul, but I was wrong. Tacita asked me to look into her mind, and I did, as much as I dared. I told myself I only wanted to be respectful, and not violate the sanctity of the monk's mind, but that wasn't true. I was timid and afraid. I failed to see the truth, and Tacita nearly died because of it."

"What about the maps? Did the King and Queen give them to you?"

Tuava-Li shook her head sorrowfully. "No, they're not going to help us. There was nothing I could say or do to convince them."

"Then the time has come for you to leave, Tuava-Li. You must go to Argant, and try to get the maps that Tomtar says are held by his Clan."

"But I was hoping that I could take you to see Tacita—"

"If Asra's taking care of her, there's no need for me to risk making things worse by showing my face where I've been forbidden to go. You must journey to the Pole and fulfill your destiny, Tuava-Li. You cannot allow Brahja-Chi to stop you. The night is nearly over. Let's awaken Neaca and go to the treetop together to greet the dawn, one last time."

Matt slept fitfully beneath the roots of another ancient tree. He turned onto his back and felt something crawl across his lower lip. *Bug*, he thought, stirring.

Automatically his hand leapt up and swatted his mouth. He sat up and spat onto the dirt. The soggy pouch of herbs he held in his cheek had broken open. He spat again. He had been lying on his left side; he could feel the bits of straw drop from his cheek. If the Mage knew, she would be mad at him. She said he had to sleep on his right side from now on. How long, he wondered, would he have to stay here like this, learning their superstitions? He pulled on his sneakers and hoisted himself out from under the tree roots where he had slept. His skin stung from the tattoos, his clothes itched, and his muscles were sore from trying to hold the strange poses that the Mage insisted he perform. The Faerie Folk were nearby. Matt could just detect the odor of cut onions; they were still worried about being exposed to human germs. They didn't want Matt and his sister Becky to interfere with their dreaming rituals, whatever they were. Nobody had bothered to explain them to Matt. He supposed they thought it was none of his business. He peered into the darkness of the forest. It didn't look like anyone was up yet, so he hurried to the nearest tree.

Matt was relieving himself when he heard the sound of the Elves singing the song they always sang when the sun came up. *Another day*, he thought, *another tattoo. Maybe once my body is entirely covered with pictures of vines and leaves and bugs, they'll sell me to the freak show and get out of my life for good.*

"Matt?"

"Whoa, you startled me," Matt said, turning away and pulling up his zipper. Maybe the faeries didn't have a sense of privacy

79

about going to the bathroom, but that didn't mean that he had lost his own. "Tomtar, what are you doing up so early?"

The Troll looked excited and worried at the same time. "As soon as the sun comes up, Matt, we're going to be leaving for Argant, to get the maps that'll lead us to the Pole, and to Helfratheim. Tuava-Li's back, and she says they refused to give her the maps in Ljosalfar."

"Oh, no," Matt groaned. He knew that everything had been leading up to this moment, just as surely as he knew that they were still completely unprepared. Time was precious, and a detour through Pittsburgh was going to set them back even more. "Becky's not going to like this," he said. "She's not going to want to stay here with the Mage and Neaca. She's going to insist on coming with us. And I still haven't managed to convince the elves that they have to help me rescue my parents before I go off with them to plant that seed in the ground. It all sounds so stupid, anyway. Do you think there's really some tree at the North Pole with a fruit on it? It's got to be a thousand degrees below zero up there. Nothing can grow."

Tomtar shrugged his shoulders. "'Tis Faerie land, not Human. Maybe it's not like you think."

"I think I'm starving," Matt said, feeling a familiar cramp in his belly. It had been days since he had eaten normal food.

"Then have some of these," Tomtar offered, holding up a cloth sack.

"What is it, mushrooms?"

"Fungus," said Tomtar. "Dried fungus. 'Tisn't bad, once you get used to it."

"I hate this stuff," Matt sighed, taking the sack. "I guess if we're going to Pittsburgh, there's a chance I can get some people food again."

"Matt?" A voice came from the base of the tree where Matt and Becky had been sleeping. "Matt, what's going on?"

Matt glanced at Tomtar, then took a deep breath. "Becky," he said. "We have to talk."

As the day began, Tuava-Li lit a small campfire within a circle of stones, and everyone gathered around. There was a shrine set up at one end of the fire. A thorny vine spiraled around an old piece of oak, and small carvings of Elfin figures were arranged on both sides. Matt, Tomtar, and Tuava-Li were instructed to prick their fingers on the vine, and then to squeeze a drop of blood into a bowl filled with scented oil. Matt went last. He realized that since most Faerie Folk were terrified of spilling blood, performing this ritual must be terribly important. He pricked his finger and his blood swirled on the surface of the oil. The Mage lit it with an amber candle. "Now you are as one," she said. "Henceforth you will act in accord with the will of the Gods, and your paths will converge in peace and harmony."

Becky, stiff with tension, sat close to her brother. She let her knee press uncomfortably against his. The little group sat within a circle of ceramic bowls, turned upside down on the dirt. Neaca had covered each bowl with incantations, written in a scrawl of ink. The bowls were meant to catch evil spirits in case they should come too close—and Neaca was certain that they would. "The greatest success requires a sacrifice," the Mage continued.

Matt stared at the old Elf. Her hair was a white cloud wreathing a gaunt, wizened face. Matt wondered what she was talking about, and hoped that Tomtar and Tuava-Li could understand her, because nothing that she ever said made any sense to him. "Sometimes," she said, "the sacrifice is of a precious dream, sometimes it is something more, but you must remember that everything is a gift, and when the time comes, you must not cling. All is for the best."

"My mother used to say that everything is a gift," Becky interrupted, "but now I know that's a lie."

Neaca and the Mage exchanged glances, and then Neaca struggled to her feet. "Come, my young friend," she said to Becky. "Will you help me gather some food for your brother and his friends to take on their journey?"

Becky got up and gave her brother's shoulder a hard squeeze. "Owww!" Matt cried.

"Sorry," Becky said. "I forgot that you were sore from all those fairy tattoos." Then she turned and stomped after Neaca into the woods.

"She didn't forget about the tattoos," Matt said to Tomtar. "She did that on purpose. She's mad at me, too, because I said she couldn't go with us."

"Remember," the Mage said, "the right words, spoken with energy and compassion, will change the energy field around you. You must remember. If you feel weak, or frightened, say these words—*I am strong. I am capable. I choose the path of truth.* The path toward the future is like one of the sacred Cords that wrap around our world. Follow the Cord, don't let go, and don't look back."

The Mage stood up. "I have three med'cine bags for your journey. Inside are gourd rattles, for calling down helpful spirits, and corncobs to offer them as gifts. There are scraps of fur to remind you that all of us, animal, Human, and Faerie, are one. Neaca and I have replenished your *Huldu*, Tomtar and Tuava-Li, so that you'll have a supply of med'cine to help offset the effects of metal, and many other things."

Tuava-Li opened her medicine bag and looked inside. "What's this?" she exclaimed, drawing out a large sapphire.

"The stones in your bags are all that remain of the Alfheim Jewels," said the Mage. "I found a single sack, probably dropped by Jardaine and her monks as they fled from the fire. Since Alfheim is no more, the Jewels have lost their original purpose. You may have need of them to help pay your way in the Human world."

"But—but the Jewels are sacred," Tuava-Li protested.

"As is the journey you are about to undertake," said the Mage. "May the stones serve you well. For me, they only bring sorrow."

Tomtar and Matt peered into their bags as the Mage got up and walked across the clearing. Matt looked scornfully at the tufts of hair and corncobs. *What a joke,* he thought.

"What are we looking for?" asked Becky, as she followed Neaca into the woods.

"Good things," Neaca replied. With a basket tucked under her arm, she was imagining the treats they might find. "What do you think your brother would like?"

Becky snorted. "I guess you could start with Snickers bars, pepperoni pizza, maybe a Coke, and, oh, some chocolate-chip cookie-dough ice cream. When Matt gets to Pittsburgh he's going to have all the food he can eat, and I'm going to be sitting out here in the woods with you, while bugs bite us and we starve to death. And when he goes to rescue my family, I won't even know about it, because I—"

Becky stopped in mid-sentence, her chin quivering. "It's not fair."

"Nooo," Neaca answered, shaking her head sadly. "'Tis up to us to try to make life more fair, to bring balance, and harmony, and trust. Each of us contributes, in her own small way."

"Then why won't you let me go with Matt?" Becky cried. "I could help!"

"Perhaps you could," soothed Neaca, as the two of them gathered berries and nuts. "But the legend of Fada tells the tale of how three individuals made the journey to save our world.

Reliving a legend is like slipping a key into a lock: If you don't have the right key, the lock won't open. If three made the ancient journey, then it should be three that undertake the quest again. As best we can, we must re-create the mission in its original form. Otherwise we risk failure. Child, this mission will be full of danger. Even if you could go, 'twould be all the more dangerous for you. The Mage has been training your brother, shaping him for survival. He's not just looking for your family, you know."

"I know, I know," Becky sighed. "It's that seed. That stupid magic seed."

"And you're learning your own magick," Neaca said, with a gentle smile. "You're learning to control your own emotions, and to bring your attention to whatever task is at hand."

As they came back into the circle of *Klumma*, Becky could hear the high, wailing song of the Mage, Tuava-Li, Matt, and Tomtar chanting together. The sound made Becky feel edgy and frightened, and angry with her brother for joining in. "What are they singing about?" she demanded.

"They're praying to the Gods," Neaca replied, "for strength, and clarity, and the power of spirit."

"But Matt doesn't believe in your gods," Becky said.

"Belief doesn't come first," Neaca said, "not for any of us. That would be foolish. The words have their effect by opening the door to belief."

"I don't know what you mean," said Becky, feeling frustrated and annoyed.

When Matt heard his sister's voice he stopped chanting. He was embarrassed, ashamed of what he felt the Elves were making him do, in exchange for their help in finding his mom and dad and baby sister. The Mage turned her head and stared. "It appears we're finished," she said.

Neaca smiled and held up a pouch, offering Tuava-Li the meager portions of raspberries and pine nuts she and Becky had gathered. "For the journey. In the name of the Mother and her Cord, may your travels be swift, and may you find what you're looking for."

"You will depart from the lake," the Mage said to Tuava-Li. "Come."

Tuava-Li, Tomtar, and Matt strapped on their packs. They weren't regular backpacks, like the kind Matt and Becky used to wear to school. These packs were more like baskets, made of thin branches and bound together with vines. Matt did his best to avoid Becky's gaze. He couldn't believe he was going to leave his sister behind after all they had been through. "Be certain that your amulets and charms all face outward," said the Mage. "Walk with your right foot first, and do not stumble. Between here and the lake you must tap each tree that we pass with your knuckles, to alert the spirits of the forest that your journey has begun, and that your intentions are good."

The three walked silently, single-file, toward a small lake. Neaca, Becky, and the Mage trailed behind. When they arrived, Becky saw that Tuava-Li had something in her hand. It was a piece of bark, and she watched as the Elf stood at the edge of the water and flung the bark as far as she could throw. Tomtar and Matt, in turn, followed the Elf's lead. "What are they doing?" Becky whispered to Neaca.

"They've written on the bark the one most important thing each of them wishes to leave behind as they begin their journey," the Elf replied. "When they abandon these things, 'twill lighten their burden, and bring them good fortune."

"What did they write?"

Neaca shook her head. "'Tis not for us to know."

"In every moment there's a beginning and an ending," the Mage announced, "and we're called upon now to honor the journey ahead. What's done is done. Therefore let there be no good-byes."

Becky felt panic welling up inside her. "But, I—"

"No," Matt called to the Mage, as he stomped up among the reeds. "You can't ask me to just—to just leave like this. I want to give my sister a hug, at least!"

"There will be no good-byes," the Mage repeated. She looked like a ragged scarecrow, stiff and straight, with her frizzy white hair sticking out of the hood of her cloak. "You will not bring bad fortune upon this quest before it's even begun. You will turn and walk toward your destination. You are all prepared, and the one thing left to do is simply to turn and go forward, without looking back."

"Matt," Becky cried, starting toward her brother. "Matt,

don't do it! Don't go! We can save Mom and Dad and Emily on our own! We can—"

The trio had already turned away. "No," Becky wailed, and collapsed on the ground. "Don't leave me, Matt, don't leave me here!" As she cried out, she knew that it was useless to argue or complain, or to try to make her brother feel guilty. Suddenly she felt very small. As she watched Matt vanish into the woods, she felt smaller, and smaller. Becky wished that she could just disappear, so that the horrible feeling in the pit of her stomach would go away. Nothing else mattered anymore, not her mother and father, not her baby sister, not the fate of the world. All that mattered was how horribly alone and abandoned she felt now that her brother had betrayed her.

Matt gritted his teeth and walked on. He followed the Elf and the Troll with short little steps. *If they walk like this the whole way, we're never going to get there.* He thought of the little piece of bark he had thrown into the lake. On it he had written, *My guilt for leaving Becky alone with the elves.* It was tearing him apart. *I can't do this*, he said to himself, fighting the urge to turn around.

Yes, you can, said a voice in his head, and Matt did not know whether the voice was coming from one of the Elves, or if it was his own. The three of them, facing forward, headed into the woods.

10

BECKY WATCHED BIRDS sail among the treetops and billowy clouds passing overhead. As the day drifted by she realized that the world was moving on without her, without regard to her misery. Her stomach still grumbled. She sat beneath a tree and flipped through the pages of a little parchment book Neaca had given her. Because Becky had expressed some interest in the plants of the forest, the old Mage had gone to the trouble of making sketches of many common plants, with descriptions of their uses. The Elfin script was difficult to read, but the drawings were neat and precise. Becky felt grateful for the gift and wondered if she could find something to give Neaca in return.

The other old Mage, though, and her tattooed apprentice, made Becky angry. They were mean, and unfriendly, and they seemed full of secrets and schemes they never wanted to share. Though Becky was heartbroken to see Tomtar and her brother go, she was glad she wouldn't have to see Tuava-Li anymore. At the moment the Mage was resting in Neaca's hut, and as far as Becky was concerned, that's where she could stay. She was old, and she complained endlessly about her powers being weak, but it was clear to Becky that she was strong. She was also rude, and stubborn, and she was always absolutely certain that her way was right, no matter what anyone else said. Why anyone would choose to follow her was a mystery that Becky couldn't begin to understand.

Sitting forward, and letting out a bored yawn, Becky slipped Neaca's nature book into her pocket. She wondered what life would be like if she had to live in the forest for very long. Summer was over, school had surely started by now, and girls like her all over the country were sitting in classrooms, or hanging out with friends, and doing things that Becky could only dream of. Here she was, lying alone on her back on a bed of pine needles and doing nothing. She wondered if she'd remain in the forest until winter. What would she wear? The only clothes she owned were the ones she had on her back. What if Matt never returned? She might not ever know if he was alive or dead, or if her mother and father and baby sister were alive or dead. Maybe Becky would spend her life out here in the woods, growing up and growing old, without ever seeing another human being again. She began to cry. "Becky," Neaca called to her from the shadows of one of the *Klumma*. "Someone's nearby!"

A moment later a figure appeared in the distance. Becky was transfixed. It was an Elf, with the most beautiful face she had ever seen. As the Elf wandered toward them, looking lost and frightened, Becky thought of the dolls in her collection, and how much she missed them. Her heart ached with longing. The Elfmaid's eyes were huge and round, her skin the same pale color of all the other Elves Becky had met; yet there was something about this Elf that was different. Her bearing was refined, almost regal. Though she was dressed in plain clothes the color of the forest, and her honey-colored hair was tied back in a long braid, she looked like a princess.

The Mage had joined Becky and Neaca, and together they watched the Elf coming toward the *Klumma*. *Do you recognize her?* Neaca asked in thought-speak.

Aye, answered the Mage. *'Tis Asra, Princess of Alfheim. I wonder if she's looking for me.*

The Mage strode toward the *Klumma* and stepped between two of the carved poles, leaving the protected area where she and the others were invisible. Then she stood and waited for the Elfmaid to see her. Asra gasped and quickly bowed before her Mage. "Thank the Gods I've found you! I've looked everywhere in the woods."

"Not quite everywhere," said the Mage. "You need not bow to me, Asra. Things are not the same as they once were."

"You're still my Mage," Asra said, and reached into the bag she wore at her side. "I've brought you something."

"A surprise!" a voice boomed from the trees behind Asra. "I love surprises!"

As the Mage and Asra stood, stunned and helpless, a battalion of soldiers leapt out of the woods and surrounded them. "I should have sensed this," the Mage moaned.

Queen Metis of Ljosalfar stepped into the clearing, a look of satisfaction on her face. "I always wondered what these old poles in the forest were for. I assumed they were ancient relics, like so many of the piles of stones and arrangements of twigs one finds in the woods. Now I see that they're something more than I'd have ever guessed!"

The Mage turned her eyes on Asra. "Asra, what have you done? Why have you brought Metis here?"

"Asra's innocent," said the Queen. "She didn't know she was being followed. She hasn't betrayed your hiding place—but she is something of a thief! After the stunt she pulled in the infirmary, stealing from the med'cine cabinets while the patients ran riot, she slipped into the map room and took some very important documents that belong to us. One of the guards saw the Princess hide the maps beneath her mother's own sickbed. If the King had found out, he would have been livid with rage; he would have had Asra locked up. I kept the information to myself, however. This morning I called Asra's guards away so that she could escape—I wanted to see where she was going, and my suspicions were entirely correct. Give me the maps, Asra."

The Elfmaid stood proudly before Queen Metis. She reached

into her sack and pulled out a folio of parchment, hesitating just a moment before returning it to the Queen. "I'm sorry," she said, "but only because I was caught."

"Why am I not surprised," the Queen said. She turned to the Mage, bowed low, and offered her the maps. "I should have insisted on giving these to you from the very start, despite my husband's feelings on the matter."

Asra looked stunned. "But I thought you were on Brahja-Chi's side, I thought—"

"If you had thought your actions through a little more clearly," said the Queen, "you might have avoided some unnecessary complications."

She turned her eyes on the Mage. "Brahja-Chi and her monks have been working their magick to try to find you out here, Kalevala, suspecting that you were sheltering Humans somewhere in the forest. Our soldiers have been scouring the woods, too, and turned up nothing. Leave it to our little Princess to find your secret lair!"

"Do not underestimate Brahja-Chi," the Mage replied. "She lets no one stand in her way. Did you know it was Tuava-Li who stopped her magickal display at the Synod meeting? Brahja-Chi poisoned Tacita, seeking revenge for what Tuava-Li did. You're not safe—no one's safe as long as Brahja-Chi lives inside the walls of Ljosalfar."

"My safety is my own concern, not yours," the Queen scoffed. "'Tis because of my concern for Tacita that I've decided to have her brought here, where you and Neaca may care for her until she's well enough to return to Ljosalfar."

"But Brahja-Chi—" said the Mage.

"Brahja-Chi is preparing to leave, even as we speak. The monk who delivered the poisoned beverage to Tacita's chambers has been . . . shall we say, *sacrificed*, in the valley beyond the woods. Brahja-Chi claims that it was the monk's own ill will toward Tacita that led her to the attempted murder. Such an offense, according to her faith, is punishable by death."

The Mage shook her head in disbelief. "And you allowed this to happen?"

"I don't interfere with the practices of others' religions," the Queen said, shrugging. "My husband was worried about insulting Brahja-Chi, so as a favor to him, I did not object. One must choose one's battles, you know."

The Queen turned again to Asra. "The time has come for my soldiers and me to return to Ljosalfar. I would ask you to come along, but I'm afraid you've outworn your welcome, my dear, with disrespect and bad temper. My parting words shall be a command. I order you, and all the Humans hidden in these woods, to leave here immediately. Go to the North Pole, if you wish, with Tuava-Li and the Troll. Keep each other company!"

"The quest must be undertaken by only three," the Mage said scornfully. "And they're already gone, by the way. They left this morning at dawn for Argant, where they hope to obtain copies of the maps which you should have given Tuava-Li when she asked for them." The Mage handed the folio back to the Queen. "Now they're of no use."

"Yes they are," came a voice behind the *Klumma*. Becky materialized from a wall of green, and approached the Queen.

Metis backed away, her face pale and tense. The soldiers withdrew arrows from their quivers and prepared to fire. Few of them had ever seen a real human being before, and they trembled in fear. The Queen pulled a silken handkerchief from her robe and held it over her face. She glared at the girl. "Is this an illusion like Brahja-Chi's, or is it the real thing?"

Becky felt as big as a giant. "I'm real," she said, "and I'll take the maps. I can use them to catch up with my brother."

"Your brother is already hours from here," said the Mage. "You'll never find him."

"Then I'll go to that other place, what did you call it, Helfratheim, and find my parents!"

The Queen laid the maps on the ground and stepped back. "You're going to find your parents," she said. "An admirable goal! And it gives me an idea."

She turned to face Asra. "As you are banished from my kingdom, I hereby order you to go with this Human on her journey to Helfratheim."

"Don't be ridiculous," said the Princess. "Me? Travel with a Human? I stole the maps for my Mage to help her. That's all. You can't ask me to do this!"

"I'm not asking you Asra, I'm commanding you. If you

succeed in the task, you may find yourself more welcome in Ljosalfar upon your return."

"Your Highness," the Mage said, "even with maps, 'tis far too dangerous for the Princess to travel to Helfratheim. The veil between our worlds is thin. She'll never be sure when she's in the Faerie world and when she's crossed over to the Human side."

"Perhaps you're right," said the Queen. She snapped her fingers and one of the guardsmen stepped from the crowd. "This is Radik. He grew up in these woods. I was prepared to send him with Tuava-Li and the others, but since I've arrived too late for that, Radik will accompany the two of you to Helfratheim."

"Do not make your decision on a whim," the Mage scolded. "'Tis an impossible task you propose."

"Nothing's impossible," said the Queen, "not in these times. For instance, here we stand in the presence of a Human, and we do not run for our very lives. Who would have thought *that* possible?"

"You're trembling," the Mage said.

"I said we stand in the presence of a Human," Metis muttered, "I didn't say we had nothing to fear."

"There's no reason to send Asra away like this," the Mage said. "Tuava-Li's already promised to help free the Humans once her quest is completed. She's strong, and she's capable. I trust her to succeed. But if you insist on sending Princess Asra with this Human child, you're sending them to their doom. Even if they manage to reach Helfratheim, they'll never get inside."

"I disagree," said the Queen. "With King Valdis and his son dead, and no heir apparent, Helfratheim will be in shambles. Even this Human child should be able to waltz right through the gates."

Asra glanced at the guard. He was the one who had ushered her from the infirmary to the Queen's chambers just the day before. She felt foolish for noticing that he was handsome, and blushed. She wondered how he felt about his new assignment. Becky, meanwhile, opened the folio and looked at the map on the top of the stack. She had studied maps in school, and had a sense of how to read them. But an Elfin map was another matter, and many of the markings were strange to her. She bit her lip and said nothing. "With any luck you'll get to Helfratheim long before your brother," said the Queen. "Complications are bound to arise on his journey to the Pole. That Seed-planting business may well be more difficult than any of us thinks."

"What about my mother?" Princess Asra demanded. "Who's going to look after her while I go on this foolish quest?"

"Perhaps you should have thought about that last night, before you made such a mess of things," Queen Metis said. "But don't worry. Your mother will be treated as well as the others in the infirmary, which is probably more than she deserves. 'Twas shameful the way she fell in line with the Dockalfars' plans."

"As I recall," said the Mage, "the entire Synod was behind Asra's marriage to Prince Macta!"

The Queen shrugged dismissively. "What's done is done.

Remember, Kalevala, we're a generous people, and we protect the weak because it's the right thing to do."

The Mage turned to Asra. "If Queen Metis will have your mother delivered here to me, I'll look after her. 'Twill be my purpose, my reason for being, to care for Shorya and Tacita and see that they're restored to health."

Asra nodded. At the same time she could feel Becky's eyes on her, and it made her shiver with disgust. "What's the Human's name?" she asked the Queen. "If we must travel with her, we should at least know what she's called."

"I have no idea," Metis said. "Ask her yourself."

Becky took a step forward, and all of the Queen's guard did the same, weapons at the ready. "I'm Becky. That's short for Rebecca. I mean, Rebecca is my real name, but people call me Becky."

"If that's what *people* call you," Asra replied, "then we'll address you as Rebecca."

"Very well," the Queen smiled. "Then all is settled."

She turned her head and nodded to one of the guards, who tossed a pack containing some of Asra's clothing and personal things onto the ground. Then Metis reached into a satchel hanging from a band around her waist and withdrew a silver box. She flicked it open with her thumb, and a Fire Sprite lifted its fiery orange head and looked around. "Take it, Radik," she commanded cheerfully. "May it bring you good fortune. You have my blessings and my best wishes for success."

"Aye, ma'am," said the guard, feeling a deep unease. In

these woods, he knew his bearings. Once he'd left the forests of Ljosalfar, however, things might be quite different. He slipped the silver box into his pocket.

Neaca stood with her hand resting on the edge of one of her *Klumma*. Though her encampment was still hidden by magick from the eyes of the intruders, she knew her presence in the woods was no longer a secret. It was a loss she would learn to bear. She never guessed that already there was someone else hiding nearby, listening intently to every word that was said. The dark figure crouched behind a tree. He had dozed the morning away, and stirred only when he heard voices in the woods beyond. His plan had been to return to Ljosalfar and find a way through the gates. But the sight of Asra, and the beautiful sound of her voice, made Macta Dockalfar change his plans. He reached into his pocket and withdrew his notebook. He grinned as he added some figures to the tally of bets he was making with himself. *Sixty-two thousand*. Macta was a gambler at heart, and though many things had changed, he still thrilled at the prospect of winning—even if it was only imaginary riches at risk. *I bet myself fifteen* dratmas *that I would find my way here. That's three ropes of coins. I bet another ten that luck would be on my side once I arrived. If only I'd known I'd see Asra here, I'd have chanced another thirty, and that would have brought the total even higher!*

The love of his life stood in his sight, and his hand tingled. *Good luck,* he thought, *I can feel it!*

Macta had to press his sleeve over his mouth to keep himself from giggling aloud.

11

A FEEBLE SUN hung over the spires of Helfratheim. Outside the King's chambers an argument was underway. Prashta, the Most Reverent Official Agent of Dockalfar Security Operations, was pointing an accusing finger at Jardaine, former monk of Alfheim. "I've had about all the interference from you that I can stand," he said. "'Tis been long enough since your return from Alfheim, and all of us in the Agency want to see for ourselves how well Prince Macta—I mean, King Macta—is recovering from his injuries. You must let us see him!"

Jardaine forced a smile. She knew that Prashta was spokesman for a powerful group, the Seven Agents who ran Helfratheim through the authority of the King. "You have nothing to fear," she said. "Macta is in full command of his faculties, though he still suffers with the pain of the burns he received in Alfheim. Rest assured that his wounds are healing quickly, with the help of my monks. However, we don't wish to risk the possibility of infection from contact with others. Since our return, I've been faithful in passing on Macta's messages, haven't I? He's just as concerned as you are about keeping the business affairs of this Kingdom running smoothly. The Seven Agents should be confident that all is well."

Prashta glowered with suspicion. He shifted uncomfortably as he stood with Jardaine in the hall outside the throne room. His advising snake lifted its head to whisper in his ear, "Who is thisss audacious young monk who claimsss the authority to ssspeak for the new King? She is a ssstranger to Helfratheim. Sssince Valdisss and mossst of hisss generalsss, advisorsss, and clossse family are dead, 'tisss impossssible to measure how much thisss monk is worthy of our trussst."

Prashta lifted his double chin and shook his head. "What you say is all well and good. Nevertheless, Jardaine, we insist on seeing Macta with our own eyes."

Jardaine's patience reached its limit. "Didn't you see Macta when we first carried him from the Arvada? Didn't I tell you of his heroism fighting the Humans, and how he killed many with his own bare hands? Macta's a hero, and he'll be a great King, now that his father is gone. We must honor his wishes, and if he desires not to meet with the Seven Agents until he's completely restored to health, then it shall be so."

"No it shall not," Prashta said, his voice quivering. "You must tell Macta that we insist on meeting with him, and soon. The security of this realm rests on the confidence of its citizens, and until we see the new King, our faith will be sorely tested."

"I'll give Macta your message," Jardaine said icily. "I don't know what his reaction will be to the news that you have so little faith in him."

Prashta bowed and turned to go. Though he wanted to tell Jardaine that it was *she*, not Macta, in whom he had little faith, he held his tongue. When he had padded away, and his footsteps were nothing more than a faint echo in the corridor, Jardaine slammed her fist against the wall. Behind the anger and fear she felt a terrible loneliness, and missed having an advising snake of her own to confide in. She was sorry she'd killed Sarette during the debacle in Alfheim. Not all of Sarette's advice had been good, but Jardaine had definitely overreacted when she'd flung her snake from the top of the wedding tower. *If not for me,* she thought, *this kingdom would lie in ruin. But if the Seven Agents find out the truth, that Macta is dead, then my life will be ruined as well. I brought the Arvada back to Helfratheim with an illusion of an injured prince, swaddled in bandages, and tales of victory in battle. The Elves' pride and hope for the future depends completely on my ability to keep the deception alive. I can create an illusion of Macta to fool them for a while, but the Seven Agents won't be deceived for long.*

Jardaine stalked along the corridor and descended a narrow flight of steps, then hurried through a hidden door at the side of the palace. She made her way across a courtyard toward the massive stone building where the Experimentalists practiced their art. Anxious for a moment's distraction from all of her troubles, Jardaine hoped that the sight of the Humans she had brought back from the house near Alfheim would cheer her. "Greetings in the name of the Mother and her Cord," she said to the guards she had posted to keep watch outside the lab.

The guards nodded and stepped aside. Jardaine entered the lift and rang the bell. As she rose to the third floor, she focused on her breath and tried, with little success, to still her troubled mind. When the door of the lift opened, several Elves rushed to hand her a white robe. She pulled it over her head and draped a protective medallion around her neck. The Experimentalists were, in Jardaine's opinion, overly cautious when it came to contamination from the Humans. "Greetings, my Mage," they smiled nervously as Jardaine strode into the lab.

She nodded and peered through the wall of glass at the back of the room. "What have you learned of the prisoners since my last visit?"

"Come and see!"

Fire Sprites blazed from sconces along the walls. Behind the glass wall lay the three Humans. Their wrists and ankles were bound, though the workers had already paralyzed their limbs with special potions. They were conscious but unable to struggle as the Elves poked and prodded their bodies from afar with an arsenal of long, pointed tools. "Interesting," Jardaine said to the chief Experimentalist. "What are your assistants doing?"

"Taking measurements, readings of temperature and nerve response. They're using highly sensitive instruments that can detect the relative solidity of the organs that lay below the flesh."

"I see," said Jardaine. "But why are they working at such a distance from the Humans? I would think their measurements would be less precise when they stand so far away."

"Ma'am," said the Experimentalist, "naturally we are concerned about the effects of contamination, and therefore—"

"I've had much exposure to the so-called vapors of the Humans," Jardaine said, her contempt for the fearful Experimentalist barely concealed. "I've suffered no ill effects. You can take my word for it that Humans are harmless."

"Ma'am, we Experimentalists are cautious by nature," the Elf said. "I pray you won't mind if we draw our own conclusions."

Charlie, Jill, and Emily McCormack lay on their backs, their staring eyes fixed on the ceiling. Emily had cried hysterically for an entire day when the Experimentalists first attempted to paralyze her. Uncertain of the right dose, they'd left the girl unable to move her arms and legs, but still capable of crying. Eventually they arrived at the proper dosage, and the racket ceased. The adult Humans had been given higher doses of paralytic agents from the very beginning, and could barely move their lips to complain. No amount of tincture or magic, however, could stop the fear and anger that was growing inside Charlie McCormack. His rage was nearly explosive as one of the Experimentalists used tools to pry his frozen lips apart, intending to count his

teeth. Charlie broke through the paralysis and screamed. His bellow was so loud that it shook the glass panes of the walls, and the Experimentalist, instrument in hand, leapt back in fear. "Where are my children?" Charlie cried. "Matt and Becky, what have you done with them?"

Quickly Jardaine focused the energy in her mind, imagined it forming a ball of concentrated power, and shot it into Charlie's brain. For a moment he seemed to black out. Then he groaned and lifted his head. *This Human is strong*, Jardaine thought. *I could try again, but the force might kill him.*

"What have you done with my kids?" Charlie demanded, his voice hoarse and full of pain. "You've got to let us go, we've done nothing to harm you! Let us go, I'm begging you!"

Jardaine stood over Charlie, shaking her head. "Your other children are safe," she lied. "They're in another room, not far from here. We only keep you here to discover if your kind is infected with anything that can harm us. We'll release you soon."

"Now!" Charlie moaned. "You've got to let us go, now!"

Lying next to Charlie, Jill made little gasping sounds. "Please," Charlie begged, "Let us go. We'll go away, and we'll never tell anyone where we've been. Just let us go!"

The strain of breaking through the magick that held him became too much, and Charlie passed out. "What else have you learned?" Jardaine turned to ask the Experimentalist. Since Dockalfar Security Operations was in the business of making weapons, Jardaine knew that an understanding of her enemy's weaknesses was crucial to good weapon design.

"We've taken samples of their hair and fingernails," he said, speaking softly so that the Humans would not hear. "The Techmagicians have cast spells on the tissue. They've chopped, boiled, and burned it, in order to see how the Humans respond from afar. We think that the subjects feel corresponding pain, though in their paralyzed state, we're not yet certain of the extent."

"Bah," said Jardaine. "The Humans have no feelings, they're just animals. We're looking for magick that will damage the most tissue at the greatest distance—keep that in mind. Just make sure you keep them alive until you've learned all you can."

"Ma'am?" said another of the Experimentalists, tugging at Jardaine's sleeve. "A message has just arrived for you. 'Tis from the Seven Agents."

Jardaine spun around. "Give that to me," she barked, and tore the wax seal from the envelope. "Well, well," she said, scanning the announcement. "It seems that King Macta is expected to make an appearance on his balcony, just three days from now. The good citizens of Helfratheim want to see their new King, and I'm to make absolutely sure that he doesn't disappoint them."

Jardaine stalked to the lift. She needed to return to the palace, where she could be alone to compose a response to this demand. *What am I going to do?* she thought. *I need help! There's no* way I can trick the thousands who'll stand beneath the King's balcony into thinking Macta's truly alive. I have no choice—I must contact Brahja-Chi. She's the only one who can manage an illusion on that scale . . . I'll send an Arvada right away to see if I can't convince the old witch to come to Helfratheim!

12

MATT MADE HIS WAY through the forest, with Tomtar and Tuava-Li trailing behind. Now that he had a purpose, some specific task to perform, Matt felt his frustration melt away. It felt good to move freely again, and to feel the dappled sun on his face. Too long he'd been suffering in silence under the watchful eye of the Mage. Too long he'd been trying to please her, to learn the postures and the incantations and the chants she said would protect him on his journey. Matt knew that once he was back in Pittsburgh there would be new obstacles to overcome. Once they had the map to Helfratheim, he'd have to find a way to make Tomtar and Tuava-Li go with him and help save his parents. He knew his chances for success were slim. He tried not to think about it in detail, but only to stay positive and focus on one goal at a time. Otherwise, the future, and all his fears and uncertainties, would overwhelm him.

Matt saw movement out of the corner of his eye, and he turned his head. A wren fluttered out of a tree and disappeared. "Did you see that, Tomtar?" he called.

"The bird?" Tomtar puffed.

"Yeah, I guess it was just a bird. For a second I thought it was . . . something else."

"What?"

"I don't know," said Matt, "it's just that once in a while I get a feeling like . . . like I don't know, something else is out here in the woods, watching us. Not just forest animals. It isn't scary, just kind of weird. Do you ever get that feeling?"

"I'd get a funny feeling if we weren't bein' watched," Tomtar said. "The woods are full of spirits, at least on the Faerie side of the border, and, there are bound to be a lot of eyes watchin' to see who's crossing their land."

"So what do you mean?" Matt asked. "What's out there, more elves, and trolls and stuff?"

"Aye," said Tomtar. "Some Faeries we know, and some we don't. This world's a mysterious place, and there are plenty of souls out here we haven't even got names for. Some of 'em are pretty shy, and they don't want other Faerie Folk to see 'em."

"They won't harm us," called Tuava-Li, struggling to keep up, "unless we harm them first."

Matt looked over his shoulder. He couldn't help but feel annoyed at everything the Elf said or did, and now that the Mage was gone, he felt free to say what he pleased. "Harm them first?

In that case, they're just the opposite of elves, aren't they? From what I can see, elves strike first, and ask questions later."

"No," Tuava-Li replied. "Elves are like Humans. They lash out when they feel threatened, even if there's no reason for it." She paused, trying to find the right words. "'Tis wrong of you to blame me for everything that's happened. The Mage and I weren't the ones who kidnapped your family and burned your house. We were *all* the target of the Dockalfars, we were *all* their victims."

"Don't give me that victim stuff," Matt said.

Tomtar forced himself to whistle a tune as he clomped along between Matt and Tuava-Li. He thought it might keep them from arguing. If he had to play the role of peacemaker, he'd figure out a way to do it so neither of them thought he was taking sides. He kept up his whistle, trying to sound jolly as they made their way up a steep hill.

At the top of the hill Matt slowed his pace and peered down through the trees to view what lay ahead—just more trees, dense and green, as far as his eyes could see, hills beyond hills beyond hills, until everything shimmered in a distant golden haze. There was no trace of civilization. No roads, no houses, no cell towers, no smokestacks or factories or industrial parks, no airplanes in the slate-blue sky. *Elf realm,* he thought. Matt took a step further and the ground gave way beneath his feet. He let out a surprised cry as he tumbled toward the bottom of the hill in a cloud of dust.

Matt was gasping for breath as he sat up and checked himself for damage. His jeans were torn, his T-shirt was ripped, and he was covered with briars. There were scrapes on his forehead and cheeks. He got up, spitting dirt. Tomtar and Tuava-Li scurried down to see if he was all right. But before they could speak, Matt saw something just ahead. It was a Cord. It was bulging out of the ground behind a large, mossy boulder, and in the dim forest light its ribbed surface seemed to throb. "It must be the Cord to Ljosalfar," Tomtar said in a hushed whisper. He reached out to touch it. "The Elves reinforced it from inside with wooden beams, so they could travel safely to the wedding in Alfheim."

Matt shook his head. "Tomtar, maybe it's the Cord to Alfheim. If this one goes to Alfheim, it's not far from my house. My—"

Matt thought of the fire, and he knew that his house, his dad's development, was gone. Still, he wanted to see with his own eyes what remained, even if it was just a pile of blackened rubble. He wasn't entirely certain that he'd ever have the chance again.

"He's right, Tomtar," Tuava-Li murmured. "'Tis the Cord to Alfheim, I can sense it."

Matt grabbed a stick from the ground. Without a moment's hesitation he thrust it into the Cord and tugged, and he could feel the gust of rushing wind blow over his face.

Matt had traveled the Cord once before, when he and Becky journeyed to the outskirts of Ljosalfar with Tuava-Li, Tomtar, and the Mage. He must have been in shock then, gripping Becky's hand the whole way, for he scarcely remembered how he had managed to do it. But since he had done it once, he was certain he could do it again.

Matt peered into the opening he'd made and looked down the length of the Cord as it disappeared into the darkness below ground. Suddenly he remembered his awful dream of falling, and the feeling of panic welled up inside him once again. But this was not a dream; it was real. The Mage had told him something while he was being tattooed. She said that each time a person makes a move, he risks his entire future on that move, so he should be sure that it is the right one. At the time it had made no sense, like most of what the Mage said, but maybe it was true. Matt put his ear to the Cord and listened for the sound of anything that might be approaching.

"We'd save a lot of time if we take the Cord," he said, glancing at Tomtar and Tuava-Li. "Once we get to Alfheim, and the place where my house used to be, it's about twenty or thirty miles to Pittsburgh. That's a couple of days' walk, if we stay on the highways, and follow the signs. I don't have any idea how far we'd have to walk if we went on foot from here."

"Are you sure the Cord's a good idea?" Tomtar asked. "What if it's damaged? What if if collapses while we're inside?"

"We'll never know until we try," replied Matt. "Who's going to go first?"

"I will," said Tuava-Li. She glanced up at Matt, and then turned to Tomtar. "You go last, to keep an eye on him, and see that he doesn't get hurt."

She lifted one leg into the Cord, then the other, stretching the walls as far as she could. One by one they dropped inside, and the wind carried them away.

Alfheim. It was just a word now, just a collection of memories, and for Tuava-Li each one was more painful than the last. When the travelers reached their destination, she rolled out of the Cord and climbed the blackened steps that once led to the Sacred Grove. It was terrible to see the damage that had been done, though she'd been haunted by the thought ever since the fire. Matt was next to tumble into the ash, and Tomtar followed after him. "You didn't do too badly, for a Human," Tomtar said.

Matt brushed the hair from his tired eyes. "Thanks, I guess."

He stood up next to the Cord and gazed across the devastated landscape. "I know where to go from here. Follow me!"

Tuava-Li was troubled. She had something to say to Matt, and she was reluctant to address him by name. To even say *Matt* out loud felt somehow too familiar, too close, and she felt as if she needed to maintain her distance from the boy. "You know, I understand what you've lost," she said, finally.

Matt snorted. "What? You didn't lose your parents, or your sister." He knew that Tuava-Li was looking up at him, but he walked ahead and refused to honor her remark with even a glance. He was as awkward and uncomfortable around the Elf as she was around him.

Self-pity is not the way of the warrior, thought Tuava-Li, but she did not say the words out loud, for she knew Matt well enough to know it would only make him angry.

"Maybe we should rest and have a bite to eat before we move on," said Tomtar.

"No," Tuava-Li replied, looking around at the ruined trees that had been her homeland. "Not here."

"Then where?" asked Matt. He could feel the anger and frustration rise in him again. Talking to Tuava-Li was just like talking to the Mage, as far as he was concerned. She was cold, and always seemed tense, even while she made a pretense at being friendly. It didn't seem to come naturally to her. Maybe that was the way Elves always were, or maybe it was just the monks; all he knew was that he didn't like her. "Maybe you'd rather stop next to the rubble where *my* home used to be? Would that make you feel better?"

"I'm sorry," said Tuava-Li. "You should know that I mean you no disrespect."

"How should I know that?" Matt demanded.

"Come on," said Tomtar. "Do you remember the hillside, Matt, where we used to sit with Becky and watch the clouds roll by? We could rest there."

"Okay," Matt sighed. "Sounds like a plan."

When they reached the old familiar hillside, there was nothing familiar about it. All that remained were skeletons of trees, blackened stumps, and charred branches on the ground. Matt had an easier time than his companions at crossing the burned

forest, but many times he was forced to lift Tomtar and Tuava-Li like children over fallen tree trunks. It wasn't long before he saw the houses, or what remained of them, in the distance. There was a grim satisfaction in seeing them again. For several nights he'd dreamed of this place, but that was all in his imagination—and his imagination was no substitute for the bleak landscape that spread out before his eyes.

Matt blinked. There must have been a little smoke or soot in the air, because his eyes teared up, and he wiped his face with the back of a dirty hand. The construction site between the ravaged woods and the ruined houses lay as raw as a fresh grave. The toppled swing set in the backyard was still intact, but the paint was discolored and bubbled. His dad's pickup truck lay on its side, burned black, the windshield shattered, the seats in tatters. His breath caught in his throat when he saw the yellow tape. *So people have been here*, he said to himself. Poles had been pounded into the ground around the foundations of each of the houses, and bright plastic ribbons reading POLICE LINE DO NOT CROSS had been stretched between them. Matt glanced out toward the road. There were tire tracks in the ash, lots of them. *Maybe fire trucks were here. Maybe somebody who could have saved us, if they'd come in time. Maybe we should have waited*, he thought, *instead of going with the elves. Maybe . . .*

"Nuts," said Tomtar. "We've got hazelnuts, walnuts, and acorns, split by Becky's own hands. Cranberries, too. A little sour, but not bad. Who wants some?"

TOMTAR, MATT, AND TUAVA-LI

Tuava-Li took a few, and Matt reluctantly held out his palm. As the three stood munching their snack, Matt wiped his hands on his dirty pants and pointed. "We're going to go left at the end of that driveway, and we'll walk down that road until we get to a bigger one. Now the only problem that I can foresee is that if anybody sees a teenage kid walking with an elf and a troll, there'll be panic in the streets. Maybe nobody will pay attention to me because of my tattoos, maybe nobody will notice you, since most people know faeries aren't real, but maybe they will. So if you have some of that stuff in your *Huldu*, Tomtar, that makes you look like a human? You'd better start chewing on it."

Tomtar shook his head. "'Tis only good if you're close enough to smell me. Remember how it works? We've got our amulets, and the tattoos. If we're along the road, and no one's payin' close attention, chances are good that we won't even be noticed."

"What about me?" Matt said. "By September kids are in school, and people will wonder what I'm doing if they see me walking along these roads in the daytime. Nobody out here walks anywhere. If you're on foot, it looks suspicious. Too bad my clothes look so shabby. People will think I'm a homeless person, which I guess I am!"

Matt looked at Tuava-Li. He still didn't want to say her name. The thought of the sound in his mouth made his lip twitch. He wondered if the Elf could read his mind, like the Mage had done. He realized that Tuava-Li wouldn't have to read his mind to know that he didn't care much for her. "I'm also thinking that the closer we get to the city, the more metal you're going to have to deal with. More cars, fences, signs. There'll be metal everywhere. I know you have *trans* for that, but maybe it would be easier for you to turn into an owl or a hawk, or whatever you do, and fly along above us."

Tuava-Li nodded. "A kestrel," she said. "I turn into a kestrel, which is a kind of hawk. But your idea is a good one . . . Matthew."

Matt was startled. *Matthew* probably wasn't that popular a name out in the elf world. He wondered how she could have known his full name, not just the nickname that everyone called him. "I'm sorry, Matt," Tomtar said. "I told her your long name. She wanted to know."

"Fine," Matt said with a sigh. "No secrets between warriors, right?"

Tuava-Li blinked. Why would he have said *"warriors"*? The word had been in her mind just a few minutes earlier. *Just a coincidence,* she said to herself, *unless . . . unless I'm planting things in his mind, or he's reading mine. Whatever it is, I must be more careful. We can pretend to be friends, if we must, but I'm an Elf, and he's a Human . . . and I know how this is going to end.*

"Don't be afraid to call me Tuava-Li," she said aloud.

"I'm not afraid," Matt replied.

"I didn't mean *afraid*, I simply meant —"

"Okay, okay, Tuava-Li," Matt said. "Forget about it, all right?"

As they made their way across the construction site and

headed toward the road, Matt found himself veering toward the charred heap of rubble that had been his house. He ripped away the yellow tape blocking his way and stepped carefully onto the wreckage of the porch. He could see that much of the house had collapsed into the basement when the floors gave way. He could see a network of bent plumbing pipes, like a brittle skeleton protruding from heaps of broken timber. Some of the window frames were still intact, though the glass was broken or melted, or both. He wondered where his bedroom was in all this ruin, if there was anything left. He thought of his music, his TV, the posters he'd just hung on his walls. He thought of Becky's dolls, and his eyes scanned the rubble for any little arms or legs that might be sticking out. But there was nothing to salvage.

"Come on, Matt," Tomtar said in a gentle voice. "There's nothing to see here. We should really be on our way!"

Then Matt saw the black case, like a coffin, sticking up from a mound of ash. It was his dad's gun safe. Nearly six feet tall and a couple of feet wide, it lay in the ruins, and it barely looked damaged at all. Matt's grandpa's old shotguns had been kept in a glass case in the hallway, but the safe had been stowed out of sight in a closet. Maybe there was something here that he could use. "Give me a minute," Matt said. "I want to check something out."

Matt crept on all fours across a blackened but sturdy-looking beam until he reached the gun safe. He tested the door and found it was locked. *Metal . . .* he thought, *something to pry with . . .*

His eyes scoured the wreckage. He inched backwards along the plank toward solid ground, and headed for the pickup truck. In the dirt behind the truck he found a crowbar and part of a car jack. "What are you looking for?" Tomtar asked. "Can I help?"

"It's not safe," Matt said, creeping back onto the plank, "not for you. Too much metal."

"But I can chew one of my *trans*—"

"No. Let me do this myself."

He jammed the crowbar into the upper edge of the door of the safe and pushed. Nothing. Then he pushed the part of the car jack underneath the crowbar to work as a lever, and he pushed again. The safe shifted in the rubble and Matt was afraid it would tip over and collapse into the basement. But the lock groaned, and the door snapped open. Everything inside had fallen from its shelf and lay in a heap in one corner. Carefully he took out each object and examined it. His dad had shown him this stuff once, so he remembered what some of it was. There was a wooden turkey call. There was a pistol magazine, a black leather powder pouch, measuring tools for powder, some things that looked like little metal pipes, some stone axheads and Native American arrowheads. There was a barrel to an old model 12-gauge shotgun. There was a powder horn, an antique hatchet, a box of hollow-point bullets, and an iron bullet mold. There were some other stone things that his grandpa had found buried in a field. But there were no guns. Matt swore silently, remembering that he and his dad had taken the shotguns into the woods when they were looking for Becky. Then he saw the knife. It was old, leather-handled, with a compass set into the top of the handle. He slipped the knife into his pocket and crept backwards along the beam. "Come on," he said to Tomtar and Tuava-Li. "Let's hit the road."

13

L IKE I WAS SAYIN', back in Argant I lived with a lot of cousins, and aunts and uncles, in an old building that *Tems* had abandoned. They said it was a schoolhouse."

The sun trailed along its well-worn route in the afternoon sky as Tomtar told his story. The air shimmered over the blacktop road. A passing truck blew past, pelting the boy and the Troll with gravel. Tomtar coughed violently at the exhaust fumes. "Makes living in the forest seem pretty good, doesn't it?" Matt asked. "You okay?"

"Aye," the Troll replied. He gazed out over the fence that separated the highway shoulder from the field beyond. Bales of hay dotted the landscape, and grain silos towered over tin-roofed barns. High above, Tuava-Li soared as a kestrel.

"It was crowded, but we had our fun," Tomtar said. "Faerie Folk were everywhere in those days. Pixies liked to live at the very top of the empty buildings, and Dwarves, of course, liked the basements. We could never figure out why *Tems* would make so many buildings, and then move away and leave 'em to rot. It wasn't like they were clearin' out to make room for us!"

"Probably not," said Matt. "Do you think you'll be able to find this place, this school building, once we get into town?"

"I think so," Tomtar said. "There's a sign on the corner with a *Tem* word printed on it. When I see the sign, I'll know."

"Once you see the sign," Matt sighed, "you'll already be there. Don't you remember what the sign said?"

"It was *Tem* language, but there are Trolls all over town; in fact there's a Troll under every bridge, and there are bridges all around Argant. You can't get into town without going over at least one bridge. One of them can tell us where to find my Clan. I'll just ask for Uncle Vollyar. Everybody knows him!"

"Your uncle's a popular guy?"

"Uncle Vollyar's head of our Clan," Tomtar said proudly. "He has three daughters, and I grew up with 'em like they were my own sisters. Megala's the oldest, and the toughest. Mitelle's the gentle one, and Delfina's the baby of the family. She was my best friend when I lived in Argant. Vollyar, though, was tough. He ran the place like an army, with soldiers stationed everywhere, and more rules and regulations than you could count, but that's the way it had to be. Trolls were on guard from moonrise to moonset."

"Why did you need guards?" Matt asked.

"They were keepin' watch over the Cords that still ran through our part of town."

"I wouldn't think there'd be Cords in cities."

"Most of the Cords were already cut," Tomtar said. "*Tems* always cut Cords when they're puttin' up their buildings, without even knowin' it. It happens everywhere the worlds overlap. But when I was little, a few of the Cords still snaked through basements and sewer pipes, and they got more protection than a fortune in jewels."

Matt glanced down at his friend. "Does your uncle keep clan jewels, like the elves do?"

"They try," Tomtar said. "Faerie Folk always kept Clan Jewels to bring 'em security, and status, you know, but most of the Trolls in the cities lost theirs a long time ago."

"You mean stolen, like the Alfheim jewels?"

"Aye," Tomtar said. "At least Uncle Vollyar was able to hold onto ours."

"What about your . . . what did you call it . . . your *wandering*? That ritual thing trolls do? You weren't supposed to go back to your home until you were done with it."

"I'm done," he coughed, holding a sleeve over his face as another truck roared past. "Trolls on their Wanderin' have to say *aye* to anybody that asks 'em to do something, and I had to say *no* when Nebiros told me to tie up Becky and leave her in the burnin' woods. That's how I knew it was over."

"Well, I'm glad for that. But wasn't there something else?

Some kind of present you're supposed to take back to your clan when you go home?"

"I've got you," Tomtar said, "you, and Tuava-Li. You're the Gift I'm bringin' back to share." He gazed up in the air, where the kestrel was drifting gracefully.

Ahead of them on the edge of the road lay a dark shape. The breeze ruffled the dead animal's black, matted fur. "Look where you're going," Matt said, stepping out of the way. "You don't want to get rat guts on your shoes."

"Poor critter," Tomtar said, stopping to look at the ragged pelt. "'Tisn't a rat, though."

"I don't know," Matt groaned, "then it's a groundhog, or a squirrel, maybe. I don't want to look."

"We can't leave it here, Matt, we should do something!"

"What can we do? We can't bury every dead animal we see."

"Not bury it, we should build a pyre and cremate the poor thing. That's what Faerie Folk do when something dies."

"Come on, Tomtar," Matt cried. "We've got to keep going."

Tomtar got down on his knees and spoke to the dead animal. "Poor opossum. At least we can move you out of the way."

Very gently, he picked up the carcass and placed it in the tall grass at the side of the gravel shoulder. He closed his eyes and said a few words, wiped his hands on some weeds, then turned to join his friend up ahead. "Opossums don't look like rats, Matt."

"Squashed flat?" Matt shrugged. "Who knows. What makes you an expert on rats, anyway?"

"I saw them in Argant when I was growin' up," Tomtar said. "Didn't you?"

"Back in Pittsburgh? In the alleys, once in a while, but I never got too close."

"Well, I got close," Tomtar confessed. "For a while the Trolls in Argant used to *eat* rats, and pigeons, too!"

"You? After all this fuss about paying respect to some roadkill, you tell me you ate rats? I thought you were a vegetarian!"

"I won't say I never tried 'em," Tomtar said, "because when you're young, and your Elders are serving you things, you just eat what's in front of you. Faerie Folk didn't start off eatin' flesh. We came to it by accident, really, and by and by, we just kind of forgot how the Gods wanted us to live. Do you want to hear the story?"

Matt sighed. "Does it have a happy ending? That's the only kind of story I want to hear these days."

"It started with my cousin Megala," Tomtar began. "She discovered a pen on the roof of one of the *Tem* buildings, and it was full of pigeons! Megala started goin' in every day to snatch the eggs the birds laid. Food was scarce in those days. We grew a lot of our own, but because of the fightin' between Clans, it was hard to get all the supplies we needed. So Megala, she brought eggs home, and it turned out the Clan loved the taste. Sometimes she'd would go up the fire escape to the roof and the *Tem* who owned the birds would still be there, talking to 'em and giving 'em treats. Megala would be quiet, and wait until the Human was gone, and then she'd get the eggs. After a while she got bold and started takin' birds, too."

"We have a word for that," Matt said. "Stealing."

"After the *Tem* caught on to us, he put a lock on the pen. Some of the old Trolls said it was the will of the Gods, to tell us that we shouldn't be eatin' flesh, but most didn't pay that any mind. One day Delfina and I thought we'd try to make a trap to catch wild pigeons—the ones that were always down on the ground peckin' for food. We built the trap from sticks and string and wire. It had a shelf inside, with a lever, and we put a chunk of stale bread inside. Then we hid behind a ledge and waited. The birds were suspicious, you know, and didn't go in, but that didn't stop us from catchin' a rat! Delfina ran over and pried the trap open, and she put her hand way down inside to get the rat out. Well, not only did the critter bite her, but her arm got stuck in the trap. She made such a racket that a *Tem* across the street came to find out what was the matter. I don't know how he saw her, but he took one look and ran away. I had to bust the trap apart to get it off Delfina's arm, and she was covered in rat bites, but we laughed like maniacs all the way home! Delfina's sisters were pretty mad at us for comin' up with the idea."

"Good times," Matt said distractedly. He was thinking about his own sisters.

Tomtar shook his head, and a shadow seemed to pass across his face. "Mitelle got sick early on. She was one of the ones who got better, but . . . once the Clan had a taste for bird, it seemed like they couldn't live without it, no matter how many Trolls got taken down by the sickness. They just wouldn't quit, even after they figured it out. I mean, we *thought* we figured it out. Some of the old Trolls still said it was the Gods' revenge for breakin' the old laws. You know, Elves always think *Tems* contaminate everything with their sicknesses and disease, but in Argant it was the birds that did it. It wasn't the Gods, it was just pigeons. That's what we decided, and that's when Sattye's Clan came over the rooftops, lookin' for a fight, and I left."

"I don't understand," Matt said, as a familiar sense of foreboding crept over him. "I thought everything was going to be fine when we got to your place. Now you say everybody got some kind of . . . what, poisoning, or bird flu? Who's Sattye?"

Tuava-Li swooped down to the fence along the roadside and perched on the end of a post. Her feathers began to shimmer and blur, and in a few seconds she was an Elf once again. "Hand me my garments," she said to Tomtar, as she squatted on the post with her arms folded in front of her.

Tomtar rummaged in his sack and found Tuava-Li's rumpled clothes. "I could hear your conversation," she said, "and it worries me. We're counting on you to get us the maps we need to take us to the Pole!"

"And to Helfratheim, to rescue my parents," Matt said.

Tuava-Li gave Matt a disapproving look before turning to the Troll. "What can we expect to find when we reach Argant, Tomtar?"

"I'm sorry," the Troll mumbled, and hung his head. "To tell the truth, I'm not completely sure."

"Why didn't you tell us this before?"

"It wouldn't have made any difference, would it?" Tomtar pleaded. "We had to do something, we couldn't just stay in the woods. I was plannin' on telling you sooner or later, really, I was."

"This is great," Matt said. "We don't know if your clan's even in Pittsburgh anymore. Our chances for getting those maps just tanked."

Without saying a word, Tuava-Li changed to a kestrel once again and flapped into the air. "We're going to have to hurry to keep up with her now," Tomtar said.

Matt shook his head and quickened his pace. He wasn't in the mood to talk.

14

MILES AWAY, Becky was on a mission of her own. She got out the maps, drawn on nearly transparent paper, and tried to pinpoint her location. The trick was simple—she placed the map of the Elf realm beneath the map of the Human realm, making sure that the corners matched. Then she held them up to the sunlight. The features of the landscape common to both worlds were now plainly visible, overlapping on the maps. The elements that varied from one map to the other would give the travelers the information they'd need to determine which side of the veil they were on.

Becky squinted. She stared up through the maps for a moment, and sighed. The script on the maps was very old-fashioned, with lots of twists and curls on the letters. Like the lettering in the book Neaca had given her, the words on the maps were hard to decipher. The numbers and calculations were worse. There were feet, yards, and miles recorded on the maps. But as far as Becky could tell, Elfin measurements were different from the human ones. "I don't understand," she announced to her companions. "Sometimes when the distances between points on the map are short, I count out feet with my steps. A hundred feet on the map isn't nearly as far as a hundred feet that I take. Are elf distances shorter than human ones?"

"The foot we measure by," said Asra, "is the measure of a Mage's foot. Perhaps our Mages have smaller feet than yours."

"We don't have mages," Becky said distractedly, still staring at the maps. "We don't believe in stuff like that."

Instantly Becky realized her mistake. She was in the company of a princess, a Faerie princess, no less, and she'd just insulted her. "I—I'm sorry, Princess," she blushed. "I didn't mean to say there was anything wrong with, like, mages, I just meant that I'll just have to try to adjust things when I'm reading the map so it makes sense. You know, since I'm a human."

Asra sat on the edge of a boulder and tapped her pack, which lay on the grass, with the toes of her shoes. Though the afternoon sun was pleasantly warm, and birds warbled in distant trees, she was far from happy. She'd spent her entire life inside the walls of Alfheim and Ljosalfar. She was used to walking on soft carpets of the finest moss, sleeping in canopied beds in elegant rooms, and dining on fine china in the company of refined and clever guests. She had longed for freedom and independence, but this wasn't what she had in mind. She felt that the Queen had made a terrible mistake in sending her on this mission. The Human child was more than she could bear. She was big, gangly, and awkward, her speech was clumsy and unrefined, and her behavior was far too familiar. Asra was used to being treated with a certain respectful distance, but Becky didn't seem to understand that. She was a Human, and she was loathsome. That was all there was to it. "Just how lost are we, by your calculations?" Asra asked.

"Not bad, your Highness," replied Becky.

"I'd like to see the maps," Asra sighed, getting up. Careful not to let the girl's fingers touch her flesh, she took them from Becky and examined them. "'Tis impossible to say for certain where we are. I know there's a river nearby—I can hear the burble of the water. But I'm not sure if it matches what I see on the map. The cliffside up ahead looks like the one in the picture, here, except for the grove of ash trees. Where could they have gone?"

"Let's take a look," Becky replied, marching ahead. "If we're on human land, somebody probably cut them down."

The Elfin guard Radik was busy watching the woods. He had a curious feeling that they were being followed. Radik knew that the woods were full of Faerie creatures, but most of them couldn't care less about the presence of Elves in their midst. This was something else, something he couldn't put his finger on. He jumped when Becky cried out. "Look at that!" she said. "It's a covered bridge. I've never seen one in person, just in books!"

Sure enough, the forest gave way to a trail ending in a covered bridge.

The walls were a faded shade of red. Someone had spray-painted big, scrawling letters on the side: KEEP AWAY. Streams of light trickled in through holes in the flimsy tarpaper roof. "Princess," Becky called as she approached the bridge, "Do you see this on either of the maps?"

"Nooo. This is a Human bridge, but the river appears in both."

Radik felt the skin prickling on the back of his neck. He knew that Trolls often lived under bridges, and exacted payment from those who ventured across. But there was no sign of any Troll. He sensed that trouble would come, but was not yet sure from which direction. He paused and scanned the forest; then he thought he saw movement in the bushes by the bridge. There were Faerie creatures hiding there, he was certain. "Stay where you are, Asra."

Becky stepped into the cool shadows of the bridge. "It's so pretty," she called. "Princess, you should see it!"

Becky wandered across, the broad wooden planks creaking and groaning beneath her feet. "Is it safe?" Asra called, stepping into the cool darkness. "Come, Radik. It looks stable enough. The girl's nearly reached the other side."

"Princess!" Radik called, "Asra, you mustn't—" but his cry came too late.

From beneath the bridge a swarm of glistening, silvery shapes appeared. "Lamia," Radik hissed, and bounded toward the bridge.

"Aaaaaah!" Becky screamed, as the tiny silver Faeries swooped and sailed around her, flapping their wings like hummingbirds, hissing like snakes. "Get off of me, you vermin, get off!" Asra roared, swatting at the Lamia with fluttering hands.

Becky smacked one of the hideous creatures and it fell at her feet. It had wings like a bat, clawed feet, and a long, dagger-like tail. Its expression was fierce, and Becky could see when the monster hissed at her that it flashed a long, forked tongue. Radik hurtled into the darkness of the bridge and slashed at the creatures with his knife. "Run!" he cried. "They'll only attack when you're in their territory. Run!"

Becky could see that Asra was completely surrounded by the awful buzzing creatures. In a blur of motion the Lamia spun around her, like piranha in a feeding frenzy. Their claws raked Asra's body, and at the first taste of blood, they closed in, their hisses changing into a horrible kind of purr. Becky knew that Asra recoiled at her touch, but this was an emergency. She reached into the swarm and grabbed the princess around her waist. Becky dashed toward the other side of the bridge, and daylight. Radik followed, still slashing at the Lamia. Suddenly Becky's foot punched through one of the rotten planks. An entire section of the bridge floor collapsed into the narrow river below, and before she knew what had happened, she was thrashing in ice-cold water. Asra sank out of sight, and Radik was dangling by his fingernails from the bridge planks above. The swarm of Lamia buzzed around his head until, screaming, he let go and

tumbled into the water. Becky felt something grab at her ankle and realized it was Asra. She pinched her nose with one hand and dove beneath the surface, moving her free arm back and forth until she found a fistful of the Elf's hair, and pulled her up. Asra coughed and gagged, spitting up water and muck from the bottom of the river as she clung to Becky's shoulders. Radik paddled close and shook his head as he swam to shore. "I warned you," he said, crawling onto the muddy bank.

Becky could see the Lamia peering from the hole where the floorboards of the bridge had collapsed. Their tiny gray heads bobbed, their eyes and teeth gleaming with menace. "Their territory is just inside the bridge," Radik said. "They won't come down here."

"Get me out of the water," Asra cried. "I can't swim."

"I know," Becky said, then added, "your Highness."

"This is a very bad omen," Asra mumbled as Becky helped her safely into the reeds along the bank of the river. She waited until Becky moved away, then busied herself squeezing water from her hair. Her clothes, soaking wet and smeared with mud, clung to her slender form. Her shoes were gone.

"I saved the life of a real princess!" Becky exclaimed, both pleased and surprised by her own bravery.

"Only after you put it in jeopardy," Asra snapped.

They both struggled to climb up the bank onto the path. "Look here," Radik called, pointing at the peaked roof of the bridge. "I think the veil between the worlds opens up right here,

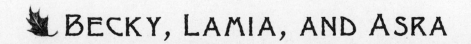

BECKY, LAMIA, AND ASRA

on this bridge. See, along the top of the roof, the shimmering, there?"

A strip of blue, slightly darker than the sky above, wavered along the edge of the roof. "The Human bridge holds the tear open, so it becomes a passage between the realms."

"How fascinating," Asra said sarcastically.

Radik walked through the tall grass and began collecting twigs and limbs that had fallen from the trees. "Help me gather some wood to make a fire. We'll need to dry off before nightfall."

"I've got to brush my hair," Asra said. "'Tis full of leaves and algae from the water. But the brush is in my pack, and I left it by the boulders on the other side of the bridge!"

"I'll get it," Becky volunteered. "I don't mind getting wet, and the water's not too deep."

"My shoes came off in the river, too," Asra added, tentatively. She wanted the girl's help, but at the same time was wary of having to feel gratitude for her aid. "Won't you . . . find them for me?"

Becky gazed into the water and shivered a little, thinking of the slippery muck along the bottom, and the tiny critters that might be waiting in the murky depths to give her toes a pinch. "Stay close to the bridge," Radik said. "I think that's the only way you'll be able to cross between the realms."

Becky climbed down through the reeds. She pictured the Princess's smiling face when she returned with her things, and hoped that Asra would appreciate her act of kindness. There wasn't really anything special about Becky, not like Asra, who was a real princess. Asra was an Elf, but she was also beautiful, and regal, and everything Becky knew she would never be. "Princess," she called, "when I've brought back your bag, may I brush your hair for you?"

Asra shuddered. "Absolutely not!"

Radik opened the silver box that Queen Metis had given him. Like all of the other provisions he carried, the Fire Sprite had been soaked when Radik fell into the stream. It took a great deal of coaxing to make the Sprite cooperate with his efforts in starting a fire. By the time Becky returned, however, it danced among the dried bits of twig and vine and withered leaves, setting them all alight. Before long there was a roaring blaze to warm the bedraggled travelers, and dry their river-soaked clothes. The Sprite settled into the heart of the fire to rest. Asra worked at brushing the tangles from her hair. Radik spread the contents of his pack out to dry along the edge of the fire. Smoke curled up into the evening sky. When a breeze turned the plume toward Becky and made her eyes burn, she circled around to the other side of the fire where Asra sat. Radik promptly got up and moved between Becky and Asra. "You don't have to protect her from me," Becky said. "I'm not going to hurt her. Don't you know that by now?"

Radik poked a stick into the blaze and watched absently as

sparks drifted upward. Asra watched the light play on the girl's face and she could see that Becky felt stung. "Sometimes we hurt without meaning to," Asra said.

Becky wasn't sure if the Elf meant that Radik hadn't intended to hurt her feelings, or if she was implying that Becky was going to contaminate them with Human germs. All she wanted was to be friendly. What was so bad about that? Were the Elves going to act like this all the way to Helfratheim? And once they got there, would they really help her rescue her parents and her baby sister? Becky didn't want thoughts like these to poison the hope she'd worked so hard to keep.

Asra felt uncomfortable. Something like empathy was tugging at her conscience, and the thought occurred to her that perhaps the time had come to take a friendly turn to the girl. She was a Human, there was no getting around it, but she didn't seem to mean any harm. For whatever reason, Rebecca had saved her life. It was amazing, when Asra thought about it. She knew that she would not have dared to do the same, had the tables been turned. She also knew it would be a long journey, indeed, if she and Radik insisted on keeping their distance. It might be wise, then, to make a gesture of kindness. "What are you thinking about, Rebecca?" she finally asked, not certain if she really wanted to know the answer.

"Nothing," Becky answered. "I mean, nothing that would be interesting to you, Princess."

"I'm having trouble with my hair," Asra offered, nearly

choking on her words. "Here in the back—there are so many tangles. Would you help me brush it?"

Radik looked alarmed, but at a nod from Asra he got up and let the girl slip past.

Just then he heard a sound from the path leading toward the covered bridge. He leapt to his feet and moved instinctively in front of Asra, in case there was danger. He breathed a sigh of relief when he saw an old Troll, dressed in brown work clothes, shuffling down the path. "Greetings," the Troll said with a nod. "Pleasant afternoon, eh? Ought to be a lovely sunset tonight."

"If you say so," Radik answered.

"'Tisn't every day that one sees a Human travelin' with Elves," the Troll noted, almost casually, as he passed.

"I must warn you, sir, we just crossed that bridge, and it isn't safe."

"Aye," said the Troll with a chuckle. "'Tis *my* bridge—I should know! I've got a flock of Lamia in there to keep watch whilst I'm gone. Since I wasn't here to collect the fee, my little friends were supposed to keep anyone from crossin' the bridge. You're clever to have gotten past them; Lamia's teeth are sharp. Now that I'm back, I'll take my toll, if you don't mind!"

"We nearly lost our lives getting across that bridge," Radik said angrily. "The floorboards are rotted through, and we almost drowned after your revolting little guardians tried to have us for lunch. We'll pay you nothing."

The Troll frowned and shook his head. "Oh, but I think you will!"

"We haven't got any money," Radik lied.

The Troll smiled slyly. "Few who cross my bridge pay with money. I'll accept that Human of yours in exchange for the damage you've done. She'll fetch a pretty penny down where the Dwarves live!"

"Don't be silly," Asra said, alarmed. She reached in her pack and withdrew a silk purse. She extracted three coins, stepped around the fire and handed them to Radik, who then dropped the coins into the Troll's upturned palm.

"That'll do," said the Troll, grinning as if an unpleasant word had never been spoken. "I wasn't going to bother about the planks, anyway. If a few unwary travelers should happen to take a plunge into the river, I might have reason to collect another fee for fishing 'em out!"

Becky crouched behind the fire. When Asra returned, she touched the girl's forearm awkwardly, and then moved away. Once she was behind Becky she wiped her hand on her smock. "There's nothing to fear," she whispered. "The old coot's harmless."

"Before you leave, there's one more thing," Radik said to the Troll.

"It'll cost you!"

"The coins I've already given you are more than enough. The flickering light around the bridge concerns me. I need to know if we're still traveling in the Faerie realm."

"Nooo," said the Troll, "not anymore. You're sitting on Human ground. But the Faerie realm is right there, on the far side of the bridge! The veil between the worlds tore open on the roof, there, like a thin piece of paper. 'Twas my lucky day! Now it's a gateway for all manner of beasties on both sides of the border."

The Troll took off his hat and knelt on the ground. "Come on, little critters," he cried, "time to pay the toll!"

Many creatures crept from their hiding places behind rocks and trees, and dropped bits of fungus, colored glass, pine cones, and flowers into the hat. They followed the Troll across the bridge, minding the rotten floorboards, and passed to the other side. A moment later, when a group of Faeries on the far side of the bridge paid their tolls, there came a clattering of tiny hoof beats, and a chorus of cheeps, bleats, and squawks. Becky stared in awe at the sight. Winged Faeries dispersed in the purple sky, as other strange creatures trotted along the ground and plunged into the undergrowth.

"They're beautiful!" Becky exclaimed.

One of the Faeries swept over Radik's head, and his arm shot into the air. "Gotcha!"

He returned to the fire with something struggling in his hand. When he held it up, Becky could see that it had glistening wings and a face like the Lamia beneath the bridge, but without the sense of menace. Its wide mouth was pulled back in fear, and tears sprung from its eyes.

"A Pawderflit," Radik grinned.

"Let it go," Becky cried. "You're hurting it!"

Asra looked over Becky's shoulder. "Don't worry, I'm sure he just wants to show it to us."

Radik grunted when the squirming creature sank its teeth into his thumb. "Why, you," he snarled, and flung the Pawderflit to the ground.

Becky ran toward the little Faerie. "You killed it!" she cried.

"Why did you do that?" Asra demanded. "You could have just let the poor thing go!"

As Becky got close to the Pawderflit, it reared back, hissed at her, and shot into the night sky. "See? I didn't hurt it," Radik said. "I spent my whole life in the forest, I know all about these beasts." He massaged the place on his hand where the Faerie had bit him.

"It was scared," Becky whimpered. "Didn't you see how it flew away? I think you hurt one of its wings!"

"Don't be stupid," Radik mumbled, disgusted at the girl's sentimental reaction.

"You're horrible," Becky cried. "Elves are horrible. I wish I'd never met you!"

She jumped up, covered her face in her hands, and ran down the path, away from the covered bridge. Radik and Asra sat awkwardly by the fire. "That was brilliant," Asra muttered.

"I just wanted to show you," Radik said. "And the Human, she'll come back. She has no choice."

"Neither do we."

"Listen," Radik said in a low voice, "why do we have to help the girl? We could leave her here, on the Human side."

"And you could live with yourself afterwards? Disobeying your Queen, abandoning her command? Leaving an innocent child to wander and starve here in the forest?"

Radik scowled. "Why put both of our lives in danger to help her? She's nothing but a Human."

"And we're Elves," Asra said. "We must stand for something, even if no one knows it but us." She sighed, then got to her feet and set out for the path. "Rebecca?" she called. "Let us talk."

On the other side of the bridge a dark figure made its way through the shadows. When the Troll demanded his fee for the stranger's passage, he was rewarded with a blow to the head that sent him reeling. Even the Lamia stayed back when Macta Dockalfar, smiling faintly, stalked across the bridge. He would keep his distance from Radik, Becky, and Asra, but he had no intention of letting them out of his sight.

15

IT WAS LATE AFTERNOON when the forest started to thin, and housing developments appeared among the trees. Matt led Tuava-Li and Tomtar around the edges of the tidy little communities, with their neat backyards, curving driveways, and garages tucked cozily beneath perfect three-story homes. Matt couldn't help but think of the development his dad had carved into the woods just a few miles north. Some children playing on a backyard swing set saw Matt out along the edge of the woods, and they began to gesture and point. Matt figured it must be after three o'clock if these kids were home from school. He ignored them and kept walking. He didn't know if the kids were able to see the Troll and the Elf following behind him. All he knew was that he had a destination, and a goal to travel as far as they could before nightfall.

It wasn't easy trudging through the woods when the highway

shoulder, in comparison, had been so smooth and flat; but Matt had decided that they should leave the main roads and continue their journey off the highways. There were several reasons for the change of plans. Whenever they passed a dead animal, struck by a passing car, Tomtar would insist on dragging the carcass into the grass and conducting a ceremony. A dead deer on the road had rattled Tomtar and Tuava-Li so badly that they looked as if they might not be able to continue the journey. A couple of drivers had honked their horns as they passed, and Matt was worried that somebody might stop and ask him what he was doing out there. Worse still, someone might see Tomtar or Tuava-Li, even though they weren't supposed to be able to. Who knew what would happen, then? "We must make the best use of our time," Tuava-Li said. "There are exercises we must practice, to keep us sharp and focused. The Mage would be glad to know we were prepared for what lies ahead. We can practice as we walk."

"I thought the tattoos and amulets were supposed to protect us," Matt replied. "I had enough of the Mage's exercises back in Neaca's camp. Maybe we should be saving our strength by *not* doing any more exercises."

Tuava-Li stopped in her tracks and closed her eyes. She imagined a circle of protection, a wheel of pure energy, spinning around her waist. She breathed in and out of the spinning wheel until she felt sure that it was strong. "What's up?" Matt asked, turning to see what had become of the Elf. "Why did you stop?"

Tomtar looked back in surprise. "Tuava-Li, is there something wrong?"

"Nooo," she breathed. "Both of you, come to me. I want to show you something."

Tomtar hurried toward Tuava-Li, but at a distance of five feet, he was thrown onto his back with a loud *ooomph!*

Matt stepped over the Troll and suffered the same fate, tossed away by an invisible force. On impact the knife he had found in the wreckage of his old house slipped out of his pocket, and fell on the ground.

"What's that?" Tomtar asked.

"It's a knife. It used to belong to my dad."

"I didn't know you had a weapon," said Tuava-Li.

"I didn't know you could toss people around like that," Matt grumbled, getting up and adjusting his pack. "All right, so you can do magic tricks. What are you trying to prove?"

"'Tis not a trick," Tuava-Li said, "but it *is* magick. You can do it, too. I'll teach you!"

Matt smirked as he slipped the knife back into his pocket. "Can I use it to toss elves around?"

"'Tis called the Belt of Power," Tuava-Li said, ignoring the boy's remark. "'Tis a method of nonviolent resistance to force."

"I want to learn!" Tomtar said.

"Okay," sighed Matt, "I guess I'll give it a try, but I'd be surprised if a human being could learn one of your faerie tricks."

Clouds rolled lazily overhead as the sun arced across the

sky. No one would have guessed that the boy and the Troll were busily trying to conjure Belts of Power into being as they traipsed over the rough terrain, guided by the Elf's instructions. The trio trudged along a ridge and Matt saw electric towers, looming like spires built from a gigantic Erector Set, leading the way into the purple distance. The towers stood in pairs. Each had a bulky, box-like top, meant to hold the power lines high above the ground. They were lined up as straight as soldiers, extending as far as the eye could see. The woods had been cut away to make room for the towers, which carried electric lines on their long journey through the farthest suburbs of Pittsburgh. The ground around the towers was flat and carpeted in grass, smooth as a billiard table. "Hey, look at that," Matt cried, glad to be distracted from the exhausting mental work of keeping the Belt of Power in motion. The others were already looking.

Through the eyes of an Elf and a Troll, the towers looked nothing like they did to Matt. To Tomtar and Tuava-Li, the electricity that raced along the cables, high in the arms of the towers, shimmered and glowed in rainbow colors. Matt heard a faint hum emanating from the cables. Tomtar and Tuava-Li heard something more like music, harsh and discordant, but full of a ringing sound that was almost like distant voices, singing. At the same time the radiating power of the electricity made them ill. "We can't pass through here," Tuava-Li said, feeling dizzy. She sat down on the ground.

"But look at the grass," Matt said, "there, underneath the

towers. It's flat, and soft, and it will make our trip a lot quicker than if we keep hiking through the woods. We can follow the trail here and still stay out of sight of people!"

"Let's try some of the *trans*," Tomtar said, rummaging in his *Huldu* for the appropriate bits of tree bark. "Here," he said, offering pieces to Tuava-Li and Matt.

Matt smiled faintly. "No, I'm okay. It's just electricity. This kind of thing doesn't bother me — I'm human, remember?"

Tomtar nodded and popped a piece of bark into his mouth. Tuava-Li did the same, and after resting on the ground for a few minutes, diligently chewing, they were ready to try hiking ahead in the shadow of the towers. "'Tis like Faerie voices," Tomtar said. "Who do you think it is, doin' the singin'?"

"What singing?" Matt replied.

"Don't you hear it? Comin' from those vines, up there?"

"Singing?" Matt controlled his urge to smile. "Vines? Those are rubber cables, full of electric wires. I guess there must be metal inside, but I don't know for sure. They carry power to light up houses, operate machines, run all the refrigerators and air conditioners and computers everywhere around here. What did you think makes all that stuff work?"

"Magick," Tuava-Li said and shuddered. "Human magick!"

"Maybe you could show us some more of your elfin magic," Matt said flippantly. "If we could rustle up a flying carpet, we could ride right into Pittsburgh, get those maps, and keep flying until we reached Helfratheim."

Tuava-Li started to speak, but Matt knew what was coming, and he cut her off.

"Or first we could go straight up to the city at the North Pole, and find the magic seed, and plant it in the middle of the earth, down where there's nothing but molten rock and iron and stuff nobody could get through in a million years. Have I got it right?"

"You don't understand," Tuava-Li explained. "'Tis not the same in the Faerie world as it is in your Human world. Fada made the journey, and so shall we. Before Fada there were others, heroes lost to time, who did their part, too—just as we shall do ours."

"So tell me the story," Matt said, "the legend, or whatever. What's the deal with this Fada guy, the one we've got to copy? What did he do? Who went with him—a kid like me?"

Tuava-Li nodded; it was a simple tale, one she'd heard and told a thousand times. There was one detail, however, she would have to omit: the sacrifice at the end of the journey. "Fada was an Elfin Prince, and a warrior. He was renowned for victory in many battles, in a time when Faerie Folk and Humans shared the earth, and had forgotten how to live in peace. The world then was torn with strife and hatred, and the Adri, the mighty trees whose roots bind the world together, began to die. The Goddess called Fada to undertake a quest to find the hidden city at the North Pole, where the Adri grew. Fada chose a Troll Mage named Desir and a Human King named Volsung to go with him.

The Goddess instructed them to pluck the last fruit of the dying Adri, and take its Seed. Then they were to travel down along the roots of the ancient tree until they came to an earthen chamber at the center of the Faerie world. There they were to plant the Seed. Fada and the others did as they were instructed. When the Seed was planted, the old tree pulled up its roots, a new tree grew to take its place, and peace and well-being were restored to all the realms."

"You mean humans and faeries were separated, like little kids who can't learn to get along. We each got a world of our own, and we weren't allowed to play together anymore. Right?"

"If you choose to see it that way."

"Couldn't your goddesses, or gods or whatever, have planted the seed themselves, if they wanted everything to be all cozy in faerie-land?"

"Of course," said Tuava-Li. "But the Goddess knows 'tis better for us to do the most important things for ourselves, so we know their real worth. The Goddess simply shows us the way."

"And what became of these characters after they did what they were supposed to do? How did they get out of the middle of the earth? Did they get to go home and live out their lives, or did the gods have other stuff for them to take care of?"

"Fada returned to tell the story, so that it would live on through time. What became of the others is not important. But the vision that the Mage and I shared was proof that the three of us are chosen to live the legend anew, and save our world."

"That's it?" asked Matt. "So your faerie goddess chose me and Tomtar to go with you?"

"As Her representative, I chose you."

"I guess I should feel flattered. I never even got chosen for the school volleyball team. The problem with your story, though, is that there aren't any details. I don't know how we're supposed to do this thing when we know so little about it. It all seems like a wild goose chase to me. We're never going to get to the North Pole, and even if we do, we won't know where to go or what to do."

Tuava-Li shook her head. "We will succeed, there will be signs. The Goddess wouldn't ask us to undertake this quest if She weren't going to guide us, and provide for us, in every way possible. We simply have to look for the signs—in the stars, in our dreams, in the journey itself, as it unfolds."

"Maybe the singing is a sign!" Tomtar said.

"Singing?" Matt looked up, squinting past the wires on the high-power lines that loomed over their heads. "Oh, yeah. You want to climb up one of those ladders that goes to the top, and see if you can find out what you're hearing? Choirs of angels, maybe?"

"Nooo," Tomtar said nervously. "'Tis far too high."

Matt laughed. "I wouldn't climb it, either, Tomtar. Not if my life depended on it."

"I don't know how you do it, Tuava-Li, flyin' like you do!"

"A kestrel has wings," Tuava-Li said, "and doesn't fear falling.

Birds are more fearful of being trapped in an enclosed space. In the sky a bird feels free to go wherever she pleases."

"I used to feel like that," Matt said, "free, I mean. Or at least, looking back, I was pretty much free to do what I wanted. All I had to do was wash a few dishes, fold some towels, go to bed by eleven on weeknights and pick up my room now and then. Now here I am, getting ready to walk north across a continent. Maybe it looks like I'm free as a bird, but I might as well be locked in a cage, for all the choices I have."

"We're free to make our own choices, Matthew," said Tuava-Li. "We choose our goals and follow them, step by step. You might think we're slaves to our goal, but this is the road you've chosen to take, of your own free will. No one forced you on this journey."

"I don't need another lecture," Matt scowled. "I know what I've signed on for."

Tuava-Li bit her lip. Somehow, once again, the conversation had gone wrong, and the boy was angry with her.

The trio walked on, passing industrial parks and enormous cinderblock warehouses, and then low brick commercial buildings, parking lots, and backyards enclosed with chain-link fences. Finally they came to a crowded, four-lane highway, busy with passing traffic. "I think I remember this road," Matt said, looking up at the signs that lined the curbside. "We're getting close. We'll have to stay on the sidewalk now and just hope that nobody sees you. Can you guys chew some of that stuff that makes you look human, just in case?"

Tomtar reached into his *Huldu* for the *trans*. Unlike the medicine that relieved symptoms of nausea from exposure to metal, the *trans* he now sought had a different effect on the user. When chewing on the bark, something in it would cause Tomtar and Tuava-Li to emit a subtle odor that would affect the perception of any person that smelled it. Faerie Folk would then appear to be nothing more or less than human beings, with eyes and ears in the correct proportion, and a convincing skin color to fool the most discriminating eye. Some might have called it magic, and some might have called it chemistry. Whatever it was, it worked. A few moments later Matt was walking down the side of the busy road with what appeared to be two human beings roughly his own age and size.

The moon was slowly rising over the muffler shops, gas stations, cell phone outlets, and fast food franchises that lined the highway. "There's a ring around the moon," Tuava-Li noted. "Rain is on the way!"

"But there's not a cloud in the sky," Matt said. "Is that, like, farmers' knowledge, from studying nature, or is it one of your superstitions?"

Tuava-Li knew she was being challenged. "What is superstition?" she asked.

Matt sighed. He had just meant to insult Tuava-Li, not get into another discussion. "Superstition is, like, a belief that isn't based on reason or knowledge. It's like the evil eye, and amulets and tattoos to protect you, and green men in the sky."

Cars and trucks sped by, distracting Tuava-Li. It was hard to concentrate when she was feeling ill and overwhelmed. "I believe one thing always leads to something else," she said.

Matt nodded. "Okay. That's called *cause and effect*. That's what humans believe in."

"I know that everything is connected, and that everything happens for a reason."

"Well, there you go," Matt said. "That's superstition. You take cause and effect to an impossible level. Sometimes, things happen for no reason at all. Coincidence. That's just a fact."

"'Tis your *belief*," Tuava-Li said, keeping an eye on the highway. She'd never seen so many vehicles at once, or traveling so fast. "We believe that once two things are connected, they are always connected, no matter what happens to separate them."

Matt let out an exasperated sigh. "I guess, sort of. That's the way memory works. For the rest of my life, for instance, whenever I think of you, I'll always remember what a pain you were!"

"Matt!" Tomtar scolded.

"Connection is the nature of magick," Tuava-Li continued, ignoring the insult. "'Tis the *foundation* of magick. If I take a lock of your hair, and I cast a spell upon it, I'll be able to hurt you, no matter where you are. If I take a clipping from your fingernail, or something that belongs to you, say, that knife you were hiding from us, I can use it to cause you pain. That's why 'tis so important that you don't lose things that belong to you."

"That's just silly," said Matt. "Of course you could use my knife to hurt me. But if I take this grubby old shirt of mine and throw it in the dumpster, who cares? It's gone off to the landfill, it rots into nothing, and nobody ever knows it had anything to do with me."

"You don't understand," said Tuava-Li. "Someone who has the shirt and knows that it was yours could use it against you."

"You mean make me smell it?" Matt said with a snort.

"No," Tuava-Li said. She could see that this conversation, like every one she had with Matt, was going nowhere. "Maybe you'll believe me when the rain comes."

"If I had any money," Matt said, "we could make a little bet. But since I don't, we'll just have to drop the whole thing." Matt knew he was being cranky. He felt a twinge of guilt, then realized his mood was the result of being famished. *Cause and effect,* he thought.

Though Tomtar and Tuava-Li were busily chewing on bits of bark intended to make them appear human, their bellies also gnawed with hunger. For Matt, the scents of pizza, charbroiled meat, and hot grease were making him feel faint. Each of the pungent odors that wafted on the evening air struck him like a punch in the stomach. It had been so long since he had eaten anything that a normal person would eat that the smells of food blowing out of the exhaust fans of the restaurants seemed incredibly rich and exotic. He scuffed his feet along the sidewalk and imagined gorging himself on everything these take-out places had to offer. Tuava-Li paused for a moment, took off her pack and rummaged inside. "Would anyone like something to eat?" she offered, holding a little sack that Matt knew was filled with withered berries, dried mushrooms, and bitter-tasting nuts.

"I'll take some," Tomtar chirped happily.

"All right," Matt said, feeling dispirited and desperate. "Me, too."

As the three stood on the sidewalk and chewed their meager meal, Tuava-Li moved as far from the road as she possibly could. She tripped over a concrete barrier at the edge of a parking lot, and toppled to the ground. For a second the illusion that she was Human vanished, and she was a scrawny, pale Elf again. The bark had fallen from her mouth and lay amid the soot, gravel, and litter. A hot breeze nudged an abandoned Styrofoam cup toward her. Tuava-Li cringed and got up. "Let me help you," Tomtar volunteered.

He found another *trans* for her, and she popped it into her mouth as she forged ahead. She couldn't get away from this place any too soon.

Matt shook his head. "Boy, you're in a hurry, all of a sudden! Look, if it's because of what I said . . ."

Tuava-Li felt faint. A truck sped past, spewing a black cloud and ruffling her hair. "The Human world is awful," she coughed. "I didn't want to insult you, but I can't help it. I'm going mad from the sound of this place, all the rumbling and roaring! 'Tis a world made by devils, only there are no devils here. There's nothing living here, at all — no trees, no grass, no birds or animals, just Humans and their horrible machines and buildings, and this hard, hard ground, for as far as I can see. Why does nothing grow on this soil? Is there some curse on this land?"

"It's called blacktop."

Tuava-Li's eyes were full of sorrow. "'Tis so ugly."

"Who cares?" Matt shrugged. "This strip has everything you could ever want — look, you can buy a car over there, or a refrigerator at that place next to it. You can get your nails done, or buy some junk for your next party, or you can fill up your belly with all the fat and salt and sugar you can tolerate. All you need is cash!"

"Cash?" Tomtar repeated.

"Something we don't have," Matt said. "But we're going to get some, just as soon as we sell those jewels. I don't know, but I think we've got enough of those precious Alfheim stones to make us rich."

A beat-up sedan squealed around a corner. A teenager in the passenger seat rolled down his window and leaned out. "Bums!" he yelled from behind his greasy bangs, and the vehicle sped away.

"I can't stand this," Tuava-Li said with a shiver.

"What?" Matt replied. "We look like bums, didn't you know? We look like homeless, crazy bums. And there isn't anything we can do about it. At least we know now that the two of you look like people when you're chewing on that tree bark.

Come on, let's keep walking. This isn't going to get any better for you, Tuava-Li, until we leave Pittsburgh. If you happen to see any weeds popping up from cracks in the concrete, that's about all the nature you're going to get, so stop and savor it, if you want."

Tomtar seemed content to gaze about, looking at the brightly colored signs that lit up the highway now that the sun had gone down. The air hummed with their fluorescent buzz. "What do the signs say, Matt?"

"Just names, mostly," Matt said, remembering that the Troll did not know how to read English. "McDonald's, Chevrolet, Taco Bell, Domino's, Midas, things like that. These same stores are all over the world!"

Tomtar's eyes widened. "The entire world?"

"Well, the human world, anyway. Come on, Tomtar, you lived in Pittsburgh. You must have seen this stuff before."

"Not like this. Not so many."

Matt smiled, feeling somehow proud of the world he lived in, in all its cheap, prefabricated complexity. "That's the 'burbs for you!"

"'Tis amazing!"

"Look at that place over there," Matt said, pointing. "They sell pizza. God, I'd sell my soul for a slice right now."

"Don't say that, Matthew," Tuava-Li scolded.

Matt wandered up into the parking lot. A man was getting out of his car, and he scowled and shook his head when he saw the boy approaching. "What are you staring at?" Matt demanded, as the man yanked open the door and stepped into the pizza place. Matt could only begin to imagine how bad he must look, with his filthy clothes and tattoos. "Ah," he said, as a cool breeze wafted past him. The air tickled his skin through the holes in his shirt. "Air conditioning!"

The trio stood outside the plate glass window and stared inside. There were people nestled into yellow plastic seats at red plastic tables, engrossed in their meals. They nibbled at the edges of bubbling-hot pizza slices and sipped their giant sodas while they chatted and laughed, oblivious to Matt and his companions. Matt remembered eating at places like this with his own family, in some other lifetime. Now here he stood, in his dirty rags, his arms and torso covered with pictures of leaves and bugs and vines. There wasn't a dime in his pocket. He found his mouth watering at the sight of strangers eating their supper. Lost in his own thoughts, Matt was startled when he heard a loud bang from behind the building. He spun around. "Something's wrong," Tuava-Li whispered.

"No," said Matt, "let's check it out!"

A young man from the kitchen was behind the restaurant, wiping his hands on a soiled apron. He had heaved a large plastic bag and a couple of pizza boxes into a dumpster by the chain-link fence. Now he was going back inside. "I can't believe I'm doing this," Matt breathed, picking up his pace as he headed for the dumpster.

"Wait," Tuava-Li warned. "You mustn't go back there. I sense something Faerie is—"

Matt lifted the lid of the dumpster, and his nostrils burned with the reek of garbage. "*Phew!*" he cried, wrinkling up his face. "Of all the things I've had to do since I met you guys, this has got to be the worst. Well, I may be a bum, but at least I'm not gonna starve."

Matt had seen the man from the restaurant throw the pizza boxes into the trash, but he couldn't believe his luck. The lid of one of the boxes had tipped open and a greasy slab of pizza slid out. "No you don't," Matt muttered, leaning into the dumpster.

"Aye, I do," a high-pitched voice answered, and Matt tumbled back. "Something—somebody's in there!" he cried.

Tuava-Li shook her head. "I warned you."

Matt opened the lid again, this time with caution, and saw a dozen eyes staring back at him. Tuava-Li climbed onto the edge of the dumpster and peered inside. "Pixies," she said.

"This is ours," shrieked one of the little voices.

"And mine," came another voice from outside.

Matt spun around. Tuava-Li dropped onto the ground and Tomtar backed away, ready to flee. It was a Troll, with bad teeth, drooping eyebrows, and bushy hair. "In the name of the Canon and the Mistress who serves the Word, what do you think you're doing here?" the Troll demanded.

"What's it to—" Matt began, but Tuava-Li cut him off.

"In the name of the Mother and her Cord, who are you to greet us in the language of the Mage Brahja-Chi?"

PIXIES AND NICK

"Look," Matt said, "there's some pizza in there, and it's got our names on it. If you don't mind, I'm going to reach in there and get it."

"Are you?" the Troll said in a mocking voice. "Then help yourself."

Matt hoisted the lid of the dumpster again and peered into the putrid gloom. The Pixies inside were gobbling bites from every slice of pizza, and they glared up at Matt with sauce-smeared, pockmarked faces. Their dull gray wings fluttered nervously, and when they saw Matt staring at them, they attacked the pizza with renewed vigor.

"What's wrong with them?" Matt cried, stepping back.

"Wrong?" the Troll said. "There's nothing wrong with them that a little food won't fix."

"But—their faces!"

"Nothin' to be done for it, eh?" the Troll said with a shrug. "Metal poisoning. We live in the world we live in, after all, and decent *trans* is hard to come by. Scarred for life, but they still have to eat!"

"So do we," Matt said, "but I wouldn't touch anything that your little friends in there wiped their filthy paws on. They've taken a bite out of every slice, so that we wouldn't dare eat it!"

The Troll laughed and tapped his forehead. "Smart, aren't they? They may not have much else goin' for them, but they're smart, I tell you!"

"Or just greedy," Tomtar volunteered.

Matt heard another bang and he flinched. This time the sound was from the kitchen door. A man with a head as shiny and hairless as a waxed floor was standing in the doorway. He had a broom handle clutched in his hands, and he was aiming it at Matt. "Get out of here, you little punk," he sneered. "Get out of here, or I'll call the cops! I know it's you that's been messing up my dumpster every night. You homeless people think you have the right to do whatever you want, but I tell you, you're not getting anything from me!"

"Come on," the Troll laughed, and he bent to squeeze through an opening at the bottom of the fence behind the dumpster. "Follow me!"

Matt watched the Pixies dart through a rusted hole in the trash bin; they flitted through the fence and were gone. "What do you think?" asked Tomtar. "Should we go?"

Tuava-Li looked nervously at Matt. "I don't trust them. It's odd, but I feel like I've met that Troll before."

"One thing's for sure, I can't fit through that little hole."

"Let's go around the fence and find out where they went," Tomtar said. "Maybe this is one of the signs we've been waiting for, Tuava-Li."

Matt walked cautiously down the side of the restaurant, keeping one eye on the man with the broom handle. He was still glaring at him. "I'm going," Matt said. "Don't bust an artery, man!"

At the end of the fence Matt made a swift turn and hurried

up the other side, followed by Tomtar and Tuava-Li. They found themselves in an alley between two rows of shops. Half a dozen Pixies fluttered around the Troll's head as he squatted on the blacktop. "If you're hungry," the Troll said, "just wait here a while. There's plenty more food where that came from! The Goddess always provides for those in need."

"Why would that guy just throw out perfectly good pizzas?" Matt asked.

The Troll snorted. "I learned the trick from watching Humans. The Pixies are always finding coins that Humans have dropped, and when we have enough of them, I climb up into the phone booth on the corner to call in my order. I ask for funny toppings, like pineapple and anchovies. When I don't show up to get my pies, the Humans wait a while, then throw 'em out because they know they'll never be able to sell 'em to anybody else. We come around and pick the pizza out of the garbage, see? That way, we get a free meal. We can't do it too often at one place, though, or they catch on to us."

"You speak of the Goddess," Tuava-Li said, "and yet you feel free to lie and steal. What kind of religion do you practice?"

"I am devoted to the Goddess, and the Mistress who serves Her," the Troll said cheerfully. "Lying and stealing isn't wrong, if it's done to Humans!"

The Pixies giggled, licking their lips as they swarmed around the Troll. Their gowns were streaked with tomato sauce and cheese, as well as countless other stains that Matt preferred not to think about. "My name's Nick," the Troll said, bowing to Tuava-Li.

"Nick?"

"I chose the name myself," the Troll said, "after I was reborn in the service of the Goddess and the One who saved me. Have you heard the good word about Brahja-Chi?"

"Now I remember," Tuava-Li exclaimed. "I knew I'd seen your face somewhere before. You sat on the bench next to me in Ljosalfar, at the Synod meeting. Why were you invited there? And how did you get back here so quickly?"

"I might ask the same of you, Mistress. I was wondering if you'd recognize me."

"We're on our way to Argant," Tomtar volunteered, "to find my family."

"Really?" said the Troll, raising an eyebrow. "Not another kind of mission? I seem to recall mention of a quest of some kind, traveling north, perhaps? Are you part of a Clan, in Argant?"

"I have an uncle named Vollyar," Tomtar said. "He's my Clan leader. I'm comin' home from my Wanderin'!"

"Is that so?" said the Troll, wearing an expression Tomtar couldn't interpret. "Just how long has it been since you've been to Argant?"

"A long while."

"Then I hope you like surprises!" The Troll turned his head and took in Tuava-Li. "I heard you speak before the Synod. Brahja-Chi, you know, doesn't approve of your little mission."

"I travel on a higher authority than Brahja-Chi."

"Listen," said the Troll with a confidential smile. "You're still too far away to reach Argant tonight. Faerie Folk in the Human realm have to stick together, even when we disagree. Have you got a place to stay?"

"We're just going to keep walking until we get there," Matt said. "We're kind of in a hurry."

"A hurry?" the Troll snorted. "The police will stop you for sure if they see you walking along this road late at night. And there are worse dangers than that out there, I promise!" He turned to Tomtar. "Listen. Tonight we're having a little celebration. Faerie Folk are coming from all over. How would the two of you like to come and spend the night with us? I know you'd find it interesting. You'd be our honored guests!"

Tomtar looked at Tuava-Li, and Tuava-Li shook her head, almost imperceptibly. The Troll threw a glance at Matt. "I can't invite *you*, understand. Humans and Faeries simply don't mix! It looks to me as if you're used to sleeping in the woods. One more night on a bed of dirt and rotten leaves won't hurt you."

"I think we're going to wait here until they throw out some more pizza," Matt said. "We're all starved. And the three of us, we kind of stick together, if you know what I mean."

The Troll turned to Tuava-Li with a grin. "I won't accept *no* for an answer. It'll be fun, I promise—a night to remember. Come by 'round midnight. Head back through this parking lot and you'll find a block of tan-colored buildings not far from here. We're in B22, just inside the U-Store-It. It's the second row, last door on your right."

"You live in a storage unit?" Matt asked. Suddenly there was a loud bang from the other side of the fence. Somebody was throwing something into the dumpster behind the pizza place.

"Suppertime," the Troll smiled. "Better hurry, boy, if you want to eat!"

16

THE THREE HUMANS lay, drugged and paralyzed, on wheeled carts in the lab. The Experimentalists' silver and bone tools were outfitted with fiber-thin sensor cables. With their protective medallions in place, and their gloves and masks pulled tight, several of the Experimentalists worked on the woman and her daughter. Busily they made calculations and sent feedback to their fellows on the other side of the glass wall. But the Elf whose job it was to examine Charlie McCormack wavered dizzily, unable to do his work. The Experimentalists had never had trouble with their instruments before. They were monitoring the man's pulse, and something was amiss. Each of the other Experimentalists took a turn. Each soon stumbled away from the Human, pale, trembling, and glassy-eyed. They were at a loss to explain it. Finally, exhausted and not a little frightened of the implications of this new development, the Experimentalists returned the McCormacks to their cell.

Charlie's arms were tingling all the way up to his shoulders by the time the guards turned the key in the lock and left the family alone. The tingling always meant that normal sensation was returning, and that soon the paralysis would fade away. Charlie lifted a trembling hand to his mouth and pulled out a medallion. He'd been holding it inside his cheek all day. The medallion was about the size of a quarter, and it had once been attached to a beaded necklace. Charlie had overheard the Elves discussing how the medallions had magical properties to protect them while they worked. A few days earlier the Elves had accidentally bumped Charlie's cart against a table leg. A box of their protective medallions had fallen over and scattered across Charlie's cart. Charlie, nearly paralyzed from their potion, had managed to grab one of the discs before his fingers went completely numb. He had slipped it into his mouth; there was nowhere else to hide it. Charlie hadn't known if the medallion would be of any use to him, but it was worth a try. He was desperate. And indeed, during the course of the next several days, their efforts to poke, prod, inject, infect, and experiment on Charlie had failed. As long as the medallion was in his mouth the instruments failed, and the Experimentalists, feeling weak and ill, were afraid to come near. In fact, Charlie noticed that he could wiggle his fingers and toes a little more each day, even after he had been forced to swallow the bitter fluid that was supposed to paralyze him.

"Well?" said Jill, as sensation crept back into her lips. She managed to sit up, slowly and painfully, and as soon as she was able she reached over to get Emily. The little girl moved her tiny, stiff arms around her mother's neck and began to cry.

"It's getting better," Charlie said, the words feeling dry and brittle in his mouth. "You see how they have a hard time experimenting on me, and I'm starting to be resistant to that poison they give us so we can't move. It's got to be the medallion. I don't know how, but it really seems to work. I want you to try it. I also want to see if the protection has any lasting effect, even after I take it out of my mouth."

Jill McCormack reluctantly slipped the wet medallion into her cheek. It didn't take more than a few seconds for her to cough it up into her hand. "It's too big," she said. "It makes me gag!"

"Maybe if you just keep the end of it in your mouth, while we're here in the cell, it'll build up some kind of effect," Charlie said gently, "like when you get a booster shot for tetanus—like some kind of immunization, you know? Then when we go into the lab you'll be protected, too. Even with Emily, we can use the thing like a little spoon, and we can feed her some of the mush they give us with the medallion. Maybe just a little contact will help protect her, too. We need to be strong enough to resist them, and their spells, and if I can get another couple of medallions, maybe we can get out of here."

"And then what?" asked Jill. "How would we ever get back home?"

"I don't know," Charlie said, shaking his head. "But we've got to try! Once we find Matt and Becky, we'll figure out what to do next."

Outside, the shadow of an Arvada swept over Helfratheim. The enormous, bloated Air Sprite that powered the vehicle spat a column of flame into the soot-choked air, then descended into the courtyard outside the palace. Members of the Elfin Air Squad leapt from the brass cab, dragging long cables to tether the airship to hooks anchored in the ground. Jardaine and her monks scurried along a mossy carpet; they were going to greet Brahja-Chi. The old Mage moved her imposing bulk down the steps of the Arvada. Followed by eight of her own monks, whose robes billowed and snapped in the winds, Brahja-Chi frowned. There was no crowd to greet her. Jardaine and her group of six got to their knees and bowed, touching their foreheads to the carpet. "In the name of the Canon and the Mistress who serves the Word," they murmured in unison.

Brahja-Chi wore a pained smile as she gazed down at Jardaine. Her chins trembled slightly as she led her own monks in the new, preferred greeting, "In the name of the Mistress, and the Canon which inspires her works."

Jardaine nodded to her monks, and nervously they repeated the Mage's words. "In the name of the Mistress, and the Canon which inspires her works."

"You may stand," Brahja-chi intoned. "'Tis good to see you again, Jardaine."

Brahja-Chi and Jardaine entered the King's war room alone, leaving the monks in the corridor outside. "You must be tired after your journey, my Mistress," Jardaine said nervously, offering a seat to the old Mage. "May I offer you some refreshment, a cup of tea, perhaps?"

Brahja-Chi let out a throaty chuckle. "It was tea that was meant to kill your disrespectful friend, Tuava-Li. The Gods work in mysterious ways, however, and Tacita, from the Synod at Ljosalfar, was the only one to pay the price for Tuava-Li's attempt to humiliate me. No matter, I'll deal with Tuava-Li later. As for your tea, I do not want any. I travel with my own refreshments!"

She reached into her voluminous robes and withdrew an elegant beaded *Huldu*. Inside the purse were a number of small, plump beetles. She popped one of the insects into her mouth and smiled demurely as she chewed. "What news have you heard of Tuava-Li, by the way? May I assume she's made little progress on her quest?"

"Tuava-Li?" said Jardaine, looking perplexed. "I haven't seen her since the fire that destroyed Alfheim. What poison are you talking about? What quest? Is Tacita dead?"

"You need to keep better track of your enemies, if I know more about them than you do," Brahja-Chi smiled. "Your Mage has sent her apprentice on some kind of mission, involving the Seed from the fruit of the Adri at the North Pole. They want to re-create the journey in the ancient legend told by Fada, and save the world. They both had some kind of *vision*."

"A vision?"

Brahja-Chi grimaced at the sound of the word, as if it left a particularly bad taste in her mouth. "Can you imagine, a vision from the Great Goddess?" Her eyes bore into Jardaine's. "You've never had one of those, have you?"

Jardaine knew Brahja-Chi was renowned for preaching about the visions that the Gods had given her. These personal messages, in fact, made up the bulk of Brahja-Chi's teaching. Though she'd never personally experienced anything like a vision, Jardaine wondered what Brahja-Chi was getting at. "Nooo, I haven't," she finally managed.

"Of course not," Brahja-Chi replied. "It seemed like a joke to me, a pathetic joke, and old King Adon went along with my wishes and refused to give her the maps she said she needed. I have an entire group of monks whose job it is to block the Mage from trying to communicate with Tuava-Li as she journeys north . . . just in case there's anything to it, of course. One can't be too careful these days."

Jardaine furrowed her brow. The thought of her old rival Tuava-Li achieving great success filled her with envy, and distracted her from her purpose. "Of course not, Mistress. I can't help but wonder, for that reason, if we should take this business seriously. If Tuava-Li intends to re-create the ancient journey, there's much glory waiting for the one who beats her to her destination. We already have access to maps, we have Arvada to take us anywhere on a moment's notice. There are many things to attend to here in Helfratheim, but maybe we need to take this so-called quest into account. We could beat Tuava-Li at her own game. She has nothing to guide her, after all, but her *vision*. How far can that get her?"

Brahja-Chi nodded distractedly. Her heart burned with anger at the thought that other Mages might be graced with real visions, for she, to her infinite regret, was not. How dare the Goddess ignore her own need to be recognized, her pleading for contact? How dare the Goddess and all the pantheon of lesser Gods ignore all her hard work, her devotion over untold thousands of moons, acting in their behalf? The Heavenly forces had, to be fair, intervened once in Brahja-Chi's life—the day she acquired the ability to change shape. *But a mole?* In her youth she had fancied becoming a snake, a glorious, regal snake, and it had been a bitter disappointment when she discovered that a small, black rodent was the Goddess's choice for her. In a lifetime of service, the voices of the Great Ones had otherwise been conspicuously, willfully, arrogantly silent.

Over endless hours of labor she had written the Canon, the Holy Book that she claimed had been dictated by the Goddess, and all the while she had prayed for inspiration and guidance. She had received nothing. Her sermons, her chants, her prayers were hollow; they were incomplete, because they were unanswered by the deities for whom they were uttered. Brahja-Chi hated the Goddess for not talking to her, and she hated herself for needing the Goddess so much. Perhaps the Goddess didn't exist at all.

Maybe, Brahja-Chi thought, her ability to change shape wasn't a gift from above, but simply a fact of life, in the way that breathing enriched the Blood, or food was transformed into energy.

But . . . no. It was almost too much to bear to think that there was no Goddess out there. Brahja-Chi knew that she would do anything to receive a vision like the one that the Mage of Alfheim and her gawky little apprentice Tuava-Li claimed to have had. They must be lying. They *must*! Brahja-Chi knew the importance of a good lie. Her entire power base was built on a foundation of lies. But what if the Mage and Tuava-Li were telling the truth? Brahja-Chi forced a smile and placed her palms on the table. "We need not worry ourselves about Tuava-Li. She is beneath contempt, and her efforts are doomed to fail. Now, tell me, Jardaine—why have you called me here? Does King Macta know that you asked for me to come, or is it a secret between one Mage and another?"

Jardaine looked at the Mage's hands, and the jeweled rings that decorated her fingers. Someday, she thought, she would have rings like those, too. "I wish to share a secret with you, Mistress. Macta is dead. Up to this point I've managed to convince the Council of Seven Agents that he's alive, but injured, and that he hides in his quarters while he recovers from the wounds he received near Alfheim."

Brahja-Chi's face darkened. "You must have done an excellent job at your deception, Jardaine, or my spies would have known about this. Macta is dead?"

"Aye, Mistress. We saw him struck by a Human vehicle along a road outside Alfheim. There's no doubt about his fate. Fortunately, the illusion I've created keeps the Council from asking too many questions. I give them orders that I insist are coming from Macta's own lips, and they believe me."

"Then what do you need from me?"

Jardaine cleared her throat. "In the interest of full disclosure, Mistress, you should know that I don't have the full powers of a Mage. I'm just a monk, and my first animal transformation has yet to occur. This illusion of Macta is very difficult for me to maintain, and I don't have the strength or the skills to keep it up much longer. I asked you here because I hoped you could help me create a permanent illusion of Macta—one that I can control. I wish to rule Helfratheim, and I need a puppet-King that everyone will believe is real. I know your powers are vast, my Mistress, and I'm hoping I can convince you to help me."

"I see," Brahja-Chi said. "How do you propose to make such an arrangement beneficial to me and my cause?"

"The best weapons in the realm are made here in Helfratheim," Jardaine said. "I can promise you that the work you did with King Valdis to bring about war between the Human and Elf realms will continue. All of our resources will be at your disposal, as long as Helfratheim is mine to rule."

"In that case," said Brahja-Chi, leaning close to the monk, "there are several things we should discuss. Your weaponry is of little interest to me, but there are other ways I believe you could be helpful to our cause. You are familiar with the tenets of the Canon, of course?"

Jardaine nodded slightly. "My studies with Kalevala Van Frier, sadly, didn't include your sacred text. Perhaps 'twould be best if you refresh me on the relevant details, Mistress."

"The Canon is the basis for the one true religion. It is *my* religion. The Canon prophesies that the Human realm will fall before an Elfin Mage with great powers. That Mage, of course, is *me*! The Canon tells how the great Mage will collect a thousand Human children, and sacrifice them to the Goddess beneath a full harvest moon. This sacrifice will signal the beginning of the final war, and the start of End Times, when the Goddess and her armies will return to destroy the Humans. As you know, the harvest celebration will take place just seven nights from now. The effort to obtain the sacrificial victims is well underway. We are calling our program the Acquisition. There are Faerie Folk all over the realm that are joining us in our work, making strategic strikes at the borders of their world. I've asked many important individuals to supervise the abduction of Human children. You should be aware that those who bring me the greatest number of children shall be richly rewarded when I'm given my rightful place in the New World. Nevertheless, Jardaine, there's only room for one to sit at my right hand. Do you know what I'm saying?"

Jardaine was perplexed. She had no desire to sit at the right hand of anyone, least of all Brahja-Chi. She was sick of being subservient, but at the same time she knew she needed Brahja-Chi's help. "I do," she said. "I'd be honored to help you to acquire your sacrificial victims. Is there anything else?"

"Indeed there is," said Brahja-Chi. "We have need of a central location to house the children until the full moon, as our facilities in Storehoj aren't large enough. Transportation presents major complications for us. You have your fleet of Arvada, which could be used to bring the children here."

"It could be done," Jardaine said, nodding, "though we would have to keep the Air Sprites working day and night to collect so many in one location."

"Bringing the children here means that the sacrifice must occur here, as well. The courtyard in which the Arvada landed seemed the perfect size for such an enterprise. Do you understand what I'm asking of you?"

"I believe I do, Mistress."

"You do not fear the contamination of Blood?"

Jardaine shook her head. "Not if it's Human Blood, my Mistress."

"In that case, I'll offer you my aid."

Jardaine's excitement was so great that it was all she could do not to spring out of her seat. "Then how soon can you give me the illusion of Macta that I need? The Council of Seven Agents demands that Macta make a speech from his window less than two days from now. If I can't fool the crowd that will gather for the event, I'll never be able to offer you my help with the Arvada and the use of the courtyard for your mass sacrifice!"

Brahja-Chi leaned back and sighed. "'Tis not as easy a task as you might imagine, Jardaine. How is it that you think I come into possession of my powers?"

"Practice, my Mistress?" Jardaine ventured. "Prayers to the Goddess? The force of your will?"

Brahja-Chi laughed bitterly. "The arsenal of a typical Mage is a pitiful thing. We have spells and incantations based upon our ability to control the world of matter with our minds. But a Mage like me, gifted from birth with many fine magickal talents, still needs something more; especially as I am very old, and much of my own magick is spent in keeping up the appearance of youth."

Jardaine nodded, wondering if Brahja-Chi might be able to read her mind. If she did, she would certainly see that Jardaine's eyes beheld an old, fat, and ugly Elf, who had left youth behind many, many moons ago. If this was an illusion, it was far from effective. "That's why," Brahja-Chi continued, "I must, at times, ask for special help."

"Special help?"

Brahja-Chi nodded. "The strongest and smartest among us employ the help of other Faeries with special abilities we can only *dream* of. The Fir Darrig, for instance."

"Fir Darrig, mistress?" Jardaine breathed. "I've heard of them, but never met one!"

"There are only a few in all the realm. They can take on

any shape they wish, at any time. They're disembodied spirits, though, until a powerful Mage utters the spells that bring them into the material world. They stay for as long as you contract them to stay, and then they disappear once again. They exact a high price for their favors, Jardaine, but success always comes with a cost!"

"What kind of cost?"

Brahja-Chi lowered her voice. "You must say nothing to anyone about this."

Slowly she hiked up the hem of her robe so that her knee was exposed.

Jardaine gasped. The old Mage's leg looked like the twisted branch of a tree, with tiny leaves budding from dark stems. Brahja-Chi wore a grim smile as she let the folds of cloth fall to the floor. "Each time that I ask for a Fir Darrig's help, I must sacrifice a little of myself. They don't exactly *eat* the flesh, but when they're done, a part of you is gone. They love Elfin flesh, and especially that of a Mage, like me. At first I gave up certain unnecessary things. I now have the use of only one ear, for instance. The sight of only one eye. Eventually I was forced to give up small lengths of bone, and the Fir Darrig replaced them with oak branches of the appropriate size. They have quite a sense of humor, these forest spirits. Now I while away the hours scraping leaves and buds from my ankle. They grow quite fast, you know. If I continue to solicit the aid of the Fir Darrigs, there will come a time when every part of me will be wooden, and I will be a tree."

BRAHJA-CHI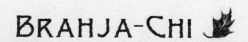

Jardaine's mouth hung open. The old Mage sat back, grinning. "But given our love of trees, 'tis not an inappropriate fate for an Elf, eh?"

Jardaine felt sick to her stomach. "Do you have sensation in the ankle, Mistress?" she choked.

"Perhaps not as much as I once had," the Mage replied, "but the sensory world never held much appeal to me, anyway. It seems to me that power is a Mage's domain, not feeling. Now. Are you ready for such a sacrifice, Jardaine? If so, then we can begin."

Jardaine swallowed the lump in her throat. "What will the Fir Darrig take from me?"

Brahja-Chi laid her hand on top of Jardaine's, and stroked her fingers slowly. The monk, unaccustomed to being touched, did her best not to recoil. "Don't be afraid, my child," Brahja-Chi soothed. "I often work with a Faerie named Jal-Maktar. Since we know each other well, he lets me call him *Jal*. Rest assured he'll start by taking something small. Your appendix, perhaps, or your tonsils, or maybe a few teeth. Maybe a kidney. Nothing you will miss, certainly. You're not asking for much, after all; just an illusion of a dead Prince! This is how the game is played. Now, shall we find out if my friend Jal is free to join us today? We'll only need a little of your Blood to summon him."

Jardaine nodded. She was too frightened to speak.

17

MATT, TOMTAR, AND TUAVA-LI ate their pizza in the alley, hunched over the boxes like starving animals. Matt gulped down fistfuls of topping, which Tomtar and Tuava-Li peeled from their greasy crust. When their hunger was sated the trio sat back in the dirt, hands on their bellies, and pondered their next move. Matt was so tired that it was hard to keep his eyes open. Tuava-Li wanted to find a place with trees and sleep in the branches. She wondered aloud if they should take turns keeping watch. Tomtar, however, wanted very badly to accept Nick's invitation and go to his party at midnight. He was curious about something the Troll had said; it was the way he asked him if he liked surprises. He felt terribly guilty that he'd led Matt and Tuava-Li to think that he could readily come up with the maps they'd need to get to the North Pole. Now any clue about what to expect when they got to Argant might make all the difference in the world. Tuava-Li was reluctant to go. She worried that since the Troll was a follower of Brahja-Chi, he might try to do something that would interfere with their quest. Still, she reasoned, caution would go a long way to protect them.

Matt kept track of the time by watching a digital clock on a bank sign across the street. They stayed out of sight in the alley, avoiding attention from passing cars, and Matt dozed off repeatedly as he sat hunched by a fence. Each time he woke up his feet hurt, and the muscles in his thighs and calves were so sore that he had trouble straightening his legs. Tomtar caught a cricket in the weeds along the fence and played a little game where he let it hop from one hand to the other. "'Tis a good time to practice some of the exercises I taught you," Tuava-Li said. "The Belt of Power, for instance."

Matt sighed. "I'm too tired for that. It's kind of hard to concentrate on an imaginary ring anyway, and it would be impossible if somebody was trying to hurt you."

"That's why it is important to practice, to sharpen your skills. Magick is all about discipline."

"I can do it," Tomtar said, standing up. He held out his arms and wriggled his waist.

Matt laughed out loud. "You look like you're spinning a hula hoop!"

Tomtar's eyes widened. "What's that?"

"It's a toy," Matt said. "It's a big plastic hoop you spin around your waist. My mom can do it really well."

At the thought of his mother, Matt grew sullen and turned away. "Maybe we should practice it together," Tuava-Li suggested. "You don't need to move your hips like that, Tomtar."

"Why don't you practice them yourself?" Matt grumbled. "I'm not in the mood."

Tomtar, embarrassed, sat down at Matt's side, and Tuava-Li did her exercises alone. When she'd finished with the Belt of Power, she knelt uncomfortably on the concrete and hummed quietly to herself. With her eyes closed and her fingertips touching, making little circles of her hands, she pictured the three of them achieving their goal, and she repeated the words the Mage had taught her—*I am strong, I am capable, I choose the path of truth.*

"Hey," Matt said, when he could stand the mind-numbing repetition no longer. "Do you have to say that out loud, Tuava-Li? You're driving me crazy!"

"You don't have to listen," said Tomtar.

"I mean, we're either going to do okay, and things will work out, or we'll screw it up and fail," Matt said. "Telling ourselves that we can do it isn't going to make any difference!"

"Aye, but it will," Tuava-Li said.

"It's eleven o'clock," Matt said, checking the sign across the street. "If we're going to do this, we'd better get going. Otherwise, I'm going to fall asleep right here on the ground. We can hang around outside the storage place for a while, if we get there too early. I'll wait outside while the two of you go in and see if you can find out anything about Argant."

"Look in the sky," Tuava-Li said. "'Tis a good omen. Khidr!"

Matt remembered the strange name, and what the Mage had told him about his vision of a figure made of diamonds. "Show it to me!"

"There," said Tuava-Li, pointing.

Matt saw a star with a faint green glow.

"Don't you know the Green Man?" Tomtar asked. "That's what *Tems* call him."

Matt stared, and shook his head. "The Mage told me, but what do you mean? Some kind of constellation? Am I supposed to be looking at stars?"

"The holes in the dome," Tuava-Li said tensely. She found it hard to accept the Human's ignorance. "The holes in the dome, where the light from Heaven shines. They're called *vindues*. The green light at the crown of his head is shining."

"Do you see the figures on the ground, beneath him?" asked Tomtar.

Matt looked carefully, and saw a horizontal line of stars. Someone with a very good imagination might see the stars as a symbol of fallen bodies. "I guess," he said.

"Khidr's struck, he's defeated his enemies, so we're ready to make our next move, as well. The Gods are tellin' us that the time is right!"

Matt remembered how his dad had tried to help him see the constellations in the night sky, and how hard it was to see the figures that ancient people had seen there in the arrangements of stars. He also realized that the Faeries had a much different view of the universe than he did. How could he ever trust them to do something sensible, when their minds were so clouded by superstition? "You know, ancient humans had a way of looking at those little points of light, which are stars, by the way, not *vindues*, or whatever you said. They're like the sun, except they're really far out in space. There's no dome out there, that's just . . . I don't know, more superstition. Anyway, people used to look at the way the stars are arranged in the sky and they saw the outlines of the gods and goddesses they believed in. People used to be so bored that they would look at the stars and think that some kind of play was going on out there, acted out by the gods, or something. There's no green man out there. No . . . whatever you call him, Khidr."

"Not for one who refuses to see," Tuava-Li grumbled.

"You think the sky is a dome?" Matt asked. "A dome, with little holes poked in it, and the gods who live on the other side move the holes around to give you clues about how to behave?"

"Aye," Tomtar said.

"What about the moon? Is that just a hole in the sky, too, with light from heaven shining through it?"

"Finally, you understand," Tuava-Li said with an exasperated sigh. "There's so much for Humans to learn!"

"We do the best we can," Matt said sarcastically.

The trio trudged through the parking lot and up an incline toward a series of industrial buildings in the distance. Security lights atop high poles threw pools of light on the concrete. Tomtar and Tuava-Li had given up the constant chewing on *trans* that made them appear to be human, and Matt thought that Tuava-Li looked like a bedraggled child. Her hair tumbled carelessly around her shoulders and she walked in a strange, shuffling gait. It was obvious that her feet hurt. Matt's feet still hurt, too. So did the healing tattoos on his shoulders, back, and chest. He felt a moment of empathy with Tuava-Li—her body bore the same kind of markings that he now had. Neaca had etched many of Tuava-Li's tattoos, as well. Tomtar had his own tattoos, of course. Though they were somewhat different from those of the Elves, all three would carry these vines, and leaves, and bugs tattooed on their skin to their graves. They were victims of the same superstition, Matt thought, a superstition that promised some kind of protection from evil, in exchange for being scarred for life. Matt felt anger and resentment rising up in him again as they approached a faded sign that read U-STORE-IT.

There was a security gate along the driveway, meant to stop unauthorized cars, and they all ducked under it. Matt had never visited a storage facility before. There were rows of low cinder-block buildings, and they reminded him somehow of the cheap motels he'd stayed in with his family on road trips. Here, however, there were no parked cars. Whatever business this place did obviously happened in the daytime. There were no lights, except for the security floods set up around the perimeter of the place. There were no windows along the sides of the buildings, just pull-down metal security doors. Everything was shrouded in darkness and shadows.

"What number did that Troll say?" Matt asked, his brain foggy from fatigue.

Tuava-Li answered. "B22."

"Okay," Matt sighed, gazing into the tunnel of darkness between the rows of buildings. "I don't see any sign of life down there."

As soon as the words were out of his mouth, a feeling of dread crept over him. *No signs of life*—maybe they were being set up for something. Maybe this was a trap. "Tuava-Li," he whispered, "you said you felt something when we got close to the pixies in the dumpster—a feeling like something was wrong. Do you feel anything now?"

Tuava-Li closed her eyes and sensed the space around her. If there were danger nearby, there would be a subtle change in the vibration of the place, and if she were sensitive enough, she would detect it. But there was nothing, and given Matt's remark, that made her feel afraid. "What is it, Matthew?"

"I don't know. I think I'm getting paranoid. Let's keep going. Just be careful, okay, we're sitting ducks here if anything happens."

"What are sitting ducks?" Tomtar whispered.

"Never mind. Let's find B22. That, or get out of here."

"B19, B20, it must be just ahead," Tomtar said, pointing. It was obvious that he wanted to keep looking for the Troll and his friends.

Matt crept silently along the front of the building. Tomtar and Tuava-Li were behind him, and the air was so quiet that he could hear the charms and medallions around his neck rattle. He wished, not for the first time, that he could throw them all away. Suddenly something *whooshed* past his head. He ducked, just in time to see the little flock of Pixies he recognized from the dumpster sailing past him. They giggled, banked upward like a flock of sparrows, then swooped into a crevice along the pavement, down at the end of the building.

"That must be the place," Tomtar said, breathing a sigh of relief. "Let's go!"

A little wooden block, inscribed B22, was nailed to the wall by the security door. Matt stared down at the strip of light that spilled from beneath the garage door; it wasn't open more than a foot. Unless he lifted it, his friends weren't going to fit under. He squatted down, put his fingers beneath the lower edge, and began to lift. "Stop that!" came a voice from inside. A little head peered out, glaring angrily at Matt. It was Nick, the Troll they'd met earlier in the evening. "Somehow I don't remember inviting you here tonight," he said, crawling from under the gate.

"Sorry," Matt said. "Just trying to make room."

"Only Faerie Folk allowed. Come back in the morning." Then he put his hands on Tomtar's and Tuava-Li's shoulders and beamed. "Come in, my friends, come in! I'm delighted to see you again!"

"Under the door?" Tomtar asked.

A pair of Brownies rounded the corner. "We've brought presents," one of them said, looking warily at Matt. He withdrew a green glass bottle, wrapped with a ribbon, from his jerkin.

"Wonderful," Nick said, accepting the bottle. "Don't worry about the Human, he's harmless. Plus, he's just leaving."

As the Brownies slipped under the door, Tuava-Li took off her pack and laid it on the ground. "I have nothing to offer as a gift," she said, "but these."

She pulled out the shakers the Mage had given her, which were designed for calling down the Gods. "Excellent!" Nick said. "You can help with the music."

"I've got a flute," Tomtar said, "and I know how to play!"

"Then squeeze under the door," said the Troll. "In the name of the Canon and the Mistress who serves the Word, we'll surely make this a night to remember!"

"Wait," Matt said. "What am I supposed to do? Where am I supposed to go?"

The old Mage had told them to stay together, and now, for the first time, he had the feeling that she was right. He didn't want to be left out here by himself. "There's a scrap of woods beyond the parking lot," Nick said. "You'll be safe there until morning."

"Don't worry, Matthew," Tuava-Li said, touching his hand. Matt felt a tingle rush up his arm. He recoiled in shock as he heard her voice speaking inside his head, though he didn't see her lips move at all. *We won't be long,* Tuava-Li said in thought-speak. *Once Tomtar has discovered what the Elf knows about Argant, we'll leave.*

Matt watched helplessly as his companions got down on the concrete and squeezed beneath the door. At that moment he experienced a strange rush of emotions. He felt scared to be left alone, he felt violated that Tuava-Li had appeared inside his head like that, and he was amazed that it was possible. There was something else. It was a very small feeling, barely recognizable. Matt felt flattered that Tuava-Li had confided in him in a way no one else could hear.

A tight little cluster of Faeries appeared out of the darkness. They were dressed in odd attire, with capes and pointed hats, velvet boots, feather boas, and lace. "He can see us!" one of them cried, and the group scattered like leaves in the wind.

"It's okay," Matt called. "I'm a friend." He realized how absurd that sounded; he couldn't even convince himself that his statement was true. "But I'm leaving. Go on and have a good party!"

"This is worse than we thought," a voice murmured behind him. "Aye," whispered another. "We knew the boundaries were coming undone. But we thought we'd have more time!"

"If Humans can see us, we've got to do something."

"But what? It isn't safe here!"

"Of course it's safe," said Nick, calling from under the garage door. "Now come in, come in! Let's see what you brought!"

Matt walked across the parking lot. There were trees ahead;

it was just a little scrap of woodland that nobody had bothered to cut down. Matt was annoyed that the Troll would send him out here, but he realized that he was going to feel more comfortable in the woods than he did back in civilization. All the concrete, the barbed-wire fences, the plastic, and the metal were getting to him in a way they never had before. Matt stepped around the corner of a painted cement barricade and headed into the darkness. He'd plop down under a tree, maybe grab a little sleep, and wait.

A pair of ornate Victorian lamps gave the inside of the storage unit a warm glow, as Tomtar and Tuava-Li gazed around. It was a big room, by anyone's standard, with several antique couches, settees, and high-backed chairs arranged around a worn Persian carpet. Two four-poster beds with canopies were crammed in against the back wall. Behind the furniture, cardboard boxes were stacked precariously up to the ceiling. "The owner's an old Human lady who pays the monthly storage bill," Nick explained, "but she never comes around. The last time she was here she dropped the key to the padlock out on the road, and when I happened to find it, I knew that the place was as good as mine!"

A Troll passed, carrying a tray stacked high with squares of pineapple pizza. "No, thank you," said Tuava-Li, as Tomtar grabbed a piece and popped it into his mouth.

Tuava-Li surveyed the furniture and realized that she would need help hoisting herself into even the lowest chair in the room.

Why, she wondered, would Faeries choose to luxuriate in the midst of all these Human things? She looked at the pockmarked complexions of the Faeries around her. Not one of them looked well, even in this feeble light. She took a piece of *trans* from her pack and began chewing it, hoping to avoid sickness from exposure to metal, and resolved not to eat any more Human food.

The Faeries who had met Matt outside the storage unit crawled underneath the door and got to their feet, smiling. There were two Elves, both young females, dressed in matching velvet smocks. Their eyes were lined with black paint to make them appear even larger and more luminous than they already were. There was a balding Dwarf with a pointed beard and tattoos on his forehead. The Pixies swooped and dove around the ceiling, giggling, "Catch me! Catch me!"

Nick was the perfect host. He moved about, introducing guests to one another, and sipping dark liquid from a paper cup. Tomtar sidled up to the Troll and grinned. "So, you mentioned Argant a while ago. Have you been there lately?"

"Have I been to Argant," the Troll repeated. "Who hasn't been to Argant? I say, have you met my friend Numi?"

"No," Tomtar said.

One by one, Tuava-Li and Tomtar were introduced to Pixies, Brownies, other Elves and Trolls, Spriggans, Trows, and a host of other Faerie creatures. A sleek white Goblin pup sat on the lap of an elderly, elegantly dressed Gnome. She seemed to be holding court on one of the couches, regaling her audience of

Shefros, all dressed in forest-green coats and red caps. Flying Faeries settled on several of the ornate chandeliers that hung from the ceiling. They peeled grapes as they chatted, and let the purple skins drop to the floor. Some shape-shifting Faeries took on the form of woodland animals and scurried to gobble them up. Tomtar followed Nick to the bar, which was a cardboard box draped with a piece of cloth. "Have some punch," he said. "'Tis made of fly agaric!"

"Isn't that poison?" Tomtar asked, shouting over the din of laughter and conversation.

"How could it be poison? We brew it ourselves from what we find in the pine and birch woods. When we drink enough, we see the Goddess in all her glory! Here, have a taste!"

A brownie filled a cup with the vermilion liquid and handed it to Tomtar. "You asked me if I liked surprises," Tomtar said, "back in the alley. What do you mean by that? Is there something I should know about Argant, before I get there?"

"Can we ever know the future before it happens?" asked Nick.

Tomtar realized that the Troll had an annoying way of answering questions with more questions. An Elf dressed in a slouchy feathered hat and a black cape stepped up and slapped Nick on the back. "You old devil," the Elf exclaimed, "How did you do it? How many have you got?"

Nick put on a smug smile. "Did you think I couldn't do it?" he whispered. "Fifteen, so far. But with any luck, by the time of the full moon, I'll have at least twice that many!"

"Where do you keep them, old boy?"

Nick laughed ominously. "Why spoil the surprise?" he said. "You'll see, soon enough, if the Goddess smiles on me. You'll see!"

"What are you talking about?" Tomtar asked.

There was an old harmonium in a dusty corner, and a trio of Phoukas, in their lynx form, pulled a cover from the instrument. One began to dance atop the keys as the other two pressed the pedals below. "It's time for some music!" Nick shouted, and all the Faeries gathered around.

A Phouka stepped forward, waving her tail, and she began to sing.

Hark, a chill wind sweeps the bend;
'Tis naught but Autumn, our dear friend.
Flecked with gold and crimson hues,
Too swift to catch up on old news,
She swoops and sails through glen and vale,
Dashing color from her pail!

When it was time for the chorus, all the Faeries joined in, filling the room with a raucous, screeching din.

My, my, hey, hey, our time is done, we must away.
Hey, hey, my, my, break the earth, and crack the sky!

One of the Gnomes leapt up onto a table, knocking over a tray of greasy sausages. He stripped off his shirt, revealing an intricate tattoo of thorny vines. Twisting and flexing his muscles, he began the second verse.

She darts and dives, and in her wake,

Leaves steam-trails dancing on the lake.

Hares soon burrow, geese take flight,

The warmth of days gives way to night.

The restless summer sun departs,

And leaves no fire to heat our hearts!

Nick jabbed Tuava-Li in the ribs with his elbow. "Get out those shakers of yours," he demanded. "Let's have some music to celebrate the Acquisition!"

"What are you talking about?" Tuava-Li asked, but she was drowned out by the revelers, shouting the chorus of the song.

My, my, hey, hey, our time is done, we must away.

Hey, hey, my, my, break the earth, and crack the sky!

"What about you," Nick said to Tomtar, leaning so close that Tomtar could feel the heat of the Troll's body and smell the fly agaric on his breath. "Come on, get out your flute and play!"

Tomtar reached into his pack for his flute, and placed it against his lips. Someone grabbed the shakers from Tuava-Li's hands and began waving them furiously about. Everyone was dancing, banging fists on the furniture and stamping little feet, keeping a frantic rhythm. The pair of Elves in matching smocks climbed up on the arms of a couch, cupping Fire Sprites in the palms of their hands. They danced and clapped, and the air was filled with sparks. Tomtar played the melody of the song. Six of the dirty little Pixies descended from the chandelier and joined in on the next verse. They acted out the music, batting their

eyelashes and waving their arms about. A Troll picked up an old
three-stringed instrument and began to strum along.

The fiery trees give up their glow,

As Autumn now too soon must go.

Oh stay, we tremble, linger, do!

Autumn swiftly fades from view.

Hark! Her voice is shrill and strange.

The only word she sings is change!

My, my, hey, hey, our time is done, we must away.

Hey, hey, my, my, break the earth, and crack the sky!

Everyone joined in the last chorus, and more than a few of
the Faerie Folk had tears in their eyes when the song was over.
Nick climbed up onto one of the couches and cried, "Who's
next? Who's next? Praise be, let's have some more music. We're
here to celebrate, aren't we? The Goddess is among us! Can you
feel it?"

Matt awoke with a start. He had fallen asleep beneath the
misshapen trunk of an old maple tree, and when he gazed about,
he couldn't remember for a moment where he was. His chest
itched and he scratched it. When the itching didn't stop, he
lifted up his T-shirt to see what was the matter. In the moonlight
he stared at the tattoo on the center of his chest. He blinked,
thinking his eyes must be playing tricks on him. He saw a tattoo
of a knife with a little compass on the top. His knife! Matt was
shocked, and horrified. His skin crawled with revulsion. He tried

to control his rising panic. He knew that Neaca hadn't tattooed a knife on him; all that had been on his chest when he left camp were tattoos of leaves and vines. He hadn't even found the knife until after they'd left the camp, and his tattoos were healing. What kind of magic was this? What kind of trick were they playing, trying to confuse him, frighten him, mess up his mind with something impossible? Matt scrambled to his feet and slung his pack back over his shoulder. He headed for the barricade that separated the trees from the parking lot. He would get Tomtar and Tuava-Li, and make them explain what was going on.

A blanket of black clouds swept across the moon. It was terribly, terribly dark, and when he looked up into the sky, a suffocating weight of darkness pressed down on him like a huge, smothering hand. *I'm just turned around,* he thought, trying not to panic. *This little scrap of woods can't be that big. I just have to find the barricade, and*—suddenly Matt realized that there was no barricade anymore. He spun around and saw nothing but trees, and shadows of trees, as far as he could see into the gloomy depths. In a moment of horror he realized that he had crossed back over the border of the Human realm into the Faerie realm, and he was lost in some great, primordial forest.

Get a hold of yourself, Matt whispered aloud. *You can do it.* He jammed his hand into his pocket and brought out the knife he'd found in the wreckage of his house. He held the little compass on the handle of the knife close to his face, so he could see which direction was north. *I can do it,* Matt said to himself. *I'm strong.*

There was a rustling from the high branch of a tree somewhere nearby. Matt tried to ignore it. *The big highway was going from east to west. I saw it on one of the signs. That means the other little road beside the storage unit goes north and south, and so does that barricade I'm looking for. If I stay on a path going perpendicular to where the fence was, I'll find my way out of here.* Slowly and carefully, eyes on the compass, Matt headed north. He stepped carefully over the rocks and sticks that littered the forest floor and tried to stay calm, breathing up through his feet. *I'm capable,* he said to himself. He wandered on for perhaps five minutes. Then he stopped. *This isn't the way. The place where I lay down next to the tree was just seconds away from the fence. I've got to go back the other direction.*

Matt heard other sounds in the night, some near and some far away, and a branch struck him on the cheek. *I'm strong,* he murmured, *I'm capable. I choose the path of—oh, man, what am I saying?*

Minutes passed, then there was a glimmer of something in the distance. Matt froze. What could it be? It looked like some kind of animal, with a pale coat, something long and scrawny, and—no, it wasn't an animal! It was the white concrete barricade, and it was going to lead him back into his own world. Matt began to run. He stumbled to the edge of the barricade and then fell over the top of it, landing hard on his side. He lifted his head from the blacktop and saw the storage facility ahead of him. Hot tears ran down his cheeks, and bloody scrapes stung his knees and hands.

"Oh, man!" he cried. "Oh man, oh man, oh man!"

By the time he got to the service road Matt's relief had already turned to anger. He was more than angry, he was indignant. That stupid Troll had told him to go back to rest in the woods, and he had to have known that Matt was going to get lost out there, maybe lost forever. The Troll's betrayal was even worse than Matt's discovery that his tattoos were changing. He bounded toward the last storage unit, charged up to the metal door marked B22 and slammed his fists against it. "Hey," he yelled. "Hey, Nick, or whatever your name is! Get out here, I want to talk to you!"

Silence. The music, the genial chatter, the din from inside the storage unit stopped cold. Matt waited a second, hearing nothing but his own harsh breath. He reached down and grabbed the bottom edge of the garage door. He began to yank. There was a rusty screech of metal, and instantly a swarm of Pixies surrounded him. Their tiny claws raked his cheeks, and Matt backed away, swatting at them. Nick crawled through the opening. "What did I tell you?" he demanded. "Didn't I tell you to wait for your friends in the woods?"

"Get them off me," Matt yelled.

With a nod from the Troll, the Pixies swirled away and gathered, hovering, behind Nick. Matt stood with his fists clenched tight. "Tell Tuava-Li and Tomtar to come out here now. We're getting out of this place!"

Nick snorted, then disappeared beneath the metal door. His

Pixies followed close behind. Matt heard whispering; a moment later somebody inside began to pound the keys of the harmonium. Soon there was clapping, and singing. Matt let out an angry cry. "You're just going to ignore me?" He was just about to try hauling the door open again when he heard Tuava-Li calling to him. She crossed the concrete like a shadow.

"Matthew, what's the matter?"

"What are you doing out here? I thought you were—"

"I wasn't comfortable in there," Tuava-Li said. "I've spent so many moons living quietly with the Mage that all their racket hurts my ears. But Tomtar's still inside. He thinks that Troll, Nick, is going to tell him something useful. Your appearance here makes that less likely now that you've made Nick angry."

"I know, I know," said Matt. "But we can't trust anything he tells us, anyway. He's got some kind of game going on here—some kind of dangerous game. Listen, can't you read his mind, or something? Like you did with me?"

Tuava-Li shook her head. "I didn't read your mind, Matthew. That would be a violation. I can move my thoughts outside of my body, just like all of us move objects with our hands. You have abilities of your own, you know, though you're not aware of them. You plucked my thoughts from the air, and then heard my words as if they were spoken inside your mind. That is the nature of thought-speak."

Matt was confused. "Okay, if you say so. But you can see

into other people's, or faeries', minds, can't you? You can see what they're thinking, if you want to?"

Tuava-Li shook her head again. "Just because I'm capable of a thing doesn't mean that I'm free to do it, or that I can do it very well, if you must know. Searching the minds of others is a power I may use only in the direst emergency, when no other choice is possible. I did it once, and misinterpreted the results, and the Mage's friend Tacita nearly died because of it."

Matt threw up his hands. "What? Either you're willing to do something, or you're not."

"I will not read his mind," Tuava-Li said. "If the Goddess favors us, Tomtar will find out what he needs to know. If you wish, I'll go back in and see if I can speed the process along."

"Fine," Matt said, "but what am I supposed to do in the meantime? The troll sent me to the woods over there, and I got lost in the faerie realm. He knew it would happen. I almost didn't make it back! I tell you, he's up to something."

Tuava-Li furrowed her brow. "You passed back through the veil?" Though her intuition did not warn her of grave danger, she wondered if perhaps there was more going on here than met the eye. "Maybe you'd feel safer waiting for us by the place we came in, near the gate."

"Somebody might see me over there," Matt said. "There are too many lights."

"Then wait on the other side of the building, at the far end. We'll come as quickly as we're able."

"Okay," Matt said with a sigh. "But before you go, there's something else. Look at this!" Matt pulled up his shirt. "What do you see?"

Tuava-Li frowned as her eyes followed the dark lines and colors of Matt's tattoos. She looked genuinely surprised. "Why would Neaca have tattooed a knife on your chest?"

"She didn't," Matt said, "and it's not just *any* knife—it's the one I found in the gun safe in the ruins of my house. I don't know when or how this happened, but the tattoo changed. You've got to tell me how you did it!"

Tuava-Li shook her head vigorously. "*I* didn't do it, Matthew! I had nothing to do with it. I promise you, I don't know why your tattoo would change. I've never heard of such a thing before. Perhaps it's the work of the Goddess. Perhaps it's a sign of some kind. Perhaps it's something that happens when a Human gets an Elfin tattoo. Maybe it happened to the Human King who went with Fada on his quest to the Pole, I don't know! I would ask the Mage, if I could, but I can't reach her in thought-speak, and we can't go back. Have you used the knife for anything?"

"Yeah," Matt said, thinking back. "I used the compass to help me find my way back here, just a few minutes ago."

"Then maybe 'tis a gift, a sign from the Goddess that She's there to help us, to direct our actions. You must keep an eye on your tattoos and see if they continue to change!"

"Duh," Matt snorted. "Of course I'm going to keep an eye

on my tattoos. I feel like I've been invaded, like some kind of parasite or something got under my skin and is moving around. Ink doesn't have a mind of its own. You don't have any idea how weird this feels."

Tuava-Li nodded. "I can imagine. Now let me go back to the party, and see if I can hurry Tomtar along."

"Make it quick, okay? This place gives me the creeps."

18

THOUGH THE MOON WAS HIGH, Matt could see clouds crawling across the night sky and blotting out the stars. He shuffled over to the next building and stood in the shadow of an awning. The air was cool as a faint breeze swept past. He sat down on the ground, pulled his knees up tight, and stared into the darkness. *I want to go home,* he thought, but quickly blocked the longing that swept over him. It was too painful to think of all that he had lost. He rested his head on his knees, yawned, and felt himself drifting away. Waking and sleeping tumbled together down the path of dreaming. He found himself sailing over a highway. He was flying over bright fields of wheat and corn, watching his own shadow move across the ground. Then he was in the Cord, flying through the milky depths. Then he heard the sound of crying. It was faint, weak, and far away. Matt opened his eyes and tried to shake himself awake. The crying continued.

He drew all of his attention to the sound. A moment later the crying stopped. Matt got to his feet and padded along the front of the building, past door after door. He heard a whimpering sound close by. Matt had two younger sisters. It wasn't hard to remember what it sounded like when a baby cried.

Matt drew up alongside one of the metal garage doors and pressed his ear to it.

He held his breath; this was the one, there was no doubt about it. Reaching down, he grabbed the padlock at the bottom of the door. Locked, of course. It looked cheap, though, and old, and sort of fragile for something meant to keep a door like this closed. Matt looked around for a rock, but there were none nearby. He took his knife from his pocket and wriggled the point into the lock, being careful not to break off the tip of the blade. He'd never picked a lock before and had no idea if this would work. Keeping a gentle pressure on the top of the lock, he pried up from below. Suddenly there was a snapping sound. The lock popped open. Matt placed it on the ground and then gripped the bottom edge of the door with both hands. Very, very slowly he lifted. The door squeaked in its tracks. It was impossible to do this quietly, but it had to be done.

Matt squeezed into the opening and stood peering into the gloom. The place stank of urine, excrement, and mold. He felt along the wall and found a switch. The overhead bulb flickered on, throwing a dim light onto the walls. Matt squinted. He took a step forward and nearly tripped over an old grocery store cart.

He gave it a push and it rolled away. There was a pool table in the middle of the room, stacked high with cardboard boxes and piles of newspapers. "Attack! Trade Towers Fall," screamed a headline. A couple of rusty lawn mowers leaned against the back wall. There was a green, rectangular plastic bin in the far corner. When the crying started again, Matt followed the sound. There, lying on a pile of damp newspapers at the bottom of the bin, was a baby. A human baby. And its diaper had obviously not been changed in quite a while. Three or four carved medallions hung on beaded necklaces around the baby's neck. *Faerie stuff,* Matt thought. The baby reached out its scrawny arms and erupted in a pitiful wail. Matt leapt back in dismay. He turned and fumbled toward the door, pausing only to shut off the light as he bolted outside.

There was music in the air and the sound of faraway laughter. Matt stalked back toward B22. Had the Faeries stolen the baby and hidden it in that room? What were they planning to do with it? He wasn't sure what his own plan was, but he knew he needed to get Tuava-Li and Tomtar to help him figure it out. Matt mouthed the words, *Tuava-Li, I need you.* He tried to make the words solid in his mind, giving them weight and urgency. He imagined that he was moving the words out of his mind and directing them through the air, and into the storage unit where the party was still going strong. *Tuava-Li, I need you,* he called again, in an urgent, silent plea. Self-doubt swept over him, and a flood of bitterness poured in. *This is a joke,* he said to himself. *It's all a useless joke. I'm not an elf. I can't do this!* He had raised his fist and was just about to start banging on the garage door when he looked down and saw Tuava-Li squeezing through the opening.

"What is it, Matthew?" she asked. "What's wrong?"

"You heard me!" Matt exclaimed, his eyes wide with astonishment.

"Where are you going, Tuava-Li?" came Nick's voice, from below the door.

Matt quickly turned to face Tuava-Li. "Read my mind," he whispered.

Tuava-Li shook her head. "Read my mind," he hissed. "It's an emergency!"

"Not *you again*," Nick sneered, as he caught sight of Matt. "I won't have you spoil my celebration. What do I have to do to make you leave?"

Tuava-Li didn't need to read Matt's mind to understand the expression on his face. "I'm sorry," she said, turning to Nick. "I'll get Tomtar and we'll leave. You've been very kind to have us here!"

Suddenly Matt was alone with the Troll. He looked away and tried to swallow the ball of anger in his throat. A moment later Tomtar and Tuava-Li crept from beneath the door. "Good night," Tuava-Li said to Nick, as she made an awkward bow and turned away.

"Good luck with your celebration," Tomtar called, and the three of them stepped into darkness.

"Good luck with your quest," Nick said sarcastically. "I hope the Gods show you what you're looking for!" He stood with his hands on his hips until they were out of sight.

"Follow me," Matt whispered. In the glow of a distant security light he could see the gate at the far end of the complex. A moment later they entered the storage unit where the baby lay crying on its bed of soiled papers. Tuava-Li shivered when she saw it. "How disgusting," she said.

"It's just a baby," Matt said defensively. "Babies are messy. I'd pick him up if I had a change of clothes."

Tomtar climbed up, reached into the bin and touched the medallions around the baby's neck. "Nick and his Pixies must have put him here," he murmured, and gave the baby a tickle under the chin. "But where would they even get a Human baby?"

"They had to have stolen him from somebody," Matt said. "And are these charms supposed to protect him from us, or the elves?"

"I heard some of them talking about celebrating something they called the Acquisition," Tuava-Li offered.

Tomtar swallowed. "And I heard Nick say that so far, he'd managed to collect *fifteen* of something. Do you think he was talking about babies?"

"I don't know," Matt said tensely. "Maybe the troll has them hidden away in different storage units. How are we going to find them all?"

"What do you want to do, Matthew?" asked Tuava-Li.

"What do you mean by that?" Matt cried, turning on Tuava-Li. "Do we have a choice? What do you think we should do? Walk away? Pretend we never found him?"

"I didn't say that. *I* wasn't the one who took the baby!"

"Yeah," Matt said, "but you're a faerie."

Tuava-Li stepped back. "What of it? Do I blame you for all the things Humans have done to my kind?"

"As a matter of fact, I think you do!" Matt said through gritted teeth.

The baby was crying again. Matt rubbed its chest with two fingers, and then reached around behind the baby's neck to find the clasps for the beaded necklaces. He tore the medallions away and tossed them across the room. "Look, we've got to get him out of here, to a hospital, or something. He needs food and water."

"Where would we take him?" Tomtar asked.

"Back down on the highway, there's got to be something open, some store, or restaurant, some place safe." Matt's eyes searched the room and fell upon the old shopping cart in the corner. He lifted the baby from the bin, carried it across the room and gently lowered it into the cart. Then he pushed it out the door and into the night. Rain had begun to fall. "Oh, great, on top of everything else, now he's gonna get soaked. Tomtar, I want you to push this cart down the hill toward the main road. Find the first place you see that's open, and take the baby inside. Leave him where you see some people. Then go to the corner where the two big roads meet, and Tuava-Li and I will meet you there as soon as we can."

"What are you going to do?" Tomtar asked.

"We're going to find out where Nick put the other babies. Tuava-Li is going to read his mind."

"No, I'm not," Tuava-Li said.

"Then I'll have to think of something," Matt said angrily. "Hurry, Tomtar, you've got to get the baby out of here before anything else happens."

The wheels on the old grocery cart squealed and shook as Tomtar pushed it past the gate and down the hill. Tuava-Li followed Matt back to the door marked B22. When he pounded on the metal with all his might, she trembled and stepped back into the shadows. The boy was angry, and scared, and Tuava-Li didn't know what he was going to do. In the blink of an eye the gang of Pixies swept under the door and swarmed around Matt's head. Matt let out an angry roar and swatted furiously at the Pixies. "Why can't you leave us alone?" asked Nick, climbing out into the drizzle.

Matt was on top of the Troll in an instant. The Pixies pulled his hair and clawed at his eyes as Matt knocked Nick to the ground and pinned him there. He had one knee on the Troll's chest, and their faces were close enough now that the Pixies couldn't get between them. "Where are the others?" Matt demanded. "Where are you hiding the other babies?"

"I don't know what you're talking about," Nick choked.

Tuava-Li looked on nervously. "The fifteen Human babies," she said, "the ones you were bragging about earlier."

Nick forced out a scornful laugh, though the weight of the boy on top of him made it hard to breathe. "I won't tell you anything. Get off me, you filthy—"

Matt released Nick and grabbed one of the Pixies that was clinging to his shoulder. He thrust the squirming creature into the Troll's face. "Then what about this," he spat, squeezing the Pixie so hard that she cried out in pain. "What do I have to do to her to get you to talk?"

"Matthew!" Tuava-Li yelled. She knew spells that might stop the boy; spells that would make him lose control over his muscles, if only for a moment. But she knew that she needed his trust, and his help, and she would ruin everything if she went to the aid of the Troll now.

"There are no more babies," Nick cried. "I lied. I was only able to capture one. I should never have let you near this place," he moaned, his eyes rolling back in his head.

"Just put the Pixie down, don't hurt her, I'll do whatever you want, please, just don't hurt her!"

By this time all the Faerie Folk at the party had climbed out from under the metal door. At the sight of Matt crouching over their friend, they scurried into the night, frightened for their lives. Two of Nick's Pixies, however, fastened themselves to Matt's cheeks, and sunk their teeth into his eyelids. The rest of them yanked out clumps of his hair and clawed at his nose and lips. Matt screamed in pain. Suddenly they all fell away. Matt felt the Pixie in his hand go limp, and he leapt to his feet, horrified. "No," he cried, "I didn't mean to—"

Tuava-Li glided past Matt and he heard her muttering in a strange language. "What are you doing?" he cried, stumbling back. The Pixies lay on the wet concrete.

Nick was twisted and still, his arms flung out at his sides like a discarded doll. Raindrops danced on his body.

"Don't worry," Tuava-Li said angrily. "You didn't kill them, but you might have, if not for the burst of energy I sent into their brains, and the spell I've cast."

"No," Matt said, "I would never have—I just threatened Nick because I needed to find out about the babies, and—"

"I suppose it's part of both of our moral codes," she said, "to go to extremes only when it's necessary for survival. 'Tis a hard lesson to learn, isn't it? At least you didn't use your knife."

"You wouldn't read his mind, but you knock him out with magic?" Matt cried, fury boiling in his veins. "Because of what you did, we've learned nothing. We don't know for sure if there are any more babies. We don't know about that—what did he call it?—the Acquisition. We learned nothing! By knocking the troll out, you protected him, and we got nothing!" Matt wiped blood and rain from his eyes with a filthy sleeve. "How long will they be unconscious? Maybe we should wait, and I can try again to get the truth out of him."

"Nooo," Tuava-Li said. "I don't think Nick was lying. Let's

find Tomtar and go. What happens here is not our business." She closed her eyes and bowed her head for a moment, as feathers began to appear on her pale flesh. A moment later she was a kestrel, flapping into the rain-filled night. Matt scooped up her robe and dashed for the road.

Meanwhile, the grocery cart was too big for Tomtar to manage. He'd narrowly avoided toppling the entire thing over while rounding the corner at the bottom of the hill. He maneuvered the cart through a parking lot outside a twenty-four hour pharmacy when, as if by magic, the doors opened. Tomtar thought it must be a gift from the Goddess. He'd been invited into a Human building, and not a word had been spoken! The fluorescent lights were nearly blinding as he stepped through the entrance and gave the cart a swift push. The baby was crying again, but Tomtar felt so happy that he had accomplished his task that the sound no longer bothered him. A man leaning on the counter at the front register glanced up at the sound of the baby's feeble wail, staring in confusion at the damp cart as it glided past him. "What the—"

Those were the only words Tomtar heard, for as he turned to face the exit, the doors opened to welcome him back into the night. *'Tis a miracle*, he said to himself, and he joyfully dashed outside.

Rain fell in great fat droplets on Tomtar's knit cap, and ran down his long nose as he scurried across the parking lot. He heard the doors glide open again behind him. "Hey," a voice

shouted, "hey, you can't leave a baby here! Come back, come back or I'll call the cops!"

Tomtar didn't know who *the cops* were, and he didn't care. He wasn't sure if the man saw him or not. He hurried down the street until he reached the corner, where he huddled against a pole beneath the street sign and felt the rain beat down on his narrow shoulders. He watched the lights changing colors. He watched the cars sail past, and he began to understand. He'd seen cars before, back when he lived in Argant, but he'd never noticed the delightful game they seemed to play with the lights, starting with green and stopping with red, and speeding through on the yellow. He waited there on the corner, hoping that Matt and Tuava-Li would join him soon. He imagined that they might all be friends, one day. For now, it was easy to see that Matt didn't like Tuava-Li. Tomtar knew that she was wary of Matt, too. She hadn't grown up around Humans, so she was more cautious. There was nothing wrong with that. Matt, of course, had lost most of his family because of the Elves, so it was only natural that he was cautious, too.

Tomtar knew that both Matt and Tuava-Li thought he was useless. It didn't bother him too much. At first they'd been angry with him, when they'd found out that he didn't really know where the maps in Argant were hidden. He thought he'd be able to get that Troll, Nick, to talk, but that hadn't gone so well, either. Maybe once they reached Argant Matt and Tuava-Li would need Tomtar's help. For now, though, it seemed like he wasn't

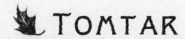 TOMTAR

good for much; except that he'd been able to get the Human baby to a safe place. That made him happy.

Tomtar heard a voice in his head, calling his name. He spun around, staring through the rain, and saw a dark shape approaching. It was Tuava-Li, in her kestrel form. She landed at the top of one of the poles on the corner. *Where is the baby,* she asked in thought-speak.

"I put him in there," Tomtar said, pointing. "A Human is going to call the cops!"

What does that mean?

"I don't know," Tomtar confessed. "But I think everything's going to be all right!"

Matt came bustling down to the corner, puffing for breath. He bent over and grabbed his knees.

"The baby's safe," Tomtar said, beaming. "What did you learn from Nick and his gang?"

Matt glanced up and scowled. "Well, we might have learned something, but Tuava-Li knocked them all out with some kind of magic, and now they're unconscious. Interesting, don't you think? Sometimes I'm not sure which side she's on."

"She's on *our* side, Matt," Tomtar said. "We're on a quest, the three of us. That's what comes first."

A voice suddenly appeared in Matt's mind. *I did what I did because you lost your temper, Matthew. You were out of control, and I had to make sure that you didn't do something you'd regret.*

"I'm sure we've all got things to regret," Matt said, touching the bite marks and scratches the Pixies had left on his face. "Let's get moving, okay? When that troll wakes up, he and his friends are going to be pretty mad that we rescued the baby."

"Do you know the way to Argant from here?" Tomtar asked.

"Look at that sign," Matt said. "It's the route south. Can you fly in this rain, Tuava-Li?"

Not very well, she replied in thought-speak, swooping down to the street. *No better than I can walk, I'm afraid.*

Tuava-Li's voice was so clear in Matt's head that he couldn't believe she wasn't inside there, somehow. Maybe what she had told him was true, that she had moved her thoughts out of her mind and into some place where Matt could pick them up and translate them into the voice he heard in his brain. But how, he wondered, could he be doing *that?* Tuava-Li said she wouldn't actually read his thoughts unless it was an emergency. Maybe it was true. Maybe it wasn't. Back when he'd first met the Elves, when he'd stared at them from his sister's window with the old diamond-covered shoe in his hand, the Mage had gone into his mind and tried to control his body, tried to make him give her the shoe. The old Elf must have believed that was an emergency. Tuava-Li may have thought of the mind as a sacred place, but she still had the power to cast spells over other living beings and knock them out, maybe even kill them, if she wanted. Matt realized the Elves would always be a mystery to him. He thought he might not be quite so rigid as Tuava-Li if he knew how to get inside somebody's head and take a look around — especially if there was something he needed to know.

A glossy pickup truck sped by. *"Aaaaaargh!"* Matt cried, as the truck's tires showered him with cold, dirty water. "That jerk should be more careful!" He leapt away from the curb and stood shivering, watching the truck pull into a gas station up ahead. The driver jumped out of the cab. He unhooked the hose and shoved the nozzle into the gas tank. Then he made a dash into the convenience store that served as the gas station's office. "We're in luck," Matt said. "I think we just found us a ride. Come on, follow me!"

He hurried across the wet concrete and slowed only as the lights above the gas station caught him in their glare. Tuava-Li returned to her Elfin form, and she and Tomtar followed. The driver had yet to come out of the building. Matt glanced around to make sure that no one was looking, then lifted Tomtar and Tuava-Li into the back of the truck. He hoisted himself over the back door and scrunched down. There was a soggy tarp jammed into the corner of the cab. Matt grabbed one edge of it and pulled it over the three of them. "Don't move," he whispered. "We don't want the driver to know we're back here."

"How do we know that this Human is going in the right direction?" Tuava-Li said, as she drew a pouch full of *trans* from her pack. Already she was feeling the effects of exposure to metal. She handed a piece to Tomtar, and the two of them began to chew.

"We don't really know anything," Matt replied. "Not for

sure. But he was going south when he pulled in here, so with any luck he'll get us a little closer to Pittsburgh. Once we get moving, I'll poke my head out the side of the tarp and make sure we're not heading in the wrong direction."

"What then?" Tuava-Li asked.

Matt shrugged. "If we turn off the main road we'll climb out of here as soon as we can. Then we'll have to figure out something else. I'd ask you to read the driver's mind and find out where he's going, but I'd be wasting my breath. Right?"

Tuava-Li nodded and looked away. "The Goddess will guide us."

"Yeah, right," Matt scoffed. "I think I remember somebody saying that if there were any gods out there, they'd want us to take care of things ourselves."

"*Ssssssh!*" said Tomtar.

The driver of the pickup truck came around the side of his vehicle, tearing the wrapper from a candy bar, and gave the nozzle on the pump a final squeeze before placing the hose back into its cradle. A few moments later the pickup truck was speeding down the road. Rain pelted the tarp, and Matt held up the edge like a visor to protect his eyes as he watched the night fly past. Tomtar and Tuava-Li, exhausted from the day's journey, were motionless at his side. Matt thought about what had happened with Nick the Troll and his Pixies. Everything had gone so terribly wrong. His eyelids were swollen and sore where the Pixies had bit him, and he wondered if he'd mastered that Belt of Power trick, if he might have been able to keep them away. He tried to imagine a spinning disc around his waist. He tried not to think about anything else. *Discipline,* he reminded himself. *Discipline.* Within ten minutes Matt's head had slumped against his chest. His eyes were closed, and as the truck headed south, all three travelers lay sleeping in the back.

19

THE MOON WAS A SILENT SIREN, calling for
the creeping things to awaken and rise from the depths of gloom.
For a few brief hours they were the kings and queens of the night.
Armored insect soldiers scurried through the dry soil, eating,
and in turn, being eaten. Scampering, slithering, scuttling, they
came. Lurking, worming, wriggling, they crept. Spiders waited
on their web thrones. The denizens of darkness went about their
loathsome business in the shadows, filling the world with their
hungry song; and the music would not let Asra sleep.

If the Gods did not favor insects, they would not have made so many,
she thought, turning uncomfortably on her pallet of leaves.
Radik had made beds for the three of them, scooping out hollows
in the earth, near the trunks of the biggest trees he could find.
He had then filled the hollows with leaves and roofed them over
with more branches, and more leaves, until they were completely

disguised. Sleep, Radik believed, was something best done in private. Thirty feet from Asra, Becky lay hidden in her own rustic bed. Fatigue had won a battle with discomfort and she slept soundly. Radik spent the night hours deep in dreaming, lost beyond the Gates of Vattar. But Asra refused to sleep. Her pride kept her awake, arguing, cajoling, shouting inside her head, demanding sympathy that never came. She heard birds and small, furry things with snouts and tails, all jabbering to each other in a language of grunts and snorts and whistles. Why did they have to be so loud? She desperately missed the princess she had once been.

Asra was not alone in her longing. Near, but not too near, and far, but not too far, a dark figure trod on silent feet. The pain in his shoulder screamed, but none could hear it, save Macta. He had already slept as much as the arm would allow him; now all he could do was wait, distracting himself with mindless pacing. Soon Radik, Asra, and Becky would awaken, and continue their journey to Helfratheim. Macta would follow. He knew that they had maps. He knew that they were cautious about travel in the Cord, for so many of the passages were worn thin, or torn, or collapsed. A bitter smile crossed Macta's face as he realized his own body was like the Cord; badly damaged, and failing fast. He could tell that the wounded arm wouldn't last. He'd have cut off what remained, if he had the courage. For now he simply lingered in the distance, biding his time, recording little bets he'd placed with himself, waiting for the moment when he could . . . what?

Macta kept coming up blank at this point in his train of thought. What was he doing? Aside from his heroic fantasies and dreams of romance, which never seemed to die, the future looked grim. If the trio of innocents wouldn't risk travel in a Cord, they'd never reach Helfratheim. It was simply too far away. He knew he, too, would never make it on foot. He could leave them behind and journey ahead in a Cord himself, for there were Techmagicians and Experimentalists in Helfratheim who could save his life, and maybe restore his arm. But something in Macta refused to let him go on ahead. He had to stay, even though he knew that it was just a matter of time until Radik realized they were being followed.

Becky was the first to creep out of her makeshift bed. Her parents were never far from her mind, and she pictured her family in the kitchen of their house, eating breakfast and talking. She could almost smell the aroma of fresh coffee and taste the sweetness of maple syrup on her pancakes. She could almost see her mother's pretty face as she fed Emily, and her dad standing by the counter, squinting at the sports page in the morning newspaper. Why did he always seem to lose his reading glasses? She could almost believe that she would find her parents, and free them from the Elves, and that life would go back to normal. She could almost believe. Almost. She pushed away the branches, letting them tumble to the ground. She wouldn't be sleeping here again. Her stomach ached with hunger, and worse, she had to go to the bathroom. This was the moment she always dreaded, and it seemed to come all too often. When she had finished her business behind a tree she returned to find the others awake. Asra nodded in Becky's direction as she and Radik gathered up their things for the day's trek.

Before long they found a stream where they could wash their hands, according to Elfin custom, and they ate what little remained of the food Neaca had given them when they began their journey. Radik, still hungry, broke a chunk of yellow fungus from a fallen tree. He offered a piece to the Elfmaid, but Asra refused to eat. An empty belly was preferable, it seemed, to the indignity of eating something so coarse. "Let me help," said Becky. She understood that Radik, who had spent his life in the woods, had a far better knowledge of edible plants than she would ever have. She was certain, however, that she'd be able to make whatever food she could find seem more appetizing than Radik. "I'll find something to eat!"

The Elves, both dubious of the wisdom of this task, were too hungry to protest. They were content to rest and let Becky wander. Radik knew there would be Faerie Folk in the woods. Some of them were potentially dangerous. Despite the orders of his Queen, Radik regarded Asra's protection as his primary obligation. If Becky were to cry out, he would hear it and go to her aid, but he didn't intend to spend his days worrying about her safety. Asra, for her part, seemed content to let others take care of her needs. As long as breakfast was more appetizing than yellow fungus, she didn't mind that it was a Human who was going to prepare it for her.

Becky soon returned with flushed cheeks and a smile, and a bundle in her arms. She set to work, and before long the breakfast was ready. She approached Asra with a broad, lime-green leaf cupped in her hands. Nestled on the leaf was a mound of tiny blackberries and raspberries, surrounded with a ring of cracked beechnuts. "Your highness," Becky said, bowing her head.

Asra smiled politely. "Very pretty," she said, and reached to take the food from Becky's hands.

"You don't have to worry about germs," Becky chirped, "because my hands were clean when I picked all the ingredients. If you wait for me to bring the rest of the food, I can say the blessing!"

Asra carefully placed the leaf, like a tray, upon her knees. She plucked several of the berries and admired them. "Where did you learn to prepare food like this, Rebecca?"

"From Neaca," Becky called. "She's the Mage's friend from the forest outside Ljosalfar. I don't remember if you met her when you came to bring the maps to the Mage. I helped Neaca gather food while Matt and I were there. She gave me a book to help me find things."

Becky carried Radik's breakfast to him, and then went to get her own portion. When she was seated, she closed her eyes and said, "In the name of the Mother and her Cord, we thank you for this blessing of food."

Asra couldn't help but smile. "If you were not a Human, Rebecca, I would say you're on your way to becoming a monk!"

"But she *is* a Human," Radik said, carefully picking at the food Becky had given him.

When they were done eating, Becky and Asra spread out the maps, discussed the swiftest route north, and the three continued on their journey. Radik kept his distance from Becky. Though he resented his assignment he felt at home, at least, among the trees and the hills. Asra, however, quickly discovered that she was not cut out for serious hiking. Her feet were blistered and the heels of her shoes were wearing thin. Radik had come to the conclusion that if they could find one of the major Cords, it might be worth considering traveling north on the old Faerie way. He convinced himself that since Becky had traveled in a Cord once before, it would not be too dangerous. He was surprised when he suggested the change of plan that Asra and Becky were quick to agree. They examined the maps more carefully and found what appeared to be a large Cord that came to the surface along a ridge several miles ahead. When they reached the ridge, however, they were met with a disappointing surprise.

"Oh," Becky cried. "What's that smell? Is that the Cord?"

"And what are those yellow ribbons?" Asra wondered aloud. "*Police Line Do Not Cross.* Human things!"

Radik walked up to the ruins of the Cord, stepped beneath

the police line and knelt on the ground. A large section of the Cord was missing where it bulged out of the ground. The cut was clean, and there were marks on the ground where the piece had been dragged to a truck. There were tire tracks in the dirt, too, and they led into the green distance. On either side of the cut, the Cord lay collapsed like greasy slabs of yellow cheese, streaked with black and green mold. The air that normally coursed through the Cord now bubbled weakly through the rot. Flies buzzed in the rank air.

"It's clear we're still in the Human realm," Radik said, stepping back. "Only a Human would stoop so low as to sever one of our Cords."

"Maybe they didn't do it on purpose," Becky offered.

"Of course they did it on purpose," Radik sneered. "Humans have always hated us!"

Becky's hands bunched into fists. "You don't know what you're talking about! People don't even know that faeries really exist. They think of you as characters in stories and pictures, that's all. If the boundaries between my world and yours are all messed up, somebody probably stumbled on the Cord and didn't know what it was. Maybe they just took a piece to try and like, study it!"

"I've got to get out of here," Asra moaned, looking ill. "The stench is too much. If we can't travel in a Cord, then we'll continue on foot, somehow. Perhaps if we follow that Human trail, 'twill be easier than moving through the woods. What do you see on the map, Rebecca? Can we go that way?"

Radik sulked as he watched Asra and Becky hold the maps up to a blue patch of sky, and he saw how easily they spoke with each other. He already knew that Becky idolized the Princess. Now he could see that Asra was warming to the girl, as well. It made him feel jealous and angry as he clomped along, following the tire tracks out of the woods. Soon they came to the road and turned onto the gravel shoulder. "You have to be careful, here," Becky said. "This is like your Cord, except it's out in the open. Just stay off to the side and you'll be okay."

"What do you mean, like our Cord?" Radik asked. When he felt the rush of air, and heard a slight hissing that grew louder with each passing second, he spun around. "Asra," he called, gripped in panic. There was no time to say another word. Radik leapt off the road and tumbled into a ravine as a car sped past. Becky turned away so that Radik wouldn't see the smile spreading across her face.

Radik grumbled, crawling up out of the weeds. "The Human realm is cursed. We shouldn't be here!"

"There's a lot more to see," Becky said. "Look at that sign!"

The Elves noted that the road was marked with a number of metal signs attached to tall poles sticking out of the ground. Each was printed with letters and numbers, in some strange shorthand that Asra couldn't understand. Radik stared glumly at the signs and waited for Becky to explain. "The road signs show we're coming to a town," Becky said, smiling. "Now you'll find out what it's like where people live!"

Radik clenched his jaw. "Can't we go around?"

"It would take too long. If we just walk through it, we can go back into the woods on the other side. Don't be afraid, if you stay by me, everything will be all right."

Another car sped by, this time from the opposite direction. It was followed by a pickup truck. Each time a vehicle went past, Radik shuddered. "What are those things? Why are there Humans inside them?"

"They're like the gondolas," Asra said, "that the royal families ride inside the Cord."

"Do royal Human families ride in these vehicles?"

"I'll explain everything later," Becky said. "If people see me talking too much, they'll think I'm crazy, since they won't be able to see you. It's better not to attract attention."

Becky glanced down at her soiled shirt and jeans as she headed along the road. After so many days in the woods without a change of clothes, she was a mess. She ran her fingers through her dirty hair, trying to pull out the knots. "Do I look all right, Princess Asra?"

Asra bit her tongue. To speak the truth, that she thought Becky's appearance was loathsome, with her huge body, gangly hands and feet, would not have been wise. With or without clean clothes, Becky was a Human, and to an Elf, she was always going to be ugly. "Aye," Asra lied. "What about me, Rebecca? Do I look presentable?"

Becky stopped walking. She looked Asra up and down and sighed, "You'll always be beautiful!"

Radik had little patience for such an exchange. "We should stop this chatter and plan what to do when the Humans see us!"

Asra shook her head. "Humans don't see Faerie Folk because they don't believe we're real. There aren't many like Rebecca. 'Twill seem odd, I'm sure, to walk on the Humans' street, but we should be able to move amongst them as if we're invisible."

"Then why do you ask if you look presentable? What does it matter?"

Asra scowled. "Is there something in particular that makes you afraid?"

"I'm not afraid," Radik said. "I just want to make sure there's no reason for *you* to be afraid. Even if the Humans can't see us, this place is still full of danger. Just the scent of metal here will sicken us if we stay long!"

"I wonder why faeries can see people, but people can't see faeries," Becky mused.

"When there's a conflict, or a battle," Asra explained, "the victors always forget about those who have lost. But the losers never forget. Our tutors teach us about Humans, so we always remember what you did, before the Goddess created a special world for us."

"But *I* didn't do anything!" Becky said.

Soon they crossed a concrete bridge and headed into town. Main Street was a corridor of two- and three-story brick buildings. There were cars, and shops, and pedestrians, awnings and flags and green wooden benches where people sat and waited for the bus. A barbershop pole spun lazily as Becky walked past, the two Elves trudging behind. They came to a crosswalk and waited for the light to change. Radik held his sleeve over his face as cars sped by, spilling exhaust into the air. There was a newspaper kiosk on the corner. Becky bent to get a closer look at the picture on the front page; it was a photograph of a girl, a little younger than Becky. The headline said that she was missing. Policemen were scouring the woods trying to find her. Her parents were afraid that she had been kidnapped, and they were awaiting some kind of ransom note. There was another article below, and Becky's breath caught in her throat when she saw the picture above the headline. "Look at this!" she whispered.

"A Fungus Among Us," the paper read. There was a line of smaller type below: "Officials concerned about environmental impact of rare growth discovered in local woodland."

"'Tis the Cord," Asra said. "The Cord we saw cut in the forest!"

"Experts ready with powerful fungicides," the paper read.

"I'd buy a copy if I had some quarters," Becky said. "Then we could read the whole story."

Radik shook his head gloomily. "'Tis unforgivable that Humans should touch our sacred Cord. None of this will end well. None of it!"

They walked on down the block, past a sporting goods outlet, a run-down hotel, a pawnshop, and a thrift store. Becky studied her reflection in the window glass and wished that she had the money to buy a change of clothes, even used ones. On the next corner they passed a bakery, and the smell of fresh bread wafted out of an air vent. The dizzying array of odors in the Human town made Asra and Radik feel slightly ill. At the same time, they realized how hungry they'd grown. "We must eat, soon," Asra said, "if we intend to keep our strength."

Becky shrugged. "We haven't got any money!" At that moment a woman stepped out of a store and gave the girl a peculiar look as she hurried to her car.

"She probably wonders why I'm not in school," Becky said.

"Or why you're talking to yourself," Asra added.

Suddenly the woman turned, reached into her pocketbook, and came back toward Becky. She held a five-dollar bill in her hand. "Here," she said, and quickly hurried away.

Becky left the Elves outside while she went into the bakery. There were several people already in line, and as she looked longingly at the doughnuts and pastries that filled the shelves, she overheard the cashier talking to one of the customers. "It wasn't just the one little girl," a woman said. "I heard on the news this morning there are more kids getting kidnapped—a few in Kittanning, more in Butler, and when you add that to the kids who were already taken in Pittsburgh, it's got to make fifty, at least!"

"Crazy," said another customer. "It's got to be a rumor. Fifty kids can't just disappear!"

The cashier shook her head. "Somebody told me there's rumors that hundreds of kids are missing up in New York, and the governor won't say anything about it because it would cause a panic."

"Oh, come on, you can't keep something like that quiet!"

"You know, whoever took the kids left a few notes behind," a woman remarked. "On the news, though, the police said they thought the notes were a hoax. Maybe all the kids are runaways. Maybe there's some new kind of cult, or something!"

Two young men in overalls stood in front of Becky. "Maybe them kids got snatched up by aliens," one of them snickered.

"You mean illegal aliens, like from some other country?" asked the other.

"No," his friend scoffed. "I mean from outer space! You know, they found some kind of weird alien stuff out in the woods. They said it was a fungus, but I don't know. You can't believe what you read in the papers. Only a fool would say there weren't aliens out there. Could be they're coming to get us all!"

When Becky came to the front of the line, the cashier took one look at her and frowned. "Where's your mother, sweetie?" she bent over the counter and asked.

Becky's eyes widened. "She's, um, out in the car, waiting for me."

"Well, it's good you're not all by yourself, because I wouldn't want something to happen to you. It's not safe out there anymore."

"I know," Becky said, putting on her best reassuring smile. "How many doughnuts with pink frosting and sprinkles can I buy with five dollars, please?"

237

Becky waltzed out of the bakery proudly holding a large paper sack. "Let's find some place where we can eat and talk without being noticed," she said to the Elves.

There was an alley midway up the block. Radik, always cautious, went ahead to make sure it was safe. He peered into the shadows between the two buildings. He held up a hand, indicating that the others should stay back. Behind a row of trash cans a figure stood, a can of spray paint in his hand. Radik backed away and gestured to Asra and Becky. "There's a Troll in there!" he hissed.

"Perhaps he can help us," Asra said.

The Troll was young, with dark hair tucked under his cap, and his face was tight with concentration. He moved his arm in a wide arc, painting something on the wall. He turned to glance at Radik just as Asra came into sight. Not a second later his skin went ashen and he dropped to one knee on the alley floor. "Princess Asra," he stammered.

At that same moment Becky appeared from around the corner. The Troll leapt up, wide-eyed, grabbed his paint can and turned to run away. "Wait," Asra called. "Please, we mean you no harm. How do you know my name?"

The Troll stopped, then turned and squinted into the light at the end of the alley. "I come from a Troll Clan south of Alfheim. My family was there at your wedding to Prince Udos—I mean, when you were supposed to be married to—"

"That was a long time ago," Asra said. "My homeland's gone

now, and I'm a Princess no more. Did you know that Alfheim was destroyed in a fire?"

"'Twas the same fire that leveled my home," the Troll said, nervously eyeing Becky. "Princess, why are you with a Human? How is it that she can see me?"

"You don't have to be afraid," Becky volunteered. "We're on a journey. We're . . . friends. The Princess calls me Rebecca, and that's Radik over there. What are you doing back in the alley?"

"I'm tagging," the Troll said shyly, holding the can of spray paint behind his back. "I've never spoken to a Human before."

"We mean you no harm," Asra said. "Rebecca is just curious."

"Well," the Troll said, "I'm marking my Clan's turf. There are a lot of Faerie Folk in town, especially after the forest fire. We find it easier to get along if we stay with our own kind. We mark our territory, and nobody gets in anybody else's way. Come look, if you want."

"Don't go in there," Radik whispered. "It might be a trap."

"Nooo," said the Troll. "I'm alone."

He stood back from his work, and Asra and Becky came close to examine the marks he'd made on the wall. Large, balloon-like letters and numbers, outlined in black, were scrawled across the brick. Becky couldn't make out what they said. "It looks like graffiti, like what kids used to spray on the walls in Pittsburgh, where I grew up."

"You mean Argant," the Troll said. "If you saw tags there, most likely they were drawn by Faerie Folk. 'Tis how we know when one block is run by Trolls, or Pixies, or Gnomes, or Elves. I wrote *Karuna,* so everybody will know that the folk from my Clan control this alley."

"The paint smells foul," Asra said, wrinkling her face. "Doesn't it make you ill?"

The Troll grinned, and Asra was startled to see that there were teeth missing from his swollen gums. Embarrassed, he drew a hand up over his mouth. "There's a price to pay for living here," he explained. 'Tisn't like the old days in the forest, when nobody ever got sick, and our lives were as long as the Cord reaching to the end of the world. Now we just make the best of what we've got, and thank the Gods for it!"

"Would you like a doughnut?" Becky asked.

The Troll looked to Asra for approval. She nodded, and he reached into the sack. "I wouldn't say no!"

Radik felt edgy and tense. He had the feeling that they were being watched, and he didn't like being trapped in an alley. "We must go," he said. "Do you know if there are any Cords around that might be safe to travel? We're trying to find our way north, toward Helfratheim."

"You're not making a delivery, are you?" the Troll asked, stealing a glance at Becky.

"We're looking for the girl's parents," Asra said. "What do you mean, a delivery?"

"Don't you know?" the Troll gulped. "There are Elves who've been taking *Tem* children and sending them up to Helfratheim in some kind of airship. There's a Mage who put out the word that she's going to sacrifice the children to the Elfin Gods, and start a war with all the *Tems*. I know it sounds crazy, but it's true. You should be careful if you're traveling in places where there might be Faerie Folk about. They might not be as friendly toward the Human as the two of you!"

"Where might we find one of these airships?" Radik asked.

"I don't know," the Troll said, brushing doughnut crumbs from his jerkin. "But if you're looking for a Cord that's still intact, I heard about some deep ones a little ways north. I met a Dwarf a while back who told me that the *Tems* were digging mines near their town. They came upon a Cord, a really big one, and they nearly cut through it. He said it was the fifth one, if anyone ever had need of it. Anyway, the *Tems* didn't know what it was, and they were just starting to investigate when a fire broke out in some of their other mines. They had to pack up and leave. If you can find the village, you might find the mine, and the Cord. The Dwarf told me his Clan still traveled in it sometimes. It might be dangerous, though, because of the fire and the gases underground. On the other hand it's a long way to Helfratheim on foot!"

"We're aware of that," said Asra. "You're sure you haven't heard of any other Cords?"

"Nooo, your Highness."

"Then thank you for your help," Asra sighed, "and . . . good luck to you. I wish you well here amongst the Humans."

"Hard times, hard times," the Troll said, bowing a little as he watched the Elves and the Human girl disappear down the street. He was just about to have another bite of doughnut when a two-by-four struck the back of his head, and he fell to the ground.

Macta Dockalfar tossed away the lumber he'd been carrying in his one good hand. While Asra and her friends had been talking to the Troll, Macta had crept around the block to the back of the alley. He waited until the Troll was alone to make his move. "Finally," he mumbled, bending to pick up the doughnut the Troll had dropped. Though there were several bites missing, Macta had given up any notion of being picky. He took his first bite and nearly swooned with pleasure. Now, he thought, he'd have the strength to continue the chase. He took out his notebook and wrote in it. He'd bet himself five dratmas that he'd get the doughnut before the Troll had taken any bites out of it. *Lost that one,* he thought, and scribbled out the new total. But he'd also bet himself another ten that the Troll would go down without a fight, and he'd been correct about that. He smiled. Life was just a game, after all, and he was going to win, if it was the last thing he ever did.

20

JARDAINE WAS SKIPPING by the time they reached the playground. *I've got a secret, I've got a secret, and his name is Jal-Maktar,* she sang to herself, so excited that her skin tingled and her breath came in shallow little gulps. Bringing Jal-Maktar into material form hadn't been as difficult as she had thought it would be. After all those many moons at the feet of the Mage of Alfheim, she was used to magick being hard work. She was used to praying for guidance, she was used to hours spent at the Discipline, at endless exercises meant to strengthen her will and bring her closer to the great Mother and all the Faerie Gods. So much energy had been wasted worrying about purity, and contamination, and the curse of Blood. Now, after sacrificing a little of her own Blood to invite Jal-Maktar into being, she knew! Blood was a pathway to a world of rare and mysterious Faerie creatures, and that was why Mage Kalevala Van Frier and all her wretched monks were so afraid of it. They were afraid of real power. They were afraid of what the alchemy of fierce desire and iron will could do to change the world. Brahja-Chi knew! Brahja-Chi knew, all along. *If only I'd gone to study with her,* Jardaine thought, *instead of the Mage of Alfheim!* But no . . . she stopped herself. This was no time for regrets.

When she'd first heard of Tuava-Li's quest to journey to the North Pole to re-create the legend of Fada, Jardaine had been worried. If the Mage's vision were true, Tuava-Li would become a living legend, powerful beyond all measure. *Why couldn't I have been chosen for such a quest,* she'd wondered to herself. But now, with the help of Jal-Maktar, everything about Jardaine's life had changed for the better. The past was dead and buried, and the world was gloriously alive, full of promise and hope, bright as a spring bouquet. Jardaine was bursting with happiness. Jal-Maktar's impersonation of Macta had come at no cost to her whatsoever. His appearance before the Council of Seven Agents had gone perfectly. And for a special fee, bits of Jardaine's flesh and Blood, he was more than willing to help abduct Human children for Brahja-Chi's cause.

Jal-Maktar, for his part, knew that he'd fallen into the job of a lifetime. In exchange for pretending to be Macta in the week leading up to the Acquisition, Brahja-Chi had agreed to pay him with the soul of a single Human child per day. Jal-Maktar would have preferred pieces of the old Mage's flesh as his reward; more appetizing than Human spirits, it was rich with the flavor of greed, hatred, lust, and contempt. But Brahja-Chi promised Jal-Maktar that on the night of the Acquisition, he would get a special treat. He would have the privilege of devouring not a hundred, not five hundred, but all one thousand souls that the Mage was going to sacrifice! This was the part of the bargain that made Jal-Maktar the happiest of creatures—not only would it be a feast like no other, but with so much of what he called his *soul food*, he would be able to leave the spirit world behind and take on a permanent material form. He was delighted beyond measure, and giddy with excitement. No longer would he have to spend his days with less substance than the wind, sensing the vitality of the world around him, but only rarely getting the opportunity to taste it.

Jal-Maktar brushed blond ringlets from his eyes. To Human eyes, he looked like a plump little boy, maybe five years old. He, Jardaine, and several of her loyal monks were skipping down a winding brick path, past fragrant garden beds and manicured shrubs and trees. They could hear the sound of children's laughter just ahead. *It is going to be so easy!* Jal-Maktar rounded the corner and saw happy toddlers in swings, pushed gently by their young mothers. Two little boys were climbing to the top of a slide. There were other children in a sandbox, and on a bench nearby sat two women, absorbed in an animated conversation. Jal-Maktar smiled; the choice was clear.

The little girl in the sandbox looked up as a shadow came between her and the warm autumn sun. Her blue eyes flashed above rosy cheeks. "Hi," said Jal-Maktar, disguised as the boy, gazing down at her.

"Hi," answered the girl. She had a plastic shovel in one hand, which she had been using to move sand into a little pink flowered pail.

"I've got a sandbox at home," said Jal-Maktar, smiling innocently. "It's as big as a desert!"

"No, you don't," the girl said.

"Have you seen the dolls?" asked Jal-Maktar. "All the girls are going to want to see them."

"What dolls?"

"They're right over here, on the other side of the bushes. Somebody must have left them here by mistake, but I don't know how anyone could forget to take dolls as beautiful as these. Come on, I'll show you!"

"Okay," said the girl, getting to her feet.

The other children in the sandbox looked up. "Come, come," said Jal-Maktar, gesturing confidently. "Come and see the dolls!"

Jardaine and the monks lay in a row along the brick walkway, just out of sight, behind the bushes. They stared blankly into the sky, watching shreds of cloud drift past in a sea of blue. They were waiting. Faint smiles decorated their frozen faces. Under normal circumstances the children would probably never have seen them, but thanks to the magick of Jal-Maktar, the Elves were now plainly visible. They looked like big dolls, even in their black robes. With their large, moon-round eyes and their hair arranged to hide their pointed ears, their faces looked almost sweet. Delicate hands lay still at their sides. "Ooooooh," the girls cooed when they saw them.

"Why are they dressed like that?" one of the children asked, leaning down to look.

Jardaine felt a stab of regret at that remark; for an extra fee, Jal-Maktar could have made the monks appear to be wearing pretty Human dresses. Jardaine knew that she could have probably created the same illusion, and at no extra cost, but it had hardly seemed worth the bother. Humans were so foolish, in the end. All the children had to do now was touch them. Just one touch, one little brush of the fingertips, and the children would belong to Jardaine and her monks . . . forever. *Touch me,* Jardaine thought, as a toddler looked down at her, hesitating. The girl's older sister, eyes wide with curiosity, stood behind her. Jardaine could tell the older girl was intrigued. *Just reach out your filthy fat finger,* Jardaine thought, *just reach out and touch me!*

"She looks so real," said the girl, and her fingers brushed Jardaine's cheek. At the same moment her little sister touched one of the other monks on the tip of her nose. Jardaine's hands shot out, grabbing the older girl's shoulders. Her little sister gasped when the monk grabbed her by the hair and pulled her down. The enchantment was instantaneous; the girls fell to the grass, unconscious. There was only one other child left to snatch. As the girl turned her horrified face away from the Elves and started to run, Jardaine called out to Jal-Maktar.

"All right, you've got me. Stop the child before her mother comes, and I'll give you something more."

"It won't hurt," he said in a kindly voice. "You have much more to give before it begins to hurt!"

Jardaine felt a twinge in her belly, and knew that Jal-Maktar had taken something from inside her. The child fell without making a sound. Her mother, one of the women on the nearby bench, was still deep in conversation with her friend, and knew nothing of what had happened.

"Four," Jardaine said. She got to her feet, and wiped her hands on her robe. "All that, for a total of four children."

Now that they had the children under their power, Jal-Maktar made a casual gesture and the children lifted off the ground, their clothes and hair flapping as if they were caught in some kind of invisible wind. He muttered something under his breath and the children disappeared.

"How long will it take for them to arrive at Helfratheim?" Jardaine asked.

"They're there already," Jal-Maktar said brightly. "I hope your monks in Helfratheim are ready to lock the loathsome brats up where they won't cause any harm. Shall we continue? Next time, I think I'll try something a little different; otherwise capturing Humans just gets so dull, you know. Just to inform you, Jardaine, our contract for this business is good for another two hours, seventeen minutes, and forty-three seconds."

"Your precision is impressive," Jardaine smiled humorlessly.

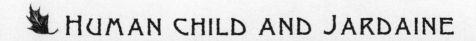 HUMAN CHILD AND JARDAINE

"Find another playground, Jal-Maktar, and we'll snatch some more. Once word gets out that children are missing, it won't be so easy for us. Parents will stop taking their children outside, or they'll watch them like hawks. We must work quickly."

Jal-Maktar sniffed the air and chuckled to himself. "Wind and water, fire and mud, Jal-Maktar smells fresh young Blood!"

"Then lead the way," Jardaine said, gathering her monks. "I don't want to waste an extra second!"

21

THE STEADY *TAP-TAP-TAP* of raindrops on the tarp did not deter Matt, Tomtar, and Tuava-Li from sleeping in the back of the pickup truck. Even when the driver pulled off the main road, wound his way through a dense pine forest, and pulled into the driveway of his bungalow, sheer exhaustion kept the trio from waking. Finally the morning sun crept through a hazy sky. Matt's arm slipped from beneath the tarp, and a puddle of cold water trickled onto his wrist. He woke up with a jolt, and swallowed a cry of despair when he squinted from under the plastic cover and realized that they were back in the woods again. He gently shook his companions awake and helped them out of the back of the truck. Matt had promised them that he would make sure they stayed on the highway, and now he had let them down. He had let himself down, too, and he felt heartsick.

Tomtar and Tuava-Li said little as they began their hike down the side of the mountain. They were both queasy from spending the night on a bed of metal, and they chewed their *trans* and waited for some relief. Tuava-Li thought it might be a good idea to view the terrain from above, and see if she could tell where they were. She changed to a kestrel and flapped into the humid air. Matt turned his head and looked up. The tip of one of Tuava-Li's wings brushed against a pine bough, still heavy with last night's rain. "Watch out!" he cried too late, as he and Tomtar were showered with icy water.

What next, Matt thought, shivering. He was surprised when Tuava-Li made a loop in the air and drifted back to the side of the road. He turned his head, not wanting to see her until she had slipped back into her clothes. "The main road is near," she said breathlessly. "If we make a path down through the woods here, we'll be back on course in no time!"

"You know," Matt said, "you don't need to change back into an elf just to talk to us. I've given up on trying to keep you out of my mind, Tuava-Li. Just go ahead and use your thought-speak, or whatever you call it. You're wasting too much energy changing back and forth like that. If you're a kestrel you won't have to limp around on those crummy shoes, and we can get where we're going a little more quickly."

Tuava-Li shrugged. "Thank you, but I wonder if you're just embarrassed to see me without my clothing when I make the change."

"Okay," said Matt. "Maybe I am. But what I'm saying is that

I'm going to try to trust you not to mess around in my mind, if you want to use thought-speak when you're up there flapping around."

"That's not how it works. Still, I appreciate your trust. I don't want you to feel violated."

"Too late for that," Matt replied, "I already feel violated. But not for the reason you think."

Tuava-Li stared blankly. "What do you mean?"

Matt was silent for a moment. He was still bothered by the tattoo of the knife on his chest. "When I look at my body, that's when I feel violated. See, when this is all over, you get to walk away, and everything will be like it was before. But not for me. I'm going to have to explain these weird tattoos to everybody I meet for the rest of my life. I—"

"Nothing will be like it was before," Tuava-Li interrupted.

"We've all got tattoos, Matt," Tomtar said, "to show what Clan we're from, to mark us for protection, for—"

"You're faeries," Matt said. "You don't know many humans. *Any* humans, except for me. People like me don't get tattoos—at least, not until they're older. And I've never heard of anybody getting tattoos that change."

Tomtar's eyes grew wide. "What?"

Matt pulled up his shirt so that the Troll could see. "I showed it to Tuava-Li last night. When we left Neaca's camp, I had tattoos of leaves and vines on my chest. Sometime later, it turned into this knife."

"I don't see a knife," Tomtar said, looking closely. "It looks like a picture of some kind of building."

Matt felt the blood pulsing in his temples as he peered down at his own chest. The knife was gone; in its place was an image of an old brick church with a steeple on top. "No," he cried, "it can't be. Last night, there was a knife there. We both saw it. I've never seen this building before. Have you?"

The Elf shook her head helplessly. "You have to believe me, Matthew, no, I haven't, and I don't know what it means."

Matt pulled down his shirt. "All right, if you say so. Do you think we're supposed to look for this building? It's not where your uncle lives, is it, Tomtar?"

"Noooo," answered the Troll. "But it might be near there!"

Matt sighed. "So what do you say, let's head for the highway, okay? Today we're going to make it to Pittsburgh. Maybe we'll see this building when we get there."

"*Argant*," Tomtar corrected with a grin.

Tuava-Li nodded as her nose and mouth began to harden into a beak, and soft feathers rippled over her skin. Matt looked away.

At the bottom of the hill they came to the back of a gas station, surrounded by a chain-link fence. They crossed along the edge, sidestepping mounds of litter and dried leaves. It was still early enough that the gas station was closed. There was a red metal box, about the size of a big refrigerator, at the side of the blacktop lot. "Look at that," Matt said. "'Clothes for Life,' it says, there on the top. It's a drop-off box. People put old clothes in there for charity."

"What's charity?" Tomtar asked.

"*We* are," Matt replied, holding out his arms. His pants and T-shirt were beyond mere ruin; his clothes were more tattered and filthy than those of the most destitute homeless person. "I'd like to get in there and see if there are any clothes that would fit me. I don't want to go into town looking like this." Matt pulled the handle on the box and tried to peer inside. "I can't tell if there's anything in here or not."

"Can I see?" asked Tomtar.

Matt turned to look at his friend. "Not unless I hold you by the ankles and lower you in."

Tomtar shrugged. He was a little worried about going headfirst into a strange metal box, but he took off his pack and laid it gently on the ground. "I'll do it."

Matt heard a voice in his mind. *What are you doing?*

"We're looking for clothes," Matt said, glancing up to see the kestrel circling high overhead. "Maybe we'll even find something for you, Tuava-Li!" Matt hoisted the Troll up as high as he could, then reached behind him to grab the little hinged door and pull it open. "Come on, Tomtar," he grunted, "just squeeze in there, okay?"

"'Tis too small," the Troll said, as he leaned forward and strained to get through the opening. "The edges are sharp!"

Suddenly his weight shifted and he tumbled into the darkness, his tattered shoes slipping off in Matt's hands. "Oh no," Matt cried.

"I'm all right," came Tomtar's muffled voice. "I fell on something soft."

A moment later the kestrel landed on the top of the box, wings flapping, fierce eyes glaring down at Matt. "He fell in," Matt said helplessly, and hurried around behind the box. He bent over and peered at the rusty hinges. "There's a door here, with a lock on it. You must have some kind of magic spell or something to open this up, don't you?"

"Is there no other way?" Tuava-Li said, changing to an Elf once more. She took her garments from Tomtar's bag and slipped them on. "You yourself said that changing form requires a great expense in energy. So does magick."

"I'm sorry," Matt said. "I know what I told you about changing. But for someone who spent her life learning magic, you're pretty cautious about using it."

Matt reached into his pocket and pulled out his knife. "Maybe I can open up the back with this!"

He angled the tip of the blade into the little round lock. He rattled it back and forth, but nothing happened. He tried again, pushing the tip of his blade as far into the lock as it would go. Nothing. "Tuava-Li, isn't there something you try, some spell, or magic words, at least? Tomtar's not coming out of there unless we get him out."

Tuava-Li closed her eyes and concentrated. She imagined the

inside of the lock, and a hazy picture took form in her mind. She moved her concentration like a kind of pry bar into the tiny, rust-brown space, feeling the little metal parts with fingers of perfect, crystalline attention. She felt sweat break out on her forehead. "Now," she said.

The latch moved into place. Matt gave the door a yank and nearly fell backwards. Tomtar tumbled out and landed on his side, followed by four or five plastic garbage bags stuffed with musty old clothes. "Eureka," Matt said, untying the knot on the biggest bag. The smell of mildew and stale body odor assaulted their nostrils, but at Matt's insistence they proceeded to open up every bag in the bin. He pulled out a lot of baby outfits, and found a pair of jeans at the bottom of a bag that he thought might fit Tomtar. Tuava-Li dug out a little girl's jumper with a flower appliqué sewn on the front. She held it up in front of her, and carefully laid it aside. Matt dragged out a lady's shirt that still had its original price tag stapled to the back. Matt chuckled as he read the words printed on the front of the shirt. "The Goddess is coming back, and boy, is she pissed!"

Tuava-Li nodded. "She *is* coming back. But what does *pissed* mean?"

"It means *angry*."

"How do *Tems* know the Goddess will be angry?" Tomtar mused.

"It's supposed to be a joke," Matt said. He pulled an old blue wool suit jacket from a bag and held it up in front of him, then put it on. He rolled his shoulders and checked the sleeves for length. "Finally, something that fits. It's not exactly my style, but it beats what I've been wearing! At least nobody will see my tattoos."

Matt searched the bag and found the pants that matched the jacket. He wasn't sure what kind of shirt would go best with the suit, but there were a couple of colored T-shirts that weren't too badly stained. He chose the brightest one, and then went around to the side of the metal box to change. The medallions and amulets around his neck jangled, and for once, Matt found the sound cheerful. He was out of his old clothes and into the new ones in a flash. After he'd tied the laces on his old sneakers he stood up and stuck his hands into the pockets of his new jacket. There was a hole in one pocket, but Matt was surprised to feel a wad of paper in the other. He pulled it out and examined it. "A ticket for the symphony, from 2001. I guess I missed that one!"

There were a few faded business cards, a piece of paper with a phone number scrawled on it, and a wad of tissue paper that crumbled in Matt's hand. He tossed them in a nearby trash can. But when he reached into the breast pocket, his eyes lit up.

It may have only been four dollars, folded in half, but Matt felt so happy that he almost burst into tears. When he leapt around the corner of the rusty metal box he saw Tomtar and Tuava-Li getting into their new clothes. It was slightly absurd to see the Faeries dressed in colorful children's outfits, looking rumpled and completely out of their element. "Wait," Matt said, "you're putting those on inside out!"

"We know," Tomtar mumbled. "It's for protection, remember?"

"Whatever," Matt answered. "But if you think I'm doing that, too, you're crazy. Guys, look at this! We've got money!"

When the bus glided in along the curb, its brakes made a satisfying hiss. Matt stepped up into the air-conditioned interior. Then he realized that Tomtar and Tuava-Li still waited on the sidewalk. He turned around and whispered, "What are you waiting for? Come on!"

"You must invite us," Tuava-Li said, "any time we enter a Human place. Did you forget our law?"

"I invite you in," Matt said, rolling his eyes. "Hurry!"

Tuava-Li climbed the steps and looked suspiciously at the automatic doors folded on their hinges. *Magick,* she said to herself, and jumped when the doors closed behind her.

Matt handed his cash to the driver and waited for the change. He shifted his weight and realized that the Faerie-woven pack on his back was going to draw unwanted attention; he'd have to get rid of it as soon as possible. "Is that your brother and sister?" the driver asked, turning his head. "They can—wait, where'd they go? I could have sworn I saw somebody besides you get on the bus!"

Matt blinked and forced a smile. "Nope, just me! You're going downtown, right?"

The driver nodded, and shifted the bus into gear.

Tomtar and Tuava-Li sat by a window toward the back of the bus, watching the road fly past. They chewed on their *trans*, feeling frightened, and dizzy, and nauseated. "It's like riding in the Cord," Matt whispered from his aisle seat. "It's sickening at first, but you get used to it."

"I'll never get used to it," Tomtar groaned. At first he had been excited to see the road signs, and the cars, and all the buildings go by in a bright blur of colors. Now it just made him feel ill. "How long must we travel like this?"

"As long as we have to," Matt said, looking around to make sure no one was paying any attention. There were only a few people on the bus, and they all seemed lost in their own thoughts. "When we get into the city, we'll find a jewelry shop, and see if we can trade in some of the Alfheim jewels for cash. You can't go anywhere in the human realm without money." Now that he had spent so much time in the company of Faerie Folk, Matt had gotten used to referring to himself as a human.

"A Troll from my Clan used to work on the Melusina Bridge," Tomtar said. "If we went over on foot, we could talk to him and find out how things are going with my uncle Vollyar. I can't wait to see the look on his face when he sees me with an Elf and a Human!"

"I've never heard of any Melusina Bridge," Matt said. "If the bus stays on this road, we'll be going over the Allegheny on 16th Street."

"Aye," said the troll, nodding his head. "That's one of the paths into Argant, it's just the *Tem* way of puttin' it."

The bus was beginning to fill with people. Matt stared out the window, remembering the town he had left behind not so long ago. As they approached the outskirts of the city, the buildings looked older, taller, and closer together. Everything was brick, or aluminum-clad, and there were pedestrians on the streets. The ride grew slower, with more stops and starts, and Tomtar's and Tuava-Li's normally pale skin was flushed white. It was plain to Matt that they couldn't tolerate much more of the ride. The bus lurched to another stop, and an old woman in a babushka made her way down the aisle. She stood beside Matt, shopping bag in hand, and let out a sigh. "Are you going to move over so I can sit down?" she asked, and Matt realized that she thought the seat next to him was empty.

He was going to have to make the old woman go away. "I'm saving it."

"Then I'll just sit down until your friend comes," the old lady said, nudging her sack into Matt's lap.

"No," Matt said, "you can't. There's—somebody left something wet on the seat, you don't want to sit there, believe me!"

"I'm going to tell the driver," the old lady warned. "I'm a senior citizen, and just because I'm old, that doesn't mean I'm stupid. I'm going to have you thrown off the bus!"

"Fine," Matt said, getting to his feet. "I'm about to get off, anyway!"

Tomtar and Tuava-Li had barely slipped into the aisle before the old woman heaved herself onto the molded plastic seat. They exited the bus at the next stop and stepped onto the curb just a block from the 16th Street Bridge. Tomtar looked up, scanning the skies. "What do you see?" Matt asked.

"Nothing!"

"I mean, what are you looking for?"

"Pigeons," answered Tomtar, seeing only a few slow-moving clouds. He raced ahead. Tuava-Li, her shoes so badly worn that they hardly clung to her feet, hobbled along beside Matt. Her backpack, too, was looking a little frayed. "We'll find some place in the city to get you some new things," he said. "Don't worry."

"I'm not worried," Tuava-Li answered with a pained grimace. "The Goddess will provide. She always does!"

Tomtar stopped when he got to the foot of the bridge and stared about. He raced down the embankment, and then scrambled up again. His expression quickly changed from puzzlement to panic. He turned, ashen-faced, to face Matt and Tuava-Li as they waited above. "There's no one here!"

"Maybe your buddy's down on the lower side of the bridge, or he's taking a break, or something," Matt said.

"No, you don't understand! There are usually a lot of Trolls down here, taking tolls when Faerie Folk cross the bridge. We have—we *had* members of all the Clans on all the bridges, all four hundred of 'em. We had little booths just in the shadows, there, with shrines for all the Gods, where folks gave thanks for their crossing, and paid their tolls. But there's nobody here, nobody at all! It's as if no one ever was!"

"Maybe this is the wrong bridge," Matt said. "There are dozens of bridges up and down the river."

"Nooo," said Tomtar. "This is the right bridge! I know it! I know it! Look at that writing there, on the pier!"

Matt wrinkled up his face. "That graffiti? Some kid spray-painted that, Tomtar. I know you can't read English. It's just, like, a tag, or something. You know, a name!"

"I can read that," said Tomtar. "It says '*Emrys.*' It means *immortal.* It's one of the Clan names. But we're *Ingeborgs.* Uncle Vollyar would never let his bridge go to another Clan. Unless . . ."

"You told us that something bad happened in Argant," Tuava-Li said, "something to do with a sickness . . . a bird flu. But if there are still Trolls marking their territory, they must be living here, don't you think? They can't all be gone. Let's just go on into the town and see what we can find! I'm sure your uncle's still here."

"All right," Tomtar said sorrowfully. "I brought you here to find the maps for our journey. If we can't get them, then—"

"We'll find your relatives, and we'll find the maps, too," Tuava-Li soothed, trying to sound cheerful. She couldn't begin to imagine what they would do if this expedition to Argant was a failure.

"I don't know this part of the city," Matt said, gazing out over the low industrial buildings and warehouses near the river. He pointed toward the jumble of skyscrapers toward the west. "I grew up on the south side. But if we follow the roads downtown, we'll find a jewelry shop for sure, and once we get some money we can buy something to eat. Then we'll all think a little more clearly. Okay?"

A trim man in a linen suit stood behind the counter. A diamond glittered on his tiepin. His habitual frown grew more pronounced as he watched the teenager enter the store. The boy was dirty and disheveled, and he looked decidedly ill at ease as he took in the elegant surroundings. The walls of the store were lined with shelves, artfully lit to reveal expensive necklaces, antique clocks, and jeweled pendants. The counters at eye level glowed with a cool light that illuminated the clerk's face from below. Matt's eyes scanned the room, alert for trouble. There was a velvet curtain behind the counter. He knew that there might be more employees in the back room and the thought of it made him feel tense.

The clerk put on a pained smile. "Is there something I can do for you?"

"I hope so," Matt said. He took off the strange pack he wore over his suit jacket and laid it on the carpet. "I've got something I want to sell."

The clerk raised an eyebrow as Matt reached into the pack and pulled out a little cloth pouch. "We're not really in the business of—"

Matt spilled the contents of the bag onto the counter. The sound of the gems rolling across the glass was almost musical, as the man stepped back in amazement. "Where did you get these?" he asked.

Matt hesitated. He realized he should have worked out a convincing story, but hunger and fatigue had kept him from thinking straight. "They're from my family," he said. "My grandmother left them to me when she died. How much are they worth?"

"Well," the man said in a tight voice, taking a little jeweler's eyepiece from the counter and using it to get a closer look, "if they're real, they're worth quite a bit."

"Oh, they're real, all right," Matt said, nodding. He noticed that the clerk's hands were shaking.

"Diamonds, rubies, sapphires, topaz, opal, jade, peridot, amethyst, and some other stones I don't even recognize," the clerk murmured. "Wait here, please."

He turned sharply and disappeared behind the velvet curtain. Matt could hear him talking in hushed tones. Then he thought he heard the sound of someone punching in numbers on a telephone. "What should we do?" Matt whispered.

We should go, Tuava-Li said in thought-speak.

Matt shoveled the Jewels back into the pouch and put it in his pocket. He was halfway to the door when the clerk swept the curtain aside and came back into the room with another man, older and fatter, with a beet-red face. "Wait," the other man said.

"You come back here, this instant! All of you, get back here!"

"All of—what are you talking about?" the clerk asked his employer, looking puzzled.

"The children!" The fat man's chin wobbled as he spoke, and he reached for a button under the counter. "The boy, and those, those two smaller kids behind him."

Matt grabbed the handle of the door and pulled, but he was too late. The fat man had activated a security lock. "The police will be here in a few minutes," he said, "and then we'll find out where you got those jewels!"

The clerk blinked as he stared at the door. All he saw was Matt, caught like a trapped rat, banging on the glass to get out. "Hey," he said to his boss, "the kid didn't steal anything from us. We can't just lock him in here!"

"Thieves," said the fat man. "How else would these punks get a hold of a fortune in jewels?"

"What are you talking about? There's only one boy there. Are you feeling okay?"

"Tuava-Li," Matt said through clenched teeth. "Come on, do it—do it now!"

Tuava-Li shut her eyes. An instant later there was a whir of gears, a snapping of fine steel springs, and a click as the lock came undone. "Yes!" Matt hollered. He flung open the door and the three raced into the street.

"Don't let them get away," the fat man screamed. He shuffled out the door in time to watch Matt disappear around the corner.

"What on earth are you doing?" the clerk demanded. "You would have thought the kid pulled a pistol on you, the way you acted in there."

The fat man withdrew a handkerchief from his back pocket and wiped it across his forehead. "Don't talk to me like I'm stupid," he mumbled. "I'm your boss. I don't know what came over me. For a second I thought those other kids were . . . I don't know what they were. I just got afraid, that's all."

"Well, when the police get here, you'd better let me do the talking. There was just one boy in here. You're seeing things!"

The fat man shook his head. "I know what I saw!"

Matt didn't stop running until he was three blocks from the jewelry store. He bent over, sucking in breath, and waited for Tomtar and Tuava-Li to catch up with him. "Well, that went well!" he puffed.

"We'll try again, some other place," Tuava-Li said.

Matt stood up, then sighed and looked down at his companions. "You got that door open fast," he said to Tuava-Li. "I guess that magic of yours works pretty good, when you decide to use it!"

Tuava-Li blushed and looked down. She curled her toes, and realized her feet were really beginning to hurt. Suddenly a businessman hurried past. The corner of his leather briefcase struck the back of Tuava-Li's head. "*Oooooh!*" she cried, and toppled to her knees.

"Watch where you're going, moron!" Matt shouted.

The man looked over his shoulder and glared. "What a jerk," Matt mumbled, and scratched his neck. "I thought all these charms and amulets we've got on were supposed to protect us, Tuava-Li. As far as I can tell, they don't do anything for me except make my neck itch."

"No one knows what kind of trouble we'd be in if not for the medallions."

"We're fooling ourselves if we think any of it's going to help," Matt argued, venting his frustration. "We're up to our knees in trouble already and I don't know how we're going to get out of it."

"You saw what the Belt of Power can do," replied Tuava-Li. "I hope you are both still practicing on your own."

"Yeah, yeah," mumbled Matt.

Tomtar gazed across the street and saw a row of striped umbrellas on the sidewalk, at the foot of a giant steel skyscraper. There were tables set up under the umbrellas, and a waiter in a white apron hurried to deliver a tray of sandwiches. Smiling people chatted and sipped their iced drinks. Pigeons bobbed along the concrete, looking for crumbs. "Food," the Troll said, staring longingly.

"How desperate are we?" Matt asked. He realized he was salivating at just the thought of something to eat. "Come on, let's cross the street."

Tomtar shook his head, and his face took on the troubled look that Matt was getting to know. Back in the woods, in the Elf realm, the Troll had always looked happy and carefree. Now that they were in the town where Tomtar had grown up, everything was different. Tomtar was different. Since the incident at the bridge, he was afraid. "I don't want to get close to the pigeons," he whispered.

"Okay," Matt said, "take it easy. I'll chase them away. I promise!"

He punched the button beneath the WALK sign and the light changed. As they approached the sidewalk café Matt waved his arms so the birds would scatter. A woman in a gray suit had left a small stack of bills tucked beneath her tray. She checked her lipstick in a little mirror before she got up from her table and hurried down the street. There was half of a turkey sandwich left on her plate, along with a piece of lettuce, some potato chip crumbs, and what looked to Matt like a pickle. He picked up the sandwich and took a bite, then handed the rest to Tomtar. "Hey, you!" a waiter shouted from the restaurant door. "Get away from there, or I'll call the cops!"

"I'm going," Matt said. "I'm going!"

Another waiter slipped out of a door on the side of the building. "Wait," he called to Matt. "There's a soup kitchen not far from here, it's in a church a couple of blocks that way. Don't make your little brother and sister eat scraps, kid, it isn't right. And you should get them off the streets; it isn't safe around here anymore. Go to the church—they'll help you out."

"But I'm—" Matt realized with a start that this man could see

Tomtar and Tuava-Li, and he thought they were children. The fat man in the jewelry store had seen them, too, and his reaction had been startling. Either they should start chewing on the *trans* to make them look human all the time, or they should keep out of sight. "Yeah," Matt said, "thanks. We'll check that out."

When they got to the church, they stopped and stared. There was no mistaking it as the image of the stone building tattooed on Matt's chest. "I guess we've come to the right place," he said.

22

HUNDREDS OF MILES north of Pittsburgh, in
another Human town near the Canadian border, a cluster of
Elves crouched warily outside the walls of a nursery school.
Hidden in the shadows of fragrant pine trees they waited. The
basement windows of the building were open so that children's
laughter spilled like jewels into the autumn air. Jardaine
watched jealously as Jal-Maktar changed once again from
Macta into a little Human boy. *Why,* she thought, *can't I change
shape, too?*

Once she was named official Mage of Helfratheim, Jardaine
felt certain that her long-awaited transformational powers would
manifest. She could almost feel the animal strength in her trying
to get out, seeking form with fang, and fur, and claw. In the
meantime she watched Jal-Maktar flex his shoulders and shift
his shape as easily as he drew breath. When the teacher's aide

came to answer the knock at the painted oak door, she saw a little boy with a turned-up nose and black ringlets of hair falling over his eyes. His face was a mask of sorrow, with tears streaming down his apple-red cheeks. "My n-n-nanny left me here, and I don't know w-where I am!" he blubbered.

"Oh, baby, poor baby," the woman crooned, gathering the helpless little boy into her arms, holding him tight against her bosom as she turned to go back into the nursery. "Don't you worry," she said, "we'll find out where you belong. You shouldn't be outside by yourself, it isn't safe!"

The boy shifted in the woman's arms, so that she would be forced to look into his eyes. What she saw there was darker and emptier than night, colder and more distant than the deepest star. The boy blinked, and a cruel smile crept across his tear-streaked face. The woman froze in terror as the boy began to change. "What's wrong?" the teacher cried, as her aide and the boy in her arms toppled to the floor.

Jal-Maktar got up and scurried across the carpet. His body was stretching, changing into something long and powerful, with sinews that snapped like steel bands, skin as red and shiny as molten lava, and a mouth as wide as a small car. "Come in, Jardaine," the creature boomed, blinking its half-dozen eyes.

Jardaine and the monks hurried down the stairs once they'd received their invitation. They stepped into the nursery just in time to see the monster swallowing the children, one by one. Jardaine knew the little ones would be safe in the creature's

JAL-MAKTAR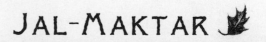

belly until its return to Helfratheim. Then they'd be spat out, none the worse for wear.

The teacher wore dangly hoop earrings and a flowered dress, and a look of fear that twisted her pretty face. She cowered against the wall, where drawings and paintings the children had made were pinned to a sheet of cork. She smeared the chalk in a dirty rainbow of color as she dragged herself slowly toward the door. "Stay where you are," Jardaine shouted.

The teacher shook her head, trying to clear her senses of the horror she was witnessing. Someone was talking to her. Someone was — suddenly the monks began to flicker into her awareness, like a candle lit in a dark room. Little people, dressed in black robes, little people with sickeningly huge eyes, and deathly pale skin, and ears stretched out to knifepoints, were gathering around her. Behind them the monster had finished its job. Seventeen children entrusted to her care, seventeen children, all gone. The woman prayed fervently that God would take her life that very moment, for the sheer weight of her terror was too much to bear. "Sit down," Jardaine demanded.

The teacher sat. She was far too big for the child-size chair and the little pink table before her, but she was too frightened to feel discomfort. Jardaine thrust a piece of paper before her and pressed a stubby pencil into her hand. "Write," she said. "Say that you have taken the children, that the Gods told you what to do, because this place is evil, and you want to save the children from having to dwell in this awful realm. Say that you have taken them to a better place, and that no one will ever find you."

The teacher stared dumbly at the empty chairs, the empty tables, where just moments before there had been seventeen smiling, happy children, sitting, playing, and talking. Her lips moved as she silently prayed for the nightmare to end. "Write!" Jardaine hissed in her ear, and forced the woman's fingers toward the paper. "Write!"

The teacher's hand trembled as she composed the note, writing the words just as Jardaine had instructed. Then she dropped the pencil on the table, and her head slumped. "Jal-Maktar," Jardaine called, and the monster, resting languidly on the floor, raised one scaly paw and gestured in the air. "I'll put the two big Humans somewhere I can have them later, at my leisure."

The teacher vanished in a swirl of dust and cinders. "'Tis done," Jardaine said, wiping her hands on her robe. She looked around the room, and everything she saw filled her with revulsion. A shudder ran down her spine as she considered her contempt for Humans. Jardaine saw the monster stretch and yawn. She saw the bulges in its belly as the children inside pushed and banged to get out. She knew that she had done well. She realized what it had cost her to gather this many children for delivery to Helfratheim, and she knew it was worth it. Who needed two kidneys, anyway? Jal-Maktar was obviously enjoying his job, and showing off, for her benefit, by taking on the form of the spectacularly ugly monster. Jardaine also knew, or at least she hoped, that Brahja-Chi would be impressed by her efforts. For a moment she thought of her old Mage, the Mage of Alfheim, and Tuava-Li and her quest. She felt a pang of jealousy and wondered how Tuava-Li was faring. She realized that in a way, she was competing with Tuava-Li for status and position. She steadied herself and imagined that it would be she, in the end, who was triumphant. How else could it turn out, after all?

Jardaine reached up to the door handle and pulled the old door wide. Jal-Maktar squeezed through the opening as the children made his belly bulge. He let out a foul belch, followed by a boisterous laugh. "That was fun," he said, "let's do it again!" Then he shot into the air, and was gone.

"Come," Jardaine sighed, gesturing to the monks. She and the others would be returning to Helfratheim on foot. Fortunately, the journey was not far. Now that the veil between worlds was so exquisitely thin, and riddled with holes, Helfratheim and this Human city were very close to one another. It had made the Acquisition much easier. At first, she had harvested children from playgrounds, but it didn't take long for the Humans to realize that their children were not safe outside. Jardaine was forced to make yet another deal with Jal-Maktar. It was going to cost her more to take children from Human buildings, but it had to be done. There was no other way. The notes she left behind were meant to throw the Humans off guard until the Elves were ready to attack. Jardaine grimaced as she stepped out into the crisp air; there were blisters on both her heels. She could have arranged some quicker way to travel, but she knew that Jal-Maktar would have charged her dearly for that, as well. Sacrifice was a good thing, Jardaine thought, as long as it didn't go *too* far. In several hours, she would be home . . . her new home, the place she belonged, Helfratheim.

Evening shadows crept over the room as Jardaine sat at her desk and soothed her feet in a bowl of warm water and herbs. She considered her good fortune. She ached all over, and the places where Jal-Maktar had removed pieces of her body were still tender. But there were one hundred and thirty-four Human children caged in the courtyard, and forty-seven of them were there because of her own hard work. Jardaine put down her quill pen. She was still composing the speech that Jal-Maktar was scheduled to give that night. During the return trip to Helfratheim she'd thought of nothing else but the speech, and the difference it was going to make. The speech was good; she was sure of it. If the Fir Darrig's delivery was as powerful as her own words, the Faeries of Helfratheim would be hers to command. "It *will* be good," she murmured.

"Will it?" came a voice from the corridor.

Jardaine spun around in her seat, as water sloshed from the bowl on the floor. "I didn't hear you coming. You surprised me!"

"Of course I did," Jal-Maktar chuckled. He had assumed the form of Macta. He was dressed in black silk, with a soft fur collar around his neck, and jeweled rings on each of his fingers. His lank hair was tucked behind beautifully formed ears, and his eyes twinkled darkly. "I've just come from the courtyard. You know the deal, one soul a day, until Brahja-Chi arrives for the main event, and then I get them all."

"I remember," said Jardaine. "But didn't you already take the souls of the Human women at the nursery school?"

Jal-Maktar smacked his lips. "They were an added bonus. You know, Human souls are just an appetizer. Now that you're becoming a Mage, you've grown far more appealing. Your kidney was even more delicious, for instance, than that bit of lung I devoured yesterday."

"I don't need to hear about that, Jal-Maktar," she gulped. "By the way, I've been wondering—that's not your real name, is it?"

"Of course not," he grinned.

"Tell me your real name!"

"You couldn't pronounce it," said Jal-Maktar. "And if you did, who knows what might happen? Worlds have been known to collapse at the proper pronunciation of my true name. If 'Jal-Maktar' is too much of a mouthful for you, you may call me Jal, as Brahja-Chi does. There's no need to be formal. We have lots of fun together, don't we?"

Jardaine swallowed and forced a smile. "Aye, we do!"

Jal-Maktar returned the smile. "Now let me see the speech."

There was a chill in the air as the sun went down over Helfratheim. In the vast stone courtyard outside the palace gates, the Elves were arriving, anxious to see their new leader deliver his first speech as King. Tall wooden pikes, decorated with Elfin heads, surrounded the courtyard. All were cheered to see the grisly sight, for it meant that the government of Helfratheim was protecting its citizens from the rabble who broke the laws of the kingdom. The first to arrive were also fortunate to get a clear view of the Human children who were penned in the corner of the courtyard. The Humans huddled there, most of them hunched and crying, all of them helpless and confused. "Mommy," a few of them cried pitifully, "Mommy!"

None dared try to escape from the jail, a dome of thorn-studded vines, a cage woven like an enormous basket. Monks were positioned along the perimeters of the cage. Deep in trance, they worked to create a spell that would hold contagion at bay, so that no Elves would have to fear being sickened by the Human stench, or the foul corruption they carried on their breath and skin.

The Techmagicians had worked overtime on the decorations that would make the first appearance of Macta as King of Helfratheim a memorable one. Members of the audience carried signs and banners welcoming the new King. Beneath the high window where Macta was expected to appear, jugglers and acrobats entertained the crowd. Costumed performers acted out grim tableaux of torture and mayhem, replete with spurting artificial blood, beheadings, and disembowelments. The audience roared its approval. Meanwhile, at the cage where the Humans were held prisoner, Faerie Folk were given sharp sticks to prod the captives.

The air was electric. From the stage at the steps of the palace, a heavily muscled Elf banged a clay gong. Musicians blew mightily into long wooden instruments, hollowed out by termites, and the low bleat reverberated in the bellies of the crowd. All of the Faerie Folk turned their eyes on the high window, which was wreathed in a halo of Fire Sprites. Suddenly the King was there. His arms were raised in greeting, and he looked strong and vibrant. If there were any traces of the injuries that had kept him away from his people for so long, they were not apparent now. "Macta!" the Faerie Folk roared. "King Macta!"

The moon was coming up, fat and nearly round, just behind a black curtain of trees. Torches lit the courtyard with flickers of orange and gold. Not a hint of a breeze stirred the air. As Jardaine stood behind him, head bowed, Jal-Maktar grinned and waved at the masses below. Their scent filled his nostrils, and he sucked it in. *Delicious*, he thought. It was the odor of life, of Blood, and it did not matter to Jal-Maktar what color the Blood; it was all the same to him. He made a gesture, and the crowd fell silent. "The time has come," he said. His words echoed off the courtyard walls. "Aye, the time has come, my children. The new era of the Elves has begun. All of nature knows it, and our prayers reach to the Goddess in the firmament of Heaven. Look, do you see the moon? She is growing full with the promise of our delivery, as we grow full of the rage that will save us from the oppression of our enemies. The infidels are at our very gates, and we are nearly ready to throw off the bonds of slavery that have held us in captivity for so long. Soon the entire world will be ours, as it was always meant to be! Take a look, my children, take a good look at the Human scum there in the cage, and know what must be done! Every day the promise grows stronger, the numbers increase, the Acquisition of Brahja-Chi is revealed in the number of Humans who cringe there, ready to be sacrificed to the Goddess.

"Look, my children, look! The moon is thirsty! She longs to see their souls set free! When their crimson Blood flows in rivers on our hallowed streets, when the Goddess hears their hapless cries and rejoices, 'twill be time for the Human world to be struck down. Your new King will reign eternal! Though my father, King Valdis, is gone, his memory will spur us to victory, his spirit will guide our steps! With the help of Jardaine, whom I have appointed the first and most glorious Mage of Helfratheim, we will vanquish our foes. Let there be no barrier between government, and religion, between Techmagick and the hard labor of our bodies. Let us be as one, spirit, and sense, mind and muscle, body and soul, as we go forward. The time has come, my children, the time has come!"

The crowd erupted in cheers once more, and even the severed heads on their pikes seemed to smile with pleasure. The Faerie Folk of Helfratheim had a new leader, and he would make them strong. There would be no room in their hearts for doubt, or fear of weakness.

Someone started a chant. "King Macta, ruler of Heaven and Earth! One world! One world! One world!"

Jardaine smiled until her cheeks hurt. She felt such happiness that she longed to lash out and hit someone. Still, she kept her head bowed, and her fists clenched at her sides. When Jal-Maktar turned and walked back into the palace, Jardaine followed. She knew that it was she who had composed the words that were spoken, and that it was she who held the reins of power. Her wildest dreams were coming true. "Well?" said Jal-Maktar, turning to face the new Mage of Helfratheim. "What do I get for giving the speech?"

Jardaine raised her robe, exposing her soft, pale belly. "Take it," she said, her teeth clenched.

"This might hurt," he said gently. "But it's just another little piece of liver, just a bit. By this time next week, you won't even be able to tell the difference!"

Jal-Maktar lifted a bony, bejeweled finger, twirled it in the air, and a rapturous look spread across his face as Jardaine cried out, and fell to the floor.

23

MACTA SLEPT ON HIS GOOD SIDE, downwind from the Elves and the Human. He didn't want Radik to detect the scent of him during the long hours of the night. He cradled his mangled arm as he lay in a shallow earthen pit, covered over with leaves, and trembled. High above the trees the stars were twinkling. When Macta entered the Gates of Vattar, he discovered that he was whole again, he was healthy and strong, and the Dragon Thunderbus he carried smelled of oil and metal and power. Images of his father, King Valdis; Powcca, his pet Goblin; Cytthandra; Druga; Baltham; and so many of the departed drifted like ghosts through his dream, each, in turn, touching him and leaving a mark that spread like a sickness over his soul. Still, in his dream, he had his weapon. A shadowy figure crept out of the gloom. Macta felt his flesh prickle with fear, and he released the Fire Sprite from its box, so that it might light the tinder. Though his hands trembled, his aim was true. In a blast of smoke and light Macta saw his enemy's face illuminated before him. It was as if he was looking into a mirror.

Macta woke with a start. He opened his mouth to cry out, but something inside stopped him. *Willpower,* he thought. *Willpower. Without that, I'm nothing.*

There were deer in the forest. Two does and five young fawns were grazing on tender leaves, not more than a hundred feet away. Macta rubbed his eyes and watched them move in the feeble light. The deer scampered off when the Human girl began to cry. It was no more than a whimper, really, but in the silence of the forest it was like a trumpet's call. Macta held his breath and listened. "All is well, Rebecca," Asra whispered, getting up to go to where the girl was camped. "We're here with you."

Becky sat up and rubbed her eyes. "I'm sorry," she murmured, "I was having a bad dream, that's all."

"What's wrong?" Radik called sleepily.

"Nothing," Asra said. "We're fine."

Radik watched the deer leaping through the foliage. When they were out of sight he turned to Asra. "We mustn't waste the morning. Now that we're all awake, we should get ready to go."

Radik could tell by the look on Asra's face that she was tired of pretending they'd ever reach Helfratheim. Becky stood up and brushed bits of dirt and leaves from her arms. The girl towered over the Elves, and Asra moved away when some of the leaves drifted down upon her head. Soon a symphony of birdcalls brightened the morning, as the three prepared for the day's journey, trying to find reasons to be cheerful. They washed their hands in a trickle of water Radik had stored in a gourd and ate a few leathery berries from Becky's pack. "Come, Rebecca," Asra said. "Let's look at the maps again."

"There's no guarantee that we'll find a Cord up ahead," Radik said, "and your shoes won't last another day. You'll be walking barefoot if we continue like this. We should try to find some Elves who can help us."

Asra shook her head and frowned as she studied the map of the Faerie realm. "Where?" she said. "Where would we find anyone to help us? We're completely on our own."

Radik looked up, startled, to see Becky ripping a thin strip of cloth from the hem of her jeans. "You can wrap this around your shoes, Princess," she said. "We'll tie a knot on the top. Denim is strong. It'll help, I know. We've got to keep moving."

"Thank you, Rebecca," Asra said. She glanced over at Radik, who gave her a knowing look. They were on a fool's errand; it was obvious to both of them. Only the girl remained oblivious to the fact.

As the morning dragged by, Macta trailed behind Asra, Becky, and Radik, watching them like a hunter stalking his prey. The ache in his shoulder seemed more bearable, somehow, as long as he kept Asra in his sight. He realized that it was his longing for Asra, more intense than the pain, that kept him going. Macta looked away for a moment to hoist himself over a fallen log. That was when he heard the distant metallic snap, and the awful howl that followed. He was filled with a terrible delight; an exquisite joy that there was someone whose suffering was greater than his own. He hurried through the underbrush, drawing closer to the source of the hideous roar, and stopped, still out of sight, when he saw Radik writhing in agony on the ground.

"What is it?" Asra cried, tugging at the steel bands that had broken and crushed the leg of their companion.

"I don't know," Becky answered, her face contorted in panic. "I think it's some kind of a trap!"

"Help me, please, help me get it off him!"

Radik clawed at the trap, his hands flailing. Blood gushed from the wound and stained the earth a rich, deep green. Becky and Asra wept as they strained to pry the jaws of the trap apart. It was no use. Asra's fingers blistered at the touch of metal, and she pulled away, sobbing. Becky realized in horror that she could see the bones in Radik's leg; they jutted through the wound like a pair of fangs. He screamed with such ferocity that no one heard the Humans as they came crashing through the woods. "We got one! We got one!" the voices hollered.

Becky looked up and saw the two men. A large golden retriever bounded up from behind them, but at the sight of the Elves, the dog stopped. The fur around its neck stood out in spikes, and it let out a menacing growl. "Careful, Rex," one of the men commanded. He had a long face and a drooping mustache, and his eyes gleamed with the thrill of conquest. The other man, shorter by at least a head, wore a hunting cap. His pudgy face was red from exertion. "I don't see—"

And then he stopped. There was Becky, kneeling by the trap, with tears streaming down her face. The man looked fearfully around. "Hey, there's just a kid here, a little girl. Where's that howling coming from?"

"Don't you see it," the man with the mustache said. "There, in the trap, we've got one of the creatures we caught a glimpse of out here the other day, look at it!"

"You've got to help us!" Becky wailed, and pointed to the trap.

The man in the hunting cap looked again, blinked, and shook his head violently, as if there were wasps buzzing around him. "Jeez," he murmured, "you're right! We caught ourselves a critter!"

Asra backed away, her face twisted in fear. "No, you don't," hissed the man with the mustache, and he leapt forward. "We caught ourselves *two* critters!"

Asra screamed as the man snatched her up in his arms. She pounded on his face with her fists, but he only laughed, a high-pitched cackle that came in explosive bursts. The man in the hunting cap lumbered toward his friend. He was fumbling with a burlap sack, trying to hold it open as wide as he could. In a moment they had forced Asra into the sack and tied the top so she couldn't escape. Becky knelt by the trap, paralyzed with dread. Radik was no longer screaming. He lay sprawled over the edge of the trap, moaning. His leg was white and bent at a right angle. "What are you doing?" Becky whimpered to the men, her eyes pleading. She wanted to run away, but didn't dare. The Elf was too badly hurt, and Asra was a captive. "Please, you've got to help him, please!"

"Friends of yours, are they? Then you must be an enemy of ours." The man with the mustache spat and turned toward his companion. "Cut another piece or two of that rope and tie up the girl, too."

The man knelt by the trap, pressed the release, and pulled the jaws apart. He turned the rusty contraption upside down and shook Radik onto the dirt. Then he tossed the trap aside. "So," he snarled, flipping Radik onto his back. "The police wouldn't believe me when I told them I saw you and your kind out in the woods. Then my little girl went missing, and I knew it had to be you. So you think you can kidnap children, do you? You're gonna tell me where you took my little girl, and you're gonna tell me fast, or I'll feed you to my dog."

"Human scum," Radik muttered, spitting blood.

"Tell me where my girl is, you little monster, tell me!" the man screamed. He squirmed on top of Radik, with one knee pressed against the Elf's chest. "Tell me!"

Radik let out a choking gurgle. His eyes clouded over, and his head fell to one side.

"NO!" Becky screamed, as the man in the cap forced her hands behind her back and roughly tied her wrists with a length of rope.

"This one's gone," the man with the mustache choked. "He didn't tell me nothin'. What are we gonna do now?"

"We'll get the other one to talk," said the short man, giving Becky a push with the heel of his boot. "I wouldn't be surprised if this here kid can tell us a thing or two about what's goin' on!"

"Come on, Rex," said the first man, calling to his dog. "Let's go, we'll take 'em home and see what we can find out. If there's any chance my little girl's still alive, we'll find her, I tell you. We'll find her!"

"Get moving, kid," said the man in the cap. He swore, gave Becky another kick, and they began shuffling down the slope.

As soon as Macta thought that the dog was far enough away that it wouldn't come back to attack him, he crept out of the woods. He threw a passing glance at the body of Radik, thrown carelessly into the brush. He paused to consider the Elf's bow and arrow. He had spent some time using a bow for a sport, though he believed it was beneath him to use the implement as a weapon. It was completely useless, however, for someone with only one arm. He went to retrieve the dead Elf's pack, and spilled its contents on the dirt. At first glance there was little of any value. No food whatsoever, a small obsidian blade, and a little wrapped package. Macta tore open the top with his teeth. *Blowguns,* he said to himself, and smiled. This was a sport he knew well. He tucked the knife and the package into his vest pocket, and wondered just how much poison was on the tips of the darts.

Then he saw something lying just outside the Elf's pocket.

It was a silver box with a royal insignia on the top. He popped open the lid, and smiled when he saw the Fire Sprite curled up inside. He closed the lid and dropped it into the pack, slung it over his good shoulder, then hurried to the place where Asra and the others had disappeared. They were still just visible halfway down the hill. Macta followed them at a safe distance. The love of his life was tied up in a sack, slung over one of the men's backs, and Becky whimpered at the other man's side. The dog was bounding on ahead, anxious to get home. A smile crept across Macta's fevered face. *Finally,* he thought, *the tides are beginning to turn.* He reached into his pocket and withdrew his notebook. He paused for a moment, knelt on the ground, and wrote something inside it. *Just a little wager,* he thought. *A thousand dratmas that I win her back. Why not? I'm on a winning streak!*

The screen door slammed as the woman flew onto the porch. "Did you find her?" she cried, her face sagging with dismay. "Who's this? What's going on?"

"I don't know," said the man with the mustache. He was coming up the walkway, dragging Becky by the arm. The other man lagged behind. He was puffing with the weight of the sack on his shoulder. "I found the kid in the woods with a couple of those little monsters we saw the other day. I told you they were real! But there's no sign of our girl. One of the creatures is dead, and we got the other one in the bag. It's a female. I've got some ideas about how we're gonna make it talk."

The golden retriever was barking now, spinning in circles around the woman's legs. There was crying from behind the screen door; two little faces peered through the mesh, toddlers longing for their mother's attention. "Is she hurt?" the woman asked, stumbling down the porch steps. She went to take Becky's face in her hands. "Honey, are you all right? Did the monsters hurt you? Do you know anything about my little girl? They took her yesterday, and I've been 'bout to lose my mind!"

"Keep off her," the man cried, giving Becky a kick. "She's not one of us, she was carryin' on with the monsters, cryin' like they was her kin. She's gonna tell us a thing or two, you can bet on that."

"But the police —" the woman said.

"The police don't know what to do," the man sneered. "They've been in the woods lookin' for our little girl and a hundred others, and they got nothin'. God answered our prayers, and now we're gonna find our daughter!"

"Please," Becky pleaded, searching the woman's face for a trace of compassion. "Please, you've got to help me! I didn't do anything wrong, I swear it! The elves are my friends, and Princess Asra would never hurt anyone, I swear! Please let us go, we're just trying to find my parents, and save them from the elves who — listen, we've got to find them, and . . . and . . ."

The man grabbed Becky by the hair. She screamed as he dragged her across the dirt and weeds of their little lawn, past a pair of plastic pink flamingoes on coat-hanger legs. With one hand the man opened the door to a rusty dog kennel that sat at the base of a tree. He forced Becky inside, as his friend tossed in the bag that held Asra. Then he slammed the door shut and shoved the latch into its slot. "Get me a padlock from the workbench," he called to his wife, who sat on the porch with her head in her hands, sobbing. "Go on, get it, quick, we can't let them get away!"

"What are we doing?" the woman cried. "What happened to our baby?"

"Joe, keep an eye on this one," the man sighed. "I guess I'll have to get the lock myself."

Becky fumbled with the knot at the top of the sack. Asra's arm punched out of the opening, and as soon as the rope was untied, she climbed awkwardly into the cage next to Becky. She was bruised, and disheveled, and her face burned with rage. "Let us out of here, I command you!"

"Well, well, what have we got here?" the short man murmured as he stared between the bars, keeping a safe distance.

Asra's eyes were huge and wild. No one had ever treated her this way before. Her muscles were tensed; she trembled uncontrollably. "Let us out!" she shrieked.

The man glanced over at Becky. "Little girl, what is this thing? Did I hear you call it an elf?"

"This is Princess Asra," Becky answered angrily, wiping hot tears from her cheek. "She's not some kind of animal. She doesn't deserve to be treated this way!"

"What about you?" asked the man. "What's your name? Where you from?"

"Why did you lock us in here?" Becky was on her hands and knees. There was blood on her knuckles, and her tangled hair fell over her face. "What are you doing this for?"

"You tell me," said the man. "Looks like you're the ones going around kidnapping children."

"I don't know what you're talking about," Becky cried.

The woman had stumbled across the yard, and now she squinted into the cage. She saw a blur of movement, a hint of color by the door, but that was all. To her, Becky was alone in the cage. "I'm going to be sick," the woman said, and dropped onto the ground. "What in God's name are we doing? This is only a little girl! What could she know?"

When she looked up again, her husband was there, forcing a lock through the latch. And she saw it. "My God, what is it? What's that thing in there?"

The figure in the cage was fading in and out of focus, growing solid, then transparent, then invisible again. It was Asra, rushing at the side of the cage, throwing her weight against the bars, and screaming. The woman's jaw dropped when she stared into Asra's raging Faerie eyes.

"Asra," Becky said, "it'll be okay, it'll be okay, these are people, like me, and they wouldn't hurt us, oh no, Asra!"

The Elf looked at her hands, raw and blistered where she had touched the steel bars. She fell back, collapsing on the empty

293

sack, and cried. Becky stroked Asra's shoulder, gently, and felt her flinch. Then the dog let out a sharp cry. Becky spun her head around in time to see the dog fall. The man with the mustache fell, too, followed by his wife. The short man next to the cage leapt up, breathing hard, and stumbled into the tall grass beyond the tree. A pitiful wail escaped his lips as the last of the poisoned darts struck him in the back of the neck. He fell as if in slow motion and landed, with a thud, on his face.

Children were still crying inside the house. Becky watched in amazement as Macta Dockalfar crept out of the bushes and stalked across the yard. "Look, Asra," she called. "It's another elf! He saved us! He's coming this way!"

Asra turned pale at the sight of him. "Nooo, it can't be!" she whispered.

Macta had seen the man drop the key to the lock in the front pocket of his jeans. He knelt by the fallen figure, retrieved the key, and went to open the cage. "I wish I had the right words to say," Macta offered, glancing at Asra, and then the lock, and then Asra again. "But I don't."

The lock opened with a snap. Asra flung herself against the door of the cage, and tried to push past Macta. He grabbed her arm with his one good hand. "I'm going to Helfratheim," he said as gently as he could, "and I know that you want to go there, too. I'll do everything in my power to make sure that we get there together."

"You're a devil," she cried, "a demon. You're supposed to be dead. Have you been following us all along?"

"At a respectful distance," Macta said.

"Then you could have saved Radik, instead of letting him die!" Asra hissed.

"How? You couldn't open the trap. How could I, with only one arm?"

Asra began to whimper. "What do you want from me?"

"No more than I've ever wanted."

"Let go of the Princess," Becky threatened. "Who are you?"

Macta laughed. "Her fiancé, and I don't take kindly to being given orders, especially by a Human. So shut your mouth, little girl, and forget you ever saw me here. When the others wake up, they can decide what to do with you. By then Asra and I will be long gone."

"No," Asra said. "I'll go with you to Helfratheim, Macta, but Rebecca's coming, too. This whole journey was for her sake. Queen Metis ordered me to go with her. I won't let her down."

Macta sighed. He was on fire with fever from the infection in his ruined arm. "Your newfound loyalty is touching," he said, too weary to fight. "You must know by now that I'd do anything to please you, Asra. If you insist on bringing the child to Helfratheim, then it shall be so. I overheard you talking to that Troll, a while back, about some old Human mines. We'll look for them, and see if we can locate a Cord big enough for a Human to travel. When we get home, there'll be parades to welcome me. I'll be crowned King of Helfratheim. We'll be greeted with flowers and chocolates, and there'll be a million reasons for you to love me, Asra, as I love you."

Asra was silent. She got to her feet, and her eyes drifted from one fallen Human to the next. She saw the babies behind the screen door bang on the mesh, and heard their cries. She had walked out of one trap into another, and there was nothing she could do about it. "Becky," she said, "this is Macta of Helfratheim. 'Twas our wedding that you were meant to see when you came to the Grove at Alfheim."

Macta grinned at Becky, and made a little bow. Rivulets of sweat ran down his forehead, stinging his eyes. "Charmed," was all he said.

24

MATT'S SHOULDERS WERE SORE. In fact, his entire body was sore. He had spent the night on a cot in a church basement near the Greyhound station. As the hours crawled by, homeless men snored and scratched themselves in the feeble light, babies whimpered in the next room beside their teenaged mothers, and a decent night's sleep was an impossible dream. Tomtar and Tuava-Li had camped out by a window in a vestibule at the top of the stairs and nobody had noticed them at all. The Troll always had a hard time sleeping indoors, but he realized it would be best to stay close to the others, as long as he could tolerate a roof over his head. Toward dawn, Tuava-Li climbed the steps to the spire of the church and performed an abbreviated version of her usual greet-the-sun routine. For breakfast in the basement there were generic energy bars that tasted like cardboard, and coffee that looked like sludge and smelled like burnt shoes. But it was free, so Matt was hardly in a position to complain.

Matt had tossed and turned all night lying on top of the sacks of Jewels, praying that nobody would try to steal them. He'd even dreamt that he was using that old Belt of Power trick and managing to keep thieves at bay. Maybe, he thought, it wasn't really a dream. He'd checked the tattoos on his chest and found that the image of the old church was unchanged; he wasn't sure whether that should comfort or worry him. Now that morning was here he decided to spend his last two dollars on a bus ride to his old neighborhood, down on East Carson Street, where he was pretty sure he knew of a pawnshop. When he was living in Pittsburgh he must have passed the place a thousand times. He'd never paid much attention. The windows were always jammed with battered musical instruments, outdated TV and video equipment, stamp collections, and cheap costume jewelry. None of this was of much interest to him. Matt's parents had said that pawnshops were for desperate people, people who would trade in their family treasures for a little money. Now Matt was desperate, too. He needed to turn some of the Alfheim Jewels into good old American cash, so they could afford to buy some food, and some new shoes, and the supplies they would need to survive. All he could do was hope that the pawnshop was still there and that the proprietor would be a little less picky than the fancy jewelry shop had been about buying stuff from a kid.

Hanging close behind Matt, Tomtar and Tuava-Li waited

298

for their invitation, then stepped onto the big green and white city bus. They followed him to the seat just behind the rear door. Matt sat in the aisle, always alert and ready for trouble. He thought a woman had given him a disapproving stare as he sauntered down the aisle. He wasn't sure what she didn't like about him; there were so many possibilities. Maybe it was the ill-fitting suit, or his weird backpack, or the amulets and charms rattling around his neck. Maybe it was the fact that he wasn't in school when most kids his age would be sitting behind a desk listening to a teacher drone on and on. Maybe it was the way he smelled, or the fact that his hair was as disheveled as a rat's nest. He didn't care. All he wanted to do was get what they needed, then head out of town. There were too many memories here. It was easier being in the woods with an Elf and a Troll that it was in this city, where chances were that sooner or later somebody would see the Faeries, even if they were chewing on their *trans*. Trouble had already put one foot in the door. Sooner or later it was going to come barging into Matt's life and take what little hope he had left.

Tomtar stared nervously out of the bus window as they crossed the Monongahela River to the south side of town. Tuava-Li sat beside him, her hands folded in her lap, and her eyes shut. Matt thought she must be doing some kind of ritual or spiritual practice, or trying once again to contact the Mage. In reality she was just trying to fight the nausea that always came with riding a bus. *It must be all the starting and stopping that bothers her,* Matt thought, *or maybe it's the bus fumes.* He glanced over at Tomtar. It occurred to him that the Troll looked like a kid with his nose pressed up against the window of a candy shop. But there was no joy in Tomtar's eyes as he peered through the dirty glass and scanned the bridge for any sign of other Trolls. When the bus rounded the corner at the far end of the bridge and rolled toward Carson Street, Tomtar sat back in his seat and stared at the grimy floor. He didn't say a word, but Matt and Tuava-Li knew what he was thinking.

Matt made a quick assessment of the passengers on the bus, and whether it was safe to talk. Even if people couldn't see his companions, it would draw unwanted attention if they thought Matt was some crazy kid, mumbling to himself. On the seat across the aisle sat a young woman with earphones, gazing absently out the window. An old man was reading the newspaper two seats ahead. Everybody else on the bus was congregated near the front door. Matt realized that no one would pay any attention to him if he started singing "The Star Spangled Banner." "Check it out," he whispered, nudging Tomtar in the ribs. He pointed out the window toward the hillside. "Did you ever ride one of the inclines when you lived here?"

"Nooo," Tomtar muttered.

A cable car ran slowly along an elevated track up the side of Mount Washington. A brick Victorian station house sat at the foot of the incline, and another one was perched at the top, just in front of an enormous cell phone tower that stood high on the hill. "You know there are only two of them left in the whole city," Matt said. "They're called funiculars. My friends and I used to ride the cars just for fun. Up and down, up and down. Cool, huh?"

"Uh huh," Tomtar mumbled sadly.

"Listen," Matt whispered, "It's not your fault everything's different than when you left here. You couldn't have known."

"I let you down," Tomtar mumbled.

"I think you caught a case of guilt from me," Matt said, and tapped Tomtar on the shoulder. He was beginning to see how important it was for them to keep up their spirits, no matter how hopeless things appeared. During the first few days of this ordeal, when he had been depressed and irritable, Tomtar had always tried to cheer him up. Now that the tables were turned, Matt was going to try to see the glass as half full, even if it killed him.

"Listen, Tomtar, if there aren't any trolls here anymore, there just aren't. You were away for a long time. If your family's gone somewhere else, moved to the woods, or whatever, we'll head back to Ljosalfar, and figure something else out. The Mage will have to do something to help us if she wants us to find that seed and plant it. And as for my parents, if they have to wait a little longer for help, well . . ."

"The Mage believes we can do it on our own," Tuava-Li whispered. "I'm sure that's the reason I'm not able to communicate with her; she wants me to know that I have to do this without her advice or help, that there's no going back."

Matt realized it was best to keep his real thoughts, and the depths of his frustration, to himself. He pictured a map, like something he'd once seen in a pirate movie. He imagined some brown and wrinkly parchment with black scrawls across it, marking the route to the treasure, where X marks the spot. X would be Helfratheim, as far as he was concerned. He could really care less about the weird fairy seed, or the North Pole, or the Mage's quest for them. All he wanted to do was find his parents. If he felt like it, he could walk into any bookstore and pick up an atlas that would have maps of the North Pole. If he could cash in the Jewels, he could buy airline tickets and they could fly anywhere that had an airport. He could find the North Pole if he had to. But there was no one, it seemed, who could tell them how to get to Helfratheim. It was that knowledge that was eating him up inside.

When the bus passed 16th Street, Matt got up and led his companions out the back door, and onto the sun-baked street. Down the block was the pawnshop. Paint flaked from the sign, and a strip of silver tape covered a crack in the glass. It hadn't changed a bit, as far as Matt could tell. It even looked like the same junk was in the window that he had seen when his family still lived in the neighborhood. The door was locked. There was a buzzer on the wooden molding, though, and he gave it a push as he stared through the window into the dim yellow light. This time, Matt was ready with a small, single diamond already clutched in his palm. He'd even made up a story to tell about

302

how he got it, in case the man behind the counter asked any questions.

There was a click, and a faint buzz. Matt took a deep breath and pulled the door open. The man behind the counter was young and had a silver stud in his nose. He took a careful look at Matt's diamond with a jeweler's loupe, made an offer of a hundred dollars, and that was that. There were no questions, and Matt didn't bother to bargain for a better deal. He would have settled for nearly anything. He filled out a form with a false name and address, as Tomtar and Tuava-Li stood quietly behind him, watching the exchange. A minute later Matt was back on the street with a smile on his face and a stack of bills clutched in his hand. "Let's get something to eat," he said.

The deli looked crowded, so Tomtar and Tuava-Li were happy to wait outside behind a bicycle rack. They always felt awkward and uncomfortable in Human places, anyway. Matt took his place in line inside the air-conditioned store. The counter was an embarrassment of riches as he contemplated his choices. Would it be chipped ham, turkey, roast beef, fresh mozzarella? Tuna salad, pasta salad, cream cheese? His mouth watered so much when he placed his order that he had to wipe his face with a sleeve to keep himself from drooling. He left the deli with a big hoagie, two veggie subs, bottles of pop, bags of chips, and ice cream bars. He still had a sizable wad of bills in his pocket.

Tomtar and Tuava-Li got up cautiously when they saw Matt

come out of the store. There was a row of newspaper kiosks on the corner, and Matt scanned the headlines as they walked past. No matter what town the papers were from, the big news was all the same—missing children. "Where Did They Go?" screamed one headline. "Gone, Baby, Gone," read another. "Officials Stumped by Disappearance." "Every Parent's Nightmare." There were pictures of the missing kids, school and church photographs of smiling kindergarteners with missing teeth, grinning toddlers, awkward-looking older kids with bad haircuts and suits. *The Acquisition,* Tuava-Li said in thought-speak. *What else could it be?*

Matt shook his head, realizing how glad he was that at least his sister Becky was safe with Neaca and the Mage, back in the Elf realm. He led his companions to the vacant lot around the corner. There the three of them could hide behind an old brick wall and eat their food. He kicked through the rubble and they squatted just out of sight of street traffic. Five minutes later, there was nothing left of their meal but greasy crumbs. Tomtar and Tuava-Li gathered up the paper wrappings and empty plastic bottles, and crammed the garbage into their packs. "Before long you're going to run out of room for that junk," Matt said.

"We'll burn it just as soon as we get the chance," Tuava-Li answered.

"I know," Matt said, with a resigned smile. "You don't want anybody to use that stuff against you."

"If Human children are being taken, there have to be Faerie Folk around," Tuava-Li said, "despite all appearances to the contrary. Brahja-Chi's influence seems to stretch far. We have enemies, and we must do what we can to protect ourselves."

She got up and hobbled around the corner of the wall. Matt looked at the Elf's shoes, which were held together by nothing more than a few threads. "Look," he said, "before we do anything else, what do you say we find a place that can fix your shoes? I think I remember a repair shop just down this block. I'll tell them they're doll shoes for my little sister. If we're lucky, maybe they can do it while we wait."

Tomtar and Tuava-Li followed Matt down the street. They craned their necks to see the faces of the pedestrians that blindly passed them by. Tuava-Li, in particular, had never seen so many people. But before they reached the next corner, a man strolled past with a bulldog on a leash. Humans might not have been able to see the Troll and the Elf, but the dog sniffed, saw the little figures hobbling past, and went berserk. It sprang forward, its nose twitching, its teeth bared in a fearsome snarl. "Butch," the man scolded, pulling back on the leash, "Butch, stop!"

The dog yanked hard against its collar, slobbering and foaming. The man grabbed the leash in both hands and pulled back. "Stop," he cried in alarm, "Stop it!"

The dog made a choking, gurgling sound as it struggled to break free, desperate to attack the strange little figures and the boy that were running for their lives along the pavement.

The sign above the door was hand-painted. SHOE REPAIR, it read. In the window were other signs, arranged around an artificial boulder, a pair of plaster garden elves, and a grinning plastic skull with a melted candle on the top. BELTS, read one of the signs. KEYS MADE, read another. SUPPORT OUR TROOPS, read another, in big, blocky letters. BRING THE POWS AND MIAS HOME. Wooden shoe molds hung from strings in the window, and there was a large red neon sign depicting a man's loafer, nearly three feet long. Matt opened the door and slipped inside. "Okay, you have my permission to come in," he whispered to his companions.

The odor of polish, leather, and oil was thick and dark as licorice. Displays of sunglasses, belts, keychains, and faded neckties cluttered the space. Tuava-Li and Tomtar slipped off their shoes and handed them to Matt. They stood there in their bare feet, flexing their tiny naked toes. A bulb sent shadows across the tin ceiling. A man lumbered through a beaded curtain. He had an open book in his hand, and he turned it face down on the counter to mark his place. "Yeah?" he asked.

The man's head was shaved. He wore a goatee, and a silver earring in one ear. Matt thought he looked like a pirate. "I want to get these fixed," Matt said, placing the shoes on the glass countertop. "They're just some old doll shoes that are coming apart. I got them at a . . . at a garage sale. I was hoping you'd be able to stitch them back together while I wait. My sister's having a birthday party, see, and—"

"Tomorrow afternoon," the man interrupted. "I couldn't get to it today for a fortune in jewels, kid. Things are pretty busy here, you know."

Tuava-Li was getting nervous. Things didn't look all that busy in the shoe repair shop. And why did he say *a fortune in jewels?* Could he sense, somehow, the Jewels that they were carrying in their packs? Her flesh tingled. There was something that bothered her about this place, something wrong. An icy chill ran down her spine as it occurred to her that if she gave up her shoes, they could be used to cast a spell on her, or worse. She berated herself for being so careless. *Let's get out of here, Matthew,* she said in thought-speak. *We don't need to do this. I don't trust the Human with our shoes. Take them now, and let's get out of here.*

The man picked up the shoes and looked at them. "You know, you could just go to a doll store and buy new ones. It would be cheaper than fixing these old things."

"But they wouldn't be as . . . as durable," Matt explained. "How long do you think it would take to make some little shoes like these from scratch? If you just measured them, then maybe you could make some new ones the same size, out of leather?"

The man shrugged. He bobbed his head slightly to the music that blared from a radio in the back room, and nudged the little shoes with his finger. "My name's Jim," he said, after a long pause. "Jim Winkler."

Matt looked back at the man, wondering what he was supposed to say now. It seemed an odd time for introductions. "What's your name, son?" the man asked.

"I'm, uh, Matt."

"And what are the names of your friends here?"

Tomtar and Tuava-Li stood rooted to the spot. Matt shook his head. "I don't have any friends."

"Come on, introduce me, Matt. I don't bite."

Matt made an effort to swallow the knot of panic in his throat. Clumsily he turned around. Five or six steps, it was just five or six steps to the door. There might be time to get away. "Don't be afraid," Winkler said. "We've got something in common. Some of my best friends are trolls and elves, too."

"How do you—"

Winkler waved his hands dismissively. "As soon as I saw your backpack, I knew where it came from. The thing's got *faerie* written all over it. Then I looked down and saw these two staring up at me."

"But most people—"

"I've been around the world," the man interrupted, "I've seen a lot of things. I did two tours of duty in the Persian Gulf, and believe it or not they've got faerie folk there, too. Look, kiddo, I'll make you some new shoes for your friends. Just don't come to me with some half-baked story about dolls. I don't like it when people lie to me."

"I'm sorry," Matt said. "It's just that, well, nobody would believe the truth."

"That's no excuse for not telling it," Winkler said. "Those who are ready to hear the truth will get it, and those that aren't, well, they won't. *I am invisible, understand, simply because people refuse to see me.* Ralph Ellison wrote that."

JIM WINKLER

SHOES
REPAIRED

while-u-wait

He leaned his elbows on the counter and smiled. "Now—what brings you to Argant, aside for the want of new shoes?"

Tomtar's heart skipped a beat. If the man knew Elves and Trolls, if he knew that the Faerie Folk called Pittsburgh *Argant*, he might have the information they needed. "I'm lookin' for my family," he said, bursting with excitement. "I'm trying to find my uncle Vollyar. Have you ever heard of him?"

"What's *your* name, friend?" Winkler asked.

"I'm Tomtar," he answered, "and this is Tuava-Li."

"I guess you've been walking a long way in those old shoes of yours."

Tuava-Li looked at the man skeptically. If he knew anything about Tomtar's uncle, he wasn't in a hurry to share it. "Is there still a Troll community in this city?" she asked.

The man glanced out the window, watching a garbage truck roll by. "Well, not like there used to be. You know what happened, right?"

Matt shrugged. "We don't really know much."

Tomtar shrank back a little, afraid of what he was about to hear. "The last couple of years have been tough on faerie folk," the man said. "Something nearly wiped 'em out. Especially the trolls. Nobody knows what it was. They had a hard time keeping up with their dead, it happened so fast. There are still a couple of pockets of troll outposts in town, but I can't tell you much about them. Elves are more my area of expertise."

Tuava-Li arched an eyebrow, waiting for the man to explain.

"Shoemaker, elves, you know what I mean? Didn't you see the plaster faeries in the window? Shoemakers and elves have a long history. Now if you need new shoes, my friends, I'll get 'em made for you, free of charge. It's only right to treat visitors to our fair city with a little hospitality."

Reaching behind the counter he pulled out a metal ruler and carefully measured the length and width of Tomtar and Tuava-Li's shoes.

"How long will it take to make new ones?" Tuava-Li asked.

"Tomorrow. Best I can do. Come back around noon. Have you got some place to stay while you're here?"

"Yeah," Matt lied. "Of course we do." The prospect of spending another night at the shelter wasn't pleasant, but at least they knew what to expect.

"Give me a number where I can reach you," Winkler said, "just in case."

"There's no phone where we're going," Matt said. "Just in case *what*?"

"Can you tell us where we might go to find some Trolls?" asked Tuava-Li. "My friend says his Clan used to live in an old school. We just don't know what part of town it's in."

"There's a club," the man said, "right here on Carson. Five or six blocks down. Back in the day, lots of faerie folk hung out there. You might check it out."

He nudged the shoes back across the counter. "Your little friends aren't going to want to leave these with me."

"Thanks," Matt said.

"Oh, one other thing. You can't walk around town with that backpack, not if you don't want to stand out. As a matter of fact, all three of you ought to have new packs. Those wicker things the elves make always need repair, anyway; it's just not worth the effort. Let me look around, I think I may have a couple of kid-sized packs on a shelf."

Winkler went to the rear of his shop and returned with three dusty backpacks. "Anything else you need," he smiled, "Sunglasses, belts, keys? I keep a lot of supplies on hand."

"No thanks," Matt said. "How much are the backpacks?"

"For you, they're on the house. Take a card, by the way. You never know if you'll need to give me a buzz!"

As the trio stepped outside, Matt glanced at the card the man had given him. EXPERT SHOE REPAIR, it read, JAMES WINKLER, PROPRIETOR. "Do you think we can trust that guy?" he asked.

"Perhaps," said Tuava-Li. "Or, perhaps not. That man has a history with Faerie Folk that we can't even begin to imagine. I didn't like the feeling I got in there."

They walked east past a tattoo parlor, a beauty salon, a hardware store, and a place that sold vintage clothes. They paused to let a young man with a hand truck push a stack of crates into a grocery store. Matt kept his eye on a cluster of people loitering in front of a deli that seemed to be doing a booming business in lottery tickets. Nobody paid the slightest bit of attention to them, and there weren't any dogs. Tomtar noted that there weren't any pigeons, either. Matt couldn't tell if this was a relief to him, or not. No pigeons, no trolls. Just people. Some tourists with maps and shopping bags ambled past. This street had always been a popular haunt for out-of-towners. Boutiques, coffee shops, and trendy restaurants had come and gone from Carson since Matt was little.

There was a fancy little toy store on the right-hand side of the block. Matt pointed out the display of dolls in the window to his companions. A temporary fix for their shoe problem would be better than nothing. They took off their threadbare shoes once more and gave them to Matt, who went into the cool, cramped storefront. The woman at the register gave Matt a pleasant smile. He placed the little worn shoes on the counter and asked the woman if she had any doll shoes about that size. A few minutes later he was back on the street. Matt took his purchases out of the drawstring bag, tore open the packages, and handed the contents to his companions. Tomtar put on a pair of black plastic dress shoes, meant for the feet of a large groom doll, and Tuava-Li put on some little silk slippers, in a pretty shade of purple. Matt had to suppress a smile. In the feminine shoes and the inside-out human dress she had taken from the charity box outside town, Tuava-Li was a walking contradiction. She still wore her own soiled shirt, and her hair was pulled back from her face, always tight with a fierce intensity. "What?" she said.

"Look!" Tomtar exclaimed. Matt spun around. He breathed a sigh of relief when he saw that there was no danger, and Tomtar

313

was merely pointing at a metal security gate, pulled down in front of some abandoned storefront. "Is it more fairy stuff?" Matt asked, studying at the graffiti that was painted there. "Can you read what is says?"

"*Erle,*" Tomtar replied, tracing the letters in the air. "That's a kind of Elf who makes mischief with Human children. 'Tis a word from one of the old countries."

The letters were big and round, with zigzagging edges that shot out from the letterforms like dagger blades. The design was painted in red and black, and when Matt went to touch one of the letters, his finger came away smudged with paint. "This is fresh."

"So the Acquisition is going on here, too," Tuava-Li said. "Someone is marking their territory on this corner, so that other Faerie Folk who are abducting children will find a different place to do their work."

"That means there may be at least enough Elves left alive to be competing with each other," Tomtar said.

Matt shook his head. "If there were only two dogs left on earth, they'd both be fighting over the same bone, Tomtar. And if the only faeries left in Pittsburgh are the kind who are stealing little kids, maybe we don't want to meet them at all."

Tomtar smiled wanly. "If they have maps, we do!"

Matt sighed. "Let's see if we can find the place the guy at the shoe repair shop told us about."

On the next corner, an old man sat in a folding chair, playing an accordion. The battered cardboard case was open on the sidewalk in front of him, and there were a few quarters inside. The man's fingers worked the keyboard, and a wheezy waltz poured out of the bellows of the old squeezebox. Tomtar and Tuava-Li hurried past, holding their ears, and Matt thought it was a good thing that the musician couldn't see his companions. He tossed a dollar into the case. The man gave Matt a nod as he tapped his foot to the music he was playing. A few doors down, a dark-eyed woman stared at Matt from the glass window of a palm reader's shop. There was a funeral parlor, a pool hall, and another deli with windows plastered in ads for beer, cigarettes, and all the legal lotteries.

And then there was the juggler. He was setting up shop in front of a brick wall with another graffiti tag on it. He wasn't much older than Matt, with pimples on his forehead and eyeliner painted around his big brown eyes. He wore a white undershirt and tuxedo pants with suspenders. Matt could tell by following the juggler's gaze that he could see Tomtar and Tuava-Li, though he said nothing, and showed no emotion. The juggler laid his gear on the concrete and covered it with a soft cloth. Then he stood and shut his eyes, and folded his hands into a little steeple as if he were deep in prayer. Tomtar tugged at Matt's pant leg as he turned to go. Matt shook his head. "No," Tomtar whispered, "Wait up! Look!"

Matt stood as far as he could from the juggler without falling over the curb into the street. On the sidewalk next to the young man was a metal box about as big as a toaster. "Fire Sprites," Tomtar whispered, as he hid behind Matt, his fingers tingling. "I can tell, they make a little sizzling sound. They're in that box!"

The juggler caught Tuava-Li's eye, and the corners of his mouth curled imperceptibly. "Catch," he said, and tossed a tennis ball at her. She ducked behind Matt, and the ball rolled into the street. "Well," he said with a shrug, "are you going to get that for me?"

Matt knew that if the juggler could see his companions, and seemed to take it in stride, that he must be another of those mysterious people who had dealings of one kind or another with the Faerie Folk. Even though Matt shared their ability, he felt strangely cautious. "My friend says you've got fire sprites in there."

"I'm a juggler. Sometimes I play with fire."

"Is there some kind of—some kind of club, or something around here, where, you know . . ."

"I'm looking for my Clan," Tomtar volunteered.

The juggler nodded, and pointed with his chin at the building across the street. It was an old brick building, painted purple. There was a big, arched wooden door in front. FIRE DEPARTMENT was etched into the sandstone doorframe. There were windows, but they were all taped over with newspapers from the inside. An awning hung over the little door to the side. ST. ELMO'S FIREHOUSE, the lettering on it read.

While the trio's backs were turned, the juggler lifted the lid of the metal box and carefully took something out. "Your friends are welcome there, after dark," he said, managing a disinterested smile. "But *Tems* like you aren't allowed. Even when they're carrying elfin backpacks."

"I'm their friend," Matt said.

"I'll be your friend if you go get that ball," the juggler said, lifting a finger toward the street.

Matt bit his lip. He left Tomtar and Tuava-Li at the curb as he ventured between two parked cars, looked both ways, and then went to retrieve the ball that was lying in the gutter at the opposite curb. He picked it up and tossed it. When the juggler caught it, he flicked his wrist and the ball disappeared in thin air. "So you do magic, too," Matt said, returning.

The juggler coughed. Matt didn't realize it was part of the act until he coughed a large Fire Sprite into his upturned hand. "Oh, that's hot!" he cried, and coughed out two more. He juggled them, slowly at first, and then faster, and higher, until the Fire Sprites began to twist and turn in the air like divers doing tricks off the high dive. He caught them in his oversized pockets, and jumped up in mock alarm as clouds of black smoke began to curl from his trousers. Tomtar laughed, and both Matt and Tuava-Li turned to give him a disapproving look. The juggler reached into one of the pockets and withdrew a bright red apple. Licking his lips, he took a bite. "Normally I like to have my apples sliced," he said, chewing with his mouth full. "It's so uncivilized to eat them whole, don't you think? Which one of you is carrying a knife? I know one of you must be armed. Come on now, don't be shy, I'm not going to bite you!"

Tomtar tugged at Matt's sleeve. "Give him your knife, Matt," he whispered.

Matt shook his head. "No way!"

Tomtar looked so disappointed that Matt relented and took his knife from his pocket. He handed it to the juggler, who promptly tossed it into the air. He caught it by the handle as it came back down, and cut a thin slice from the apple. "That's not very challenging now, is it?" he said, and plucked a shiny meat cleaver and a butcher knife from beneath the cloth he'd spread on the ground. One by one he tossed them into the air, followed by Matt's knife. He juggled all three, tossing them high enough that he had time to catch Matt's knife, cut a slice from the apple, pop it in his mouth and continue juggling effortlessly. Tomtar applauded. "Bravo!" he cried.

"That's nothing," the juggler said. "I've juggled more than a dozen at once."

He put his knives back with his equipment and handed Matt the knife he'd borrowed. Then he quickly picked up a top hat from the ground and, bending low, held it out in front of him. "A token of your appreciation?" he murmured.

Matt sighed and fished around in his pocket for a dollar bill. "Now that you've seen what I can do," the juggler said with a grin, and pocketed his money, "why don't you tell me what makes *you* so special?"

"What?" Matt said, taken aback. The juggler gave Matt a funny feeling; was he a human, or some kind of Faerie in disguise? He didn't seem to be chewing on a *trans*, like Tomtar and Tuava-Li did when they wanted to appear to be human. "I'm not special. I'm just a kid."

"A kid who travels with faerie folk," the juggler noted, holding out a hand. "I'm Stefan."

Matt reluctantly shook the stranger's hand. "My name's Matt. Don't you see many people hanging out with faerie folk around here?"

"No," Stefan replied, "but sometimes I see faerie folk who hang out with humans! I'll bet you a dollar that I can tell you something you don't know."

Matt sighed. He wasn't in the mood for games. "I've got to go," he said, glad at least that they'd found the club where they might talk to some Trolls. "See you around. Thanks for the act."

He gestured to Tomtar and Tuava-Li as they set off down the block, back the way they had come. "This is our lucky day," Tomtar said cheerfully.

"I don't see what's so lucky about it," Matt muttered, walking briskly. He'd already forgotten he was trying to think positively. "Everybody we meet seems like trouble."

"Not the woman at the doll shop," the Troll replied, struggling to keep up the pace in his new plastic shoes.

"I mean everybody that can see faerie folk seems like trouble," Matt said.

"Under the circumstances," Tuava-Li offered, "'tis wise to regard everyone we meet with suspicion, until it's proven otherwise that we can trust them."

Matt realized that he could be cranky and say something mean to Tuava-Li. But he was beginning to feel that the time for sarcasm and division was over. Just because he didn't like her Mage didn't mean he shouldn't give Tuava-Li a chance. She might have been annoying, she might have had her own agenda, but it was looking more and more like they were on the same team. Uncertainty and the threat of danger were slowly turning them into allies. Matt stopped at the corner to wait for the light to change. "Look, we've still got hours to kill before nightfall. We're only a little way from the place I used to live. You guys want to see where I grew up?"

25

TUAVA-LI AND TOMTAR were puffing hard as they struggled up the hillside with Matt in the lead, making their way along winding streets, a wooden stairway, and five long blocks to Jerome Street. Since the streets were nearly deserted, they stopped along the way to transfer their belongings from the rough woven packs to the canvas ones that the shoe repairman had given them. Then, behind some pine trees, in an old metal trash can, Matt lit a match and set fire to the garbage and old backpacks. They waited until there was nothing left but cinders. Tomtar and Tuava-Li spread the ashes with sticks, and Tuava-Li said a prayer. "This reminds me of what you do with roadkill," Matt noted.

Tuava-Li looked up at him. "The past is never really done with, unless you consciously close the door to it with ritual and prayer. Otherwise, it will follow you forever."

The view of Pittsburgh that spread along the river grew more spectacular as they climbed higher on the hillside. Matt felt a twinge of pride in his hometown as his companions oohed and aahed at the sight of the rivers and bridges. The funicular and the cell tower were still visible to the east. Matt approached his old block with a strange mix of apprehension and nostalgia. The apartment building sat on the crest of the hill, in the midst of a maze of winding streets lined with parked cars. "There it is," he said, stopping to point at the window of the room he and Becky used to share, back before everything changed.

The building looked small and dull. It was just two stories, with a pair of apartments at the front of each floor and another pair in back. Matt knew there were new people living in the apartment now that this place that had once been his home belonged to somebody else. Matt was, in fact, a boy with no home at all, a boy who carried the idea of home in his mind, like a life preserver floating on a stormy sea. That was all. Tomtar saw a man struggling with his keys at the door of the building. The lock had always been a little tricky. Behind him, a young woman with a stroller waited.

"Can we go in, Matt?" Tomtar asked. "We could follow them!"

Matt snorted. "I don't think so. I don't live there anymore!"

Tuava-Li brightened. "In our realm, a home is always a home. Even if we move somewhere far away, we're always welcomed back to the place we once lived, despite the fact that someone else might live there."

"That's nice," Matt said. "But we're not in your realm anymore."

"Matthew, is that you?" came a wavering voice from the building next to Matt's.

He glanced over to see a white-haired lady inching her walker down the sidewalk. "Who's that?" Tomtar whispered.

"She's a neighbor. She's a little crazy. My dad used to help her out sometimes."

Matt walked over to the woman. "Mrs. Babcek! How are you?"

"I'm all right," she said. "My back bothers me so much, I don't hardly get out. But they say there might be a curfew, what with all the kids goin' missing, so I thought I'd better get a little sun before they shut the town down! What are you doin' out, Matthew? Aren't you supposed to be in school?"

Matt's smile was strained. "Mrs. Babcek, don't you remember, we moved. I'm just here for a visit!"

The woman furrowed her brow. Matt could see her searching her memory, and coming up blank. "You moved? Oh, now I remember!"

Matt figured she probably didn't remember. "Just came back for the afternoon, for some family business. We live in the country now, a ways north. Nice new house and all. But you look good, Mrs. Babcek! I'll tell my dad we ran into you."

"You look handsome in a suit," the old lady said, as Matt started to turn away. "You remind me of my son. Why don't you come up and have a piece of cake? You could bring the rest of your family. The apartment's a little gommed up, but if you don't mind, I don't either!"

Matt thought fast, trying to come up with an excuse. "My, uh, folks are busy, they're downtown, so it's just me, Mrs. Babcek. I've really got to go, I'm sorry. Maybe next time, okay?"

"I could do with a little company," the old woman sighed. "Your dad was always good to me. The new tenants aren't too friendly, you know. The guy smokes a stogie, and stinks up the whole neighborhood."

"Doesn't your son live nearby?"

"John? He's always workin'. Hasn't got time for his old mom."

Matt took a deep breath. It was still early, hours before dark, and he didn't really have any other plans. He realized it wouldn't hurt to go inside. "You know, Mrs. Babcek, we'll come in, just for some cake."

"We?" she said, looking confused. "I thought you said your family—"

"I meant, me," Matt corrected himself. "I'm free."

Tuava-Li gave Matt's pant leg a sharp yank. *What are you doing,* came the words in thought-speak.

"It'll be good to get out of the sun for a while," Matt said. "It's a hot one, for September!"

At the door to the old lady's apartment Tomtar and Tuava-Li hesitated. "Come on," Matt whispered, as Mrs. Babcek left her walker by the door and hobbled into the living room. "I'm inviting you in!"

The apartment was dark and musty. The walls were papered in a floral pattern that hadn't been changed in half a century, and the worn, overstuffed furniture looked misshapen and sad. Matt had been in the apartment a few times, back when they were neighbors. He'd gone there with his sister when she'd made the rounds of the building to sell Girl Scout cookies, and once in a while he'd delivered mail when it was put in the wrong box. He was a little surprised at how shabby things had become since then. There were stacks of newspapers next to the couch, old catalogs and mail strewn on the coffee table. A calendar, long out of date, hung on a nail next to the door. "Sit down," Mrs. Babcek said, as she flicked on the TV in the corner. "I'll make coffee."

"Do you want some help?" Matt asked.

The old lady chuckled as she headed into the kitchen. "I can take care of myself!"

Matt cleared away some of the debris on the couch and sat uneasily on the edge. Tomtar came to sit next to him, but Tuava-Li crouched by the door, wide-eyed, transfixed by the flickering images on the television screen. "What kind of magick is this?" she whispered.

"It's nothing," Tomtar said. He had seen plenty of television when he visited Matt's house back in the suburbs. "Human stuff, that's all. You'll get used to it!"

"*Sssssssh!*" Matt put a finger to his lips. The newsman on the

TV screen was talking about children being abducted. He warned that people should keep a close watch over young children until officials figured out what was going on. Matt thought of the Troll, Nick, and the baby they rescued outside of town, and he felt sick to his stomach. He heard Mrs. Babcek rattling around in the kitchen. "I'm going to see if I can give her a hand," he whispered to Tomtar and Tuava-Li. "I'll be back in a minute."

He found Mrs. Babcek leaning on the edge of the table. "Now, where did I put that cake?" she said absently.

Matt looked around through the clutter, wondering if there was a cake at all. "Maybe in the refrigerator?"

"John, you always know where to find things," she said, and lifted a can of coffee from the counter.

Matt opened the refrigerator, feeling awkward and embarrassed; now she was calling him by her son's name. Was it just a slip of the tongue, or was the old lady really losing her grip? He saw a boxed pound cake on the top shelf next to a loaf of bread and a jar of mustard with a missing lid. He took the cake out and put it on a platter he found in the dish drainer. He found knives and forks in the second drawer he checked. "There are paper plates in the bottom cupboard," Mrs. Babcek said. "Take them all, so there'll be enough for your brother and sister."

"Oh, but I have two sisters, and they're not—"

Matt's breath caught in his throat. Tomtar and Tuava-Li were there in the next room. He'd assumed that the old lady, like most people, wouldn't be able to see the Faeries, even when they were right in front of her face. The human brain seemed to gloss over and ignore things that weren't part of the normal belief system, after all. But when Mrs. Babcek mentioned serving cake to his brother and sister, Matt realized she'd really *seen* Tomtar and Tuava-Li, and concluded that they were human children. Matt didn't know what to think. He didn't know what to say, or do. It all depended on what Mrs. Babcek was thinking, and that seemed to change from moment to moment. Did she think Matt was her son, or the kid who used to live next door? Did she think Tomtar and Tuava-Li were his brother and sister, or was she thinking about something else? As he stepped into the hallway, carrying the cake, she touched his forearm. "I forgot your brother and sister's names!"

"Oh, they're, ah, Tom and Lee, uh, Leah."

Matt felt depressed. It was like the old lady was seeing the world through a broken windowpane. Some things on the other side looked bright and clear, while other things were cracked and distorted. "Tom and Leah," he said, moving papers out of the way so that he could put the platter on the coffee table. "I brought you some cake!"

I think she can see you, Matt said in his mind, and tried to move the words out into space, like he'd done before. He hoped that Tuava-Li would be able to hear his words. *It's okay, though. She thinks you're my brother and sister.*

Tomtar and Tuava-Li eyed Matt and the old lady suspiciously.

Still, they sat quietly on the floor and ate their cake, hoping that Matt knew what he was doing.

Matt sat on the edge of the couch and nudged crumbs around on his paper plate. "When was the last time you saw your son, Mrs. Babcek?" he asked, making conversation.

"Oh, it's been a while."

"Doesn't he call?"

"I got a card on Mother's Day," she smiled. "Do you want to see it?"

"You know," Matt said, "if you give me his phone number, I could call him for you, and tell him that you could use a little help around here."

Mrs. Babcek shook her head. "I don't want to bother him, no. Say, I wouldn't mind one more little piece of cake, if you'll cut it for me!"

For the next several hours Matt sat with Mrs. Babcek as the television droned on in the background. With half an ear he listened to what the newscasters were saying, but he felt obliged to be polite, too, and smiled as the old lady talked. She reminisced about the good old days, when Pittsburgh was a steel town and she was just a girl. Matt told her a little about the houses his dad had built in the country. Several times the old woman called him "John," and he felt obliged to drink cup after cup of her strong, bitter coffee. *When are we going,* Tuava-Li asked Matt in thought-speak. *We've got things to do.*

Matt looked at her and shrugged. *Soon,* he mouthed.

Tomtar fidgeted as he sat in front of the television, watching the news. Everywhere it was the same. Children were disappearing throughout Pennsylvania, up into New York State, and as far west as Ohio. In some towns, entire classes of nursery school kids and kindergartens had vanished. Notes had been left behind, with confessions and explanations, but the police weren't buying it. Hundreds of children, maybe more, were missing. Caretakers, too, were gone. Everyone was talking about terrorists. National Guard troops had been called into several towns near the Canadian border, and the president came on to say that he was declaring a national security alert, and the borders were being closed to make sure that missing children weren't taken out of the country. In Pittsburgh they were setting up a curfew at dusk for anyone under twenty-one, and children weren't allowed on the streets at all unless accompanied by an adult.

Matt watched Tomtar squirm. Maybe all the news about the Acquisition was bothering him; maybe it just pained him to be in cramped quarters for too long. The old lady must have picked up on it too, because she turned to Matt and whispered, "Your brother and sister are so well-behaved! They don't have to just sit here while we talk, though. You know there are a lot of your old toys still in your bedroom, if they want to play."

Matt wondered if this was a good time to go. "Listen, Mrs. Babcek, I think we ought to be heading out. Thanks for the cake, and all, but we should be on our way."

"I'll make your bed up," the old woman said, shuffling down

the hallway toward the rear of the apartment. "It's a long way back, and with the curfew and all, you shouldn't be out on the street after dark."

"But—"

"I don't know what the world's coming to! After dinner, John, maybe you can help me with the bills. My eyes are acting up. Since I can't read my mail, I just keep the bills in a pile on the coffee table. I've got some extra blankets in the cupboard, your brother and sister could sleep on those!"

Matt felt trapped. He found himself wishing that they'd spent the afternoon at the public library, instead of agreeing to visit the old woman. What could he do to help her? She didn't seem to want to give him her son's phone number. Even if she did, what would he say? How could he explain what he was doing there in her apartment? This was not part of his journey, not part of his plan to rescue his parents. It was just a distraction. He followed her into the bedroom as she flicked the light switch, then bent to straighten the comforter on the old mattress in the corner. He could see past the curtains that the sun was going down. The alley behind the building was settling into purple shadows. *Maybe we could stay the night,* he thought. *It would have to be better than the shelter. Plus it's closer to Carson Street, and the club where that juggler said we might find some trolls.*

Tuava-Li's voice appeared in his head. *We should leave the Alfheim Jewels here. It may be safer than carrying them with us to the club, and we can come back for them when we leave town.*

330

"Okay," Matt said out loud.

"What's that?" asked Mrs. Babcek.

"Oh, nothing! I mean, this looks just fine."

Beneath the bedroom window there was a stack of cardboard boxes, stuffed with Legos, Lincoln Logs, and Tinkertoys. Matt realized there must be a hundred places to hide things in here. When the old woman's back was turned, he pulled the little sack of Jewels from his pocket and handed it to Tomtar. "You guys want to play in here while I make Mrs. Babcek some supper?"

Matt coaxed the old lady into the kitchen, where he tried to help her clean up and put things away. He whipped up some pancakes from a box of powdered mix in the pantry, but when he put the plate in front of her, she pushed it away. "Past my bedtime," she said wearily. "You workin' the nightshift down at the mill again?"

"Uh—" Matt said, uncertain of how to respond. He tried to convince himself that if he could do something to help the old woman, maybe it wasn't so bad to take advantage of her confused mental state, and use her apartment as a temporary hiding place. "Uh, yeah."

"Well, I'd best turn in," she mumbled, hoisting herself painfully out of her seat. "Sleep tight!"

Matt watched the old lady retreat into her bedroom. As soon as she'd closed the door behind her, he gobbled up the pancakes on her plate, then grabbed a few extra for Tomtar and Tuava-Li.

"Can we get out of here now?" Tomtar pleaded as he stepped into sight.

"Relax," Matt said. "We'll be out of here in a minute. What did you do with the jewels?"

"We hid all three pouches in the closet," Tuava-Li said, gesturing.

Matt went to look into the cluttered darkness. A faded old wedding gown, wrapped in yellowed plastic, hung on a hook on the back of the door. There were shoeboxes stacked amid heaps of dust on the floor. "Yours are in the bottom box," Tuava-Li said, "inside her old wedding shoes."

"Great," Matt said. He felt his mood sink. All of the business that had transpired because of wedding shoes was something he preferred to put behind him. "Listen," he whispered, heading back to the living room, "I don't feel right about what we're doing here. I'm going to try to find out where her son lives, and call him. Somebody's got to take care of Mrs. Babcek, and it can't be me!"

"Her spirit is lost," Tuava-Li said, "somewhere outside of her body. When we're old, our bodies lose the strength to keep the soul inside."

"Yeah?" Matt said distractedly, noticing the old woman's pocketbook on a chair by the door. There were some worn envelopes sticking out of the top. He pulled them out, checking the return addresses. Then he took out her key ring.

"Come on, Matt," Tomtar pleaded. "We've got to go, we've

got to find out if there are any Trolls left in Argant. The juggler said—"

"I know what he said," Matt interrupted. "All right. If I take her keys, I can let us in when we get back. Everybody okay with that?"

"If it's all right with you," Tuava-Li answered.

"Not really, but I don't think we have too many options here."

Tuava-Li slung her new, kid-size backpack over one shoulder. "Let's leave our packs here, too," Matt said, "since we'll be back later tonight. Take some of your *trans* and I'll take the cash from the pawnshop. I've got my knife in my jacket pocket, just in case. We probably won't need anything else."

The three slipped into the hallway and Matt quietly turned the key in the lock. Each of them felt a strange, nervous energy. They were exhilarated, yet exhausted at the same time. "Once I heard an old curse," Tomtar whispered, "*may you be born in interesting times.*"

"Are you saying we're cursed?" Matt asked, traipsing down the stairs.

"I hope not," Tomtar answered. Instinctively he touched the amulets around his neck. "But things are starting to get a little too interesting for me."

26

BECKY STUMBLED in the darkness. "Can't we stop for just a little while?" she cried.

"No," Macta said. He held the box with the Fire Sprite in it open before him, like a candle to light his way. In broad daylight the terrain would have been rough going. In the dark, it was nearly impossible. At Macta's insistence they kept up their weary march, as the moon sent silver daggers through the trees. Becky was glad that it was too dark to see Asra's face. She had worn the same frozen expression of shock and disgust for the entire day. Macta's eyes had glowed intermittently with the fire of madness and obsession. At other times he looked dull and sickly, and beads of sweat raced down the length of his pale forehead.

Becky's emotions were on an endless roller coaster ride. She was on her way to a Cord, big enough to take them all the way to Helfratheim. That was good. But the Cord might be lost to fires deep in some abandoned coal mine. That was bad. Once, near morning, Macta thought he saw a Goblin leaping through the woods. Though his beloved pet Powcca was dead, Macta's fevered brain imagined that he was still alive, and that he must catch him. Asra took the opportunity to run in the opposite direction. "Princess, where are you going? What are you doing?" Becky had cried, and Macta came to his senses.

The animal he'd seen was just a squirrel, and as it leapt into the branches of a tree, Macta turned and raced after Asra, swearing that she would never get away from him again. When he'd caught her, he took a length of rope from Radik's sack and demanded that Becky tie one end around Asra's neck, and the other end around his wrist. When Becky refused, he threatened to leave her alone in the woods, and to let her parents rot in prison when they reached Helfratheim. Becky dissolved in helpless tears. Asra, realizing that their choices were few, gave Becky her permission to do as Macta said. With trembling fingers, the girl tied the knots as best she could.

Awkwardly they continued to trek on through the woods. In his clearer moments, Macta begged Asra for forgiveness for the death of her father. He claimed over and over that when the Dragon Thunderbus had gone off, on that terrible day in Alfheim, it had been an accident—nothing more than a terrible accident. He explained that his motives toward her had always been pure, that he still wanted to spend his life with her, that their marriage would be a good one, that she would find true happiness as his

Queen. At other times Macta seemed lost in his own fevered dreams, and he would pause, sometimes laughing to himself, sometimes grumbling, to make notes in his book. He would rattle the knucklebones he kept in his pocket and talk about his bets. He would say that the fingers on his right hand were tingling, which showed that his good luck was just beginning. Neither Becky nor Asra reminded Macta that it was his right hand that was missing.

That afternoon they came upon a hunter's cabin. Inside they found a few cans of beans and a rusty old can opener. They devoured the food in minutes, eating with their bare hands. Afterwards, Macta fell into a fevered sleep on an old army cot. Asra begged Becky to untie her. Becky tried, fumbling with the knot, but Macta woke up. "You try to escape again," he swore, "and you'll never find your way out of the woods. I memorized the route through the forest, but you'll be lost forever!"

He took the maps that Queen Metis had given them, and holding them in his teeth, tore the parchments into little pieces. *"No!"* Becky and Asra cried together. "They're all we have!"

It was obvious that Macta's mental condition was flagging. He looked sicker than before, and his wound smelled of decay. Tiny flies buzzed around his shoulder. Becky thought Asra would never stop crying. Macta blathered on, trying to console her, telling her how much he loved her, and how soon she would help rule one of the oldest and mightiest kingdoms in all of Elf realm. But Asra recoiled from him. She strained against the rope to keep as far away from Macta as she could.

They spent the rest of the afternoon slowly making their way up and down one hill after another. Though there were many animals in the woods they didn't see any more people, or Faerie Folk, and Becky felt glad for that. She didn't think she could take any more surprises. Frequently she would stop to pluck a leaf, or a stalk or a berry, hoping to find something to eat. She glanced at the book Neaca had made for her. She wanted to be sure her impressions were right about the shapes and colors of the things she was collecting. She plucked edible plants, nuts, and berries for herself and her companions, as well as herbs that might be used medicinally if Macta's condition worsened, and if he'd allow her to help. She stuffed her discoveries in an old burlap sack she'd found in the hunter's cabin. Because Asra and Macta seemed to move ever more slowly, Becky was able to gather many useful things. Her most valuable possession, however, was tucked safely in her back pocket. It was a brochure for a little amusement park called Fairytale Village.

She had taken it from the back of an old display rack in the bakery they'd visited the previous day, when Radik had still been alive, and the world had seemed a brighter place. She'd grabbed the flyer on a whim, never expecting to actually go there. She hadn't even bothered to look at it until they'd stopped for a rest. The paper was yellowed and bent. The people in the pictures were wearing clothes that were no longer in style. Maybe the place wasn't even there anymore, maybe it had gone out of business as the big chains of amusement parks had taken over. It didn't matter. The only thing that mattered was the map on the back of the brochure. The old mining town they were looking for, the one where deep Cords were supposed to be, was there on the map. It was just east of Fairytale Village. The fact that Macta had torn up their other maps didn't matter anymore. Becky knew that whatever happened now, she could find the path that would take them to Helfratheim, and her parents.

When night came, Becky's ears felt like they were attuned to every subtle brush of a branch, every distant, scampering mouse, every blink of an owl's eye. But when the toe of her shoe jammed under a tree root, she nearly fell. "We've got to stop," she said. "It isn't safe to walk in the woods like this. Can't we finish the trip in the morning? We've got to make camp, gather pine needles to sleep in, we've got to—"

"We've got to do what I say," Macta growled, holding his Fire Sprite high. "It isn't far now, I know. There's a Human road up ahead. Can't you hear their vehicles roaring through the night?"

Becky could. Her heart leapt at the sound of a truck speeding along the highway—the highway that ran past Fairytale Village. They stumbled on through the woods until the trees opened up, revealing a grassy shoulder, and moonlight spilling down on the blacktop road.

Macta grinned. He shut the Fire Sprite back in its box and dropped it into a pocket. "Perhaps my father's gondola will be waiting for me! I'll take it, this time."

"What?" asked Becky.

"It's very hot out," Macta continued. "Powcca hates it in the kennel when it's this hot. I'll sneak him into my room, and if Mother doesn't come in to say good night, then he can sleep in bed right next to me. Good old boy, I love him so!"

Becky looked at Asra; the Prince was sliding into madness. Macta suddenly stopped. He leaned sideways, like a tree in a strong wind, and then caught himself before he fell. "Stay back, Powcca," he cried. "Stay out of the road, you don't know how fast the vehicles are coming."

He clutched at his shoulder and whimpered. "Perhaps we should stop for the night, after all. I'm getting a bit of a chill."

It was then that his legs went out from under him. Asra clutched the rope around her neck, still bound to Macta's wrist, and she toppled onto his still form. "Do something," she choked, "he's unconscious! Help me, Rebecca!"

"He keeps Radik's knife in his pocket," Becky said, rushing to Asra's side. "Get it out, and I'll cut you loose."

"I won't touch him," Asra shuddered violently, pulling on the rope. "You do it!"

"All right," Becky said, and knelt beside the Elf. The bandage on his shoulder was soaked though and clotted with blood. She held her breath and wrinkled her face as she slipped a hand into his pocket. "He smells bad!"

"This is our chance," Asra cried. "We've got to get away, while we can. Hurry!"

Becky withdrew the blade. Carefully she sawed through the

rope around Asra's neck. "We can't just run away, Princess! We can't leave him here to die. When we get to Helfratheim, we're going to need his help. I know you don't like him, but you have to forget about that, at least for now!"

Asra shook her head. "I don't dislike him, *I despise him!* 'Tis time you were honest with yourself, Rebecca. You know as well as I do, we're never going to reach Helfratheim."

"I know how to get to Helfratheim," Becky said, her eyes filling up with tears. "I've got a map of my own. I'm going to find my parents. Run away if you want to, but I'm still going! I've got to!"

Asra stood up, rubbing her neck where the rope had scraped her flesh. "What do you mean, you have a map of your own?"

Becky pulled the Fairytale Village brochure from her pocket and thrust it at the princess. A torrent of conflicting thoughts rushed through Asra's mind as Becky stood sobbing. She peered at the map on the back of the brochure, studying the winding lines that represented the Human world. She looked at the names of the small towns, and the roadside attractions featured there. "Why do they call it Fairytale Village? Humans don't believe in Faerie Folk."

"It just means *stories*," Becky said, wiping her eyes with her hand. "Stories for little kids. There aren't any faeries there."

"You think this path will lead us to the Cord?"

"Yes. I know it will."

"I don't know what to say," Asra sighed, and handed the

brochure back to Becky. "I suppose . . . I suppose I owe it to you to keep going."

Becky looked up. Asra's face was lost in shadows. "It amazes me that we've come this far. Truly it does. I wouldn't have thought it possible."

"Will you help me, then?"

Asra looked down at Macta and scowled. "Queen Metis ordered me to help you, but she didn't know about Macta. She also didn't know about this business with Brahja-Chi, and her Acquisition. If the Mage is organizing some kind of Human sacrifice, Helfratheim may be more of a fortress than we've anticipated. We might not just waltz right through the gates, like Metis said. Macta may offer us our only hope of getting in, but what are we supposed to do? Carry him? What good will he be to us if he reaches his homeland barely alive?"

"I've got herbs," Becky said, "things I gathered today—things that Neaca told me would be helpful for fever, and infection, and blood. I've even got things to counteract spells, if somebody's put a curse on him."

Asra shook her head. "That's not enough. How could you know what to give him, and how much? You might end up killing him, not that he doesn't deserve to die."

"He saved our lives!" Becky cried. "Don't forget, those men would have killed us today if Macta hadn't come!"

"I know, I know," Asra muttered. "He didn't save us because he's kind, though, or because it was the right thing to do.

Nothing's changed. He brought those Humans down because he wanted me to himself."

"It doesn't matter what he wants," Becky said. "It just matters that he gets well enough to travel the rest of the way. I've got echinacea, licorice root, cranberries, thyme, dandelion, and burdock. I've got some other things with names I can't remember, but I know them from their shape. Some things are pungent, some are cool, some are bitter."

Asra shook her head. "And you know how to prepare them, the doses, the spells to say?"

"I don't know any spells," Becky answered. "I remember lots of things Neaca told me, though, and she wrote lots of things in this book. I'm not sure, but I think I can help Macta; *we* can help Macta. We've got to make compresses, teas, we've got to get things into his system, but we can't do anything without water."

"All right," Asra sighed. "But once we get to Helfratheim, I'm done. You have to promise to help me get away. I can't spend the rest of my life tied to this . . . this . . . pathetic creature."

"Okay," Becky said, "once Macta orders the elves to let my parents go. For now, we'll hike down the road, and see if we can't find some water. Maybe we'll find a gas station, or something. Maybe even somebody's house, with a hose."

Asra turned her head left and right. "Which way do we go?"

"I'm not sure," Becky said, struggling to pull Macta into a sitting position. He was a limp doll, with his head flopped down on his chest. "We need to go east from Fairytale Village, but I'm not sure which way we are, compared to that. We're just going to have to guess. And I'm going to have to figure out the best way to carry Macta!"

"Look up there," Asra said, "in the sky! 'Tis Khidr! Whenever I've seen him, he's been in the east."

"Where do you mean?" Becky asked, as she peered into the star-scattered sky. The Milky Way was bright, with tens of millions of stars streaking the heavens. "I see the Big Dipper," she said. "What are you looking at?"

"There, right there, do you see the greenish light?"

"I guess," Becky replied.

"That's Khidr's head. The lights below that are his body, his many arms, and there, below his feet, are his enemies, vanquished in battle."

Becky furrowed her brow, squinting at the lights for some kind of pattern. "I think I see them! And those stars are always in the east?"

"I don't know that word *stars*. The lights are holes in the dome of Heaven, *vindues*, where the Goddess and the other Gods look down upon us. But I think that direction is east. I can take Macta's pack, so it makes it easier for you to carry him."

"Wait," Becky said. "You don't know about stars? Do elves think the Earth is flat?"

"Of course not," Asra huffed, "but where do you think the Goddess lives, if not on the other side of the dome?"

"I don't know," Becky said. "I never really thought about it.

But if the stars are just holes poked into a dome, how can they move around?"

"The Goddess can do anything!" Asra explained. "When we were little we learned that the lights are there to tell us stories, to teach us lessons. When we go through the Gates of Vattar, the lights shine down on us, and that's how the Goddess renews our strength for another day."

Becky nodded. She'd never heard anything like this before, but if it was what the princess believed, then she would show Asra the respect she deserved. "How many gods do you have?"

Asra waved her hand across the sky. "Many!"

"What about goddesses?"

Asra smiled. "When I say *Gods*, I mean both male and female deities; but there is one Great Goddess. They're all depicted there, across the dome of Heaven. Look there, 'tis Anahita, the Giver of blessings and rain. She's right below Khidr. Maybe that's the way we'll find water!"

"Then let's go," Becky said. She got down on her knees with her back to Macta, and took him by his one good arm. Hoisting him up onto her shoulder, she wrapped her other arm around one of his legs, then struggled to her feet. "Tell me more about your gods and goddesses! It'll make it easier for me to walk like this, with Macta on my back, if I'm thinking about something else."

"There are Nuwa and Fuxi," Asra said, pointing. "They're the snake Gods, the founders of the world. Their tails are twined together. The descendants of the Dragons live in the west. The

BECKY AND MACTA

five Supremes are the judges of everything moral, the arbiters of right and wrong. Look, I'll show them to you!"

"I can't look now," Becky said. She was hunched over with Macta on her back and could barely lift her head to see the road that unfolded before them in the darkness. "Just tell me their stories, Princess, won't you? I want to know everything!"

As Becky and Asra hiked along the roadside, the land stretching into the night was no more than dull patterns of black and gray. Since it was late there were no cars on the highway, just a lone truck, now and then, speeding through the night. But the sky burned with lights that told the stories of nature gods, animal gods, the triple deities, the warriors and martyrs that populated the mythology of the Elfin Clans. Asra shared what she knew, and they stopped to rest and admire the *vindues* more than once as they headed east. Each time, Becky would carefully lay Macta on his back and check to make sure he was still breathing. Remembering what Neaca had taught her, she chewed some of the leaves she'd collected in order to soften them and release their oils, then pressed the mass into Macta's cheek. By the time the moon was at its highest point they passed an old wooden sign, half-hidden by overgrown trees. "Fairytale Village, a half a mile ahead!" Becky cried. "Let's hurry!"

She and Asra were breathing hard when they reached the entrance to the amusement park. A fiberglass Humpty Dumpty, making an inviting gesture with his little white-gloved hands, grinned down from an archway over the ticket booth. A cyclone fence with a rusty padlock on it barred the way inside. "All right," Becky sighed. "I didn't think it would be open this time of night. But I thought we might be able to get in, at least, and find a drinking fountain, or something."

"It looks deserted," Asra said, "abandoned." Her enormous eyes made it easier for her to see in the dim light. "Look there, the towers have fallen from the corners of a castle. They're lying on their side."

Becky pressed her face up against the fence. A pair of gray concrete towers, crudely painted with black lines for bricks, lay broken on the ground just inside the entrance. Bits of rubble lay around them, and rusty metal pipes stuck out of the broken battlements. Flags lay near the towers, their fabric tattered and rotten. Behind the fallen towers Becky could just make out a fountain, overgrown with weeds, and a number of small buildings that were shuttered. "You're right. Maybe it's closed for the season, or maybe it's closed forever. But we still might find water in there. We've got to make poultices for Macta, something to clean his wound, at least. Help me find a way in!"

Along the side of the park Becky and Asra discovered a tree that had fallen and pushed the chain-link fence to the ground. They hauled Macta over the branches and placed him on the overgrown grass inside the park. Before them stood a little playground, with slides and swings and climbing bars. A slight breeze made the chains on the swings groan eerily. There was a concrete drinking fountain on a stand near the monkey bars.

When Becky saw it she hurried to turn the knob. It made a choked little squeak, and nothing more. "This might not be so easy," she said.

Reluctantly, Asra stayed beside Macta while Becky took the Fire Sprite and began her search for water. There was a fountain at the center of the park. Fiberglass mermaids were frozen in mid-stroke in the concrete pool, which was full of dried leaves and pools of algae and fetid water, too foul to use. There was a fifty-gallon drum behind a snack shack, and it, too, was full of water. Becky stood on tiptoes and forced herself to sink a hand into the black liquid and swirl it around. *It looks greasy*, she thought, watching the water dribble from her fingers.

She found an aluminum bucket with a handle behind another shed, and carried it with her. As she peered around a tree, with the silver box held high so that the Fire Sprite could light the darkness, she saw three figures. They were silhouetted in black, and though they didn't move, Becky held her breath and waited in the shadows until she was sure that they were just statues. When she crept closer she smiled to realize that she was looking at the Three Little Pigs. Each of them wore a flat blue cap, and rainwater had collected on the shallow lip of each of them. She wasn't prepared to drink any of the water herself, but if it were boiled, it might be all right. It would certainly be better than nothing. She closed the Fire Sprite in its box and slipped it into her pocket. Then, using her hand, she managed to scoop several cups of water into her pail. She hurried back to the playground and found Asra sitting by the fence where they had come in. "I thought that you might run away and leave me here alone," Becky said.

Asra shook her head slowly. "You wouldn't be alone, you'd have Macta, to help you find your way to a place where you'd probably be thrown in jail and left to rot."

"Don't say that," Becky cried.

"I'm sorry, Rebecca," Asra said, getting to her feet. "I didn't go anywhere, did I? I won't say I didn't think about it, but I stayed right here beside Macta, like I promised. Did you find enough water?"

"Yes," Becky said, putting down her bucket. "Now we need to find some place to put it, where the fire sprite can heat up the water. Then I'll make some things to help him get better."

Asra was impressed by Becky's ability to remain positive and more or less cheerful. She helped her find some large, flat stones to use to prop up the corners of the bucket. As the Fire Sprite boiled the water, Asra watched Becky take her roots and leaves from the canvas sack and arrange them on the ground. Together they tore strips of cloth from another sack that Becky found behind a counter, soaked them in the hot water, and applied compresses to his forehead. They made tea from strong, bitter herbs, brewed in an old Styrofoam cup. While Becky lifted Macta's head a little, Asra used a plastic spoon to pour some into his mouth. Both of them chewed other herbs, making thick masses that could be slipped into Macta's cheeks. "I guess we should take off the old bandages and clean up his shoulder and arm," Becky said, when everything else had been done. "I'm kind of scared to look at it, though."

"His arm is beyond saving," Asra murmured. "I'm afraid there's one last thing we have to do."

She reached into Macta's pocket and withdrew the obsidian blade. "If we don't cut off what remains of his damaged arm, the rot will spread to the rest of his body. It may have done so already, but if there's any chance at all of his recovering from this, we're going to need to do something drastic."

Becky's eyes were large as saucers in the moonlight. "I can't—"

"I'll do it," Asra said, steeling herself. "While I kept watch over my mother in the infirmary I saw far worse things than this. If the monks can saw off arms and legs to save lives, then I can do it, too. Believe me, I'm well beyond worrying about contamination from Blood, or what a princess should or shouldn't do. You'll have to hold Macta down, in case he tries to move. I don't know if he'll feel pain or not, at this point."

Carefully Asra peeled away the old bandages, while Becky sterilized the obsidian blade in the Fire Sprite's red-hot blaze. Then Asra sawed away the fragments of sinew and bone of Macta's ruined arm, while he groaned and cried weakly, and Becky looked the other way. Soon Asra was finished. The Fire Sprite pranced across the wound to stop the bleeding, and Becky wrapped Macta's shoulder in fresh bandages. Tears sprang from her eyes; she hoped she'd never have to take part in something like this again. "We need to sleep," Asra said. "After we burn this dead tissue, we should find a place to lay him so that he's not bothered by animals that might smell his Blood."

Becky looked around. "There," she said, pointing to a large, concrete structure on the other side of the playground. There were posts on the corners, a ladder climbing up the back, and a slide attached to the front. A drooping canopy hung from above. "It's a bed," she said. "It's a slide, and a bed. It's a big pile of concrete mattresses stacked up on a four-poster bed. Isn't that funny? We need a place to sleep, and here it is. It's the bed from 'The Princess and the Pea'!"

"What's that?" Asra asked. She had taken what remained of Macta's arm and placed it in a cardboard tray Becky found in a trash can.

"It's a fairy tale," Becky said. She opened the lid of the silver box and coaxed the Fire Sprite to set the tray, and its sorry contents, alight.

"With no Faeries, right?"

"No faeries," Becky said. "But you might like it, anyway, since it's about a princess."

When the breeze began to take the ashes and spread them along the ground, Becky and Asra hoisted Macta up the ladder of the concrete bed and placed him at the foot of the highest slab. They covered him with the rest of the bag and tucked in the corners. Then they lay back on the hard, flat surface, their heads resting on concrete pillows, and stared at the heavens through a hole in the canopy above them. "Tell me about the princess and the pea, Rebecca," Asra said, shivering a little.

"Come a little closer," Becky said, "and I'll tell it to you."

The Faerie princess lay next to Becky, huddling close for warmth. She was asleep before Becky had finished the story.

27

THE OLD ELVES WERE GATHERED in a high tower room. All seven of the officials were dressed in black and yellow, with high collars and sculpted shoulders on their long felt jackets. "Shut the window," ordered Prashta, the Most Reverent Official Agent of Dockalfar Security Operations. He wrinkled his nose and shuddered. "I can't stand the odor of Humans coming from the courtyard."

"And I can't stand the racket," complained another of the Agents. "All they seem to do is wail and cry. Don't they ever sleep?"

"I've ordered a few changes that should make things easier to bear," said Lehtinen, Director of Operations. "We're building a stone wall to shield our view from the courtyard so that we don't have to look at them until the sacrifice. We're also building sanitary facilities to reduce the odor."

"You're not working fast enough," said Prashta, making a face.

A servant hurried to shutter the window. The old Elves glanced at each other across the table, their eyes darting nervously. Prashta cleared his throat. "We're here to discuss our new King," he said quietly. "Since Macta's return from Alfheim, things haven't been the same. Of course, we can't expect him to be the same kind of leader as his father, Valdis, was. He's young and inexperienced. Yet he rejects our counsel, and these are perilous times. Perhaps we should consider taking steps to rein him in."

"He spends too much time in the company of that monk, Jardaine," said one of the Agents.

"She's not a monk anymore," said Prashta. "Don't forget, Macta appointed her Mage of Helfratheim."

Lehtinen shook his head. "It takes more than an appointment to make a Mage. Macta should be paying more attention to the family business, and not trying to win favor with that witch Brahja-Chi. We need him to be ready to travel to the sites of our clients' battles, to assure them that their weapons systems are in order, and that they can feel safe under our protection. If we can't send our leader, we stand to lose important business."

"Aye," said another. "We should be selling our products to those who wish to battle other Faerie Folk, not squandering our own resources in fighting Humans. Perhaps one day we'll be prepared for a confrontation, but for now—"

All of the Elves jumped when the door burst open with a loud bang. Into the cramped chamber stalked Jardaine, accompanied by Jal-Maktar, in his guise as Macta Dockalfar. "Greetings," he said, "in the name of the Mistress, and the Canon which inspires her works."

"My King," Jardaine purred, "I believe I overheard these gentle Elves suggesting that we stand to lose business by attending to the Acquisition!"

Prashta's advising snake lifted its head from the collar of his jacket and whispered in his ear. The old Elf nodded, and then cleared his throat. "You honor us with your presence, your Majesty. Won't you sit down and join us?"

"Gladly," said Jal-Maktar, pulling up a chair first for Jardaine, and then himself. "But I insist you open that window. There's no air in here, and the place is full of the stink of conspiracy."

"Sir, we just closed the window, because of the rank odor and the infernal racket coming from the courtyard below. The Human children are an abomination, we simply —"

"I *want* you to smell the Humans," Jal-Maktar said enthusiastically. "I want you to hear their voices! The odor you detect is the smell of victory. The noise the children make is the sound of glad tidings. Now open the window, and gaze upon our great success!"

One of the servants pulled the window open again, and a gust of fetid air wafted in. "Come, look!" insisted Jal-Maktar.

All of the Agents got up awkwardly and moved to the

window. They clustered there, reluctantly peering down into the courtyard. In the moonlight it was plain to see hundreds of children, some little more than toddlers, huddled against each other in the cramped confines of their thorny cage. All of them had been brought to Helfratheim by Faerie Folk who wished to impress the Mage Brahja-Chi. Though the children tried to sleep, the pathetic wails of a few kept the many awake. Some of the older ones tried to quiet the smaller children, but there was scant comfort there on the cold stone courtyard. The autumn air was brisk at night, and the children shivered. There were no bathroom facilities, though large piles of bricks were piled at the corners of their pen so that walls could be built. Their food was tossed over the top of the cage. Many of them refused to eat, so that piles of trash lay rotting. The stench was overpowering. "There," said Jal-Maktar. He sucked in air through his delicate nostrils and grinned. "'Tis the smell of goals being realized. Now sit down, all of you. Tell me the truth. What was the nature of your discussion before my arrival?"

"Your Highness," said one of the Agents, his long, bony nose quivering as he spoke. "There are kingdoms at the far-flung corners of the Realm that need our services, but they are wary of doing business with us, without personal assurances from our leader about the safety and efficacy of our weapons systems. The Plodorms, for instance, in the western region of Abbar, are fighting a war with their neighbors, the Vishuas. They have need of explosives, and even wish to order a fleet of their own Arvada.

But they want to meet with you, to attach a friendly and reliable face to their investment. Since your return from Alfheim, you've refused to cooperate. We have competitors, Clans that have copied our success, and they'd be glad to take our business away from us. We'll lose our position in the industry if we fail to honor our obligations."

Jal-Maktar glared at the Agents, a smile twisting his features. "Obligations," he said. "I have an obligation for you—loyalty! I feel that since my return to Helfratheim I've been faced with nothing but disrespect and distrust from the lot of you. I've come here tonight not to listen to your pathetic drivel, but to demand an oath of loyalty to *me*. Jardaine, show the gentle Elves the apparatus."

Jardaine smiled pleasantly and opened up a black deerskin bag that she held in her lap. Piece by piece, she assembled a device on the table that was meant to draw Blood. Glass tubes twisted around themselves in a complicated matrix, and a long rubber coil, outfitted at its tip with a gleaming sliver of metal, wrapped like a snake around the bottom of the strange invention. Deep inside the labyrinth of glass the terrified Agents could see a slick black shape pulsing ominously. "What is *that*?" Prashta asked in a trembling voice.

Jal-Maktar shrugged. "Something the Experimentalists have devised. There's a morphologically enhanced slug at the heart of the apparatus. It's a holding device for the fluids that the machine collects. It has seven valves, and there are seven of you. Who will be first to volunteer?"

"This is an outrage," said one of the Agents, rising from his seat. "Why would you take our precious Blood, when we have already proven our loyalty?"

"If I have in my possession a portion of Blood from each of you," Jal-Maktar said calmly, "'twill be my insurance that you do not dare to disappoint me. Jardaine is a master of the dark arts, and knows what to do with your precious Blood, in case that should become necessary. Do I make myself clear?"

Prashta shook his head, as his advising snake coiled anxiously inside the collar of his garment. "We need to discuss business, King Macta. Your father would have wanted us to focus on our financial affairs, and not on a dubious alliance with a Mage from another kingdom. Brahja-Chi is nothing but a hindrance to us. Our business is selling weapons!"

"Indeed," said Jal-Maktar. "Remember, sirs, that our ancestors were gaming folk, and the origins of our empire lie in our willingness to accept a certain measure of risk, in order to win. 'Tis all a gamble! Imagine, for instance, that we're placing wagers on rats that run along a track. The odds of our rat winning the race increase if the other rats are afraid. Brahja-Chi has made the Humans afraid by abducting their children. They will fight us, but their fear will make them careless."

"Or perhapsss it will make them fiercer," said Prashta's advising snake.

As the other Agents nodded, their snakes, too, bobbed their heads sagely. "What Brahja-Chi is doing is wrong," said

Lehtinen. "What are the chances the Gods will truly be on our side if we undertake to fight the Humans? What makes us think that they'll accept the sacrifice of the Human children, as Brahja-Chi says?"

Jal-Maktar scratched his chin and thought. "You're absolutely right, my friend. Look at the sky, and tell me if the lights from the *vindues* there have changed. Perhaps the Gods have written a message on the dome of night for us, perhaps there is some wisdom there for us to decipher!"

Warily, Lehtinen crossed the chamber and leaned out the window, the breeze ruffling his wispy gray hair. His eyes searched the night sky, looking for clues from the Gods.

"Do you see anything of interest?" Jal-Maktar asked, sliding in behind.

In one swift move he reached around his victim's waist, took hold of the hem of his cape with his other hand, and heaved the old Elf out the window. Still holding on to the cape, he peered over the ledge and savored the sight of Lehtinen hanging upside down, choking on his own collar. "What's the magick word?" Jal-Maktar laughed, giving the corners of the cape a tug. "What's the magick word?"

"Please," Lehtinen gagged. His emerald blood rushed to his head and he turned a deep, sickly green. "Please, my King, I'm sorry for —"

With a grunt Jal-Maktar hoisted the Agent back into the chamber and dropped him on the floor. "You know *two* magick words," Jal-Maktar chuckled, "*please* and *sorry*. How proud I am of my staff."

He glanced up to see the look of horror on the faces of the Seven Agents. "Come now," he said. "It was just a little joke. You didn't think I'd toss my own Head of Operations to his death, did you?"

The others sat frozen in their chairs, their eyes darting like small birds around the room. Jal-Maktar helped the Elf to his feet and guided him to his seat. "Ah, well," Jal-Maktar sighed. "So the Gods have nothing to add . . . nothing in the stars can tell us what to do. As usual, we're left to our own devices, and we are wise to heed our own counsel on important matters! Isn't that right, Jardaine?"

"As you say, my lord. The device is ready!"

"Then give me your arms, gentle Elves," Jal-Maktar beamed, "and let us find out who among you is loyal to the cause of freedom—freedom from having to share a world with the Human scum!"

28

THE AIR HAD TURNED CHILLY in Argant as a breeze floated south over the river. Matt saw a police car trawling slowly along East Carson Street, and he hid in the shadows between buildings until it passed. Tomtar and Tuava-Li huddled behind his legs. There was an odd thrill in the air, even though the streets were nearly deserted. Maybe it was a sense of danger, or of possibility, or simply the hope that their fortunes might turn that night. Whatever it was, Matt felt a shiver run down his spine, and he wondered for a moment if his companions felt it, too. A pair of men stood in the doorway of St. Elmo's Firehouse, talking quietly, their hands stuffed into the pockets of their jeans. Matt slowed his gait when he felt the men's gaze burning into him. *They're not Humans,* Tuava-Li said in thought-speak. *They're Trolls.*

"Keep walkin', kid," one of the figures said.

Tuava-Li stepped forward and stood tall before the pair in the doorway. She could see through the illusion that made them appear to be Human, and her eyes met theirs, just a few feet from the ground. "Greetings, in the name of the Mother and her Cord," she said. "May we enter?"

"Do you know my uncle Vollyar?" asked Tomtar, stepping out of the shadows. "I'm from his Clan! I've just come back from my Wanderin'."

"Congratulations," said one of the Trolls, disinterestedly.

"You two can come in," said the other, nodding to Tuava-Li. "The Human keeps walking. Boss's orders."

"We're together," Matt said.

The Troll snorted, glancing up at the boy. "Then you can all take a hike!"

Matt heard a sound from behind, and spun around to see an odd young woman approaching, her high heels clicking on the sidewalk. She wore a bright pink wig with bangs that fell over eyes caked in mascara, and a pair of fashionably dressed Elves strolled comfortably at her side. The Elves chattered animatedly, and the woman threw her head back with a throaty laugh. The figures in the doorway stepped aside to let them pass. Throbbing music spilled out onto the street. "What's going on?" Matt said. "You let *that one* in, and she was human."

"Not like you," said one of the Trolls. "Not everything you see is as it appears."

"Maybe we should just go in, Matt, while you wait outside,"

Tomtar suggested, eager to talk to any Trolls that might help him find his Clan.

Matt shook his head. "I remember what happened at that storage place outside of town. I think we ought to stay together, if we can."

Take off your jacket. The words appeared in his mind. *Show them that you're one of us.*

"I'm *not* one of you," Matt answered in a whisper, glancing at Tuava-Li.

More than you know.

Matt peeled away his jacket and handed it to Tomtar.

The shirt, too.

"What?" Matt mumbled.

Let them see your tattoos.

The amulets and charms Matt wore around his neck rattled as he pulled the T-shirt over his head. He shivered a little in the chilly autumn air, feeling naked and exposed. As he twitched the muscles in his arms, the richly colored vines and leaves seemed to have a life of their own. There were little blue beetles, and a wispy daddy longlegs, and spiders in webs that stretched over his shoulders and disappeared along his back. Matt glanced down and thought he saw something like a wooden figure, with bare limbs like branches, where the tattoo of the church had been. *Now what*, he thought.

The Trolls in the doorway stood slack-jawed as they gazed at Matt's flesh. "Mage's marks," they said, stepping aside.

Matt began to pull his T-shirt back on. "No," said Tuava-Li. "Keep it off. The tattoos are the key to your entry. They may yet open more doors."

"Forget about it," Matt said. "I'll leave the jacket off, but I'm not going in there without a shirt. You'll still be able to see the tattoos on my arms, okay?"

At the end of the hallway they found nothing but a stairwell winding down into darkness. "I thought all these charms and tattoos were supposed to make us inconspicuous," Matt said, "so nobody would get in our way, and now you have me showing off to strangers."

Tuava-Li blinked. "It all depends on the situation, doesn't it?"

"I'll remember you said that, next time I need you to do some of your Mage tricks."

The steps were narrow and a little steep, so Tomtar and Tuava-Li made their way backwards down the old wooden staircase. Matt followed slowly, his hand on the wall for balance. They reached a landing, found a locked door, then turned and followed the pulse of the music down another set of steps. Matt's mind churned with questions. "Why would the trolls change their minds about letting us in, just because of my tattoos?"

"They're not just tattoos," Tuava-Li said, breathing hard. "A Mage wouldn't mark you that way unless you were a very important person."

"Really?" Matt said. "I guess I should feel flattered. Why do you think that tree-man is on my chest?"

"Time will tell," Tuava-Li muttered.

Matt ducked as a pair of Pixies fluttered past his head, giggling and pointing. Finally, three floors beneath the street, they passed a cluster of Elves, Trolls, and Pixies sitting on the steps, slouching against the walls, and talking in boisterous tones. Beyond them was a door. More Faerie Folk moved aside to let Matt and his companions enter. Pools of colored light glowed from niches in the walls of a large, round room. The air pulsed with a deep, hypnotic beat, a booming, liquid sound that enveloped Matt as he stood and stared. *It's a nightclub,* he thought. *And I'm not the only human being in here!*

Matt peered past the crowd of Faerie Folk who were gathered inside the doorway. He noticed the woman with pink hair he had seen outside. He also thought he saw the juggler, Stefan, that they'd met earlier in the day. There were men and women towering over the Faeries, some of them kneeling, some sitting, some standing. All of them looked bizarre and more than a little scary. There was a pair of men dressed in leather, with their black hair shaved halfway up their heads. An older woman wore a headdress that appeared to be made from a tangle of vines. Her earrings were so heavy that her earlobes hung to her shoulders like stretched taffy. The people in the place seemed strange and otherworldly, as if their human identities were just a cover for something else. Matt wondered if he looked as weird to everyone else as they all did to him, but no one seemed to pay the slightest bit of attention as he stood by the door with Tomtar and

Tuava-Li. He realized how far he'd come when it was the humans who looked strange to him, and not the Trolls and Elves and Pixies and Dwarves clustered all around. If some kind of sickness or disease had wiped out a large part of the Faerie population, it was hard to tell from the crowd in this place. "I'm going to see if I can find anyone I know," Tomtar shouted.

Tuava-Li stayed with Matt as he peered into the dim light and tried to make out his surroundings. The walls were painted black. Padded booths were positioned so that customers could eat, drink, and talk in privacy. The most unusual feature of the room was the massive dark object at its center. It looked like a heap of boulders, tree branches, and vines, many times Matt's height. It seemed to be resting in a shallow pool of black water. Figures waited in line to take turns kneeling in a circle around it. "What's that?" he asked Tuava-Li.

"Don't go near it," she replied.

"But why not?" Matt said, feeling strangely drawn toward the base of the mound. "Aren't you curious?"

Tuava-Li watched Matt go on ahead, but didn't try to stop him. Her resistance didn't spring from fear, but an almost infinite sadness that the monstrous dark shape exuded like an odor. The light was very dim. Still, Matt could see the thing was covered with frail roots, like an old potato at the bottom of a pantry, and the Faerie Folk, gathered around the pool, were sucking on them.

It looks like they're drinking through straws, Matt thought, *but*

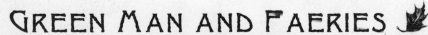

GREEN MAN AND FAERIES

what are they drinking? He reached over a row of Elves and Trolls and touched the mound. It shifted slightly, and Matt yanked back his hand as he realized the thing was alive. Someone laughed and tapped him on the shoulder. Matt turned around to see the juggler, his face gleaming with delight. "Never seen a Green Man?" Stefan shouted.

The music was so loud that Matt thought he'd misheard. "A what?"

"A Green Man. Of course, he's not very green anymore. He used to live in the old railroad tunnels under town, and before that, when humans were still just a gleam in the gods' eyes, he and his kind filled the forests. Most of the faerie folk call him Khidr."

Matt remembered his vision of the figure made from diamonds. He remembered his conversation with Tuava-Li about the constellation in the sky, the one she had called Khidr. The Green Man. Creatures like this one, he thought, must have been the source of the myth reflected in the stars. Now there was an image of something like a green man tattooed on his chest. He glanced at the thing in the pool and shuddered. He stepped away from it, trying to ignore the musty, earthy odor it gave off. "It doesn't look like a man!"

"You haven't seen him when he stands up! Of course, he doesn't do much standing these days. His branches used to be covered with leaves, like a tree—but they've fallen off, after living down here for a while. They had to do some pretty tricky construction work just to get him in here!"

"What are the faerie folk doing with those little roots in their mouths? Are they . . . *eating them*?"

"No," Stefan chuckled. "The Green Man is like one of the gods to them. In fact, he *is* one of the gods, and they're just sharing in its . . . its vital essence, you might say. It's almost like a religious ritual."

"This is a weird place for a religious ritual."

Stefan shrugged. "You take what you can get!"

"Why does the thing stay here? Doesn't it mind having its vital essence sucked away?"

"The folks who own the club say they saved the poor soul from drying out down in the tunnels, and now I suppose he's repaying his debt. Oh, and if you look closely, you'll see he's chained to the floor. Even if he wasn't, though, Green Men are known for their generosity. It's the way things have always been. *Green Man gives, faerie takes.* It used to be that the Green Men had more than enough to share. Their reserves were endless. Sipping from their roots was a faerie's birthright, like drinking water from a cool stream, or nibbling on sweet berries. 'Tis the nature of the Goddess to share the fruits of nature, you know. But now?"

Stefan gestured toward the massive creature. "Everything's changed. The well is nearly dry. You can have a taste if you want," he said. "They haven't sucked the life out of him completely, yet. Go on, no one would mind."

"You've got to be kidding me," Matt said in revulsion.

"It's just like, oh, spinach juice," Stefan said, his eyes twinkling, "or a glass of V8, sucked through a straw. Gives you energy to fight your battles, to find missing clans!"

Matt felt the room closing in around him. For a moment he thought of the tattoo on his chest, and he was anxious to have a moment to look at it again. "See ya around," he said, "I've got to catch up with my people."

"You use the word *people* rather loosely," Stefan said, standing a little too close to Matt. "Your troll friend's in the back. Come with me, I'll take you to him!"

Matt turned away for a moment and tried to form a thought that might be transmitted to Tuava-Li. He'd done it before, and perhaps he could do it again. He let the words take shape in his brain, then let them drift out beyond his own skin and towards the door where he'd left the Elf, like a message in a bottle dropped into an ocean of endless mind. *Is it safe?*

There was an almost immediate reply. *The Belt of Power*, she answered. *You should be able to do it.*

Matt looked at Tuava-Li across the room and now he could feel that there was a subtle force emanating from her body, an invisible field of energy that radiated out from her. He didn't know why he hadn't noticed it before. The corners of her mouth turned up slightly. "Okay," Matt said to Stefan. He focused his energy and imagined a broad belt of energy spinning around his own midsection, a force field to protect him from whatever dangers might lie ahead.

Stefan led Matt down a short flight of steps and along a narrow corridor. Fire Sprites rested on a high ledge, and in the feeble light Matt saw many Faerie creatures he'd never seen before. Some were slumped in corners, weeping softly to themselves, others laughed with manic glee as they swept past Matt's ankles. He was growing used to the sight of Elves, Trolls, Pixies, and Dwarves, but there were many Faeries here that he had no names for. There was a strange mood in the place, like nothing he'd felt before. He kept his focus on the imaginary disc rotating around his waist, while his eyes registered strange and wondrous things, too many to absorb at once. Matt soon found himself in another dank chamber, this one lit primarily by a pair of enormous television screens suspended from the ceiling. Faerie Folk were clustered around tables, and Matt scanned the room for Tomtar. The energy here was coarse and chaotic; the noise was nearly deafening. He saw that Tuava-Li had followed through the crowd to join them. "This is the heart of it all," Stefan said, his arm sweeping the room. "Or perhaps I should say the broken heart of it all."

Matt had to shout to be heard over the hubbub. "What do the faerie folk do down here?"

"You could call it gaming, I suppose, if the stakes weren't so high!"

A woman appeared on the television screens, and the camera panned back to reveal a mechanical device with bouncing plastic balls inside. "And the winning lottery numbers tonight are . . ."

All sound in the room ceased, as abruptly as if someone had flicked a switch.

The woman on the screen read a series of digits, and the numbers flashed on the screen. Squeals of delight erupted from one corner of the room, and the raucous chatter of the others soon returned to its previous volume, as someone switched the channel on the television and a baseball game appeared. Many of the Faerie Folk immediately began to make notes, jotting down numbers and odds. "What are they doing?" asked Matt, incredulous. "Are they . . . are they *gambling*?"

"That they are," said Stefan. "Their addiction here in Argant is . . . Well. You know, of course, about clan jewels? Their importance? Their value?"

"Go on," Matt said warily. He was suddenly glad that he had left the treasure in the old woman's apartment.

The juggler winked. "The faerie folk in Argant no longer have a social structure. No one's secure, no one feels truly at home, ever since the plague that wiped out so many of them." Stefan paused to sip from his drink. "You know, the bird flu. You must have heard about it. It started with the pigeons. It wiped out most of the trolls, and plenty of others, too. Most of them think they've displeased the gods, somehow, and now they're paying the price for it. In any event, with their clans decimated, their treasures scattered and stolen, everyone's desperate. Money's the substitute for the security they once got from their clan jewels, and they'll risk anything to get more of it."

372

"They're gambling for human money? Playing human games?"

"Not just human games," Stefan said. "Faerie games, too. A little Bisanik, a little Hatiya. Everybody wants a piece! Once faerie folk enter the wide world of chance, everything comes into play. They'll bet on something, then bet on who will be the winner of the bet. It's a path with no end! It just goes 'round and 'round."

A group of Elves tossed knucklebones in one corner of the room, as others sat at tables rubbing the foil from lottery tickets, and still others played a game that looked a little like bingo. In Faerie tradition they spit on their knucklebones, breathed on their playing cards, made elaborate gestures and stroked their charms, hoping to invite luck to their tables. A Troll scuttled along the floor on his hands and knees, pushing a battered tennis ball with his nose. Gales of laughter erupted from the gang of Faeries who watched. "When they run out of things to gamble," Stefan said, "they pledge forfeit. They gamble away their pride, until they're reduced to complete humiliation, as you can see."

"Isn't that one of your tennis balls?" Matt asked, watching the Troll squirm through the filth on the dank concrete floor.

"You're clever," Stefan purred. "How would you like to make a small wager with me, just to stay in the spirit of things? Is there something you require? I know your friend wants to find what's left of his clan."

"What do you know about Tomtar's clan?"

Stefan smiled and drew a pair of knucklebones from his pocket. Matt felt the skin on his cheeks growing tight. "Can't you just tell me where the Vollyar clan lives?"

The juggler tossed one of his knucklebones high into the air, spun around, and caught it in his teeth. "Cha-*chiiing*," he sang.

"Look, I'm not going to gamble with you," Matt said. "I haven't got anything you want, anyway."

The juggler scowled. "We both know that's not so! Each of us has something we want from the other."

"All right," Matt conceded, as doubt flooded his brain. He turned to Tuava-Li, who stood as still as a block of stone. *Read his mind*, he said in thought-speak. *Read his mind, and we can get out of here. He knows where Tomtar's clan lives. Come on, Tuava-Li, read his mind!*

When the Elf failed to respond, Matt realized his own thoughts were too confused, too troubled to reach her. He tried to still the rising panic in his brain, but it was no use. The room was full of doubt and suspicion, anger, resentment, and fear riding on the back of fragile hope. He was picking up on it; he was letting it overwhelm him. Tuava-Li could help him, if she wanted, but the odds of that weren't good. She wouldn't consider this to be enough of an emergency to bend her own precious rules. "Why can't you be straight with me?" he asked Stefan. "What are you even doing here? You're just a human, like me! Why do the faerie folk accept you in their world?"

"My, my," Stefan laughed nervously, his hands fluttering

before him. "I might ask the same of you! Come on, just for fun. You pick out three numbers, between one and seven. I'll roll the die, and if it lands on one of the numbers you've chosen, I'll answer one of your questions."

Matt narrowed his eyes. "And what do I have to give you if I lose?"

Stefan shrugged. "You answer one of mine."

"*Ooookay*," Matt said tentatively. He glanced at Tuava-Li for confirmation that this wasn't a very bad idea. Her head was turned away, her face buried in shadows. Was she doing one of her exercises? Was she listening for something? He realized it was his own judgment that he would have to rely on. Better not to count on Tuava-Li too much, even here in this strange place. "All right, I choose . . . two, three, and five."

Stefan tossed one of the knucklebones onto the edge of a table and watched it roll. "Five! You win. That wasn't too hard, was it?" He leaned back in his seat. "Now for your reward. I'll answer one of your questions, and tell you what I'm doing here."

"No," Matt said, "I want you to tell me where we can find Tomtar's clan!"

"I didn't promise which of your questions I'd answer," Stefan said. "Now as I was saying, I was raised from an early age by a family of elves, who stole me from my human family when I was just a baby. They replaced me with a little doll made of straw. I imagine my birth mother wasn't very happy about it, but my elfin mother was delighted. I may be a human in body, but in spirit, I'm all elf! I've lived here in Argant for nearly two hundred years."

"That's a stupid story," Matt said, turning away. "If you're going to lie to me, you might as well make it interesting. You probably don't even know where Tomtar's clan is. I'm going to find my friend."

"Suit yourself!"

"Come," whispered Tuava-Li. "They're talking about Brahja-Chi, right over there in the corner. Tomtar's with them, by the far wall."

Tomtar stood in the shadows, his back turned to Matt. He flinched when his friend touched his shoulder. Elves and Trolls crowded around a table, placing their bets.

"I say she gets five hundred," an Elf said.

"A thousand," snorted a Troll, scribbling on a piece of paper.

"Twelve hundred," said another.

"Anybody else in?" asked a Dwarf in a silk vest with a ruffled tie around his neck. He was apparently the one collecting the wagers. "How many will Brahja-Chi take in the Acquisition? Place your bets now!"

A thought occurred to Matt. "If I wanted to go to Helfratheim to see the Acquisition, how would I get there?"

Everyone at the table, except for Tuava-Li and Tomtar, began to laugh.

"Nobody knows that," the Dwarf said, his chin jiggling over the collar of his shirt.

"Yes they do," Matt replied. "If children are being stolen and taken to Helfratheim, there have to be a lot of faeries who know how to get there."

"Not here, there're not," said the Dwarf. "We're not players in *that* game. We're just laying odds on the outcome. Now if you want to make a bet, you do it through me. One of Brahja-Chi's monks will bring the results after it's all over and done with."

"What outcome?" Matt asked. "What happens when she's done collecting kids?"

"So many questions," came a voice over Matt's shoulder, "so little time!"

Matt turned around to see Stefan, smiling innocently. He stroked his chin. "I don't know what Brahja-Chi's plans are, but I *do* know where the troll's clan is holed up here in Argant. What's it worth to you to find out?"

Matt turned to Tomtar. "Have you been asking around? What have you learned?"

"No one would tell me anything."

"No one here is *affiliated*," Stefan explained. "They're all without a clan, or they wouldn't be here. They'd be with their own kind. We love the castoffs, the vagabonds, the wanderers, the lost and homeless. That's why *you're* here, after all!"

"We're not lost," Matt said impatiently. "We just haven't reached our destination yet."

"Whatever," said Stefan, turning to Tomtar. "If anyone here besides me knows anything about your uncle, my good troll, there must be reasons for them to keep their lips sealed. I have no reason *not* to tell you, except that it pleases me to make a little sport of it!"

"If you know where Tomtar's uncle lives," Matt said, "I'll pay you to tell me. I've got money. How much do you want?"

Stefan chucked. "That's not how it's done," he said. "Come!"

He led Matt to a long table, where a Dwarf with a long black beard sat. The Dwarf handed each of them a pair of wooden cups, a fistful of small gray knucklebones, and two pouches of wooden chips. "I'll go first," Stefan said, "to show you how the game is played."

Stefan placed the knucklebones in the cup, shook it, and then turned the cup over on the table. He lifted the lid just enough so that he could see the results of the toss, but Matt could not. "I have a pair of fours," he said. "Your toss has to beat mine, or I win one of your chips. We play until the chips are gone. The ranking is standard for knucklebones."

"What does that mean?" Matt asked.

"It's just like a game of cards. It shouldn't be hard to beat a pair of fours."

"I don't know how to play your stupid game!"

"I do," Tomtar said. "I'll help you."

"Very good," said Stefan. "Now put your money on the table."

Matt threw a wad of bills on the table. "That's all we have."

Faerie Folk began to gather around. "Five on Stefan," said an Elf.

A group of Pixies, fluttering in the air, placed a small bet on Matt. Matt furrowed his brow. He knew it was likely he was going to be cheated, or tricked, somehow. Still, if Stefan knew about Tomtar's uncle, Matt had to take the chance. He would have gladly paid the money outright for the information they needed. But if he lost the game, he'd end up with nothing. "This game stinks," he said. "How do I know you're telling the truth about the numbers on the dice you rolled, if you won't let me see them?"

"You don't," Stefan grinned. "The game's not called Liar's Knucklebones for nothing. If you think I'm lying, you can challenge me, and I'll show you the knucklebones. If you're correct, I give you a chip. But if it turns out I was telling the truth, you give a chip to me. See?"

Matt rolled the knucklebones. He won the first chip. He couldn't help but wonder if Stefan was toying with him, and he searched the juggler's eyes, hoping to gain some advantage. He lost the next two rounds. When Stefan claimed to have rolled five of a kind, Matt challenged him, and lost another chip. A few of the Faerie Folk in the crowd placed small bets on Matt, but the tide soon turned in Stefan's favor; it was clear that Matt was going to lose. They gathered in a great circle around the contestants just to relish the Human's defeat. When he handed his last chip to Stefan, the crowd roared with delight. Stefan pocketed Matt's roll of money.

"I'm done," Matt said, grabbing his jacket from the back

of his chair. He looked out over a sea of pale faces, and each pockmarked and grimacing Faerie leered at him with scorn and contempt. "Loser," one of them muttered, as Matt pushed his way through the crowd.

"What?" he said, and his feet stopped moving.

"Keep going," Tomtar said.

Don't, Tuava-Li warned in thought-speak.

Matt glared at the Elf who had insulted him and grabbed him by his collar. Before he had a chance to utter a word of reproach, another Elf had leapt onto his back, pounding with hard little fists. Dwarves, Brownies, and Trolls kicked him in the shins, and Matt screamed when he felt someone's teeth on his thigh. He thought of the Belt of Power, and tried to imagine it spinning in a wheel of protection around him, but it was too late. Suddenly everyone was screaming, punching, and clawing, and Matt fell to the filthy concrete floor. When he got up, he was tossing Faerie Folk out of his way, struggling for the stairwell and escape. Tomtar and Tuava-Li were left behind. They were helpless to stop the melee between the Human and the Faeries, though Tuava-Li tried to spread feelings of peace into the heart of the battle. The Faeries were out of control, channeling all their hatred for the Human species into this assault on one boy.

Matt fought his way to the door, forgetting his anger, fending off the Faeries' blows as best he could. When he got to the stairwell he lunged up the stairs two at a time. Pixies fluttered in the air and let out cries of dismay as Matt rushed past them.

He tumbled onto the street as the Troll bouncers cursed him and gave him a final kick in the pants. "Don't ever come back," they cried. Matt made his way across the street, and stood panting in an alley. *Tuava-Li,* he thought, trying to use thought-speak like the Elf did. *If you can hear me, get Tomtar and come out. I'm all alone out here.*

Stefan stood by the gaming table in the depths of the building, surrounded by Faerie Folk, and shuddered. "I hope you're not planning to treat me that way," he said to Tomtar. "I'm not really a human, you know. I just play one, professionally."

"Play with me!" Tomtar said.

Stefan grinned and shook his head. "You've got nothing left to gamble with, my friend. I've got all your money right here in my pocket!"

"Not quite." Tomtar moved in close to Stefan and revealed a glittering diamond, the size of a small grape, in the palm of his hand.

"Where did you get that?" Tuava-Li demanded, knowing full well that the Troll must have taken it from one of the pouches they'd hidden in the old lady's closet.

"Please," Tomtar said, looking up at the juggler. "Play with me, and if I win, you tell me where I can find my uncle. If I lose, this Jewel belongs to you."

"Fair enough," Stefan crooned, eyeing the diamond with

greedy delight. He passed Tomtar a wooden cup, a stack of chips, and five tiny knucklebones.

Half an hour later, Tomtar and Tuava-Li greeted Matt in the alley across from the club. Tomtar was beaming, and clutching a scrap of paper in his hand. On the paper was the address of an abandoned school building, just a half a mile away. "What took you guys so long?" Matt asked. "And what's that?"

"The address of Vollyar's headquarters, and I won it fair and square," Tomtar answered. "I found a diamond in my pocket and Stefan wanted to keep playing. We played Liar's Knucklebones, and I won! Tuava-Li made me give him the diamond, though, to keep him quiet."

"Why would we want to keep him quiet?" Matt asked, a little angry that the Troll had taken something from their stash without telling him, and angrier still that Tuava-Li had given it away.

"'Twould be best if Stefan doesn't tell the world that we have Jewels," Tuava-Li said. "I suggested that Tomtar give him the stone, on his promise to keep it to himself."

"And you trust Stefan?"

"We have to," Tomtar said.

"The guy's a cheat. I'm surprised he let you win, Tomtar."

"He didn't *let* me win," exclaimed the Troll. "I may not be clever, like Tuava-Li and you, but I know how to play games! 'Tis all right, Matt, I know how you felt about me bringing you here, about how dumb it made me look when we couldn't find

Uncle Vollyar and the maps. But now we've got the address, and it's all because of me!" Grinning from ear to ear, he poked his chest with a thumb as he marched along the pavement.

"You made more than a few enemies at the club tonight," Tuava-Li said to Matt. "I don't know why you have to get into a fight every time you're around Faerie Folk."

"It wasn't my fault," Matt said. "I never want to go back in there, anyway. The place gave me the creeps."

Headlights appeared on the brick beside them, and Matt turned to see a police car approaching. "In here," he hissed, and pulled his companions back into the alley. A few seconds later the vehicle crawled past. A flashlight beam from the passenger side swept along the brick wall, and was gone. There was a sound, further down the alley, and Matt stiffened. "'Tis only a rat," whispered Tuava-Li. "I saw it scampering in the garbage there."

Matt poked his head back onto the street. "All clear," he said. "You know we're going to be in deep trouble if Stefan and his buddies come after us for the rest of the jewels. It only makes sense. Where there's one jewel, there are bound to be more."

The street was dark and still. The tired old buildings lining the sidewalks were locked and shuttered, their lights extinguished. The only sound was the faint rustle of the wind. "You don't have to worry, we're not being followed," Tuava-Li said. She gazed above the scattered trees and buildings and pointed into the night sky. "Look, 'tis the Green Man!"

Matt thought he saw the faint green glow of a distant star,

but the rest of the configuration was only a jumble of twinkling lights. "Like that thing in the basement? I'll tell you, Tuava-Li, that pathetic lump down there isn't some kind of god. It's pitiful, the way it just lies there in a pool of muck and lets all of the faerie folk suck its blood, or its essence, or whatever. It's disgusting. When I think of it being tattooed on my chest, I feel like it's some cosmic joke, like the world's trying to tell me I'm weak and powerless, too. I think Stefan was being sarcastic when he called it a green man, just because it's nothing at all like what you said about the myth. Look, if you want to believe in fairy tales, go ahead, but really—if that thing in the basement is so powerful, why doesn't it yank up its chains and walk away?"

"His power is gone," said Tuava-Li. "He's suffered the same fate as the Cord, if you think about it."

"Please," Tomtar said. "I'm happy tonight. I'm going to see my uncle, who's going to help us get where were going. I did something right, and I feel good. Let's be cheerful, all right?"

"I am cheerful," said Matt, frowning.

Tuava-Li scuffed along on her satin slippers. They were already coming apart. "I believe I'd be better off flying."

"Whatever," Matt said, staring ahead. Before him he saw a traffic light turn from red to green. Leaves swayed imperceptibly on dark trees lining the sidewalk. Behind he could hear the pulling, scratching sounds that the Elf made when she underwent her transformation. The change always made him feel awkward and disturbed. He looked over at Tomtar, and forced himself to smile.

29

THE SCHOOL BUILDING LOOKED LONELY and forlorn in the moonlight. Its windows were boarded up with rotting plywood, its roof sagged, and the chimneys on either end were toppled. An eight-foot chain-link fence capped with razor wire wrapped the entire structure neatly, separating it from the other derelict buildings that were its neighbors. Tuava-Li swooped down to the broken concrete on the ground and began her transformation. "When I left," Tomtar whispered, handing over her wrinkled dress and plastic shoes, "anybody could walk right up to this place. Sure, the Humans had abandoned it, it wasn't perfect, but . . ." He shook his head, as his memories of growing up began to falter in the face of the ruined building that stood before them now. He took some *trans* from his pocket and handed a piece to the Elf. Both of them put the slivers of bark in their mouths and began to chew.

Matt watched their little jaws moving up and down, like they were working on wads of gum. He could almost see the bubbles they'd blow. "Is that for the metal?" he asked.

Tomtar nodded. "It's more or less the same stuff we used to chew when I lived here. Let's walk around back and see if there's anywhere we can get in."

"It looks deserted," Matt said. "I wonder if we've been had."

"Nooo," said Tomtar, mired in memories of his childhood. "This is the place. This is where I lived."

"I don't mean, like, we have the wrong building, Tomtar, I mean there's no sign of life here, at all!"

"Someone's here," Tuava-Li whispered, "I can feel danger. 'Tis time to use the Belt of Power."

Matt looked up at the darkened building and shivered a little. *I guess it can't hurt to try*, he thought, *though it didn't do me much good at St. Elmo's Firehouse.* He pictured a rotating disc of protective energy around him, and crept along the chain-link fence.

Carefully they made their way around the side of the old brick building, looking for any movement in the weeds and rubble. The moonlight threw long shadows on the ground. Tuava-Li kept an eye on the roofline, three stories up, while Matt and Tomtar searched for an opening in the fence. In the back, where the parking lot was overgrown with scrub bushes and grass that stretched up past his head, Tomtar found a gate with a series of locks on it. "Look," he whispered excitedly. "Maybe Tuava-Li can open these up, like she did before!"

There was an imposing padlock tethered to a steel chain. A little farther down the pole were a couple of rusty combination locks, the kind Matt used to have on his locker at school. "These locks don't mean anything," Matt said, forgetting once more the protective wheel around his waist. "Anybody with a decent pair of metal clippers could get into this place in a second, just by cutting through the fence."

"We don't have anything like that," Tomtar said. "Tuava-Li, can you—"

When the Troll stopped in mid-sentence, Matt glanced down to see the look of panic on Tuava-Li's face. "Look out," she cried as she lunged sideways.

A blow across Matt's back sent him reeling. He found himself face down on the ground, with strong hands pulling his arms behind his back. A group of Trolls, twelve in all, had sprung from the darkness. Matt could smell their sharp odor, strong and oppressive, and he felt like he was being suffocated. He heard Tomtar cry out, and a scream caught in his own throat as pain sliced at his wrists. They were binding him up with wire. "Get off me," he cried, his voice muffled beneath the rough clothing of his attackers. He wished that he'd had his knife in his hand instead of in his pocket.

Suddenly one of the Trolls fell, like a marionette that had been cut from its strings. Another fell, and then another. "The female," shouted their leader. "Stop her! She's—"

As the fourth Troll fell to the ground, the others surrounding Tuava-Li backed away, fearful of what she might do. Though

Matt was lying with his cheek pressed against the broken concrete, he thought he could actually see the Belt of Power spinning around Tuava-Li. No one dared get too close to her. Whatever she had done to the Elf and Pixies back at the storage facility outside of town, she had done once again, and the Trolls were afraid. One of them pressed a knife against Tomtar's throat. "Stop what you're doing, witch, or this one dies!"

Tomtar cried out. "I grew up here, Vollyar is my uncle! Doesn't anybody recognize me? I'm Tomtar!"

"What do you want?" one of the Trolls demanded, as several others hoisted Tomtar to his feet. They all kept their distance from Tuava-Li.

"I've come to see my uncle. I'm back from my Wanderin'. This is my—this was my home, I—I—"

"Why are you with an Elf and a Human?" the Troll demanded. "Tell the truth—why are you really here? Are you one of Sattye's spies?"

"We came here for a map," Matt said, his voice full of pain as he worked himself up on his knees. Once again he imagined the Belt of Power spinning around him. He felt the force radiating outward, and this time the Trolls who had been holding him down jerked away like they'd received an electric shock. "We just wanted to get a map that Tomtar told us his uncle Vollyar used to have. That's all we want. We just want to get the map, and then get out of this town. We have to find a place called Helfratheim. That's the only reason we're here. I swear!"

"And we need maps to take us to the North Pole, too," Tuava-Li added, irked by Matt's omission. "We need maps of the Faerie realm as well as the Human realm. We're on a quest, at the command of the Mage of Alfheim."

"Alfheim?" one of the Trolls smirked. "You're a long way from home."

"This *was* my home," Tomtar said helplessly. "Who are you? What happened to my uncle?"

"We're soldiers. And Vollyar's dead."

Tomtar's face sagged. A low moan, meanwhile, came from one of the Trolls that Tuava-Li had struck down with her magick. He lifted his head and looked around. The others came to their senses, too, and slowly got to their feet. Tuava-Li kept her eyes on them, ready to knock them out again if necessary. "Look," Matt said, "we don't mean you any harm. Can you help us? Can you take us to whoever's in charge here?"

Several of the Trolls laughed mirthlessly. One of the others stepped forward and grabbed Tomtar by the arm. Tomtar could see that he was missing one of his ears; a ragged scar ran down his cheek. "Don't let your eyes off these two," the Troll commanded, glancing at Matt and Tuava-Li. "Keep your blade against the Human's throat. I'll take this one to the boss."

A pair of Trolls unlocked the gate and lifted a sheet of plywood that lay on the ground, just inside the fence. Under the plywood was a hole, no more than two feet wide, descending into blackness. "Down you go," the Troll with the scar growled. He shoved Tomtar into the opening.

Matt watched his friend disappear into the hole and he wished that he'd been able to give him his knife. He wondered if Tomtar would have been willing or able to use it, if the need arose, but at least he'd be armed. Of course, with a blade pressed against his own throat, Matt knew that having a knife in his pocket wasn't doing him much good.

Tomtar spit dirt from his mouth as he crept along the narrow passage on his hands and knees. Nothing had gone like he had hoped it would, and now he felt certain that it would all end very badly, and possibly very soon. The Troll behind him jabbed his back with a sharp finger. "Get moving!"

Before long the passage turned upward. Tomtar saw a short wooden ladder ahead of him. "We've got company," the Troll shouted, and the sound of his voice made Tomtar jump. A ring of Fire Sprites hovered at the top of the hole, lighting the view for the Trolls that stood above, their hands twitching on the handles of wicked-looking daggers.

Tomtar hesitated, then felt the finger of the Troll prodding him once more. "I didn't say *stop*! Climb up that ladder and tell the boss your name!"

Rough hands grabbed Tomtar as he exited from the hole. They forced him to the cracked linoleum floor and held him there, face down. "Who are you?" boomed a powerful voice.

Tomtar's cheek stung. He felt wetness, and couldn't tell if it was tears or blood. "I'm Tomtar, nephew of Vollyar Ingeborg. Please, I didn't do anything wrong!"

"Coming here was wrong," the voice said. "Let him up. He's harmless."

Tomtar stared in astonishment at the figure standing before him in the flickering light.

"Uncle Orin!" he cried. "Am I glad to see you!"

The Troll stood with his hands on his hips and he shook his head. His grim smile was nearly lost in a long black beard. "I didn't recognize you, Tomtar. You've grown!"

Tomtar took in the sight of his uncle Orin, who cast an enormous shadow on the peeling wall. They were in what had once been the principal's office of the old school. Later, it had been Vollyar's private quarters; now it appeared to be the home of Orin and his band of soldiers. Orin pressed Tomtar into a chair facing the principal's desk. All of the chair and table legs had been sawed down to make them the right height for a Troll. Orin went to the other side of the desk, sloshed some greenish liquid into a glass, and pushed it across the splintered wood. He gestured for Tomtar to drink. "Why are you here?" he asked.

"Well, first of all, I'm back from my Wanderin'," Tomtar said hesitantly, perched on the edge of his chair. He hoped that he might hear some congratulation from his uncle for completing the coming-of-age ritual practiced by all Trolls his age. After a moment of awkward silence he took a sip of the liquid and continued. "Secondly, I was hoping that I could get some maps. I know Uncle Vollyar kept the important documents and the Clan Jewels in a safe place, and I thought that he would share the maps with me. I have to—"

"The maps and Clan Jewels are all gone," Orin interrupted.

Tomtar's heart sank. "Gone?"

Orin shrugged. "Everything's changed. We thought *you* were gone. When you left, none of us thought we'd ever see your face again."

"I—I was on my Wanderin'," he said. "A Troll always comes back from his Wanderin'. I brought back my friends, Tuava-Li and Matt, as my Gift. I have many stories to tell!"

Orin sat back in his chair and shook his head. "Then it's too bad that we have no time to listen. The world you knew is gone, Tomtar. Vollyar's dead. He and his daughters survived the plague that tore through Argant in the days right after you left, but we were weak and couldn't stand up to Sattye when his Clan came to fight. They took over most of our territory. They stole the Clan Jewels, the documents, the maps, the treasures we'd managed to hide away, and many of us were killed. If you'd returned just a little earlier, you'd have found Vollyar still alive. But Sattye's Trolls cut off my brother's head, and that's why you're looking at me now instead of him."

Tomtar turned away, sorrow fluttering in his throat. He blinked back tears. "How did it happen?"

"It was a raid," Orin said. "Argant is carved into two factions now. 'Tis us, and them. You'd think that controlling half of everything would be enough for the greedy scum, but it isn't."

"What about my cousins?" Tomtar whispered, terrified at what the answer might be. "Megala, Mitelle, Delfina? Are they dead, too?"

"They might as well be," Orin said darkly. "They're traitors, the three of them. They turned your uncle over to the Sattye Clan, for a handful of Clan Jewels."

"What?" Tomtar gasped. "It's not true! They'd never, it can't be, it . . ."

"It is what it is," Orin said dismissively.

Tomtar swallowed. "I want to help! For Vollyar's sake!"

Orin's face hardened. "Then take your friends and leave. We have no use for you here. Go back where you came from and leave the fighting to us."

"But Vollyar—"

"Vollyar's gone, and there's nothing you can do to avenge him. You're not a soldier, Tomtar, you never were. That's why Vollyar sent you on your Wandering, so you'd be safe from what he knew would happen here after the plague."

Orin nodded to his soldiers, who stood in a line behind Tomtar with their knives, hatchets, and cleavers held in twitching hands. "Take him back outside."

Someone gave Tomtar's chair a yank and he fell forward. Catching himself, he watched his uncle come around from behind the desk. "Good-bye," Orin said, offering a hand to his nephew.

"'Tis hard being a Troll in these times. I apologize for being harsh. I wish we had time to honor your return. We fight too much, and celebrate too little. That's how the game of survival is played. Too bad your Wandering was for nothing."

"It wasn't for nothing," Tomtar said. "Good-bye, Uncle."

His voice felt hollow and distant. He followed a soldier back down the ladder into the earthen tunnel. It felt like miles as he crept through the blackness, utterly defeated. The soldier scurried ahead, lifted the plywood lid that hid the entrance to the hole, and ordered the Trolls guarding Matt and Tuava-Li to release them. By the time Tomtar reached the end of the tunnel, his companions were waiting just outside the gate. Tuava-Li glowered in the cold moonlight as Matt rubbed his wrists where the wire had cut his skin. The Trolls kept their eyes on Tomtar and his friends until they were out of sight.

Tomtar hurried ahead of his companions on the empty sidewalk. He pumped his arms and legs to keep his distance, and he made sure they couldn't see his face. "Wait up," Matt said.

Both Matt and Tuava-Li knew that their situation looked bad. If Tomtar had come out of that dirty tunnel wearing a smile, if he'd had the courage to meet their gaze, they might have had some reason to hope. "What did you discover?" Tuava-Li called.

Tomtar stopped and spun around, his face stricken. "My uncle's dead, and the maps are gone. My other uncle, Orin, is in charge now. But he doesn't like me, and he never has. He ordered me to leave and not come back. There. Does that make you happy?"

"No," Matt said bitterly. "We're not happy at all. I don't even know why you'd say something like that. It's not our fault you got everything wrong. This whole trip has been a joke, and now we're worse off than we were when we started! What are we supposed to do now?"

Tuava-Li blew out a weary gust of breath. "We have to move forward. We must continue to the Pole, even without a map. No one said this would be easy."

"Easy?" Matt said. "What about *possible*?"

"We don't know what's possible until we try."

"Okay, we can get maps to show us the way to the North Pole," Matt said. "I'll just go into a bookstore tomorrow and pick up an atlas, or something. Or maybe we can find what we need at the public library. But that won't tell us how to get to Helfratheim. There has to be somebody in this town that's been there, taking kidnapped kids for Brahja-Chi! We've got to find somebody who knows!"

Tomtar saw his friend's despair and what was left of his confidence collapsed. "This is the end of the road," he cried. "'Tis all my fault."

"No, it isn't," Matt replied wearily. He put a hand on Tomtar's shoulder.

"This isn't about you, and I guess it's not about me, either. I'm sorry for getting upset. This is way too big a job for the three of us. But I said it before, we'll get through it . . . somehow." Matt could feel the falseness in what he was saying; he didn't even believe it himself. He was far too tired to try very hard. "We'll do what we can, and maybe, just maybe, it'll be enough."

"I'll try again to contact the Mage," said Tuava-Li. "If only she knew it was urgent, maybe she'd hear my thought-speak."

"Next step," Matt sighed. "We'll go back to Mrs. Babcek's and get some rest. Maybe my tattoos will give us some more clues about what we can expect, who knows? We'll pick up your new shoes tomorrow, and cash in some more jewels, and see if we can't figure out what to do from there."

"And what?" Tomtar asked in a shaking voice. "What will we do from there? Just go north? Just stay on Human roads, and hope that we can find a way back into the Faerie realm when we get near the Pole?"

"That may be what Fada did in ancient times," Tuava-Li said. "He didn't have maps, either. Maybe the heroes of our legends were forced to act with more faith than sense. Quests don't come with handbooks."

"Let's get a move on," Matt said. "I'm tired, and it's way after curfew. I don't want to spend the night in jail."

Inside the crumbling school building, Orin gulped a glass of the green liquid. He waved his soldiers away and headed down a flight of stairs to the dank and mildewed basement. His Fire Sprite hovered in front of his shoulder, lighting the way in the darkness. There were a few inches of foul water on the floor. Rats scampered along overhead pipes, and the sound of their chatter echoed down the corridors. Orin sloshed ahead, humming to himself. Finally he came to the custodian's office. An old broom leaned against the wall and a faded newspaper clipping hung from a strip of tape on the door. Orin turned the rusty handle and a groan echoed inside the room. "Vollyar," Orin called, "time for supper. I hope you're hungry!"

The smell in the room was rank. A Troll was strapped to a steel-topped school desk, tipped on its side in the darkness. "Look what I've brought you," Orin said.

As the Fire Sprite hovered above the brothers' heads, Orin broke the eyes from a withered potato and placed the little white stumps between Vollyar's lips. Though his teeth were gray and loose, a toxic effect of a Faerie's exposure to metal, Vollyar did his best to gum the little pieces of vegetable matter that his brother offered. He was slowly starving, after all.

"Have you given any more thought to telling me where you hid the rest of the Clan treasure?" Orin asked with icy calm. "'Tis not good to keep secrets. Here's something you *don't* know, brother! Guess who came to visit here today—our young nephew Tomtar, back from his Wandering! He brought a Human and an Elf with him, as the Gift he wanted to share with the Clan. In return he asked me to give him maps of Elf realm, and the Human realm, and Gods know what else. Funny, I never thought that one would amount to anything. I still don't, as a matter of fact. But if you'd told me where you hid all of the valuables of this Clan, perhaps I'd have been willing to help the lad with a few of the things he needed. Instead, I told him you were dead, and sent him on his way."

Vollyar mumbled incoherently. He was strapped to the desktop with vines, strong and thick as barbed wire, and the thorns pricked his flesh whenever he attempted to move. His back was covered in sores where it touched the metal; his hands trembled convulsively. "Some say the only true wealth is one's health," Orin said. "I'm inclined to disagree, but maybe that's just me. I *do* know that it's hard to hold on to the truly valuable things in life. I've done my best to protect the part of the treasure my Trolls managed to find; you'd be proud, Vollyar, of the way I've beaten you at your own game. You hid the Jewels well from us, but not well enough. We think we must have about half of them now. Whilst searching for the rest of the Clan Jewels, we came upon a pair of Green Men in an old railroad tunnel underground. They're brothers, Vollyar, just like the two of us! I imagine there aren't too many of them left in the world anymore. It wasn't easy, but we abducted the weaker of the pair. We let the other one know that we'd kill his brother unless he agreed to safeguard our hidden treasure."

Orin paused, pursing his lips. "I'll tell you, Vollyar, I don't spend half the night now worrying that someone's going to steal my Jewels. Now I just toss and turn, worrying about finding the rest of the treasure, and what will happen to you if you don't tell me where it is. What can I do to convince you that I need to know? Vollyar? Vollyar?"

Orin touched his brother's face. "Ah, unconscious again." He turned a crank at the side of the desk, which had been adapted to rotate the steel top on a pivot.

"I hate to do this, I really do," he said, as he lowered the Troll headfirst into the mucky water on the floor. After a moment of watching bubbles rise from the darkness he gave the crank another turn and Vollyar came up, sputtering. "You monster," he coughed, "I'll never tell you where the rest of the Clan treasure is. I'll never tell you anything!"

"More's the pity," Orin said with a wry smile. "I'll let you in on a little secret. Sattye's been our enemy for as long as I can remember, but you've become my enemy too, I'm afraid, since you got in the way of my taking the reins of power. Sometimes, as they say, my enemy's enemy is my friend. That's why I'm giving Sattye a sack of Clan Jewels in exchange for one of your daughters. I'll bet you didn't know they all ran over to his side after I took command and locked you up! Don't look so sad, Vollyar, they had nowhere else to go, really, you can't blame them. Sattye's agreed to let us make a 'surprise' attack tomorrow, and he's making sure that we take at least one of your daughters alive. I think maybe when I've got my clutches on someone you care about, you'll tell me what I want to know."

"Never!" Vollyar spat.

Orin sighed. "Never is a very long time, my brother, a very long time!"

30

THE FIRST THING MACTA SAW when he woke up was a goldfinch flitting in the branches of a maple tree, high overhead. Oddly, the sight made him think of breakfast. It seemed a long, long time since he had savored the taste of wild bird flesh. He did not have the strength, at first, to move, so he lay on his back and stared up at the brightening sky. The sun had already been up for an hour or so; the trees were alive with many delicious-looking birds. A breeze drifted past, brushing Macta's sticky face like soft, cool fingers. There was a dull pain in his shoulder, but it seemed at first to float somewhere far away. He felt his chest rising and falling, and as he breathed he grew aware that the inside of his nose was crusty. So were his eyes. He blinked, and went to rub his eyes with the back of his hand.

Macta's screams woke Asra and Becky from their own

exhausted, uncomfortable sleep. They jerked up on their concrete bed and saw the Elf clutching wildly at the crude bandages wrapped around his shoulder. "My arm!" he cried. "My arm! Where did it go?"

Asra raised an eyebrow at Becky, and sighed. "Whatever your herbs did, they brought him around. Now we're bound to have a whole new set of problems to contend with."

Becky scooted closer to Macta so that she could make sure he didn't fall over the edge of the concrete platform. "Macta," she soothed, stroking his forehead, "you've got to lie down and be still. Everything's going to be all right. Asra's right here, with me."

"Where am I?" Macta cried, as tears spilled from his enormous green eyes. "What happened to my arm? What have you done to me, you monster?"

"*I* did it," Asra said matter-of-factly, and brushed the hair from her face. She leaned back against the concrete headboard of the four-poster bed. "I sawed off what was left of your arm so that you wouldn't die, and Becky treated your fever with herbs. It appears you're going to get better now, may the Gods forgive us."

Macta felt woozy, and he lay back down on his hard, cold bed to make the world stop spinning. "I—I wanted your Mage to heal me," he murmured, "but I didn't think she'd cooperate, after all that's happened. Then I thought that if I got home to Helfratheim, the Experimentalists could save my arm. As long as there was some tissue left, I thought they could do something to make it grow back. But if you've cut it off at the shoulder, I'm doomed. It's hopeless. I'll spend the rest of my life as a cripple."

Asra snorted. "There are many different kinds of cripple. Some of them you see with your eyes, and some keep their damage inside."

Once more Macta began to weep. Becky rummaged in her sack and drew out a small pile of leaves. "Here," she said, dangling them over his face to get his attention. "Chew on these, it'll help keep the fever down. I'll make you some special tea, that should make the healing go a little faster."

"Y-you could have killed me with the knife, if you'd wanted," Macta choked, turning his head to steal a glance at Asra. As sunlight streamed down through the torn canopy, her beauty overwhelmed him. Weakly, he took the leaves from Becky and pushed them into his cheek. Chewing them released a bitter juice that burned as it ran down his throat. "You used the knife to save me, in your own misguided way. I would have made it to Helfratheim without your interference, though. A little fever wouldn't have stopped me. I—"

Macta closed his eyes. He felt the sun's warmth on his face, and for a brief moment it seemed to soften his heart. "I realize you only wanted to save me. If you didn't love me, how could you have stood to cut off that rotten meat that hung from my shoulder? That's no job for a Princess. If you didn't love me, you would have left me by the side of the road to die." He turned his head toward Asra and smiled. "Who says that I'm not a lucky fellow?"

"I'm not saying anything," Asra mumbled. "Ask Becky."

Becky went down the ladder and set the Fire Sprite to work beneath the bucket of water. Beyond a row of shrubs, crude concrete turrets rose from another fairy-tale castle. A misshapen dragon, its concrete tongue lolling out of a jagged mouth, was a silent sentinel towering over the trees. In the daylight the amusement park looked neglected and sad. Nature was taking over, pushing up weeds from cracks and littering the attractions in fallen leaves. "Where are we?" Macta asked.

Asra looked out toward the east, and shrugged imperceptibly. "Close to the Cord, I presume, but I'm not absolutely sure. How is your memory of the map you tore to bits?"

Macta felt stung. "Just fine," he said, getting up on his elbow. "How's your memory of the incident in which I saved your life? 'Twas only yesterday that the Humans locked you in a cage like some kind of animal. You showed your gratitude by trying to run away. Remember?"

"You killed my father," Asra said bitterly. "You burned my homeland, you destroyed my mother's mind, you humiliated me, deceived me, and made a mockery of everything I've ever believed. You didn't save my life—you ruined it!"

Macta was sitting up now, his face tight with emotion. "You're wrong, Asra, you're wrong. I set you free! Now you owe me *my* freedom, too . . . *the freedom to reach you. You're* the only

403

obstacle left in my path to you, and if you don't get out of my way—"

"Stop your gibberish," Asra spat. "You're insane!"

"Quit it, both of you!" Becky shouted. The water in the bucket was close to boiling as the Fire Sprite stroked the underside of the pail with fingers of flame. Becky leapt up from the place where she worked to separate the leaves and stood with her hands clenched. "I can't concentrate with the two of you fighting! If I can't get these plants organized, or if I make a mistake, everything will be ruined. Macta will die, and my parents will die, and I might as well just die, too. Don't you understand? Can't we work together, just a little? Can't you control yourselves?"

Asra was green with fury. She got up from the concrete mattress, looked over the edge at the ladder, and realized it was far too steep for her to climb down safely. She had never gone down a slide before, but she sat on the edge of the winding metal ramp and let gravity do its work. When she reached the bottom she sucked in her breath, amazed that anyone would go down a slide for the sake of amusement. She turned angrily toward Becky, her finger pointing. "Don't you dare tell me to control myself! I'm only here now because I felt I owed you my help. This whole journey has been nothing but an exercise in controlling myself, ever since we left the forest of Ljosalfar. If you're going to speak to me in this way, I'll—"

"Please don't point your finger at me," Becky interrupted. "The Mage said that's how you put curses on people."

"*I* don't put curses on people," Asra said. She swept her hair back over her shoulders and tried to regain her composure. "If I had the talent for curses, though, I might have used the skill to my advantage once or twice!"

"Let the girl get back to her work," Macta said, leaning over the edge of the bed. "Please."

Breathing out an exhausted sigh, he rolled over onto his back and watched scraps of cloud drifting overhead. Too many times his hopes, like the clouds, had floated past just out of reach. "I apologize to both of you," he murmured. "Please forgive my rudeness, my ungratefulness, and Asra, please forgive me for my very existence. My little book is filled with marks showing the outcome of my bets, and 'tis true, I have always loved to win. But I've never learned how to win your heart, and I've never been very good at learning from my many mistakes. I am truly sorry."

"He's still delirious," Asra said. "Otherwise he'd never say such things."

"Maybe he's not as bad as he seems," Becky mused, stirring the herbs in the pot with a twig.

"Nooo," Asra said. "He's not as bad as he seems . . . he's worse."

By the time the sun was directly overhead Macta felt well enough to walk. His recollection of the Elfin map, combined with Becky's diagram on the back of the Fairytale Village brochure, made their trip through the woods relatively easy. They followed along the edge of the highway just out of sight of an occasional passing car. Though they stopped to rest many times, Macta seemed to be growing stronger and more confident with each passing hour. As his pain diminished, his bravado seemed to return. But he managed to avoid any speculation about Asra's role in the kingdom he was about to inherit, and he refrained from his endless reminders about how he had saved her life.

After a while the road on which they were traveling narrowed and curved to the right. The foliage had already grown dry and skimpy by the time they passed a roadblock and saw their first WARNING—DANGER! sign. Becky led the Elves over the cracked and buckled concrete road into the town. The few remaining houses were deserted, with falling shingles and collapsed porches. There were abandoned cars, too, sitting on flattened tires by curbsides and in crumbling driveways.

"The Human world is horrible," Asra said, gazing about. "Everything here is so ugly. What do we do now?"

Becky held a hand over her eyes and scanned the wasted landscape. "We have to find the mines."

"The Troll back in the other Human town said that you'd have to find the fifth mine," Macta volunteered. "The farthest from the others."

Asra's eyes grew wide. "How would you know what the Troll said? Were you there?"

"I won't deny that I was following you," Macta said.

"*Stalking me*, you mean."

"As unsavory as it seems, 'twas the only way. I would have

spoken to you earlier, if I'd known what to say. The sight of you, Asra, makes it hard for me to think clearly."

Asra clenched her jaw. "You would have spoken to us earlier, only you were afraid to come near until Radik was dead. You're a coward, Macta, admit it."

Macta spat out the herbs he'd been chewing. "Would a coward have taken down those Humans with the blowguns I found in Radik's sack?"

Asra stalked ahead, unable to bear any more bickering. "Look there," Becky cried. She was pointing to a rusty railroad track that disappeared around a hillside, covered in dead and stunted trees. "I think that's the way to the mines!"

They trudged along the abandoned track until it forked, and Macta volunteered to roll his knucklebones to help choose the path they'd follow next. Becky decided to humor him as she had no idea of which way to go, and one path seemed as good as the other. Asra stood with her back to the pair of them. She was anxious, and impatient, and knew that they were approaching the last leg of their journey together. The thought of escaping still loomed large in her mind, despite her promise to Becky. If she were going to risk running away, it would have to be soon. She studied a row of metal pipes that jutted from the hillside. Smoke rolled from the tops and drifted heavily over blackened treetops. The air was ominously hot.

"There's too much metal around here," Macta complained, squatting in the weeds twenty feet from the iron rails. "'Tis making me sick. Girl, give me some more of those herbs. Somehow they make me feel better."

Asra turned with an expression of mock surprise. "What? Even the mighty King of Helfratheim is sickened by metal?"

Macta scowled. "Without the tinctures the Experimentalists prepare for us, we're as weak as any other Elves. You've been privileged to see many of my flaws, Asra, but my greatest weakness, should you need to be reminded, is my weakness for you."

Asra looked away, ignoring Macta's attempt at sweet talk. It seemed he would keep up his pathetic pursuit of her, no matter what. "Do you want to play your little game with the dice, again, so we know which way to go?" Becky asked, wiping sweat from her eyes.

"My little game?" Macta said, still jiggling the knucklebones in his hand. "'Tis no game."

"But you believe everything's a game!" Asra said.

"A very serious game," Macta scowled. "The way the child says it, it sounds frivolous. I weigh my risks, and I act. 'Tis not child's play. The knucklebones say we'll go east."

"I know you, Macta," Asra said. "The outcome of a toss of bones has nothing to do with which direction we go. Your knucklebones are shaved, so that the numbers you roll are the ones you choose."

"So they are," Macta replied. "Do you think fate is an accident? 'Tis small things, nearly imperceptible things, which determine the outcome of the most important events. I shave the corners of the knucklebones in order to challenge the rule of chance, and shape the world according to my desires."

"So you had a feeling, or a hunch that we ought to go east," Asra scoffed, "and then you rolled the knucklebones, and now you claim the outcome of the toss shows that we should go east? Maybe you can fool some people with that nonsense, but not with me. 'Tis a cheat, what you do. You even cheat yourself. You have no moral code."

Macta smiled. "Ah, but I do the work of the Gods when I roll the bones. No one knows what the Gods desire when they make the smallest changes . . . a tiny clot in the Blood that kills a King, or the fate of an Empress who chokes on a harmless little grape. Others think that there are rules in life, and if they play by them, they have a chance of coming out ahead in the game. But no one ever knows all the rules, and the most important rule is unknown to most—that in the end, we make our own rules."

"Can we go now?" Becky pleaded.

Old roadways, covered with dried mud and scarred with tire tracks, soon converged by a long bunker-like building made of cinderblocks, topped with sheets of steel. Steam billowed from vents in the ground and curled around the metal doors that barred the way into the mine marked with a sign: NUMBER THREE. The path ended here. There was no place to go but back the way they had come. Macta took the book from his pocket again, opened it to the page where he was making notes of his latest bets, and balanced it on his knee. He made several tiny, awkward marks, grunted in satisfaction, and slipped the book back into his vest. He spat out a ball of pulpy greens.

"More herbs, girl," he commanded.

Becky took another handful of leaves and twigs from her sack and handed them to the Elf. "You're always writing in your gambling book, Macta. Do you think we're going to start having good luck?"

"You must address me as *King*," Macta said.

Asra shook her head. "I wonder if you placed a little wager with yourself that the number-three mine would be the first we found?"

"No," Macta replied. "But I won a bet with myself that we wouldn't find the mines in consecutive order. We started with three. Odds are now that we're just as likely to find number one as we are to find number two, but it's more likely that we'll find five than it was the first time, because there are fewer choices. Do you see?"

"I see that you busy yourself with your bets when you're overwhelmed with fear and worry, and don't know what else to do," Asra said scornfully.

"Nonsense," said Macta. "Dockalfars are afraid of nothing."

A smile lifted the corners of Asra's mouth. "You're afraid you won't make it back home."

"We'd better be getting back," Becky said. "We'll take the other trail, and hope we do better."

They walked beside the railroad tracks, retracing their steps to the place where the rails forked. They trekked along the new path for another half hour. Finally they passed mine portal number four, and seeing that the railroad tracks continued into the woods, and the air still stank of smoke, they followed them. Dead trees eventually gave way to live ones, and the ground no longer felt hot to the touch. At last they came around a curve and saw a low building with the number 5 painted on it. The wide steel doors stood ajar. Becky gulped, and tried to put on a brave face. If she hadn't been desperate, she never would have even considered walking into danger like this. She poked her head into the opening and sniffed the air. No fumes, as far as she could tell, and no scent of burning. Still, the blackness in the shaft was all consuming. "I've never seen a place so dark," Asra said, peering through the doors. "I can't imagine walking through this portal without some kind of light."

"The Fire Sprite will help us," said Macta.

"No," said Asra. "If there are any gases in there, just a spark could blow us all to pieces. We'll have to leave the Sprite behind."

"The Fire Sprite is mine," Macta said. "'Tis up to me to determine its fate."

Asra laughed coldly. "You stole it from Radik's corpse. It's dangerous to take into the mine, so we leave it here. There's no discussion."

She tore the sack from Macta's shoulder and pulled out the silver box. "Give that to me," Macta growled, grabbing Asra's arm.

She struggled free, opened the lid and shook out the Fire Sprite. "Go," she said, waving it away. "We don't need you anymore!"

It took to the air, glowing faintly as it disappeared over the treetops. "I was going to let it go," Macta muttered. "I just wanted to be the one to do it."

Asra flung the silver box into the bushes and glanced at the girl. "What next, Rebecca?"

"We go into the mine," Macta said, making a pained face as he massaged the flesh around his shoulder. "Elves' eyes are designed to see in darkness."

"You didn't look beyond the doors, like I did," Asra said. "'Tis too dark for even you to see."

"If the Dwarves can do it, then so can we. They're a foolish, pathetic race."

"There are some sheds over there," Becky said, gazing at the hillside beyond the portal. She had a fleeting thought that she might find a flashlight in one of the sheds. She didn't dare give up hope, no matter how absurd it might be. "It's probably a waste of time, but let's just take a look, okay?"

The doors to the sheds hung on their hinges like broken wings. Inside, past rows of lockers, dusty bins of safety equipment lay inside wire cages. Becky gasped when she saw a row of yellow metal helmets with lights over the visors. She searched one of the helmets for some kind of switch, found none, and then realized that there was a shelf lined with battery packs, just below. *I wonder how they attach these,* she said to herself. She tried hooking a helmet to a battery with a long black cable. Nothing. She tried another battery, and another, and not one of them worked. Then she tried plugging a battery into a different helmet. A dim glow rose up from the face of the lamp. She tried another battery, and found that it, too, still held a faint charge. "Can you carry these?" she asked, as Macta and Asra stood waiting in the doorway. "They're metal, and they're heavy. We can use one until it goes out, and then plug in another."

"I'll need to wrap something around my hand, for protection," Asra said.

Macta nodded his head. "What about that cart, over there? You can push it!"

There was an old wheelbarrow propped against the far wall. "Great!" Becky exclaimed. "That's perfect!"

"You're welcome," Macta said, rubbing his fingernails lazily along the front of his jacket.

Becky wheeled the cart outside and loaded it up with batteries, then pushed it over to the entrance to the mine. There she unloaded the batteries in a pile, turned the wheelbarrow on its side, and angled it through the opening. Asra wrapped a rag around her hand and helped move the batteries back into the cart. "Okay," Becky said, when all the batteries were loaded. "It's time."

"Wait," said Macta, narrowing his eyes at Asra. He reached into Radik's sack and pulled out a length of rope. "We should tie

413

ourselves together, so that we're not separated in the darkness. If one of us gets lost, 'twould be a tragedy."

"A tragedy," Asra repeated, and looked out across the distant hills. It was now or never. She exhaled wearily, then held out her hand. For some reason it wasn't in her to escape, after all. "Give me the end of the rope, Macta."

Even with the helmet, the light in the shaft was very, very dim. Becky saw nothing but rocks and boulders, and long shadows jumping across the walls and low ceiling. Thick wooden beams propped up a roof that looked as if it had been smeared in concrete. There was a conveyor belt against the far wall, and Asra and Macta walked along behind Becky using the rim of the belt as a guardrail. Becky couldn't help but wonder if they would reach the Cord before the batteries ran out, or how they'd manage to find their way back in the darkness if there was no Cord to be found. She knew that Asra and Macta must have certainly been thinking the same thing. The wheelbarrow rattled. It was hard to push it along the rough floor, and Becky's arms felt weak and tired before even a few minutes had passed. Her helmet was loose, and the strap rubbed her chin. There were scuttling sounds in the darkness; Becky caught a glimpse of something moving in the shadows. "Rats," Macta whispered.

"You would know," Asra said mockingly.

"There's nothing wrong with rats," Macta said, "my father's chef used to prepare a delicious pâté from their livers."

"Be quiet," Becky cried, her stomach knotted with disgust

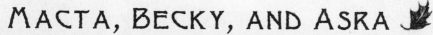 MACTA, BECKY, AND ASRA

and fear. "Please! How will we know when we get to the Cord? What will it look like?"

"I thought you traveled in a Cord to Ljosalfar," Asra said.

"I did," Becky replied. "But I was kind of . . . distracted. I'd just lost my family and my house."

Asra nodded, though it was too dark for Becky to see her. "The surface will be smooth, not like this rough stone. You'll know, when the light from the helmet finds it. *We'll* know because Faerie Folk feel a slight tingling in the fingertips when we get very close."

"Will I feel it, too?"

"Nooo," Asra said. "Elves feel it. Not Humans."

The three fell into silence as they descended deeper into the shaft. Since they could see so little, all of their attention was concentrated on the tiniest sounds, the slightest telltale odors. They were on constant alert for a hint of gas, or any faint rumble that would indicate a tunnel about to collapse. Becky tried hard to suppress the feeling of panic as they went deeper and deeper. She looked over her shoulder and found that it was as dark behind her as it was in front. The light from the helmet was just enough to make her realize how impenetrable the blackness had become. The cart rumbled on. Becky exhausted one battery after another, tossing them aside, then selecting new ones from the cart. Her fingers worked at the wire connections, fumbling in the dark. There were only a few batteries left. It made the cart easier to push, but Becky was finding it difficult to breathe. She wanted desperately to turn around and go back, to see the sky and smell the grass and the trees, to feel the breeze and to suck the fresh air into her lungs.

"My fingers are tingling," Asra gasped.

And then, suddenly, it was there. Becky ran her hand across the surface of the Cord. It bulged slightly as it pressed against the crumbling rock. "Home we go," Macta said, digging in a sharp fingernail.

Asra widened the slit, and a faint gray light spilled from inside. The air rushed through the Cord as it curved and snaked into the dark distance, working its way back through the mountain. "Don't be afraid, Rebecca," Asra said. She touched Becky's arm.

Becky looked into the Elf's dark eyes, as tendrils of hair whipped her careworn face. "As long as you're here, Princess, I'm not afraid."

"Nor am I," said Macta, yanking on the rope that tied them together.

31

MATT THREW AWAY HIS COVERS and lay sweating on the single bed, sprawled like someone who had been tossed from a roof. Sunlight streamed in, oppressive in the airless room. Voices chattered at the edges of his consciousness. Something in him realized that it was only the sound of a television turned up as high as it would go. Just because it was daytime, he thought, was no reason to get out of the first real bed he'd slept in since the Elves destroyed his home. He rubbed his eyes and yawned. Then someone tapped at the window. Matt jumped up and saw Tomtar's troubled face staring at him from the other side of the glass. He hoisted the window open and whispered, "Is something wrong?"

"Nooo."

"Do you need my permission to come in?"

Tomtar and Tuava-Li had chosen to spend the night on the

fire escape, on a bed of blankets that Matt found in the closet. They woke at sunrise and waited for Matt to get up. But now it was nearly noon, and they had lost their patience. "Maybe you should get dressed and come out," Tomtar said. "Tuava-Li says we have to decide what we're going to do today."

Matt rolled his eyes. "Look, I'm sorry I overslept. Blame the bed. Give me a couple of minutes, okay?"

He was just pulling on his T-shirt when he noticed something strange. The tattoo on his chest was different, again; it must have changed during the night, while he was sleeping. A pile of tiny Jewels, all different shapes and colors, now spilled across his chest. Matt felt his skin crawl. Each time the tattoos changed an ominous feeling came over him; he hated feeling like what was happening to his body was out of his control. *Jewels*, he said to himself, *clan jewels. These weren't here before. What's it supposed to mean now? I've got to talk to Tuava-Li and Tomtar about this.*

Matt knew it was a good time to leave. If Mrs. Babcek found him walking around her apartment, she might not remember she'd invited him to stay, or even who he was. Since they'd discovered that Tomtar's uncle was dead, and that the maps he'd been keeping were gone, there was no use lingering in Pittsburgh. Matt pulled his jacket on over his T-shirt. He took the Jewels from the shoeboxes in the closet and dropped the sacks into his pockets, then strapped on his backpack. He opened the door a little and saw that the old lady was sitting in her recliner with her back to him. The TV was turned up so high that she'd never hear him leaving. He crept toward the door as the news reporters blathered on endlessly, speculating about who was abducting America's children. *If they only knew*, he thought.

There was a cluttered end table by the front door. It had occurred to Matt that amid the jumble of bills and junk mail he might find an address book. Mrs. Babcek never budged from her recliner, as Matt went through the papers as quietly as he could. There, beneath a catalog, he found a small red book. He flipped through the index looking for the letter *J*. He copied the phone number he found next to the name *John* onto a scrap of paper and slipped it into his pocket, then dropped the old lady's key ring back into her purse. He squeezed the door shut behind him, hurried down the stairs, and went around the side of the building into the alley. Tomtar and Tuava-Li were waiting for him there.

"I got her son's phone number," Matt said. "Now I can let him know what shape his mom's in, and—hey, is everything okay?"

"Aye," Tomtar answered in a somber voice.

"I don't think so. What is it? You're still upset about your uncle and all, aren't you? You feel bad about the maps?"

Tomtar sighed. "I wish I could help my Clan. It isn't right that Uncle Orin sent me away. If I can't stand up for my own kin, what kind of Troll am I?"

"You're the kind who wants to do the right thing, Tomtar. People should stand up for their families, watch their backs. You know Mrs. Babcek told me that her own son hardly ever talks to her. It isn't right."

Matt realized he was thinking about his own family. He still held on to the hope that he'd meet someone, somewhere, who could tell him how to get to Helfratheim, where his parents and baby sister were most likely held captive. He swallowed and tried to look cheerful. "I want to tell the two of you something. My tattoos have changed again."

Tuava-Li narrowed her eyes. "Changed to what?"

Matt pulled up his shirt. "It has to mean something. Maybe it's what I'm supposed to do something about, some task, like I'm supposed to sell all the jewels today. Maybe I'm going to need a lot of cash for something."

"Maybe it means we're going to need the Jewels," Tuava-Li said, looking closely at Matt's tattoos. "Maybe it means we're supposed to hold on to them. There's simply not enough information for us to go on. The Mage wanted you to be tattooed so that you'd be protected from danger. She couldn't have known this would happen. Maybe it's part of the ancient myth, maybe it's what happened to the Human King who went with Fada on the quest to save our world. We have to learn how to read the clues properly, so that we're working in harmony with the wishes of the Goddess."

"How are we going to know that?" Matt said.

"We must pray for guidance."

Matt shook his head and snorted. "That's it? I don't know about you, but I can't think straight on an empty stomach. I need to get some breakfast in me. Are you guys hungry?"

"I'm starved!" said Tomtar.

"Then let's eat, and figure everything out afterwards."

They made their way down the hill and stopped at the deli on the corner of Carson Street. In the alley next to the deli they gorged themselves on bagels smeared with strawberry jam, and argued about what Matt's changing tattoos might mean to their journey. Matt convinced Tomtar and Tuava-Li that they couldn't survive for long without money, and that they needed to trade in at least a few of the Jewels for cash. Then they headed to the pawnshop down the block. As they stood outside Matt handed the sacks of Jewels to Tomtar and Tuava-Li. He kept two diamonds for himself, and felt their icy hardness in the palm of his hand as he pushed the buzzer. Five minutes later, he was back out on the street. "Well?" Tuava-Li asked.

"Good news," Matt said. "I got some money for the diamonds, and the guy said he'd be interested in cutting a deal on all the jewels we've got."

Tuava-Li felt her jaw tense. "All of them?"

"Yep. Problem is he doesn't have any more cash in the store, and he said he needs his partner to see what we have to sell if it's going to be a big transaction. He asked to see the jewels now, so he'd have an idea of how much money he needed to come up with, but I felt a little uncomfortable about that."

"As you should," Tuava-Li said. "The fewer who know about the Jewels, the better."

"This must be why my tattoos have changed—to get us to the

pawnshop. Based on what he gave me for the two diamonds, I figured we've got to have at least ten thousand dollars' worth of jewels in our pockets—probably a lot more, but we don't have time to find a better deal. I gave him the number I was thinking, and he said fine, we should come back tomorrow morning and he and his partner would be ready to trade."

"Tomorrow morning?"

"Yeah," Matt said, "I know. That means another night in Pittsburgh, and I wonder if we can risk staying at Mrs. Babcek's again."

Tuava-Li nodded. "'Twould be good to have some place to hide the Jewels, though, until you've . . . sold them. The Human's place seemed safe enough." Once again she felt a pang of sorrow that her Clan Jewels were about to be dispersed, and once again she wondered what the image of jewels on Matt's chest meant, and if they were reading the signs correctly.

"We'll figure it out," Matt said. "Tomorrow we'll be rich, and until then, we have a lot to do. Why don't we go over and pick up your new shoes? The guy at the repair place said they'd be ready by now."

Tuava-Li felt a growing sense of apprehension as they made their way down the block. There was something about the shoe repairman that made her uncomfortable. He knew more than a Human ought to know about Faerie Folk, and despite the fact that he was doing something helpful, she couldn't bring herself to trust him. Was it just because he was a Human, she wondered, or was it something else? She stopped a few doors away from the repair shop. "You go on in, Matthew," she said. "Tomtar and I will wait outside."

"I'll invite you in," Matt said.

"Nooo, that's not it."

Matt shrugged. "Suit yourself!"

He pulled open the door and stepped inside. "Hello," he called as he walked between the sunglasses display and the rack of leather belts.

There was a conversation going on in the back. He caught a glimpse of several faces behind the beaded curtain, but they disappeared as the shoemaker pushed the curtain aside and stepped into the light. "Oh, it's you," Winkler said with a smile. "I'm sorry, kid, I wish you would have given me a call, because I got busy and couldn't finish your shoes. You're going to have to come back tomorrow."

"But you said—"

"First thing tomorrow. I'm going to get right on it. You know what Ben Franklin wrote: *'Lost time is never found again.'* But listen, there's always a chance I'll get them done sooner, and if you let me know where you're staying tonight, I'll drop them by for you!"

"I don't know," Matt said.

"You're not staying up on the hill again?"

"Tomorrow morning will be fine."

"I'm just trying to help you, kid!" Winkler called, as Matt hurried out the door.

"There's something weird about that guy," Matt said, when he joined Tomtar and Tuava-Li on the sidewalk. "I don't remember telling him we were staying up on the hill, but he knew. I can see why you don't trust him."

"Where are our shoes?" Tomtar asked.

Matt shook his head. "Tomorrow morning. Everything's tomorrow morning. I'm thinking maybe we ought to forget about the new shoes, at least from that guy, and find somewhere else to do our business." With his hands in his pockets, he fingered some coins and remembered there was something else he'd been meaning to do. Compared to a trip to the North Pole, an unpleasant phone call was going to be a piece of cake. "Come on guys, I've got to call Mrs. Babcek's son. I bought a phone card at the pawnshop."

"What do you mean, *call* him?" asked Tuava-Li.

"On a telephone," Matt said. "Haven't you ever seen a telephone? Telephones let us talk to people who are far away—sort of like how you try to talk to the Mage, even though she's a thousand miles away. We use telephone lines, though, or satellites to do it, not magic."

"It *is* magick," Tuava-Li said. "Very powerful magick."

"Whatever."

Matt found a pay phone on the corner and called the number he'd taken from the old woman's address book. "Is this John Babcek?" he asked, and pressed his free hand to his ear to block out the traffic noise.

"I'm calling about your mom," he said. "I think she needs some help."

When he hung up a minute later, Matt had the distinct impression that Mrs. Babcek's son wasn't really interested in what he had to say. He crumpled the phone number and shoved it in his pocket. *So much for family,* he said to himself. He punched in the number for the operator and waited for the automated response. "Thank you for using our service," the voice said robotically. "What number do you wish to call?"

"American Airlines," he said.

Matt cradled the receiver under his chin while he got a ballpoint pen from his pocket and wrote the number on his hand, then made the call. He drummed his fingers on the phone as he waited for a real person to pick up. "Hi there, I want to know how I can get to the North Pole. Do you have any flights that go up there? Yeah, I said the North Pole. No, this isn't a joke. Okay, I'll give that a try. Thanks."

Matt wrote another number on his hand. He pressed his finger on the bar at the top of the pay phone to disconnect the call, and dialed the new number. "Alaska Airlines? I want to fly to the North Pole. Do you guys—what? Oh, okay. I'd have to transfer to another airline? From where? How much does it cost? No, I don't have a credit card. Don't you take cash?"

Tomtar and Tuava-Li could tell that Matt was getting frustrated. "You have to be twenty-one just to make a reservation? But why, I've got money, I—"

Matt's face turned red, and he slammed the receiver into its cradle. "I don't know how we're going to get to the North Pole. I don't know how we're even going to get close. I don't see how that legend about Fada, or whatever, is true. It must have taken those guys *months* to make it, if they ever did. If it takes us that long, my parents will be cold and dead before I can get to them. It'll be a hundred degrees below zero once we get north, anyway, and then we'll be dead, too. This is crap, all of it."

A man walked past the pay phone, saw Matt ranting to himself, and quickened his pace. Tomtar and Tuava-Li were invisible to him. "Who were you talking to, Matthew?" Tuava-Li whispered.

"I was trying to find a way to really *do* this thing," Matt cried. "I called two different airlines. We're not gonna be flying to the North Pole, that's for sure. Everything's too complicated. We could take the bus, maybe get across the country, but we can't even head up through Canada unless I can show a passport, which I can't. So we're stuck. We'll have to walk, or hitch rides from strangers, and try to sneak over the border. This is the dumbest thing I've ever done, coming with you two!"

Matt stalked ahead, and turned south on the first street that led back up the hill.

"Where are you going, Matt?" Tomtar puffed, trying to keep up.

"Back to Mrs. Babcek's, I guess. If we're going to spend another night in this town, it's better to sleep there than in an alley or a homeless shelter. There'll be plenty of time for that later. We'll take off tomorrow after I get the money for the jewels. I've already decided I'm going to leave some money for Mrs. Babcek, so don't try to talk me out of it. She needs help, and there's nobody but me who can give it to her."

"You feel guilty," Tuava-Li said.

"Of course I feel guilty!" Matt cried. "Don't you?"

"Aye," Tuava-Li said, not wanting to let Matt know that she felt guilty for another reason. If her plans went the way she hoped and prayed they would, Matt would be dead before long, sacrificed to the Seed of the Adri. "I have an idea, Matthew. Since we're not leaving Argant today, Tomtar and I could go back to St. Elmo's Firehouse and see if we can find out anything useful. There were Faerie Folk last night who weren't telling us everything they knew. If we can find a Faerie who knows of a Cord, or someone who's been north before, then—"

"Don't you remember," Matt said, "they threw us out of there last night!"

"They threw *you* out," Tuava-Li corrected.

"Stefan said they're not even open until after dark."

"There must be a few Faerie Folk there, even in the daytime; surely the ones who work there. It wouldn't hurt just to go and find out!"

"You can't go back there by yourselves," Matt said. "It's not safe. If you refuse to give mind-reading a shot, they'll all just take advantage of you there. You won't learn anything."

"You keep thinking that I can pull information from Humans' minds like one pulls wildflowers from the dirt," Tuava-Li said. "'Tis not like you imagine. The clever ones can shield their thoughts, or twist them around. A monk's obliged to use her intelligence, her reason, to find the truth in things. 'Tis the same with you."

"Well, I don't have to read minds to know that club is dangerous. The juggler guy, Stefan, he's nothing but trouble. The guy in the shoe repair shop, he's up to no good, too. I can't wait till we get out of this town."

"Don't worry, Matt," Tomtar said. "If we go to St. Elmo's now, things are sure to be calmer than they were last night. We've got no other plans until tomorrow. 'Tis worth a try, isn't it?"

"We could take a few of the Jewels," Tuava-Li suggested, "just some little ones. Maybe some of your Human money, too. We'll loosen a few tongues at St. Elmo's, I'm sure of it!"

Matt frowned. "I don't like it. We ought to stay together."

"What are you planning to say to the old woman?" Tuava-Li asked. "She may not even remember you today."

"Or she might come to her senses and wonder why you want to spend the night at her place," Tomtar said, "when you said your family was nearby!"

"You're right," Matt said, "but since I don't really have a home or a family at the moment, I'm going to Mrs. Babcek's. I'm going to tell her I'm there to help her out. I'm going to offer to go to the grocery store for her, and help her pay her bills, and by nighttime she'll probably be so grateful she'll be asking me to move in. Don't worry about me. Just come back to her apartment when you're done."

"We can't go in without a Human's permission," Tomtar said.

"Then I'll give you my permission now, in advance. I'll make sure the window in the bedroom's open for you, and you can come in from the fire escape. If you're going back to that club, I'm going to give you this, Tomtar."

Matt pulled the leather knife case from his pocket and offered it to his friend. "You have a better chance of needing this than I do today."

Tomtar swallowed. "I can't take your knife, Matt. It was your father's!"

"It's not a gift, it's a loan. Just until you get back. You're all the family I've got here, Tomtar. So take it, okay?"

"Okay."

They stepped into an alley and Matt peeled a handful of twenties from his wad of cash. He gave Tomtar and Tuava-Li the money and a few Jewels that they might be able to use to trade for information. They handed Matt their backpacks, and he slung them over his shoulder. Then they all stepped back into the daylight. "I guess I'll see you guys later," Matt said. "Be careful, and good luck. Don't do anything I wouldn't do."

"Good luck to you, too, Matt!" Tomtar said, and he and Tuava-Li watched the boy turn and walk up the hill.

32

THE WIND ROARED in Becky's ears as it carried her, weightless, over the endless miles. She hurtled through the Cord, swept on a tidal wave of air, flung headlong in its relentless current. The wind raked her eyes, tugged at her clothes, tore at her hair. Asra was just ahead of her, and Macta was at the lead; the three of them were still bound together with a long rope tied around their waists. Becky studied Asra to see how she held her body—head lifted slightly, arms and legs out straight, so that her progress was quickened by the wind. At first Becky had taken a beating as her body crashed again and again against the walls of the Cord. Until she began to get a feel for how it was done, the three of them were flung together repeatedly in a tangle of arms and legs.

Painfully they ricocheted off the walls. Macta screamed at Becky, barked orders, berated her for her size and her clumsiness. Her body was bruised; her muscles ached as she learned to navigate the merciless wind. In the end she had to learn to feel the place where she wasn't being pulled or pushed, but both pulled and pushed at the same time. It was the way a surfer has to be in harmony with the wave, the way the edge of a sharp knife makes its cut without resistance. Becky had to learn to navigate the Cord and not think about it, she had to learn by intuition, and she had to do it fast.

The passage was wide, deep in the earth, and they were not alone. Most of the Faeries that swept past her kept their distance. They glanced at Becky with surprise or contempt, for Humans were never meant to ride in the Cord. Once in a while Asra would glance over her shoulder to see how Becky was holding up. "Good catch," cried a Dwarf to Macta, pointing to the Human tied to a rope. "May the Mage get her wish tonight!"

He thinks we're bringing Rebecca for the Acquisition, Asra thought. *'Twill be a good ruse to get us into Helfratheim.*

Several times Macta leaned to the left or right and sped into branches that forked from the main Cord, pulling his companions with him into the milky distance. The journey was long, but like all Elves, Macta could feel the way to his own homeland. When many hours had passed Becky sensed that the wind as well as the Cord were rising to the surface. The Cord took on a sickly smell as the passage grew brighter. The air began to pulse, like someone sucking breath in and out, in and out. They were still a short distance from the official exit to Helfratheim. "Now bank to the right," Macta hollered.

Becky and Asra did as they were told. "Grab the surface, Rebecca," Asra called.

When Becky's fingers clutched the fragile membrane, a rank fluid seeped onto her palm. She pulled back in disgust. "Take my blade," Macta said to Asra, as the three of them huddled together, hanging on to the wall of the Cord. "'Tis in my pocket. The Cord may be too thick to cut without it."

The Princess hesitated, glaring at him, and dug a sharp fingernail deep into the surface. She dragged her fingernail along, then yanked the Cord open with no more effort than it takes to rip a piece of soggy paper. The three of them spilled out into the dirt. Becky tumbled head over heels into a patch of brambles, and cried out as thorns raked her face. Painfully she climbed to her feet in a dark forest of pines. The trunks were tall but scrawny and bent, as if their growth had been a tortuous struggle for survival. The torn wall of the Cord flapped like a sheet hung to dry on a laundry line. Asra went to smooth the tear but it flapped open once again, and she turned away resignedly, wiping her hands on her dress. "Why didn't we wait until we reached the official exit at Helfratheim?"

"The Cord was looking sickly," Macta replied. "Couldn't you tell?"

"Cut us loose," Asra said, wishing that she had taken Macta's knife, after all.

"I'll cut myself free, of course, and you, too, Asra," Macta said, "as long as you promise to be on your best behavior. The girl will remain, tied, however. I want you to bring her in on a leash, Asra, like she's your prisoner. I'll look more commanding if I walk twenty paces ahead, with the two of you trailing behind!"

Macta was giddy with excitement, and his eyes gleamed with a crazy optimism that made his careworn face seem suddenly fresh and alive. "From now on, you must address me as *Your Highness*. 'Twill set a good example for the others to follow."

"What about my parents?" Becky asked.

"*My parents, Your Highness*," Macta corrected. "There will be plenty of time for that. When Jardaine sees that I'm alive and well, she'll be happy to reunite your little family and send you on your merry way, if that's what I command."

Asra's eyes narrowed. "What do you mean, *if that's what you command?*"

"*If that's what you command, Your Highness!*" Macta said, correcting her.

The spires of Helfratheim loomed over the city walls. Flags snapped in the breeze along the ramparts, and guards dressed in ceremonial uniforms stood in a row before the finely wrought iron gates. "'Tis like they're waiting for me," Macta whispered to his companions as they stood at the edge of the forest, gazing across the great lawn that led to Helfratheim. "I can't wait to see the guards' faces when they realize who I am!"

Macta walked proudly across the grass. He held his chest high and took slow, measured steps, like he was marching in a procession. Becky and Asra followed, Becky's heart thumping with anticipation, and Asra's with dread. As they grew closer to the gates Macta was surprised to discover that the soldiers continued to wear masks of stony indifference. Even as they raised their pikes in warning they showed no sign of recognition. "Who goes there?" barked the captain of the guard.

Macta raised his one arm in greeting. "Who do you *think* is there?"

The guards saw a gaunt, scrawny Elf dressed in rags, with matted hair and filthy bandages tied to the shoulder where an arm should have been. Behind him they saw a Human girl bound in ropes and a female Elf holding the tether. All of them looked bedraggled and malnourished. "Around the side," said the captain, assuming that the Elves were bringing a Human victim for Brahja-Chi's sacrifice. "You got here in the nick of time."

"Look at me," Macta growled, "look at my face. Don't you recognize your own King? King Macta?"

The guards laughed mirthlessly. "Get out of here, you pathetic peasant. King Macta is in his throne room at this very moment, preparing for the event that will start the final battle with the Humans. If he heard you compare yourself to him, he'd have your head on a spike in the courtyard before you could blink."

Macta turned and stalked away, confusion tearing at his mind. "Good work," Asra said.

"Which of you knows the first law of strategy?" Macta demanded.

Asra and Becky glanced at one another. "The first law is to know your opponent's weakness," he muttered. "There are thirteen separate entrances to the walls surrounding Helfratheim. If these fools don't recognize me at the main gates, we'll try another."

"Why don't you just tell them you're delivering a Human for the Acquisition," Asra said. "That's what they thought when they saw us, anyway. Once we're inside, you can find someone who knows you. Trouble has taken a toll on you, Macta. You don't look the same anymore."

"Thanks to you," Macta said angrily, clutching at his shoulder. "They said something about King Macta being in his chambers. What could they have meant by that?"

"You must have misheard him," Asra said.

After trying two more gates, and receiving the same welcome, Macta was seething. "We're tired," Asra said. "Can't we just go to the Acquisition gate, as the guard told us to?"

"I will not enter my own kingdom like some peasant," Macta

muttered through clenched teeth, "There's another place, a secret entrance to my chambers. I was foolish for not thinking of it before. I will ascend to the court from my own rooms, and then they will know me."

Cloaked by shadows, Macta led the others around the perimeter of the fortress. He slipped behind a tangle of briars and with his one good hand felt for the loose stone. Behind it was a hidden lever. A minute later, all three were inside the palace walls. Macta led Becky and Asra through the darkness and up a broad flight of steps. They could hear the teeming throngs of Elves who were gathering for the sacrifice in the great courtyard at the front of the palace. "Is there a dungeon, or a prison, or something where they'd be keeping my mom and dad and sister?" Becky bent down and whispered to Macta.

When he shot her a withering look she added, "Your Highness," but Macta had his own agenda, and he refused to answer the girl. They passed beneath an arch and turned a corner, and suddenly the rough walls gave way to polished marble, the slate floors were laid with soft woven carpets, and statues were built into deep niches. Macta stepped proudly into the light and cleared his throat, so that the guards standing on the steps below would take notice.

They spun around, spear points at the ready, and gasped at the sight of the Human girl standing so close. "Don't breathe the Human's vapors," the Captain cried, "they're poisonous!"

Asra, desperate to tell the guards that they were simply bringing another contribution for the Acquisition, tried to push her way past the spears. "Sir, I—"

"Silence," the captain commanded.

Macta was livid. "Look at my face. Look at my face," he said insistently. "I know you, you're Captain Daen. Can't you tell who I am? I've spent my entire life here, everyone knows me. I'm Macta Dockalfar, the new King of Helfratheim. Can't you see? Are you all under some kind of spell?"

"Lock him up," the captain ordered his troops. "He's mad. We'll deal with him when this night is done. Lock the female up, too, in the women's prison."

"W-w-what about the Human, sir?" asked one of the guards, trembling in fear.

The point of his spear shook, and Becky pushed it away with her hand. Instantly the soldiers lunged forward, ready to impale her with their weapons.

"Stop it!" Becky cried, and shocked by the authority in her voice, the Elves stepped back momentarily.

"She's just a child," the captain hollered. "Force her out to the courtyard and toss her in with the rest. The more, the merrier!"

"Macta!" Becky screamed. "You promised me! You promised you'd help me!"

Macta struggled as he was hauled to the dungeon. He knew what awaited him there: rot, filth, and the stench of death and despair. "I'm your King, I command you to let me go!" he screamed, his words twisted and unintelligible with grief. The guards tossed Macta into the blackness and slammed the door behind him.

A dozen guards forced Becky at spearpoint down the steps to the courtyard. She blinked back tears, and what she saw made her gasp. She could see, beyond a circle of black-robed monks, a domed enclosure. It was a cage made entirely of tough, interwoven vines, and inside it, past piles of haphazardly stacked stone blocks, were children. Hundreds of human children were in the cage, huddled in terror. In another moment Becky would join them.

33

W E'RE NOT OPEN," the Troll on guard outside St. Elmo's Firehouse muttered as Tomtar and Tuava-Li stepped toward the doorway. "You'll have to come back later."

"We just want to see if there's anyone who can answer a few questions," Tuava-Li said, handing the Troll a folded twenty-dollar bill.

The guard pocketed the cash and stepped aside. "That's different. Good thing you didn't bring your Human friend with you, though, or I wouldn't have let you in at all."

"How did you know to do that?" Tomtar whispered as they went inside.

"I didn't spend my entire life as a monk," she replied.

In the foyer they heard a clatter coming from one of the upper floors; someone was hurrying down the stairs. Tuava-Li looked up to see Stefan, the juggler, hauling his prop bags through the narrow stairwell. "Well, hello," he said, "I didn't think I'd see you here again!"

"We didn't expect to see you, either," Tuava-Li replied, glancing up the stairs.

Stefan noted curiosity in her eyes. "I live up there. Want to see?"

Tuava-Li shook her head. "Nooo."

"Listen, I was on my way to do a little show in the park, but with all this *abduction* business going on, I probably won't have an audience, anyway. Perhaps I could interest you in another game of Liar's Knucklebones, instead?"

"No thanks," Tomtar said.

"You know I've been treasuring that diamond you gave me," Stefan confided. "Where's your Human friend, by the way? He's certainly a diamond in the rough! He could stand a little polishing, perhaps. But it's plain to see he's the genuine article!"

"Matt's up on the hill," Tomtar said, "he's—"

Tuava-Li *sssshed* him with a nudge in the ribs. Just then a group of Brownies squeezed past, on their way to the club two floors down. Stefan rolled his eyes.

"Everybody's after a taste of the Green Man's essence. They can't wait for regular club hours to begin—the guard's making a good profit in bribes today! You'd better hurry if you want a sip; they say Khidr's fading fast. I don't know what the club owner's going to do when he runs dry."

Tuava-Li shook her head. "Unless you can tell us the safest, quickest way to the North Pole—"

"Or who's abducting Human children in Argant," Tomtar interrupted, "and how they're transporting them out of here, then—"

"Then we'd best go inside and see if anyone's willing to talk to us."

"As you wish," Stefan said, and moved his bags through the door. "But watch out, there are thieves down there, and they'll take advantage of you if you're not careful!"

In the gloom of the basement the Green Man slumped in his shallow pool. A long line of Faerie Folk waited for a taste of his rare and precious nectar. The misery of the hulking creature was almost palpable. "Let's start down the hall," Tuava-Li said with a shudder.

A handful of Pixies and Phoukas, left over from the previous night's revelries, dozed in the corridors. Tomtar and Tuava-Li heard the blaring televisions long before they reached the gaming rooms, where a few stragglers watched the news. "Schools have shut their doors," the newscasters intoned, "corporations are beefing up private security, and parents are in a panic today as officials released the newest figures—nearly a thousand children have been reported missing from the Northeast, despite the presence of National Guard troops, and no one knows when the terror will end."

"She's done it," someone laughed.

"Not so fast," said another. "The Human said *nearly* a thousand. No one wins until Brahja-Chi sends down word herself that she got a thousand."

"We'll know for sure when the Gods have struck down the Humans," cried an Elf.

"We won't have to wait for anyone to tell us. Their Blood will run in the streets, there'll be plagues, wailing, and gnashing of teeth!"

A wiry Troll nudged his pudgy friend. "Sattye's been working overtime," he chortled, "I heard he rounded up half a hundred in just the last week!"

"What's that?" Tomtar cried, as he and Tuava-Li entered the room. "Did you say Sattye?"

"What of it?" the Troll scowled.

"Do you know where I can find Sattye's headquarters? My cousins are—"

"I'll bet you ten to one that he's a spy," said the fat Troll.

"You're on," said his friend.

The Trolls got close enough to Tomtar that he could smell the green nectar on their breath. "Are you one of Orin's spies?" they demanded, their eyes flickering with malice. "Is that why you're so curious about Sattye?"

"Nooo," Tomtar said, stumbling backwards. He felt for Matt's knife in his pocket and fear flooded over him; suddenly he knew with certainty he didn't have the makings of a fighter.

Protect yourself, Tuava-Li said in thought-speak. *Use the Belt of Power.*

A moment later the Trolls had backed away, and Tomtar and Tuava-Li stood by themselves in front of the big screens. *Sattye's not important to us now. We have to find out if there are still Cords anywhere around here that can lead us north.*

"Sattye's important to *me*," Tomtar mumbled. "My cousins are with him!"

They sidled up to a table where some Elves were taking turns laying out cards on a green felt board. *Let me try something,* Tuava-Li said, then cleared her throat. "Would anyone here care to settle a bet? My friend claims there aren't any Cords left in Argant, and I told him there must be a few hidden away somewhere, elsewise how would Faerie Folk ever be able to get from town to town? I bet him twenty Human dollars that I could find somebody in this club who could prove me right."

One of the Elves made a snorting sound. "Cords? In Argant? You just lost twenty bucks, friend. There haven't been Cords here in a hundred moons. In this town, if you can't get from place to place on foot, you deserve to die."

As the hands on the clock spun around, the club swelled with hordes of Faerie Folk. The air was full of nervous energy, and the televisions blared. Plastic lottery bubbles on one screen bounced in their pneumatic tubes. On the other television, talking heads droned on and on about the missing children and the panic that held America in its grip. Everyone was eager to place bets on

444

how soon Brahja-Chi's thousand would be confirmed, when the president's somber face would appear again, even on what product would show up in the next commercial break. Would it be shampoo, car insurance, room deodorizer? Feelings of elation and despair filled the room, and Tuava-Li felt the pull of strong emotions. Temptation gnawed at her defenses, urging her to reach into the minds of the Faerie Folk and grab hold of their thoughts. She knew that the voices in her mind were the weakness and selfishness of others seeping into her, draining her own integrity, and she did her best to stand strong. She couldn't afford to be overwhelmed now. The Goddess had given her intuition to read meaning in the eyes and words of others, without invading the privacy of their minds, and that is what she would do. She came out of her reverie when she felt a hand slipping into her robe. "What—"

The Pixie had his fingers deep in Tuava-Li's pocket, and his fist closed around the roll of dollar bills he found there. Then he was overhead, fluttering toward the hallway with his prize, before Tuava-Li could cry out. As soon as she did, Tomtar was shoving through the masses of Faerie Folk, clawing his way toward the exit, grabbing for the Pixie and shouting, "Thief! Stop, thief! Somebody stop him!"

Past the Green Man he struggled, forcing his way to the open door and the stairway that led to the street. It was then that two female Trolls stumbled into Tomtar's path. "Get out of my way," he shouted, only to freeze in wide-eyed amazement.

"Get out of *my* way, you," the Troll hollered back at him, "you — *Tomtar*?"

"Megala?" Tomtar's mouth hung open. "And Mitelle?"

Tomtar fell into the arms of his cousins as they stood blocking the entry to St. Elmo's Firehouse. "Gangway!" cried an Elf waiting to get in. "If you don't make room, I'm going to —"

"You're going to shut your trap," Megala snarled. She smacked Tomtar on the back and hooted, her attitude changing from fierce to jubilant in an instant.

The three Trolls turned into the cool darkness of the club. Tuava-Li had pushed her way to the door, and she stood there, breathing hard. "Did you stop the Pixie, Tomtar?" she cried. "That was all the money we had!"

"Look who I found," Tomtar beamed. "Forget about the money, my cousins are here!"

They made their way to a table and sat down. It was only after Tomtar had introduced everyone that he noticed Megala had a bandage wrapped around one swollen hand, and Mitelle's neck was discolored and bruised. "We're outcasts now," Mitelle said, looking around. "We've got no home anymore. That's why we came here, where all of the rejects end up when there's no place left to go!"

"That's not the complete truth," Megala laughed, "although it's true we haven't got a home anymore. We're here for information, Tomtar, not pity."

"What kind of information?"

 Megala, Tomtar, and Mitelle

"We heard that Orin has a stake in this place, and we thought maybe we'd find someone we could bribe to help us break into his compound. First he took our father, and now, with Sattye's help, he's got Delfina. But believe me, we're going to rescue them!"

"Uncle Vollyar's alive?" Tomtar gasped. "When I saw Uncle Orin at the old school, he said that he'd taken over as Clan leader because Vollyar had been killed in a sneak attack. He told me you'd betrayed your own father for a handful of Clan Jewels, and that you were working with Sattye to take over all of Argant. I knew it wasn't true!"

"The lying sack of slime," Megala sneered. "You got into the school? That place is a fortress. Ah, well. I suppose you look about as threatening as a buttered bun, cousin."

"Orin had been gathering his own troops for a long time before he made his move," Mitelle explained. "He took Father by surprise, killed his generals, and locked up the soldiers who wouldn't pledge their loyalty to him. When he came after us, we fled into the night. We had nowhere to go, and Sattye gave us shelter. He'd always been Father's enemy, but he claimed that he hated Uncle Orin even more. He gave us a job working for a Mage from Storehoj, snatching up Human children, and with our pay we were going to offer Orin money to release Father."

Tuava-Li couldn't believe her ears. "You're stealing children for the Acquisition?"

"Call it what you will," Megala said dismissively. "They're only Humans; what does it matter? Father will never tell Orin where he hid the Clan Jewels. But if Orin will settle for money, we'll give it to him."

"Why did he take Delfina?" Tomtar asked.

"Brahja-Chi's troops have been coming every day to pick up the Humans we've captured," Mitelle said. "This morning we took half a dozen down to the train yards, and Orin's thugs were waiting to attack us. They had our sister hog-tied before we knew what was happening. We couldn't stop them, but we gave them some lumps they won't forget! After they were gone we realized it had to have been a setup. Orin must have paid Sattye a pretty sum to get him to say where we could be found, so he could kidnap one of us. Our enemies have joined forces against us. Now Orin will torture Delfina, hoping that father will break down and tell him where to find the rest of the Jewels. We've got no choice but to go on the attack."

Megala put one arm around her sister, and the other arm around her cousin. "We came here looking for information but we found you, Tomtar, and you're going to help us. You're going to be a hero, cousin, a real hero!"

34

DEEP WITHIN THE PALACE a pair of guards hurried Asra down a corridor. The place was luxurious, and reminded the Princess of her days at Ljosalfar. If the guards had not had their rough hands on her shoulders she might have imagined they were servants, escorting her to her private chambers. The walls were sculpted in bas-relief, with scenes from Elfin history and the realm of the Gods. Ljosalfar was filled with artwork meant to teach moral lessons. The activities depicted here, though, were different. Frozen in moments of conquest, anxiety, or defeat, the figures along the wall held knucklebones in fists raised forever overhead, or gleefully watched rats and roosters fighting to the death in stone pens. Asra felt her freedom slipping away. Her body was numb; her feet were blocks of stone. How long would it be, she wondered, before they reached the cellar, and the prison where she'd probably spend the rest of her life?

Asra had always thought of her life as a series of choices made by others. There were only two real choices she had ever made on her own. One was to run away from home when her parents told her that she would be forced to marry Prince Macta, and that decision had resulted in the death of her best friend. The other choice had been to stay with Becky when she could have easily fled and started her life over, some place where no one knew her name or expected anything of her. What had she been thinking? Was it her fear of taking a chance that had made her stay with the girl, or was it just the opposite? Was it the thought of traveling with a Human, the possibility of adventure, and the thrill of danger that led her to this point? No, she realized. It was the girl. She cared about the girl, and now Rebecca was lost. There was no way for Asra to save her, or herself. It had all been for nothing. *At least when I die*, she thought, *it won't be as Macta's wife.*

A moment later a group of servants, led by the palace chef, approached. Each of them carried a silver tray laden with fruits and sweetmeats for the party of the King. "Godswrath," the chef gasped as they passed Asra and her rough guards. "Where do you think you're going?"

"We're taking this prisoner to the dungeon," said a guard.

"You fools, don't you realize who this is?"

They stared dumbly.

451

"'Tis Princess Asra of Alfheim," the Chef cried, "the King's own true love!"

Prashta's hands were shaking as he threw his head back and downed yet another glass of deep aquamarine liquid. He grimaced and wiped his mouth with his long, embroidered sleeve. "We need a real plan," he cried, "a contingency plan for when this all goes terribly wrong."

The Seven Agents were once again cloistered in their high tower room, sitting around an oaken table piled high with documents. Each of them had been busy compiling facts, statistics, and projections for what would happen after the sacrifice. Yet none of them had been able to devise a way to change the course that had led inexorably to this night. Since Jardaine had collected samples of their Blood to frighten them into submission, the Agents had been afraid to meet. This hadn't stopped Prashta from secretly asking the Experimentalists of the Techmagick labs to devise some special amulets for him and the other Agents. The Experimentalists often used amulets and charms to protect them from exposure to harmful vapors in the lab. But the new medallions were devised to protect the wearer from enchantments and spells, which might prove useful in case King Macta and Jardaine decided that the Agents were their enemies, and should be eliminated. Prashta nervously fingered the medallion around his neck as he contemplated the slaughter of the Humans that was about to take place.

"We've got to stop this, somehow," he said. "We can't believe that witch Brahja-Chi when she says the Gods are going to come down from the Heavens to help us obliterate the Humans and take over their world . . . can we?"

"Trussst thossse who ssseek the truth, but be wary of thossse who sssay they know what is true," Prashta's advising snake hissed, as it nosed away one of the bulky medallions.

"We're simply not prepared," said another of the Agents, his eyes glazed with anxiety. He clutched at the medallions and amulets that hung beneath the collar of his robes. "Just because Brahja-Chi says that the Gods will be so pleased with the sacrificial offering tonight that they'll lead us in conquering the Human realm, we can't trust that it will happen that way. We have to rely on ourselves. We've positioned our armies along the borders, but I fear there won't be enough troops, and their weapons won't suffice, if the Gods don't intervene on our behalf. At least we can be grateful to the Techmagicians. They've developed some new airborne poisons and infectious agents for us to use against the Humans when we strike. We've mobilized all the forces at our command, but I fear it still won't be enough."

"'Tis safer to provide weapons for others' battles than to fight one's own," Prashta said. "Weapon-sellers win in every war, but those who fight valiant causes often lose. Brahja-Chi says the Gods will guide us, and their Heavenly forces will be at our sides when we go to strike the Humans down, but what if she's wrong?"

Another of the Agents stroked his muttonchop sideburns. "Fear is our best weapon," he said. "That, and the element of surprise. The Humans don't know who their enemy is, so they see danger in every shadow. Even if we must strike without the help of the Gods, the Humans won't know what hit them, or how to fight back. The Humans can't see Elves, so they'll blame each other for the terror attack we're about to launch. Understand, there are two nation states right on the other side of the veil between our world and theirs. They're called the Union of States and Kanada, I believe. Each nation will most likely assume that the other is attacking. I don't mean to take Brahja-Chi's side in all this, but we don't need contingency plans. We're as ready as we need to be, no matter what happens after Brahja-Chi orchestrates the slaughter of all those Human children. We'll strike at them and then stand back and watch the terror unfold. They'll destroy themselves, you'll see!"

There was a sharp knock on the door. "I'll get it," said the Agent. "My friends have come to deliver a little good cheer!"

Three Elves from the Gaming Commission slipped into the room and laid their massive gambling books out on top of the table, already stacked high with war plans. "In recent days I've placed a number of bets on the outcome of the sacrifice," the Agent said. "There's still time, you know, to make this evening a little more interesting."

The Elves leaned over the books, examining the many possible scenarios envisioned by the Commissioners, and the odds on each. Murmuring approval, they seemed to forget their worries. The thrill of the game quickened their senses and brought sly smiles to their faces. "Gentle Elves," said the Gaming Commissioner, "'tis time to place your bets!"

Jardaine's face was a mask of fury. The guard cowered at her feet, trembling as he spoke. "We've made ten separate counts, my Mage, and we still come up short. There are only nine hundred and ninety-eight Human children."

"It won't do," said Brahja-Chi, smoldering in rage.

She sat, slouched in the King's throne, with her chin resting on one well-manicured hand. The Most Revered Royal Beautician was hunched over her other hand, filing the old Mage's nails into spikes. Next to her rested the Troll called Nick. He had ingratiated himself into the Mage's company by the number of Human children he and his Pixies had managed to abduct. Reveling in his success, he'd left the Pixies behind. "I brought in eighty-nine myself," he bragged, "and I would have managed ninety, if not for that trio of dolts that the Mage of Alfheim sent to ruin my plans."

"The Mage of Alfheim didn't send those fools to ruin your plans," Jardaine sneered.

Not for the first time that day Jardaine thought about her rival Tuava-Li, and her vision-inspired quest to save the world. She was plagued with doubt about Brahja-Chi's abilities to bring the Acquisition to its completion, and she found herself secretly wishing that *she* could be on a quest to the North Pole, and show Tuava-Li who was the most powerful monk of all. "It's not all about you, Nick," she said. "No, it has to be Jal-Maktar's fault that there aren't enough children. Our agreement specified that he be permitted to consume the soul of one child per day, until the great sacrifice. He must have taken more than he was allowed—that's why we're two children short!"

Brahja-Chi shook her head. "Faeries like Jal-Maktar are cruel, but they're honorable. Jal-Maktar made a promise to you, and he'll live up to every detail of your contract. No, Jardaine, this is *your* fault. The slaughter cannot begin until we have a thousand children. You know that there are a thousand citizens who won the right to take a Human's life in the Acquisition Lottery, the special knives and protective potions have already been distributed, and the crowds are waiting to see Human Blood spilled in the courtyard. Jal-Maktar would be furious if he knew that you're not living up to your end of the bargain. We can't proceed until you find two more children! Let's summon another Fir Darrig, who can snatch them for you from one of the Human towns nearby."

"Noooo," Jardaine moaned. "Can you imagine what it would cost me now to acquire two more children? Every Faerie creature within a thousand miles is waiting to see what happens here tonight, everyone knows how important this is. It would cost me both my legs to do what you ask."

"I could try to get another child," Nick offered, getting up from his seat.

456

"'Tis too late," Jardaine moaned. "There's not enough time."

Be quiet, Brahja-Chi said in thought-speak. *I feel him near!*

Someone was whistling in the hallway that led to the King's chambers. Jardaine held her breath as he approached, his slippered feet padding quietly on the flagstone floor. Armed guards stepped aside as he entered through the massive carved doors, singing a little tune. "Wind and water, fire and mud, Jal-Maktar smells fresh young Blood!"

He was the very image of Macta, from the suspicious cast of his eyes to the sneer that curled one side of his mouth, from the silky black hair tucked behind his perfectly shaped ears to his bejeweled fingers. His shoulders were draped in the robe of the King, and he wore his crown at a jaunty angle. "I'm getting hungry," he said, licking his lips. "You may have noticed, I haven't taken a soul today, even though our contract allowed it. 'Tis always best to go to a feast with an empty belly, so they say!"

"Do they?" Brahja-Chi mused.

"I wonder, Jal-Maktar," said Jardaine, "did you happen to hear any of our conversation before your arrival?"

"And how would I have done that?" Jal-Maktar answered with a derisive snort. "When I'm in Elfin form my ears are no better than yours. I hate being an Elf. 'Twould be a terrible punishment to be trapped in this body forever."

"Well, there's certainly no danger of that," Jardaine said. "We were just discussing how smoothly everything is proceeding, and what form you plan to take when you devour the children's souls. If you can't do it in the guise of the King, then we'll have to hide you—"

Footsteps echoed loudly in the corridor; all heads turned toward the door. "My Mage," cried one of the guards, excited and breathless as he appeared in the archway. Then he saw the King, and got down on his knee. "Your Highness," he murmured.

"You may rise," said Jal-Maktar, with a wave of his hand. The guard got up and turned awkwardly toward Jardaine. "Another child has been delivered to the gates since we last spoke, my Mage. The total now numbers nine hundred and ninety-nine!"

"You don't yet have the thousand we agreed upon?" Jal-Maktar asked Jardaine, narrowing his eyes. "The sacrifice is scheduled to begin within the hour. A bargain is a bargain!"

Jardaine smiled tensely. She was about to make some excuse, when a flash of inspiration struck. She nearly swooned with pleasure at her own cleverness. "Thank you for the news," she said, smiling at the guard. Her eyes flashed like diamonds. "Have you taken the last child, yet, from the Techmagick laboratories? The very young one who's been our captive there since our return from Alfheim?"

"No, my Mage," the guard said with a puzzled expression. "I didn't think she was supposed to be—"

"The first shall be the last, and the last shall be the first," Jardaine interrupted. "This has been our plan from the beginning, of course! Nick, go with the guards and fetch the little girl now. Jal-Maktar is getting very hungry!"

The guard shook his head. "Jal who? What do you mean, my Mage?"

Jardaine stiffened at her slip of the tongue. The guard, of course, believed that it was King Macta who stood before him with his scepter and crown. Both Brahja-Chi and Jal-Maktar shot withering glances at the young Mage. "Go now," Jardaine barked at the guard, suddenly losing her good humor.

"We're going," Nick said, scurrying toward the doors, and the guards were close behind.

"Hurry," Jardaine screamed after them, "if you wish to keep your heads!"

"Quickly now," the chief Experimentalist cried in a tremulous voice as his technicians wheeled Charlie, Jill, and Emily McCormack back to their cell. The long day's investigations were over, at last. Lights flickered in the narrow corridor as shadows swept behind them. "We don't want to miss the sacrifice," he squealed, his eyes flickering with Bloodlust.

Charlie no longer held the protective amulet in his mouth, but the sensation in his arms and legs was nearly back to normal by the time they reached the door of their cell. All his efforts to resist the control of the paralytic agents were paying off. With a few more days of practice, he'd be ready to carry out his family's escape. The sudden sound of pounding boots, however, made him twist his head in alarm. His eyes darted nervously as he saw a group of palace guardsmen surrounding the mild-mannered Experimentalist. "We're here for the little one," the leader of the guards commanded.

"B-b-but, you c-c-can't," the Experimentalist stammered, shrinking back.

"Jardaine's orders."

A hoarse cry rose from Jill's paralyzed mouth as she saw her youngest child carried away, a pair of Elves hoisting her arms, while another pair struggled with the weight of her legs. "Mo-mom-my!" the girl managed to call through frozen lips.

"I thought these three were completely paralyzed," said the leader of the guard, calling over his shoulder. "How do you experiment on them when they can thrash about and make so much racket?"

The chief Experimentalist adjusted his glasses and cleared his throat. "Well, you see, it's—"

"Never mind," the guard said dismissively. "After tonight your experiments will be over. The battle with the Human realm is about to begin!"

Charlie's mind raced desperately as he and his wife were wheeled into their cell. With his hands clenched into fists, he turned to look at Jill. Her eyes burned into his with an intensity he'd never seen before. "Nooooowwww," she mouthed silently.

The Techmagician in charge of locking Charlie and Jill into their cell fumbled with his key ring, too nervous to find the right key. "Come on, make it snappy," the others cried excitedly. They were anxious to reach the courtyard to witness the festivities, and they didn't want to miss a single minute.

"Oh, all right," the Elf said in exasperation, and shoved the key ring into his coat pocket. What harm could it do, he thought, if security was a little slack tonight? There were more important things, to be sure, than locking a couple of helpless Humans into a cell. They'd been poisoned and beaten down so much, by now it was doubtful they'd have the strength to lift a finger. Besides, he hadn't bothered to untie them from their slabs. There was no chance they'd escape. He hurried after his companions, and the echo of his footsteps disappeared down the corridor.

Charlie raised his hands, each of which seemed to weigh a hundred pounds, and with fingers as stiff and unyielding as tree branches he began to work at the vines that tied him down. Tears ran down Jill's cheeks as she spit the amulet onto the floor. "Don't cry," Charlie mumbled, his mouth as dry as ashes. "We're going to get out of here. All of us!"

35

THE DELI WAS ABOUT to shut down for the night by the time Matt crossed to East Carson Street. He'd spent the afternoon helping Mrs. Babcek make sense of her bills, then gone to the post office to get stamps, to the bank to deposit her Social Security checks, and to the library to look at books about the North Pole. He found a travel section in a little bookstore downtown, and browsed there until they closed. Now it was long past suppertime, and according to the curfew, he shouldn't even be on the street. He'd promised the old lady he would buy some groceries and make her dinner. He felt guilty that he'd lost track of time; Mrs. Babcek might not even be awake. He had the keys to her apartment, though, and he figured he'd just go back and wait for Tomtar and Tuava-Li to return from St. Elmo's Firehouse. Tomorrow morning they'd sell the rest of the Clan Jewels. Matt thought that maybe he'd see if he could find somebody who could make him a fake passport for when they crossed the border into Canada. It was either that, or risk chewing on some of the Elfin *trans* that was meant to make Faerie Folk invisible to each other. He had no idea if *trans* would work on humans. His tattoos and amulets were supposed to make him inconspicuous and protect him from harm, but he certainly couldn't count on them to get him across the border.

Matt bought two bags of groceries and headed up the hill. Behind him, the owner of the store pulled down the graffiti-covered security gates with a loud bang. Matt jumped at the sound. He realized how tense he'd become. He didn't know if he'd be able to sleep, thinking about how unprepared he and his friends were for traveling north. Despite everything, he'd still thought there was a chance he'd make it to Helfratheim to find his parents, and that Tomtar would be able to come up with maps to help them on the journey. But now they were about to venture into unknown territory without maps, without any kind of guide or direction, and Matt felt angry and depressed. He was angry with himself, with Tomtar and Tuava-Li, with the whole world. He was angry with Mrs. Babcek's son for not looking out for her. When he cared so much about his own mother and father, and felt so horribly guilty for what had happened to them on his account, he couldn't understand how someone else could be so indifferent. A wave of bitterness swept over him. *Maybe everybody in life is only out for himself,* he thought, *faerie folk, too. The trolls and the elves with their jewels and money, Tomtar's uncle and his lust for power. Everybody's greedy and selfish and nobody cares about other people's problems and pain.*

Matt was guilty of it himself, of course. He wouldn't have ever considered going on this farce of a quest with Tuava-Li and Tomtar unless they'd promised him that they would help find his parents. "You scratch my back, I'll scratch yours," he mumbled aloud. That was what life was about. It made him feel hollow and sad. And then he heard the breaking glass.

He was within sight of Mrs. Babcek's apartment building. He saw the two dark figures slipping through the door, and a chill raced up his spine. Matt loped through the shadows, dashing from tree trunk to shrub, alert and on guard. He came to the door and saw that it was ajar. Pieces of glass crunched beneath his feet, glimmering in the light of the full moon. He knew instinctively that the men were going to break into Mrs. Babcek's apartment. They were looking for the Jewels; maybe they'd been following Matt and planning this since he arrived.

Matt set the groceries down. He grabbed a brick from the garden bed by the door and slipped into the building. He crept up the stairs, hugging the railing, avoiding the middle of the steps where the wood might groan with his weight and give him away. He peered around the landing on the third floor and saw the two men huddled at the old lady's door. One of them was prying at the lock with a screwdriver. Matt backed up slightly, his hand slipping on the banister, making the tiniest squeak. His breath caught in his throat as the robbers spun around. Their eyes bored into his, and Matt realized it was the guy from the pawnshop, and one of the men he'd seen in the back of the shoe repair shop. One of them lunged. "Quick," the other hissed, pointing his screwdriver. "Don't let him get away!"

Matt reared back on the stairs and stumbled, losing his balance. But just as a hand reached for his throat, he smashed the brick against the man's cheekbone.

"*Aaaarrrrgh!*" the robber shrieked, and fell against Matt. Both of them tumbled down half a flight of steps. The man was on top of Matt, gripping him by the collar of his jacket as he jackknifed his legs and stopped their fall. Matt squeezed out from beneath the man's bulk and the front of his jacket tore away. The robber lunged at him again. Matt pushed against the coarse, unshaven face, so close to his, and his hand came away slick with blood. He bolted down the steps. Both men were after him now. One hurled himself over the railing and came down hard in front of Matt. He stumbled but got up, panting hard, his face twisted in fury. Matt spun around, looking one way, then another. Trapped. At the end of the hall a door creaked open, and for a second he saw a face peering out of the crack. "Call the cops," Matt cried, but the door slammed shut.

Both robbers turned toward the sound and Matt made a dash for freedom. One of the men grabbed a handful of Matt's hair and wrenched his head back. "This could have been easy," a hoarse voice whispered into his ear, "but you had to make it

hard, didn't you? Give us the jewels, kid, or you're going to be sorry you were—"

There was a rush of wind. Something swept over Matt's head, and the kestrel's scream pierced the air. Its talons raked the robber's face. The other man stumbled and fell, and when he got up, he cried out at the sight of the bird swooping toward him. The robbers covered their heads with their hands. They stumbled down the steps and hurried out of the building, glass crackling beneath their feet.

Matt hurried through the door and saw the two men climb into a pickup truck at the end of the block. He sucked in the night air and found himself laughing in relief. "That was amazing, Tuava-Li," he called over his shoulder.

The bird squawked in response, and settled at the top of the banister on the first floor. Matt heard her thought-speak. *I see I can't trust you alone for even a few hours!*

"Yeah, I'm glad to see you, too," he murmured, and noticed a car door swing open along the curb just outside. Winkler, the shoe repairman, got out of the driver's seat and walked slowly toward him. Matt knelt by the garden, never letting the man out of his sight, and picked up another brick.

Winkler reached into his pocket and withdrew two pairs of small leather shoes. "I finished these things up a little earlier than I thought, so I wanted to drop by and see that you got them."

"Don't lie to me," Matt said, hoisting the brick in his hand. "I

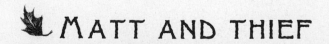

MATT AND THIEF

know what you and those two other guys are up to. I never even told you where I was staying."

Winkler nodded, then stopped in his tracks. "Do you know the writer Alexandre Dumas? *The Count of Monte Cristo? The Three Musketeers?* Ah, well. He said, *'Business? It's quite simple. It's other people's money.'* You see, my business is taking other people's money. A smart man has to have his fingers in a lot of different pies, these days, if he's going to stay ahead of the game. My partner down at the pawnshop told me about those jewels of yours. I knew they were clan jewels as soon as I saw them, and I decided it might be a good idea to have you tailed. My partner was willing to wait until tomorrow for you to bring them in to the shop, where he figured he'd buy them from you at a rock-bottom price. But why pay for something, I thought, when you can get it for free? When my boys saw you down on Carson, one of them came to tell me. I sent him and my partner to check out the old lady's apartment. If they couldn't find what they were looking for, they were supposed to wait for you to come back."

Winkler dropped the shoes onto the pavement, then reached into his pocket and withdrew a slim revolver. "Sometimes things don't go exactly according to plan. Now here we are! Let's go upstairs and get the jewels, son."

"I'm not afraid of you," Matt said, as Tuava-Li sailed out through the door and made a wide circle over their heads.

Winkler glanced up. In one quick movement Matt lifted the brick in his hand and smashed it with all his might through the windshield of the nearest car. The alarm that sounded was shrill and urgent. "That was stupid," Winkler said, rushing at Matt. "Get inside the building!"

Winkler threw Matt into the vestibule and pushed him against the wall. His arm was tight against the boy's throat. Screeching, the kestrel rocketed through the broken window of the door, clawing at the man's scalp. "I'm not leaving without the jewels," Winkler growled. A thin line of red ran down his forehead. "Tell your little bird friend to change back into an elf. Otherwise you're going to get—"

The light suddenly went out of Winkler's eyes. He groaned and fell to the floor. "Tuava-Li," Matt cried, "did you—?"

Aye, came the words in thought-speak. *Like I did before, with Nick and his Pixies outside of Argant, like I did with the Trolls outside the old school. I made sure that the burst of energy was greater this time, because of the Human's size.*

Matt searched the man's neck for a pulse. "You really did it this time."

We should get your things from upstairs and go. Winkler may not be unconscious for long.

"Longer than you think," Matt answered. The car alarm still rang shrilly. "He's dead."

Tuava-Li was still in her kestrel form; she couldn't scream. Instead she flapped her wings and shot out of the building and into the air, pumping her way closer toward the lights that twinkled and shone in the darkness, the lights that Faerie Folk believed were windows in the dome of heaven. "Tuava-Li," Matt cried, stepping into the night, "come back!"

Someone inched his window open and yelled out. "What's going on out there? I'm calling the cops!"

Tuava-Li turned in the black sky and shot toward the ground. She was a bullet, careening out of control, spiraling downwards as the earth rose up to swallow her. Just inches from the ground she arched her back, climbed out of her descent, and shot past Matt and the body of the man she had killed. At the end of the block she banked again and came toward Matt. She was turning back to an Elf as her claws touched the sidewalk and she scurried into the darkness behind a shrub. "This place is defiled," she wailed, "'tis corrupted by murder, by the life I took here this night." Tuava-Li fell to her knees and began to pray as the last of the feathers faded from her pale flesh. "I'm not worthy of your blessings, my Goddess, I'm not worthy of your love. Forever I'll live in the shadow of the awful thing I've done."

Matt heard Tuava-Li sobbing behind the bushes. "It was an accident," he said, moving awkwardly toward her hiding place. "You didn't know what it would take to stop him. He was a bad man, Tuava-Li, he might have killed me. He might have killed Mrs. Babcek, and you, too. You stopped him for my sake. You did it for the Earth, for the Cord, for your Mage, your quest. It's okay, Tuava-Li, it's really okay!"

Tuava-Li knew it had been an accident, but that didn't stop her from being overwhelmed with guilt. She was not only guilty of taking the man's life, but she was guilty of knowing that she was leading Matt to his own death, which would come when the Seed was planted at the center of the Earth. She was guilty of keeping the secret that was going to haunt her the rest of her life.

"What's going on?" a familiar voice rang out down the street.

Matt turned around to see Tomtar approaching, with two female Trolls beside him. All three pressed their hands to their ears to block out the wail of the car alarm. "Tomtar!" Matt cried.

Matt's eyes darted from one of the females to the other. "The Human can see us," Megala said, drawing a dagger from her belt.

"'Tis all right," Tomtar said. "He's the friend I told you about."

"Matt, these are two of my cousins, Megala and Mitelle. What happened to Mr. Winkler? Where's Tuava-Li? She was flying just ahead of us when we heard the siren."

Matt shook his head. "Winkler's dead. He knew we had the Alfheim jewels, and he was trying to steal them. Tuava-Li just wanted to knock him out, but I guess she didn't know her own strength. She's behind the bushes, over there."

Tomtar hurried to find his friend. "Let's get out of the light," Matt said to the Trolls. "That car alarm's driving me nuts, and the cops will be here soon."

They fled to the alley alongside the building. "Tomtar told us that the Elf is a Mage, and that she can read minds," Mitelle said, brushing the hair from her eyes and her long, pointed ears.

"She can," Matt said, "but she won't. It's against her principles, or something."

"He also said that you had *Huldus* full of *trans*, and that some of them are for invisibility. If we can sneak into Orin's headquarters without being seen, we can rescue our father and Delfina."

Matt frowned. "Your *father* and your sister? I thought your father was dead!"

"No. Our uncle captured both of them to find out where all the Clan Jewels are hidden. He'll kill them if they don't tell him what he wants to know. He'll probably kill them anyway, even if they talk! You've got to convince your Elf friend that she has to help us. Once we save our father, we'll make sure he gives you the maps you came for. Our victory will be to your advantage, as well!"

"I'll talk to her. But first I have to get my things from the apartment upstairs. I don't think we'll be coming back. The shoe repair guy tossed a couple of pairs of shoes into the grass, over there, by the way. You should get them for Tomtar and Tuava-Li."

Matt had Mrs. Babcek's key in his pocket, but he decided it was more polite to knock on the door instead. There was a hint of annoyance in her pale eyes when she answered. "What's all that racket outside, Matthew? It's so loud out there I could barely hear John's voice when he called me on the telephone."

"Your son called you?" Matt exclaimed.

"Sure he did," the old lady grumbled, shaking her head, "but I had to hang up because of that awful noise out on the street."

She had been looking at Matt, but suddenly her eyes seemed to clear. "What happened to your jacket? It's all tore up! Is that blood on your shirt? Are you in some kind of trouble? You look terrible!"

"No, Mrs. Babcek," Matt said. "I'm okay. You should call your son back, before you forget."

The old lady shook her head. "Children are supposed to call their mothers, not the other way around. Now why don't you come in and wash up? *Your* mom won't be very happy if she sees you looking like this."

Matt sighed in frustration and went to the bedroom where he'd hidden the Jewels. He realized his chest had been itching, and he went to scratch it. He shook his head as a thought passed through his mind. *No,* he said to himself. He tugged up his T-shirt and looked at his skin, more annoyed than surprised. The Jewels were gone. In their place was that Green Man, Khidr, once again. This time the Green Man was big. He looked strong, and he was covered in a thick coat of leaves. His eyes peered angrily from beneath the foliage and his mouth curled up in a snarl. *What's this all about?* Matt wondered. *Why would that Green Man be back now? Am I supposed to do something about the Green Man in the basement of St. Elmo's Firehouse, or is it just a symbol of something else? Is it telling me I have to be fierce, like the Green Man, to survive all of this? If somebody—or something—is trying to tell me something, why is so hard to understand?*

Matt grabbed the backpacks in the corner and the pouches of

Jewels from the closet. Nearly overwhelmed with frustration, he stepped back into the hall. He counted out five hundred dollars from the roll in his pocket and slipped the money underneath the keys on the table by the doorway. "Good-bye, Mrs. Babcek," he called. "Thanks for everything."

He could see her wrinkled hands on the arms of the easy chair that faced the TV in the corner. If she heard what Matt had said, he couldn't tell. The man on TV wore a troubled face. "It's official, there are now at least a thousand children and dozens of caretakers reported missing throughout the Northeast. The president spoke again this evening from the White House, assuring the American people that this is not the work of any known terrorist group, and that everything possible is being done to find the children and bring them home."

From inside the building, the car alarm was a muted throb; but Matt thought he heard sirens coming closer. He closed the apartment door behind him and hurried down the stairs. Tuava-Li, Tomtar, and his cousins were waiting outside in the alley.

36

TUAVA-LI WAS SEVERAL PACES behind the others as they rushed along East Carson Street. Her head was down, shrouded in sorrow. Matt hung back and waited for her, and touched her shoulder. "The tattoos changed again, Tuava-Li. The Green Man is back, and he looks bigger and meaner than before."

"Slow down," Megala called, holding out her arm like a crossing guard. "The Elf's not keeping up. What's wrong?"

"Wrong?" Tuava-Li answered. "Everything's wrong. Someone is dead, thanks to me."

"'Twas only a Human you killed," Megala said scornfully. "Just one Human. You have no spine, little Elf, if you let a thing like that stop you from helping us. However you do it, you've got to go into Orin's mind and find out what we need to know."

"Cut her a break," said Matt, coming to Tuava-Li's defense.

"This is hard for her. She's a Mage, after all. At least, she was training to be a mage before Alfheim was destroyed."

Tuava-Li shook her head. "When a monk becomes a Mage her Clan has a special ceremony to honor the transformation. That didn't happen to me."

"Whatever," Matt said. "She's not some kind of warrior princess, or whatever, like you guys. She's all about, well, love, and spirit, and stuff like that, she's —"

"I can speak for myself, Matthew," Tuava-Li interrupted. "My moral code is based on the teachings of my Master. We may be strong, but we choose to be gentle. We choose to act with compassion and respect. We don't believe in treading where we don't belong. Aye, I may be capable of seeing into the minds of others, but 'tis trespassing, 'tis a violation of their dignity to do so. Just because we're capable of doing things doesn't mean that we should use our power indiscriminately. In the same way that Faerie Folk can't enter buildings belonging to Humans without their permission, I know it dishonors another to step into his mind and take what is his alone to give. That's why I won't attempt to enter your uncle Orin's mind, no matter how much you beg."

Megala sneered. "You talk so that no one will understand you. You hide your cowardice behind a wall of words."

"She says she'll only do it if it's a real emergency," Matt added.

Megala stopped and stood with her fists clenched. "But this *is* a real emergency!"

"'Tisn't a real emergency to *her*," Mitelle said, "That's clear."

Tuava-Li looked away. "You don't understand," she said. "I don't—I mean my talents, or my powers, aren't refined, they're not precise. Because of my actions a living being is dead. I violated every tenant of my beliefs, my heritage, my . . . my . . ."

"She doesn't trust herself," Matt said, hoping to clarify things.

"Please," Tuava-Li said, glaring at Matt.

"Practice builds confidence," Megala said. "Help us, and you'll see."

"I've got an idea," Mitelle said. "Monks have lots of different powers. Can't you feel the presence of someone nearby, even if you can't see them?"

"Are you talking about Vollyar?" asked Tomtar.

Mitelle nodded. "And Delfina, too. We're not asking you to go against your beliefs, Tuava-Li. Maybe you don't need to go into Orin's mind to pry out his secrets. Will you be able to tell when our father's close?"

"I don't know," Tuava-Li said. "I've never met your uncle. I'm not sure how I could distinguish his energy from anyone else's. I suppose . . . I could try."

"You have to do better than try," Megala said.

"You temper your ferocity with wisdom," Tuava-Li smiled glumly. "At times your words remind me of my Mage."

"We grew up in that schoolhouse," Megala said. "There must be a hundred places in there where Orin could be keeping hostages. If we manage to get inside, we need to know where to look. We have to be stealthy; we have to make this a strategic strike. Otherwise our father and sister are doomed. We have to know where to find them before we break into the school."

"Then I'll change to a kestrel and fly ahead," Tuava-Li said. "If I stay high enough above the building, none will see me."

A door burst open and a dull, throbbing music spilled out onto the street. St. Elmo's Firehouse was just ahead. A pickup truck was parked out in front, and a pair of men lumbered across the sidewalk carrying a large barrel. They heaved it onto the bed of the truck and climbed inside. "Wait," Matt whispered. "Those are the guys who were trying to rob Mrs. Babcek before Winkler showed up! What are they doing here?"

"Who knows?" Megala spat. "Maybe they work for Orin, as well as for the Human Tuava-Li killed. There are some who serve many masters."

As the truck pulled away the club door burst open again. A trio of Elves, singing out of key, staggered into the night. Behind them came the juggler, Stefan.

"Good evening, old friends," Stefan cried, noticing Matt and the others. "Pleasant evening for a stroll, full moon and all!"

"Aye," Megala said, stepping around him.

"Tonight's the night!" Stefan said, grabbing Matt by the wrist. "They say Brahja-Chi's got her thousand, and I stand to win big if it's true!"

"I heard something about it on the TV," Matt said. "If only we could have gotten to Helfratheim . . . My parents—"

"Come on," Megala muttered, waving impatiently. "This one's nothing but a distraction."

"We could use a distraction when we get to the school," Mitelle exclaimed. "Tomtar, you know this Human?"

"Aye, I'm afraid I do!" Tomtar whispered in her ear. "He calls himself Stefan. He's a juggler; he says he was raised by Elves. He does tricks with knives and Fire Sprites."

"How much would your loyalty cost for a few hours this night, juggler?" she asked.

Stefan's eyes flashed at Matt. "A clan jewel would buy you a fair amount of trust," he answered.

Mitelle glanced at Matt, too. "All right?"

"All right," he repeated, and rolled his eyes in resignation. "A small one, okay?"

"Then come with us," Mitelle said. "I want you to put on a show for some friends of ours."

37

SPEAR POINTS AT HER BACK, Becky crossed the courtyard. Crowds of wide-eyed Elves parted before her. Some shielded their eyes at the sight of the Human, some held their noses, as if that would stop the contamination that was bound to accompany the girl. Becky saw bleachers and scaffolding to her right, guttering torches and signs inscribed with strange symbols, and scores of Elves waiting anxiously, daggers clutched in their hands. They were all dressed in black robes and wore rectangular headdresses so large that they bumped into each other as they sat in close quarters on rows of bleachers.

Festooned with flags and banners, the viewing stands hugged the palace wall. Guards plumped the cushions of the padded thrones reserved for Brahja-Chi and Jardaine. Jal-Maktar, according to plan, would watch the proceedings from his high window. The sound of Human cries rose above the noise and confusion and Becky's eyes flew to the cage where the children were held. Brahja-Chi's monks were stationed every ten feet or so around the cage, their arms stiff and extended, a circle of black scarecrows. Their faces were frozen in concentration. Their great eyes were squeezed shut, as they silently mouthed the incantations meant to protect the masses from Human germs.

The guards opened a gate in the cage and thrust Becky inside. She tumbled over several small children and a pile of stones, and landed on her back. Everything was happening too fast for her to make sense of it, or to feel the crushing weight of failure. The Elfin Queen had predicted they would march right through the gates of Helfratheim, and Macta had promised that he would reunite Becky with her parents. Both of them were wrong, and nothing had gone the way she'd hoped. The smell of fear and despair was thick inside the pen. Becky saw the eyes of the children, wide and deranged, staring down at her. "She's got a pack," a voice cried. "Take it and see if there's anything to eat!"

Becky pressed her elbow against the bag but hands clawed at her, tugging and tearing, and she let go. A boy, no more than six, stared down at Becky as she struggled to her feet. Becky was at least several years older than most of the other children in the pen; the Elves had obviously done their best to abduct the smallest and most helpless children they could find. "Can you help us get out of here?" the boy asked plaintively.

"I'll try," Becky sighed, "but there are a lot of elves out there, and they've got weapons."

"What do you mean, *elves*?" demanded one of the older children.

"You don't know?" Becky asked. The blank stares on the faces of the boys and girls told Becky the sad truth. None of them had any idea what was happening, or who was responsible for their imprisonment. "They're elves," Becky said, as other children began to gather around, anxious to hear what the big girl had to say.

"Where are we?" someone cried. "What's going on?" cried another.

Becky nodded. "I'll tell you all I know."

She quickly told the children who the Elves were, explaining their rituals, fear of germs, and everything else she could think of. "At first they were invisible," a child cried. "When we first got here, we couldn't see anyone, really, but we thought we heard their voices. That's why we didn't know if they were real, or if everything was just make-believe."

"They're real," Becky said. "It's not just pretend. We can't see them at first because it's hard for us to accept that they're real. It's not like they have special powers to *make* themselves invisible, or anything like that. We just have to learn to see them."

"We heard they can fly," a little girl said in a terrified voice. "They can cast spells and stop our hearts with magic words, and turn themselves into animals!"

"No—" Becky started, and then caught herself. "Well, there are a few who can do some kind of magic. They're called Mages.

They have special potions and things that they use sometimes, to create illusions and tricks, but most of the elves can't do anything like that. Look out there—can't you see that they're as frightened of you as you are of them? There are hundreds of us in here, and we're just as big—bigger than they are. We can get out of here; we can overpower them. We've got to try!"

The whimpers and moans of the children and the revelry of the Elves in the courtyard made it hard for anyone more than a few feet from Becky to understand her words. But when she heard a toddler's cry, something made her turn her head around. The guards had unlocked the gate again, and they were heaving another small child into the crowd. Becky pushed her way past the others as her breath caught in her throat. "Emily!" she cried, recognizing her little sister. She hadn't seen her in weeks, since their home was destroyed in the fire and Jardaine took Emily and her parents away in their flying ships. The girl looked thin, and tired, but her eyes came to life when she saw her big sister. Becky gathered up Emily in her arms and squeezed her tight. Her face, wet with tears, pressed against the soft pillows of the toddler's cheeks. "If you're here, then Mommy and Daddy must be here, too." She drew back just enough to look Emily in the eyes. "Are Mommy and Daddy here?"

The toddler nodded. She looked around, and then pointed a pudgy finger back the way she had come, from the laboratory building. "Sweetie, are they all right?" Becky asked, clutching her sister's arms.

Emily scrunched up her face. It was dark, and crowded here, there were too many people she'd never seen before, and her memories of the last few weeks colored her tangled thoughts with fear. She lifted her head to the sky. "Moon," she said, and looked wide-eyed at Becky.

"Yes, I know it's the moon. It's a big, full moon. What about Mom and Dad? Are they okay?"

Someone was tugging on Becky's sleeve. "What can we do to get away?"

Becky thought about her experiences with the Elves, and tried to remember anything that might be useful. She thought of her house, and how Tomtar used to come and visit, and she thought of the strange ghost-girl, Anna, whom the Elves had used to gain entry to her home. It all seemed like a million years ago. Then a realization struck her and she shivered with a thrill of hope. "I just thought of something. Faeries can't go into people's homes without a human giving them permission. You have to invite an elf or a troll to come into the place where you live, or they have to stay outside. It's one of their laws. They never break their own laws."

"What happens if they just come in without being invited?" a boy asked.

"I don't know," Becky said, "but they never risk it. Maybe there's some kind of force field that stops them, maybe they just drop dead. I don't know. Listen, what are these heaps of stone for, all around the inside of the fence?"

"We overheard them saying they were going to build walls so

that the bad smell wouldn't get out there and bother everyone," a girl offered, "and they were going to build special places to go to the bathroom, too."

"Why didn't they do it?" Becky asked.

"The builders were afraid to get too close to us, so they gave up. Now there are just these heaps of stones."

"Well, we're going to build a house," Becky said, her words bursting with excitement and hope. "Not a house, exactly, but walls, and walls make a house. If they're *our* walls, if we build them, then the Elves won't be able to come in here and get us, or force us to come out. We'll be able to tell them what to do, and they'll have to let us go!"

"But we don't have any food," an older girl cried. "If we're trapped in here, and we don't do what they want, they'll starve us to death!"

Becky shook her head. "Come on, let's give it a try, at least," she coaxed. "The moon's full tonight. I think if we can hold them off until tomorrow, we'll be okay. I don't have time to explain. Tell everybody to take the stones and build walls around us. Even if they're not very tall, they'll still be walls, and the Elves won't be able to get us. Come on! Just do it!"

Becky got the older children working to move the stones and stack them like blocks. She hurried up and down the long length of the cage, explaining to the other children what was happening. She ordered some of the bigger kids to move the younger children and toddlers into the center of the cage; there they were to sit on the ground and be quiet. Soon, as Becky had imagined, the guards outside the fence grew curious. They rushed to find their superior, who hurried to the scene. "What do you think you're doing?" the captain called. He knew it was he who would pay the price for the Human's misbehavior. "Put those stones back, I command you!"

The captain was reluctant to order his soldiers to enter the pen; soon the prisoners would be herded into the courtyard for sacrifice. Until then, there was no reason to risk any unnecessary confrontations. From outside the barrier the Elves watched, fascinated, as the captain threatened the children with a dozen fates he assured them were worse than death. Becky waited until the final stones were set in place, forming a large rectangle nearly three feet high. She went up to the single opening and called to the captain. "Go away," she said, "we're in our house and you're bothering us."

"Shut your mouth, foolish girl," the captain yelled, as his guards tittered in amusement. "It won't be long before we bring you out into the open, where you won't dare disrespect us with your nonsense."

"This is our house, and you can't come in," Becky insisted. "Everybody knows that elves can't go into a human dwelling without permission, and we want you to go away and leave us alone."

The Elves were laughing at Becky's effrontery, but the captain felt a twinge of concern gnawing at the corner of his mind. "Those are our stones," he said uncertainly, "and it's our courtyard. If those walls make a house, it's not yours!"

"Yes it is," Becky said, with her hands planted on her hips, "because we built it. I'll prove it to you. Try to come inside, and see what happens!"

The guards backed away. All of them had been taught the law, but none were certain what the consequences were of breaking it. None of the Elves had ever been in the Human world before. "Go and get Jardaine," the captain ordered a pair of guards. "She'll know what to do about this."

In the throne room an excited crowd of Royal Propagandists, Image Consultants, and Most Revered personal assistants were clustered around Jal-Maktar and the Mages. Nick had returned from his errand to deliver the little Human girl from the laboratory to the pen where the rest of the children were kept. Now it was time for them all to go to the courtyard and begin the final stage of Brahja-Chi's Acquisition—the sacrifice. "How do I look?" asked Jal-Maktar, flexing his shoulders.

"You look like King Macta," said Jardaine. "In some ways you appear to be very pleased with yourself, and yet, somehow, I think you betray a hint of anxiety, as well. You ought to stand up straighter. If it's hunger that makes you look a little hunched over, you might—"

"All right, that's enough," Jal-Maktar said, and adjusted the collar of his cape. "A simple *fantastic* would have sufficed."

The false King and his entourage were assembling by the

door when the guards from the courtyard burst in. "Jardaine, Mistress Jardaine," one of them cried breathlessly, "there's trouble outside! The Humans have built a wall around the inside of their cage. They refuse to come out, and we can't go in to get them without their permission. What should we do?"

"*Permission*?" Jardaine spat. "*Make* them come out, you superstitious fool. We're already running late. We can't afford any more delays!"

She glanced at Jal-Maktar, realizing that it wouldn't be long before his contract ran out. He had pledged to wait to take the children's souls until they'd been sacrificed by the Elves in the courtyard; if he decided that he was in a hurry, and wanted his reward before it was time, everything would be ruined. "Will you come, ma'am?" pleaded the guard. "The captain asked for you to make an appearance and show everyone that the prisoners are harmless, and that we can go into the cage without risking our lives!"

Jardaine fought to control her rage. "Who's in charge out there, you, or a bunch of Human children? I will give you ten minutes to remedy this situation. At that time the King will go to the high balcony, and Brahja-Chi and I will make our way down the palace steps. If the Humans aren't in place for the sacrifice, you and the other guards will pay with your heads. Do I make myself clear?"

The guards hurried away and Jardaine shut the doors behind them. "Can we still manage to get this all done before the stroke of midnight?" she asked the Propagandists.

Jal-Maktar flung himself onto his throne and sighed at the delay. He soothed himself with the thought that soon he would be standing on the balcony of the high tower, where he would feed on the souls of the Human children as they were sacrificed in the courtyard below. At the right moment he would squat out of sight, so that none would see the suckered tentacles hanging from the maw of a scaly lizard face. It was the form he always took when drawing in souls lost in battle, natural catastrophes, and terrible accidents, where victims met their demise together in what Jal-Maktar liked to call *La Grande Mort*, or the Big Death.

Jardaine gathered the members of the procession by the door. In just another minute they would begin their march toward the destiny that the Great Goddess intended for them. Brahja-Chi sat by the wall, her eyes squeezed shut, her hands folded on her lap. *Forgive me, Great Ones,* she prayed silently, *for my anger and my impatience. 'Tis only for the sake of Your love and attention that I have labored so long. Please accept the sacrifice that I am about to offer in Your name. I am only Your humble servant, and all I ask is that You show me the respect I deserve. All I ask is —*

There was another knock at the door. "Now what?" Jardaine cried angrily.

A group of palace guards stalked into the chamber, and the crowd parted to let them past. Walking in the midst of a dozen white robed servants was a female Elf. She was dirty and bedraggled, but despite her appearance she held her head high. "How dare you bring that filthy creature into King Macta's throne room," Jardaine barked, "don't you—"

Jardaine's words caught in her throat as she saw another shambling, wounded figure enter the room. There was something familiar in the Elf's face, something that frightened her more than anything in the world. "In the name of the Canon, and the Mistress who serves its Word," the captain said with a bow. "We found these two Elves downstairs. The female identifies herself as Princess Asra of Alfheim, daughter of Thorgier and Shorya, and fiancée of King Macta. Some of the servants confirm her identity. The other Elf, the one with a missing arm, claims to be King Macta himself!"

All of the Elves in the room gasped. Some stifled laughter, and others groaned in disbelief and outrage. "What are you thinking, bringing these ruffians here?" Jardaine cried, her voice trembling. "If not for the ruckus in the courtyard with the Human children, we'd have been gone before you ever showed up here with these impostors. We have no time for this nonsense. King Macta stands at my side, as any fool can see. Our King is healthy and strong, not a crippled weakling. How dare you—"

"Let me speak for myself," said Jal-Maktar, stepping forward and adjusting his crown. "Captain, this interruption is an outrage. Take these Elves to the dungeon and execute them at once. I shall consider what an appropriate punishment might be for you, insulting the King by bringing these pathetic frauds into our company."

"Nooo," said Prashta, of the Seven Agents, stepping out of the group. "Let us speak with the one who claims to be Macta Dockalfar. Bring him here, Captain."

The guards shoved Macta roughly across the room. When he was standing before the Agents, he lifted his head so that the light fell on his gaunt face, and spoke. "Prashta, 'tis a relief to see you again. I beg you, will you end this charade now, before it is too late?"

Prashta fingered his amulets as a thousand thoughts, and hopes, and fears, swept through his mind. "If you are who you claim to be, then tell me, who is the one who stands before us, wearing your crown?"

Macta glanced at Jal-Maktar and saw the image of himself in better days. He swallowed his disgust. "That I do not know, other than that he's an impostor. Obviously he was paid by Brahja-Chi and Jardaine to impersonate me. I can think of only one way for you to prove which of us is the real King of Helfratheim. Test our knowledge. Perhaps this pretender who stands so proudly at Jardaine's side knows all the details of my life, but I doubt it. Go on, ask!"

Prashta cleared his throat and looked Jal-Maktar in the eye. "What is your mother's name, your Highness?"

Jal-Maktar smiled thinly. "My mother's name was Jodwa. She's dead. Why do you entertain such nonsense, Prashta? My faith in you is sorely tested by your behavior. If you value your own head, you'll stop this foolishness."

Prashta and the other Agents stole troubled glances at one another. "This is an insult to the King," one whispered. "We must stop!"

Jal-Maktar glanced at Jardaine and Brahja-Chi to see what their response was to this unexpected situation. Was the true Macta still alive, he wondered, and could this wretch be the real King of Helfratheim? What were the Mages planning to do about it?

Prashta turned to Macta, who stood clutching his wounded shoulder. "What is the name of your mother?" he asked.

"My real mother's name was Jodwa," Macta said.

Jal-Maktar rolled his eyes. "And wherever did you learn that?"

"But I have had seven stepmothers since my true mother was killed in an unfortunate accident," Macta continued, "when I was just an Elflad. My stepmothers' names were Gondel, Bittuva, Sinoay, Carladine, Farnelle, and Proavelle. Oh, wait, that's only six. The seventh was Sindu. After her untimely demise, my father chose to remain . . . let us say, emotionally unattached."

Jardaine pointed a finger at Prashta and approached him, her face twisted into a mask of fear and rage. "All of that is public record. The fool could have memorized any number of facts about our King. This little quiz is absurd. Enough now! If you don't kill him, I will!"

"You will do no such thing," said the Most Revered Agent, rattling his amulets. "And don't point your finger at me. I might get the impression that you intend to do me harm. There's still plenty of room in the dungeon for you, Jardaine."

Prashta turned toward Jal-Maktar. "Tell me, sir, what was the name of your pet?"

Jal-Maktar's breath caught in his throat. Though Jardaine had coached him on the details of Macta's life as a Prince, she hadn't mentioned anything about a pet. He felt his cheeks growing warm. "For weeks we have waited for this moment," he said, ignoring the question, "when Brahja-Chi would make this offering to the Gods, to enlist their help in our onslaught against the Human world. I will have no more of this nonsense, Prashta. I will rule without your interference from now on. You are my enemies, and betrayers of the realm. Guards, I order you to arrest these Elves at once!"

The guards raised their spears and backed the Seven Agents against the wall, but when they got too close, they discovered there might as well have been a glass shield between them. The new medallions were working, better than the Agents could have imagined. "Now it's your turn," Prashta said to Macta. "Tell me the name, sir, of your most beloved pet!"

"There is a head mounted on a plaque on the wall of my private chambers," Macta murmured, his voice raw with emotion. "'Tis the head of a Goblin. He was killed on a Human roadway when Baltham, Druga, and I were chasing that old Mage Kalevala Van Frier through the forest near Alfheim." Macta sniffled as his eyes welled up with tears.

"My pet's name was Powcca, and my heart still aches at the thought of him."

Prashta looked down at his hands, still clutching a protective amulet, and shook his head. "I do not know how this was done," he said, "or what kind of magick has created the impostor who wears the crown of the true King, but the time for little games has ended. The real Macta has appeared, and just in time. Jardaine and Brahja-Chi, I know that you're responsible for this charade, and therefore as of this moment, I am canceling the sacrifice of the Humans, in the name of the Seven Most Revered Agents of Helfratheim."

"You can't—" Jardaine began, leaping up. But something caught in her throat and she fell back in her seat. Her toes were tingling, her legs felt like they were caught in a vise.

"You," Prashta said, pointing to one group of guards, "go to the courtyard and release the children. Lead them back across the border into the Human realm. I'll find something to say to the crowd about why this has been done. And as for you, Jardaine and Brahja-Chi, I hereby banish you from this kingdom. If you ever try to enter Helfratheim again, you'll pay with your lives." Prashta stared at Jardaine as her eyes bulged out. He wasn't sure, but they seemed to be slipping across her face, moving to the sides of her head. With a look of embarrassment and disgust he turned to the other Agents. "What in the names of the Gods is happening to her?"

Jardaine clutched her throat. Scales were forming on her

neck, and they quickly spread all the way up to the top of her head. She gagged as her body convulsed, her weight shifting so that her torso grew thinner and thinner, her arms and legs seemed to shrivel, and she slipped beneath the table. "My transformation!" she choked, and as she spoke the words her tongue, black and narrow, flicked out of her mouth. Jardaine was on her way to becoming a full-fledged Mage, her animal transformation finally brought on by the height of her emotions — shame, fear, and hatred. She hadn't chosen the form she took; that was a matter of destiny. Once she learned to control the change, the power to shape-shift would be hers forever. But what an awful disappointment it was, the form that she'd been given! She wasn't one of the regal birds or fierce predators she'd hoped to become. She was a common chameleon, small and harmless. She slithered miserably behind the King's throne.

Macta snatched his crown from Jal-Maktar's head and stepped backwards across the stone floor. "Now that we've seen Jardaine's true colors," he sneered, "we must insist on seeing what this impostor looks like when he's not pretending to be me! Show your true form, monster, before we send you back to hell!"

"My true form?" Jal-Maktar said in a whisper, though there was something stirring in his voice that everyone felt like the wind that precedes a storm. His lips curled away from gritted teeth. "You think I have only one true form? Foolish Elves! I am *all* forms. Behold the power of the Fir Darrig, Jal-Maktar!"

The Faerie Folk in the chamber began to creep anxiously

toward the doors. Jal-Maktar bellowed, "I forbid any of you to leave!" and all movement ceased.

The crowd cried out as Jal-Maktar's head burst into flames. Within the fire it began to grow, until it loomed like an enormous, grinning jack-o'-lantern. Everyone recoiled from the heat, the blinding light, and a nauseating stench that filled the room. White worms of flame danced around the Fir Darrig's head. Everyone watched, frozen in horror, as a crack split the creature's body and another monster emerged, like an insect from a cocoon. It was a sinewy, hunchbacked thing with black, ashen pits where eyes should have been. It opened its twisted mouth and disgorged a cloud of black, buzzing insects. The creature disappeared as the insects swarmed together at the center of the chamber and formed a huge black shape, with arms and legs and a shriveled head set atop lumpy shoulders. Its mouth opened and it let out a shriek of triumph. A second head popped from its shoulder, then a third burst from its chest, and a fourth from its swollen abdomen. All of them opened their mouths and screamed in a hideous cacophony.

The monster dissolved into a pool of dark liquid. Out of the pool rose a spinning column, which shot into the air and spread over the vaulted ceiling. The Elves looked up in terror as an inky rain began to fall. Jal-Maktar's laughter sounded in the air. He became a metallic obelisk covered in thousands of red, blinking eyes. He became a beautiful Human child in a pink party dress with ribbons in her hair, who opened her little pocketbook to reveal a sleek serpent hiding inside. The serpent flew into the

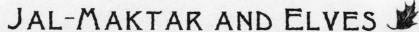

JAL-MAKTAR AND ELVES

chamber to spew the Elves with toxic, burning droppings. The image of the girl in the party dress disappeared. "Stop this display at once," shouted Macta, holding his one good hand over his head. "I am the King of this realm, and I command you to cease and show your true form! Your so-called power is nothing but an illusion!"

The serpent landed in the middle of the room and quickly took on the form of King Macta once again. "Is that what you think?" Jal Maktar chortled. He held out one hand, and it began to mushroom into a huge, gray boulder, an enormous fist carved in stone. "I shall deal with you later," he said, and swung the fist at the real Macta. "Be gone!"

When the fist struck, Macta flew backwards. Asra was standing behind him and she, too, was thrown off her feet. The pair of them disappeared in a puff of ash. "Now," he said, turning to face Brahja-Chi, "you promised me a thousand souls, old friend, and you have broken your contract."

"I did nothing of the sort," Brahja-Chi cried, pointing at the Council of Seven. "'Tis *their* fault, not mine, that the contract is broken. Take them, instead of me, in the name of the Mistress and the Canon which inspires her works!"

"I'm not interested in your Canon, and your works are as meaningless as your promises," Jal-Maktar sneered. "I, on the other hand, take my promises very seriously. According to our contract, if the terms are violated, you must pay with your own beating heart. Do you remember signing the contract, Brahja-Chi?"

Tentacles rolled from Jal-Maktar's mouth, shot across the throne room and grabbed the old Mage around the waist as she tried to escape. "Hold still," he said, his words a thick mass of syllables, "and it won't even hurt. You'll feel a little pinch, and then it will all be over."

Brahja-Chi's eyes bulged, then shrunk back into her skull. "Stop it," Jal-Maktar ordered. "Stop it! You can change your shape, but you can't change your fate!"

As downy black fur sprouted from Brahja-Chi's face, her body darkened and collapsed on itself, and her hands became paws with long claws that scratched and tore at Jal-Maktar's tentacles. She had turned to a mole, and she was fighting for her life.

"Don't shame yourself like this," Jal-Maktar slurred. "Be still!"

The mole was a blur of struggling limbs as she shot out of Jal-Maktar's grip and landed on the marble floor. With the wind knocked out of her, she lay helplessly, her legs splayed out at her sides. Jal-Maktar simply pointed a finger at the stunned little animal. "That's better," he said.

The mole twisted up and stiffened as her heart disappeared from her chest. Jal-Maktar swallowed and shook his head. "I was promised the heart of a Mage, and all I got was the heart of a mole. 'Tis not fair!" Jal-Maktar glanced around and saw the rest of the Faerie Folk trembling before him. "What are you still doing here?" He waved a hand. "Get out of my sight!"

There was a mad rush for the doors, and the seven Agents

crept through their secret exit in the back. Nick cowered behind a curtain, with one eye on the door, and the other on the tail of the chameleon that he saw protruding from behind the throne. He still desperately hoped there was something more he could do to win the favor of someone important. If there was nothing he could do to impress Jal-Maktar, perhaps it was not too late to save Jardaine. He scurried from his hiding place, dashed behind the throne, and scooped up the lizard, then headed for the door. Jal-Maktar sighed. "Silly Troll, you flatter yourself to think I'd be interested in doing you any harm," he called to Nick. "I've got a real King to deal with now."

He shut his eyes, sucked in his breath, and disappeared. As soon as he was gone Jardaine began her transformation to an Elf. Nick, frightened at the sight of the chameleon writhing and changing in the palm of his hand, quickly placed her on the floor. He ran to find her robe as she grew, stretching, her skin smoothing, her hair flowing from her pale scalp. The chamber was silent as a tomb as Nick returned and bowed before Jardaine. "I am yours to command, my Mage," he said.

"Oh, stop it," she snapped, as she pulled her robe over her head. "You don't fool me with your bowing and scraping. You're looking for an opportunity."

Nick got to his feet, not yet certain of how to talk to Jardaine. "Well . . . what shall we do now?"

Jardaine stroked her chin. "*We*?" she said. "Funny you

should ask. 'Tis said that every disaster is an opportunity. With Brahja-Chi dead, there's no use staying in Helfratheim, there's no use pretending that I could achieve any power here, there's no use in trying to carry on with plans of conquest in the Human realm. All of that is finished; but I believe the Goddess has other plans for *us*, Nick."

"The Goddess . . . ?" the Troll said cautiously.

For a long moment Jardaine said nothing, though her face bore an intensity that frightened him. "This is what we shall do," she murmured. "We'll tell the Elves of Helfratheim and Brahja-Chi's followers that the Goddess was simply testing our faith by demanding the Human sacrifice, and now they have welcomed Brahja-Chi into Paradise as thanks for what she did here. But a new task awaits us now, a new challenge. You and I are going to find a Human, and the three of us are going to travel to the North Pole to take a Seed from the fruit of the Holy Adri. We will plant it at the center of the Earth, as Fada did with his companions in ancient legend."

"What?" Nick cried. "That's what your old Mage planned, by sending Tuava-Li, Tomtar, and that horrible boy to the Pole. They must be halfway there by now. We'd never catch up. You're not serious . . . are you?"

Jardaine clenched her jaw. "We'll beat Tuava-Li to the Pole, and we'll plant the Seed, and we'll live in legend, for all time. They're traveling on foot. We have Arvada, and we have maps. 'Tis said that the Adri grows at the heart of a city at the top of the world, hidden by mountains and cloaked by magick, but if anyone can find it, 'twill be me!"

"But what if the legends are wrong?" Nick asked. "What if the Mage's vision was just a delusion? What if there *is* no Seed, what if there's no Goddess, and nothing at the top of the world but ice and snow? What then?"

Jardaine shook her head impatiently. "I've given this much thought. Listen to what I say, Nick. Stories and legends are what make us real; they give us purpose. And if I wish to rule the Elf realm, I must have the best stories. More than that, I must be at the center of the best story of them all. Brahja-Chi thought that my old Mage was a fool, and that re-creating the myth was a joke. But if the story is true, if there's the smallest, tiniest chance, if there's any sliver of possibility that re-creating the legend of Fada will force the Gods to act, then it's worth all of the risk I must endure. I'll become the most beloved, the most feared Mage in the entire realm! Plus, I will beat Tuava-Li at her own game. I cannot allow her to win."

Nick shook his head in disbelief. "But what if we find the Seed, and plant it, and nothing happens?"

Jardaine's eyes gleamed with an almost maniacal certainty. "Come, Nick, we must snatch one of the children of the Acquisition before they all get away. We'll need a Human for our quest—an Elf, a Troll, and a Human, as it was in ancient times!"

Macta and Asra came to their senses in a damp, dark cellar far below the palace.

Macta got up from the floor. Carefully he brushed the hair from his eyes and the dirt from the rags he wore. Then he raised his fist and banged on the rough wooden door, bellowing for help that would not come. Asra sat on the ground with her head in her hands. She was too tired, too weary to cry. She was locked up with the Elf who had ruined her life. Suddenly a shadow passed beneath the door. Macta leapt back as Jal-Maktar began to materialize, forming in the midst of a cloud of green smoke. "So you've come to torment me some more?" Macta said, as the Fir Darrig took on the form of a healthier, cleaner Macta, grinning cruelly. "You want to gloat?"

Jal-Maktar shook his head. "You know nothing. My contract is set to expire at any moment, and my life in the material world will be over, until some Mage calls me back. Brahja-Chi promised me the souls of a thousand Human children, which would have guaranteed me a permanent body in your realm. Now I'm left with nothing."

Asra glanced up. "Better to be invisible and free than trapped forever in a cell with—with—"

"Stop your whining and listen to me," Jal-Maktar said. "This is important. Under my contract with Brahja-Chi, while I'm in Helfratheim I'm entitled to eat a soul a day; Human or Faerie, the wording isn't specific. Though she's broken her side of the bargain, I will not break mine. I could take both of your lives, but the contract specifies *one* soul, and so it shall be. I'm entirely within my rights to take one of you. The only question is, which of you shall walk away from here, and which of you will die?"

Macta cringed as Asra turned her deadened eyes at Jal-Maktar. "Do what you will," she mumbled.

Jal-Maktar reached into his pocket and withdrew a pair of knucklebones. As he jiggled them in his palm, one of the dice fell to pieces in his hand. "Drat!" he cried. "I was going to play a little game of chance to decide which of you to take. After pretending to be Macta, I've developed a particular fondness for gambling."

"I've got a pair," Macta volunteered. He took the knucklebones from his pocket and handed them to Jal-Maktar. Asra glanced up, knowing that Macta's dice were shaved, and that odds were he would roll a seven. "Whichever of you chooses the number that's closest to the toss of the knucklebones belongs to me," Jal-Maktar said. "What's your lucky number, Macta?"

"Seven."

"And yours, Princess?"

"Twelve," Asra said, knowing what the outcome of the toss would be. She was stunned that Macta would choose to give his life for her.

"Fair enough," Jal-Maktar said.

He rolled the knucklebones, letting them bounce off the damp wall, and they landed, still as death, near his feet. "Five and two," said Jal-Maktar. "Lucky seven. Tough for you, Macta. Say good-bye to the Princess!"

Macta backed away, groped for the right words to say, and for a moment his eyes met Asra's. What she saw there was fear, and regret, and something she was surprised to recognize as love. "Ah," said Jal-Maktar. "Perhaps it would be disrespectful to take your soul in front of the one you adore. This dungeon has many chambers; Macta, why don't you slip around the corner, where the lovely Princess will be spared the spectacle? I'll join you there in a moment."

Macta walked mechanically into the darkness, and turned down the corridor that led to the next vaulted chamber. Jal-Maktar looked at Asra and shook his head. "He must love you very much to be willing to sacrifice himself like that, with those trick dice."

Asra shook her head. "You knew about the dice?"

"Come, come, I'm not stupid," Jal-Maktar interrupted. "Tell me, Princess, isn't there some affection in your heart for what Macta did to save your life? Don't you love him just a little bit?"

"No," Asra said softly, searching inside for any feeling whatsoever. "Perhaps . . . perhaps I hate him just a little less."

"Well, that's better than nothing," Jal-Maktar chuckled wryly. He turned in the direction Macta had gone and shouted, "Air and water, fire and flood, Jal-Maktar smells fresh young Blood!"

Asra sat in silence. A moment later an awful roar of anguish filled the chamber, echoing along the stone walls. The Princess choked back a sob for all that had gone wrong. Then she heard footsteps approaching.

38

ORIN'S SOLDIERS KEPT WATCH from the yard outside the old school. While a few had their eyes on the streets and alleys, most of them gathered inside the fence, laughing and bragging about their exploits. Since it seemed that Orin and Sattye had struck a kind of bargain, there was little threat of danger tonight. Some of the Trolls hunched around campfires, singing songs of battle. Others slumped with their chins against their chests, snoring loudly. Still others tossed knucklebones by the brick wall, gambling away their meager pay. The full moon threw its light down upon the army as a solitary kestrel made an arc in the sky and circled, high above.

"Nectar of the Gods," a soldier shouted, hoisting a paper cup.

At Orin's command, a pair of Humans had delivered a barrel of the green stuff from the basement of St. Elmo's Firehouse. Now everyone who tasted it was feeling a healthy glow. "Straight from Khidr himself," another soldier said, throwing back his own cup of the emerald liquid. Out of the corner of his eye he saw a tennis ball bouncing across the concrete.

"Toss me that ball, will you, mate?" a voice called from outside the fence.

Spinning around, the soldier drew his dagger. His companions leapt up from the fireside. Stefan stood innocently in the shadows by the gate, grinning pleasantly. He gave a little wave. The soldier who had retrieved the ball relaxed at the sight of him. "Ah, I've seen him down at St. Elmo's. He's all right."

He tossed the ball over the fence. The juggler shot out a hand, caught it, and with a twist of his fingers made it disappear. "Do that again!" the Trolls cried. "Where did you put that ball? Is it in your sleeve?"

"*Unnnnnh,*" one of them grunted, as the tennis ball fell from above and bounced off the top of his head.

The rest erupted in cheers and laughter. Someone picked up the ball and lobbed it to Stefan, who snapped his fingers and made it disappear once more. Then the juggler turned his head and began to cough. A Fire Sprite, big as an orange, shot from Stefan's mouth and landed in his hand. He coughed again, and again, and there were three Fire Sprites, dancing in his upturned palm. "Oooooooh, that's hot!"

He began to juggle them, slowly at first, and then faster and faster. He pitched them into the air and they spun like Fourth of

July fireworks, sending out showers of sparks. "More! More!" the Trolls cried, glad for the unexpected entertainment.

They unlocked the gate to let Stefan inside, slapping his extended hands in welcome, laughing and chortling. Quickly he opened up his pack and spread his juggling props on the ground. *Pay attention to me,* Tuava-Li's voice appeared in his mind. *Are you prepared to do your trick with the knives and the apple?*

"Aye," he answered softly, looking about for the sound of the voice.

Entertain the troops. Make them laugh, keep them distracted. When I tell you to, see if you can gather as many of their weapons as you can.

Stefan nodded. Then he stood up before the crowd, grinning foolishly. "Ouch!" he cried, and plucked a Fire Sprite from his smoking armpit. The Trolls roared with laughter.

On the other side of the building, Megala worked with the blunt end of an axe to dig a hole under the fence. The guards who were stationed there had abandoned their posts to watch Stefan's show. Tomtar and Mitelle scooped away the dirt with their hands, and Matt, at Megala's orders, stood out of sight behind a tree trunk. The rest of them were chewing on the bits of bark that would make them temporarily invisible to the soldiers. When they had moved enough earth, they got down on their bellies and squeezed to the other side of the fence. Matt looked distraught. "What about me?"

"Stay where you are," Megala said. "Without *trans* you'll be seen, and spoil everything."

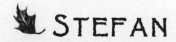 STEFAN

"It's not fair! What if something happens to you in there?"

"Don't worry," Tomtar said, "we'll be all right. I promise you, Matt, we're going to get those maps, and we're going to get to the Pole!"

"And to Helfratheim," Matt added, knowing that once they had the maps, there was still going to be a battle over where they would go first.

There was a rush of air as a shadow swept down from the sky. *I sense the heartbeats of many,* Tuava-Li said in thought-speak, landing on the edge of the fence.

Megala and Mitelle reared back, their eyes wide with disbelief. "She does that all the time," Tomtar said.

"Stay out of our brains, little bird," Megala hissed.

Tuava-Li's thoughts appeared again. *You mustn't be afraid of thought-speak. The world of thought is like a spider's web, and each of us is connected to it. The smallest vibration sends a message along the strands of the web, so all can understand.*

"I don't like it," Megala said. "Turn yourself back into an Elf and talk to us normally."

Tuava-Li hesitated. *Material transformation is very taxing. One can't do it too often. If you get used to hearing my voice in your head, you'll come to understand that I —*

"I understand that you might not make any friends when you start reading their minds," Megala interrupted. "Get on with it, then, and tell us who's inside the building."

I sense dozens, maybe more. They're at the center of the building, toward the back.

"That would be Vollyar's soldiers," Megala said, "the loyal ones who wouldn't side with Orin when he took command. They must be in the old gymnasium, where we used to play when we were young."

Many others move about inside, always in pairs, back and forth, back and forth on the same short paths.

"Probably guards patrolling the hallways."

Then there are three at the lowest level of the building. Two are stationary, one is moving about. One of them has a very faint heartbeat. At first, I couldn't detect it at all.

"Father," Mitelle whispered, "and Delfina. They must be with Orin."

"There's a chimney on the roof, which leads down to the furnace in the basement," Megala said. "If the path is clear we have a direct route to our father."

"But how will we get to the roof?" asked Tomtar.

I saw loops of braided vine lying in the grass, Tuava-Li volunteered.

"That's the rope they use to secure prisoners after a battle," Megala said. "Let's see how much of it's left."

When they found the rope, Tomtar used Matt's knife to cut away the knotted and tangled pieces. They tied the remaining lengths together to make one long rope, with a new knot every several feet to make climbing easier. "You're pretty good with that blade," Megala said to Tomtar. "Maybe you'd have been a good soldier, after all."

Tomtar blushed and shrugged, but kept on with his work. When they were done Tuava-Li flapped to the rooftop with one end of the rope gripped in her claws. There she changed to an Elf and looped the rope securely around the base of the chimney.

Megala, Mitelle, and Tomtar quickly scaled the side of the building, and pulled the rope up after them. Megala then dropped the end of it into the chimney and was the first to descend into the darkness. She found her feet dangling in the void long before she'd reached solid ground, so she dropped the rest of the way, trusting her instincts. She landed in a mound of coal and slid to the bottom. Carefully she felt her way around the inside of the iron drum, her fingertips burning with every touch. When she found the open grate that led into the basement she called up the chimney for the others to follow. Mitelle came next, followed by Tomtar and Tuava-Li. By the time they reached the bottom Megala was already halfway down a dark corridor. They all froze as a scream pierced the rank air. "It's Delfina!" Mitelle whispered hoarsely. "Where are they, Tuava-Li?"

The Elf listened for the heartbeats of those on the other side of the basement. *That way!*

At the end of the corridor was a door, and beyond it they could just hear the muted voice of their uncle Orin. There was also a faint whimpering that could be none other than their sister,

Delfina. Megala mouthed the word *now*, then grabbed the handle of the door and pulled.

Orin's hand, clutching a rusty blade, flew to Delfina's throat. He had already cut her cheek, and a trickle of Blood ran onto the old school desk where he had tied her next to her father, Vollyar. The scene was lit by Orin's Fire Sprite. It sat, glowing cheerfully, atop a light fixture hanging from the ceiling. "Who's there?" Orin called, his eyes searching beyond the open door.

Megala spit out the *trans* in her cheek and slowly materialized, so that her uncle would see who had come to kill him.

"Noooo," he murmured. "How did you get in here?" He pressed the blade tighter against Delfina's neck. "If you came to save your sister and your father, forget about it. They're not leaving here until I know where the rest of the Jewels are hidden. Put down your weapons, or I'll cut Delfina's throat. Do you want to see your sister die?"

Megala laughed scornfully. "Everyone dies, Uncle. Delfina's a soldier; she knows the cost of her choices. So do you. Give me your knife and step away."

There was a wild look in Orin's eye; Megala wasn't at all sure he wouldn't kill her sister. "Kill him," Delfina hissed, though the blade scraped her neck. "I don't care about myself. Kill him!"

Megala's lips drew back. "Uncle Orin, hand me your knife or—"

"*Noooooo!*" Vollyar's voice was a rasping gasp. "Do what Orin says! Give him your weapons!"

"But he'll—"

"I am your father!" Vollyar cried. "I won't let my daughter be killed for my sake. You have to give him your weapons, now!"

"Start by putting your knife onto the floor," Orin demanded.

Megala chewed her lip, her eyes darting from Orin to Delfina to her father. Finally she sighed in defeat, and dropped her blade. "Aye, Father."

"There's a sack, hanging over there." Orin nodded toward an open locker in the corner of the room. "Get it, and you can all put your weapons inside. There's also a length of rope. You'll use it to tie everyone up, Megala. Then I'll tie you up, and Delfina and I will go upstairs and find out why my soldiers didn't stop you from getting in here."

Tomtar watched his cousins disarm. They pulled hunting knives, boot knives, combat daggers, and stilettos from hidden places in their garments. Begrudgingly they dropped them all into the sack. A smile tugged at the corners of Orin's mouth.

"Obedience is a valuable trait," he said, "for daughters and soldiers alike."

Vollyar lifted his head. His face was haggard, his eyes dark and bloodshot. "You shouldn't have come, Megala," he mumbled, spitting out a tooth. "Or at least you shouldn't have come so late. Who's that with you, in the shadows? Who else is there?"

"'Tis I, Father, Mitelle."

Tomtar shuffled nervously behind his cousins as Tuava-Li

lingered in the darkness. "Aah, Tomtar, here," he said, waving a hand, "your nephew, Tomtar!"

The old Troll moaned. "Tomtar? I sent you away from here when things started to go bad. Why did you come back? You're not a soldier!"

"I've finished my Wanderin'," Tomtar said earnestly. "For my Gift I brought back a—"

"That's enough," Orin said. "Really, this is no time for a family reunion. Tomtar, I'm surprised you had the courage to return here. And Megala, I know you've got a favorite razor you haven't yet put in the sack. Come on, I know you still have it on you."

Megala fumbled in a back pocket and withdrew the last of her weapons. She held it up so that its edge flickered feebly, then tossed it into the sack with the others. "Good," Orin said. "Now take the rope, and tie them up."

"Never," Megala spat. "How do I know you won't kill us all?"

Orin's face darkened; he knew he could press them only so far. "Mitelle," he demanded, "come to me."

He grabbed his niece around the waist and squeezed his knife against her throat.

"I'm going to take this sack of weapons upstairs, and Mitelle will come along. If the rest of you want to see her alive again, you'll stay down here until I return with some of my guards. I promise I'll let the lot of you go, once I know where to find the Jewels."

"Don't hurt her," Megala said. "Wait, you haven't got all of the weapons yet. Tomtar, didn't I see you with a knife? You're not holding anything back, are you?"

She turned and forced her hand into her cousin's pocket. Tomtar stumbled, his eyes wide with surprise. "But, I—it's not mine, I—"

In one swift move Megala withdrew the blade and flung it with all her might. It missed Mitelle by just an inch and sank up to the hilt in Orin's chest. He stood quivering, his eyes stark and dumb, and then fell to the floor.

Megala turned to Tomtar. "You were wrong to think that the Gift you brought back from your Wanderin' was a visit from your new friends. In truth, your Gift to us was the knife you brought to kill your uncle Orin!"

With a grunt Megala yanked the blade from the Troll's chest and wiped it on her trousers. Then she handed it to Tomtar. Tuava-Li backed out the door, her face twisted in disgust. Tomtar stood frozen to the spot as Megala grabbed her razor from the top of the sack and used it to cut the cord that bound her father. "I told you to give him your weapons," Vollyar grumbled, his lips drawn back in pain. "You disobeyed me. He would have killed Delfina if he'd known you were holding back!"

"He didn't know," Megala said. "I was only trying to save your life!"

Vollyar shook his head. "You took a terrible risk. Now I have a question for you, daughter, and I expect the truth. Is it true, what Orin said, that you joined Sattye's Clan?"

"Only in the hopes of saving you, Father!"

Mitelle, meanwhile, cut her sister Delfina free. "That's a nasty gash on your cheek," she murmured. "'Tis about time you got a decent battle scar!"

"Aye," Delfina said proudly. Her eyes were full of contempt as she stepped over Orin's body. "At least I have a wound to thank him for. What's a soldier without scars to prove her courage?"

Megala hoisted her father onto a broken chair and looked him in the eye. "We've got to free the troops who are being held captive in the gymnasium. They're going to need a leader. Do you think you're ready to face them, to lead them to victory over the rest of Orin's soldiers?"

"What do you take me for?" Vollyar growled.

"You're injured," she soothed, touching the angry welts on his chest. "I could lead the troops, if you're not up to the task."

Vollyar scowled and pulled away. "A warlord never rests."

"All right, then," Megala said. "Tomtar, where's your Elf friend?"

"She's in the hall, outside the door," Tomtar said, feeling sick to his stomach. "She's not—she's not used to so much violence."

"Well, there's plenty more where that came from," Megala said. "Tell the gentle soul that it's time she changed back into a kestrel and let the juggler know that if he hasn't gathered up the weapons from Orin's gang for his last little trick, he'd better get started. We're going to need those weapons for our soldiers, once we've freed them from the room upstairs. Understand?"

Matt was still hiding behind the tree trunk where the Trolls had left him when he heard the cries of astonishment from Orin's troops, and the savage roars that followed. Even on the other side of the school building Matt could feel the spreading wave of rage as Vollyar's warriors, freed from their prison, descended upon their enemies. Matt heard the dull sound of feet pounding on the ground and saw Stefan rushing toward him in the shadow of the building. Tomtar followed, running with all his might, and a kestrel flapped overhead. "Time to go," Stefan yelled. "This is more than I bargained for!"

"What's going on?"

'Tis a Bloodbath, Tuava-Li said, her voice shaking even in thought-speak. *They're all mad with it. If slaughter like this had happened in Alfheim, the Mage would not have allowed us to return to the scene for ten thousand moons.*

Matt turned to Tomtar. "What about your uncle? I mean, Vollyar? Was he there?"

He's getting his revenge, said Tuava-Li. *Orin's dead, and Vollyar and his daughters have led the attack against his troops. There will be few survivors.*

With his face lined in guilt, Tomtar handed Matt the knife. "Here," he said. "I'm sorry to have to tell you, Megala used the knife to kill my uncle Orin. They say that once a knife has tasted

Blood, it won't be satisfied until it does again. I know the knife belonged to your father, but I wonder if you ought to keep it now. The knife will lead us to trouble."

"What does it matter," Matt said. "We're up to our necks in trouble already!"

He slipped the knife into his pocket as the sound of battle continued on the far side of the school. The kestrel perched on a branch and quivered helplessly as she felt the souls of the dead rush past her, searching for the low road. *We must go,* she said. *This is no place for the living.*

Tomtar grabbed Matt by the wrist as they headed for the street. "We know where the maps are hidden," he whispered. "Vollyar told us! He said he trusted us to go and get them!"

And he said he'd hunt you down and cut your head off if you took a single Jewel from the Clan treasure, Tuava-Li added, so that only Matt and Tomtar could hear.

"I'm going this way," Stefan said, mopping his brow and pointing back toward St. Elmo's Firehouse. "Does anyone care to join me?"

We still have something to do tonight, Tuava-Li said in thought-speak, *something we've been working toward for a very long time.*

"Then good luck," Stefan said. "Just one thing—the payment you promised me for my assistance tonight? I must say, I had those Trolls in the palm of my hand."

Matt opened up his pack and pulled out one of the sacks of Alfheim Clan Jewels.

The diamond he selected glimmered in the moonlight. "This should do," he said, thinking only about the maps, and how he might be able to get to Helfratheim to save his parents after all.

Theatrically Stefan took the diamond between two fingers and flicked his wrist. He held out his empty palm; the Jewel had disappeared. "That one was no good," he cried, "it disappeared. Another, please?"

"I don't think so," Matt said. He was in no mood for more of the juggler's jokes.

"Oh well," Stefan sighed. "Easy come, easy go." He put on a comic grin, made a bow, and pranced away.

As soon as Stefan was out of sight Matt got down on his knees and looked into the Troll's eyes. "What's this about the maps, Tomtar?"

"Vollyar told us he'd hidden his Clan treasure all over town," Tomtar said. "That way, it would be harder for any of his enemies to get their hands on the whole thing. Vollyar's brother Orin betrayed him, locked him up, and sent soldiers looking for the Clan treasure. They managed to find a lot of it, and Orin was torturing Vollyar to tell him where the rest is hidden."

"What about the maps?" Matt asked impatiently.

"I'm getting to that," Tomtar said. "It turns out that the maps were part of the treasure Orin found. He told Vollyar that he left a lot of the treasure just where he'd discovered it, because it was in such a good hiding place. *That's* where the maps are, Matt."

"And we're going to trust your lying, backstabbing uncle's

word about the treasure and the maps?" Matt cried. "Where? Where are they supposed to be?"

Tomtar pointed. "Over there, at the top of that tower."

Matt's eyes scanned the dark hillside. "What tower? I don't see any buildings!"

"The cell tower, he called it. Look there, with the flashing lights!"

Matt shook his head. "That thing? Tomtar, you can't get up there. Nobody can. It's got to be a thousand feet high! Who's going to be able to climb it?"

"You are," Tuava-Li said. "There's a ladder, but 'tis built for Humans to climb, not Elves or Trolls. Vollyar did it with ropes and pulleys, but we don't have that kind of equipment. You must do it, Matt. You have to do it now."

39

CHARLIE McCORMACK MADE his way bare-
foot through the silent corridors of the Techmagick labs, trying
to find an exit. He was breathing hard; his muscles were still
tight and stiff from the Elfin drugs. Worse yet, he had to hunch
down to avoid hitting his head on the low ceiling. He carried a
wooden plank in his hands in case he saw any Elves along the
way. Though he'd seen no sign of life, so far, he knew that he
needed to take at least one Elf hostage to use as leverage when he
went to find Emily. Perhaps they'd give him his daughter back if
he threatened to kill one of their own. Jill followed her husband,
her eyes darting left and right, alert for any sounds from the
rooms along the halls. Both Jill and Charlie wore several of
the Elves' carved medallions around their necks; Charlie had
grabbed them from a desk in the room where the experiments
were done. "Where has everyone gone?" Jill whispered tensely,

looking around the corner at another empty hallway. "You'd think they'd want to stop us!"

"When everything looks too easy, that's the time to worry," Charlie muttered through gritted teeth. "We're not out of here yet, and we have no idea where they took Emily."

A muted roar came from outside the building. Charlie and Jill glanced at each other; it sounded like a crowd in a stadium when somebody runs a touchdown, only the voices were all high and childlike. "Come on," Charlie said, and bolted toward a stairwell at the end of the hallway. At the bottom of the stairs there was a low door, just the right height for Elves. Charlie heaved it open and blinked as he glanced into the moonlit world. A river of children was rushing past, no more than a hundred feet ahead of him. Elfin guards stood back, shouting at the children to hurry, as they swept into the forest beyond the gates of the palace. Black-robed figures stood at the edge of the woods. Their eyes were closed in concentration, their pale hands held high. "What's happening?" Jill cried.

Charlie shook his head and took his wife's hand. They stumbled to the edge of the fleeing crowd and watched helplessly as the children disappeared among the trees. Some of the older children carried toddlers in their arms, while others held hands and tried to hurry each other on in the mad rush to escape. "If Emily's in that bunch, we'll never find her," Charlie hollered over the cries of the children, and the shouting of the guards. He reached out and grabbed a boy by the arm. "What's going on? Where are you all headed?"

In the moonlight, the boy's eyes gleamed with mad hope. "They're letting us go, mister, we're going home!"

He pulled away from Charlie and rejoined the surging crowd. "Emily!" Jill shouted, "Emily!"

A girl glanced up and stared as the wave of children carried her along. "Mommy?" she cried, and was swept away in the flow.

Charlie knifed himself into the crowd, working his way through the tide, as a cluster of small children fell, trampled by the masses trying to escape. "Move!" he bellowed, reaching through the jumble of arms and legs to pull some of the fallen children out of harm's way. "Clear a path, don't you see what you're doing? Who was it who cried *Mommy*?"

"Emily!" Jill hollered again. She turned to her husband, her face stricken. "I don't think the voice we heard was *our* Emily, it didn't sound right!"

The children's eyes brightened, seeming to wake from a dream, as the grown-ups' voices boomed in their ears. They had not seen an adult human in this place before, and they slowed their flight to listen to Charlie. "People are going to get hurt if you're not careful," he warned. "Listen, you've got to—"

"Keep moving," screamed the guards, their anxious voices high and wild. When they saw the pair of grown Humans in the midst of the children, they backed away. One of them hurried to the courtyard to inform his superiors.

Charlie and Jill were still caught in the rush of fleeing children. There was a faint, milky light ahead, a shimmering among the branches. Jill wanted to slow her pace but the children were plowing forward, desperate to get away from the Elves and the fortress behind them. When they passed the faint light, the road grew rougher. The trees seemed to tighten around them. "Did the elves say where you're going?" Charlie huffed, calling to the children as he pushed through the brambles.

"There's a girl back in the courtyard, named Becky," someone said, "and she knows all about the elves. Maybe they told her!"

"Becky saved our lives," another child said between gulps of breath. "She helped keep them away from us until we got to leave. She has a little sister. I saw a boy carrying her, just a minute ago!"

"Becky?" Jill cried. "You said there's a girl named Becky, with a little sister? Did you hear anything about an older boy, named Matt?"

"Mama!" a familiar voice trilled from the crowd.

Though the forest was dark, nothing could stop Jill from recognizing her daughter's voice. Her heart was thumping as she turned and angled her way into the sea of small, lost bodies. She lifted Emily from the boy's arms and squeezed the toddler to her chest. "Mama!" Emily cried.

Jill sobbed, stumbled, and moved out of the path behind a tree. "Charlie, we're over here," she cried, and a moment later her husband joined them there. Charlie hugged them both and then stood back, pointing past the crowd, toward the Elfin fortress.

"Becky's still alive! Did you hear a kid say that she's back there? I've got to go and get her—you go on ahead with the others and I'll catch up with you, Jill!"

"No," she cried, heartsick at the thought of losing her husband, even as her hopes soared at the thought that Becky was alive. She hadn't dared to entertain the thought, all the time she'd been held captive in the lab. "All right," she said, choking on the words, "go on, but be careful, Charlie, I love you! Look for Matt, too!"

The flood of children making their way through the woods had slowed to a trickle by now. Charlie trudged up the hill where the feeble milky light had shone. He flung himself through bushes and briars as branches swept at his face, calling out, "Becky! Matt! Can you hear me?" The forest went on and on and he saw no sign of the great fortress. There was nothing in the darkness he recognized, no sign of a road or clearing, no high stone wall, nothing but the moon and the trees and the moaning of the wind in the branches. He had no way of knowing that the veil between the two worlds was strong near the walls of Helfratheim, and that the monks had opened a passage for the children to pass. Now that passage was closed, and there was no going back. Charlie was alone.

"Becky!" he shouted. He fell to his knees in the dark woods and wept. "Matt!" Angrily he tore the medallions from his neck and flung them away. Then he climbed to his feet, turned and fumbled downhill through the darkness. Before long he heard the faint sounds of the fleeing children. There were hundreds and hundreds of them, and their cries were full of hope as they made their way back to civilization and their families. Charlie hurried to rejoin his wife and daughter. If Becky was all right, then perhaps Matt was, too. He prayed they had what it took to stay alive, and find their way back home somehow.

Inside the walls of the fortress Becky hurried across the courtyard toward the laboratory building. She didn't know that two pairs of eyes were following her every move from the nearby shadows. "That's the Human who led the children in revolt," Nick said to Jardaine.

"'Tis a sign from the Goddess," hissed Jardaine. "I remember her face. That girl's brother is the one who's traveling with Tuava-Li and Tomtar to the North Pole!"

"This is our chance," said Nick. "Everything is falling into place!"

Breathing hard, Becky hurried toward the entrance of the building. She still held a flicker of hope that she'd find her parents somewhere inside. "Child," a gentle voice called from behind.

She turned around to see an Elf in monk's robes, and a Troll. They both smiled sweetly. "Child, why haven't you gone with the others? You mustn't be trapped here, when the veil between the worlds closes again!"

"Who are you?" Becky asked warily.

"We're the ones who set the children free, when the other monks wanted to sacrifice them to their false gods."

"You set the children free?"

"Aye, we did," said Jardaine. "We couldn't let them be killed."

"My parents are here," Becky said. "I think they're in that building. I'm going to look for them."

"Your parents *were* in there, but they've gone. All the Humans are gone; they're safe now. There's only one Human still in danger—a boy who's been tricked into going on a secret mission with an Elf and a Troll, to journey to the North Pole. We're on our way to try to stop Tuava-Li and Tomtar, before they kill the poor boy."

"What?" Becky cried. "What did you say? That's my brother Matt you're talking about! He's the one who's going to the North Pole with Tuava-Li and Tomtar!"

"Oh, my child," Jardaine said sorrowfully. "I'm so sorry to hear that."

"You've got to let me come with you," Becky said. "I can help. I know all about Tuava-Li, and Tomtar, and the old Mage who sent them."

"We would love to have your help," said Jardaine. "Praise the Goddess for bringing us together!"

Becky's face grew dark. "I knew I couldn't trust that old Mage from Alfheim. She's mean, and cold, and she hates humans. Tuava-Li was just the same. How are we going to find them?"

Nick and Jardaine exchanged glances. "Some of the Techmagicians may still be in the courtyard," Jardaine said.

"Maybe they'll have some mode of transportation that can help us travel north. An Arvada, perhaps."

Becky shuddered as she thought of the metal cab, tight as a coffin, and the huge translucent slug that powered the thing and moved it through the sky. "Whatever you want," she said. "I'll do anything."

Jardaine smiled. She thought of the chameleon she had become earlier in the evening; perhaps she and her totem animal were a better match than she'd imagined. It was time, after all, for a change. She realized she ought to introduce herself; but what if by some chance the girl had ever heard her real name? "You may call me . . . Astrid. My name means 'strength of the Goddess.' This is my friend Nick. He hates Tuava-Li and Tomtar as much as you and I do, for the terrible things their religion teaches, and the awful things they've done in the name of the Goddess. Together we shall defeat these enemies of ours, and save your brother."

Nick bowed before Becky. "I'm honored to meet you," he said.

Becky bowed, too, her eyes bright with hope.

40

MATT RODE THE FUNICULAR to the top of the
hill in silence. Tomtar and Tuava-Li sat at his side and looked
down at the river below, and the twinkling lights of town. They
got to the top and stepped out into the night. Matt wanted to
say that the wind was too strong, that he was sure he'd be blown
from the peak of the cell tower and die. But there wasn't more
than a ghost of a breeze to rustle the autumn air. Matt wanted
to say that the fence around the tower was locked so securely
that he'd never be able to get close enough to the ladder to
climb. But Tuava-Li had become an expert at opening locks
with the power of her mind, and they entered the base station
of the tower with ease. Matt wanted to say that they should do
this the following night, when he felt rested, and he'd had time
to bolster his courage. He wanted to say that it wasn't fair to
make him do something that terrified him, he wanted to say a

thousand things, but all he could manage to do was ask Tuava-Li and Tomtar about his tattoos, and the image of the Green Man on his chest. Tuava-Li said she thought it was probably a good sign, because she knew Matt was afraid, and she didn't want to make him worry any more. But in reality she had no idea what it meant. Now the three of them stood looking up at the tower, with the aluminum drums affixed high on its beams, with the flashing lights to alert passing aircraft of its presence, with the narrow white ladder that ascended into the starlit sky.

"Khidr has vanquished his enemies," Tomtar said, pointing toward the constellation whose stars represented Elfin victory. "'Tis a good omen! That's what your tattoo means, Matt. We're going to get what we came here for!"

Matt glanced up, then let his eyes fall to his hands. Even in the darkness his skin looked very, very pale. "That guy always seems to win his battles. Not me, though. My parents and baby sister are in who knows what kind of trouble, and I've been sidetracked into looking for a seed. I try to find something to be thankful for, and all I can think of is how glad I am that Becky's still back in the forest eating weeds and fungus with those old Mages. She might be bored out of her mind, but at least she's safe."

"Do you remember what the Mage taught you?" Tuava-Li asked. "Breathing up from your feet, centering yourself, balancing your energy so that your awareness isn't just in your head? You'll need to stay focused on the climb, on the motions of your arms and legs, you'll have to let go of your fear, if you have any, you—"

"If I have any?" Matt repeated. "I've never been so scared in my life. Yeah, I remember those things the Mage taught me. I don't know if any of them will help. I have to trust that I've made up my mind to do this, and everything else will follow from there. No matter what."

"I'll come with you," Tuava-Li said. She put a *trans* for exposure to metal into her mouth and began to chew it. "As a kestrel I can fly from one level to the next, and keep you company. I can talk to you in thought-speak and help you stay on task as you climb."

For a while Matt had felt his insides turning to water. "I don't know," he said, trying to stop the tremble in his voice. "I guess that'll be okay. Listen, I need to go to the bathroom. Would you guys look the other way for a minute?"

Matt went into the bushes by the side of the fence and did his business. He returned, flexing his shoulders and rolling his head. "My back is killing me," he said. "My shoulders are tensing up. And my legs feel weak. I don't know if I can do this."

"Maybe you need to remember your parents," Tomtar said. "If *I* were climbin', I'd think about the Cord, and the Seed, and the Adri at the pole. I'd remember my purpose."

"Got it," Matt said with a sigh. "My purpose." He walked the final ten feet to the ladder and hoisted himself up onto the bottom rung. "How many steps do you think this is?" he asked. "I'd guess fifteen hundred. Anybody want to make a bet?"

"If Stefan were here," Tuava-Li said, "he'd probably make a little wager on it. But perhaps 'tis best if you don't count them. It might be distracting."

"Let's do it, then." Matt said, looking up. He adjusted his backpack one final time; he'd need it to store the maps once he'd found them.

Tomtar waved. "My cousins always say that when you climb a tree, 'tis best if you never look down!"

"Thanks," Matt said, putting on a brave smile. "I guess I'll just think of this as the world's tallest tree."

Tuava-Li changed into a kestrel and flapped to the first big horizontal bar, fifteen feet above Matt's head. *Oh, this is nothing! Wait until we come to the hidden city and you see the Holy Adri at the Pole!*

"Great," Matt mumbled.

Remember: Take your first step with your right foot. All of life is happening now, one moment, one step at a time. Just one step.

Matt put his right foot on the rung and started up the ladder. Tuava-Li listened for the sound of his breath, and tried to synchronize her own to his, and she heard his beating heart, and she vowed to stay with it for the entire climb. Matt kept his eyes on his hands and tried not to think about anything. He knew he was getting higher, because he saw the lights of the hillside drop out of his peripheral vision, and he felt the wind pick up as he climbed. It rushed in his ears as his breath quickened and grew more labored. Matt felt like a machine, a climbing machine made of muscle and bone and pumping blood. When he inhaled he imagined the air rushing into his body through his feet, moving up through his heart and filling his body. When he exhaled he imagined his breath flowing out of the top of his head like a fountain. *Crimson chalice, cave of spirit,* he thought, just like the Mage had taught him. It felt good to do the exercises, if only to distract him from his fear.

He passed the first of the antennas, the aluminum drums that looked puny from the ground, but were in reality as big as cars. He reached out and rapped his knuckles on the metallic surface. He heard the dull echo from inside. He wondered what the drum closest to the top of the tower would be like, once he'd opened the little panel door that Tomtar's uncle had said would be there. He pictured things he'd seen in movies and illustrated books, things like treasure chests brimming with glittering jewels, gilded swords with precious stones in their scabbards, and antique statues of gold and silver. He imagined the clan maps, delicate illuminated manuscripts, and he thought of his parents. At this point his imagination emptied out, and he was left with nothing but a bad feeling that wrenched his stomach. He didn't really know where his parents were, or what might have happened to them. He wondered if he would know it, if he would feel it if they died. *One step at a time,* he told himself. *I am strong, I am capable. Soon I will be there.*

Yes, you will, Tuava-Li said in thought-speak. Matt knew she was perched somewhere above him, but he didn't dare look up, because if he looked up, he might look down, and that would be the end of him. "You're reading my mind," he called, panic gripping his heart. "Is this an emergency?"

Nooo. You're broadcasting your thoughts for all that have ears to hear. Your voice is loud and clear.

Indeed, Matt's thoughts carried on the wind, and drifted down the hillside, merging with all the signals of all the cell phone calls, the television broadcasts, the thoughts of tens of thousands of people and animals, billions of insects working busily amid forests of grass, and finally the slow, dim mind of the Green Man, who slumbered in his cave near the foot of the cell tower. Tomtar's uncle Orin had abducted the Green Man's brother, and imprisoned him in the basement of St. Elmo's Firehouse. In return for keeping him alive, the Green Man who lived in the bowels of the mountain had agreed to guard Orin's treasure and see that it was undisturbed. Now he turned on his bed of earth and rock and something like an alarm rang in the thick, vegetable mind. He had heard Matt tapping on the aluminum drum, and he had seen the picture Matt had imagined of the inside of the drum, with its strange and vast treasure. He opened an eye wreathed in thick, green leaves, and stared into the darkness . . . listening.

Matt reached the top of the tower. He hadn't looked down, and he hadn't completely lost his mind to fear and panic. His legs, though, felt stiff and numb, like bricks attached to his aching hips, and his hands were already blistered with the friction of his grip on the bars of the ladder. The wind was strong; it turned tendrils of his hair into whips, stinging his forehead. *We seem no closer to the Dome of Heaven than we did on the ground,* Tuava-Li noted. She'd never flown so high at night. *I would have thought that from here, we could have seen through the* vindues, *the openings in the Dome, but it's not so.*

"You thought your gods would be close enough for you to see them blink?" Matt laughed nervously. "The gods are still a long, long way away, Tuava-Li. Up here, it's just us."

He stepped onto a catwalk, straightened himself and began creeping around the metal frame of the tower. The lights around the top flashed with a brightness and intensity Matt could not have imagined back on the ground. Tuava-Li gripped the upper rail with her kestrel claws. The wind tore at her feathers and threatened to blow her from the tower into the void of night. Still she clung, her beady black eyes narrowed against the wind, and watched Matt as he approached the drum that held the maps they'd come to Pittsburgh to find. At the front of the drum there was a circular disc, about two feet in diameter, with handles on it. Matt reached past the railing, gripped the handles, and turned the disc. There was a groan; a rumble of metal on metal, and the subtlest vibration ricocheted down the legs of the tower and deep into the soil. "This is it," Matt breathed, and swung the door open on its hinge.

Khidr was out of his hole in a heartbeat. Like a man grown from soil, his limbs like roots, his body like the trunk of an enormous tree, he began his climb up the steel lattice of the tower. He was covered in thick green leaves, from his huge block of a head to his massive feet. His arms, like branches, were many, and covered with fingers that curled snake-like around the horizontal bars of the tower. Matt had just crept into the drum when the aluminum rattled with the creature's awful roar. It wasn't like the sound of a lion, or any other animal Matt had ever heard. It was more like the groan of an avalanche, or thunder in a terrible storm. *Something's wrong*, Tuava-Li said in thought-speak.

"You think?" cried Matt. "What was that?"

Tuava-Li's claws lost their grip and she fell back into the night, flapping her wings to stay close to the tower. Matt crept around just inside the drum and peered out over the edge, trying to see what had happened. Vertigo came over him in waves. He grabbed the edges of the doorway and shifted back, his breath frozen in his chest. He glanced down again and saw the tops of roofs and cars moving like ants on narrow ribbons of highway far, far below. Then he caught a glimpse of movement and blinked in disbelief at the sight of the strange, nightmare creature scaling the tower. An image flashed in his mind of the being in the pool in the basement of St. Elmo's, the lumpy thing with the roots that grew everywhere from its skin, with its massive head sunken against a hollow chest. He realized it couldn't be the same

537

creature, though, for this one was covered in leaves, like some kind of animate tree, a man-tree, scaling the tower. Like the one tattooed on his chest. This one was vital and powerful, this one was angry. This one's luminous emerald eyes were fixed on Matt. *Khidr!* Tuava-Li cried in thought-speak.

"What's going on?" Matt cried. "What does it want?"

The creature reached up and grabbed at Matt with one of his awful hands. Matt ducked back inside the drum and squeezed himself against the wall. He saw the thing insert a gigantic finger into the drum, the way a bear would reach into a beehive for honey. Then he heard the kestrel's fierce cry, and the finger whipped away. Peering into the night Matt saw Tuava-Li diving at the thing's face, trying to rake her talons over his eyes. Thin branches like tendrils of hair shot out and grasped at the little bird. She flapped out of range as a branch nearly caught her by the leg. But then another branch came up from behind, and with lightning speed, coiled around her wing. "Noooo!" Matt screamed. Oblivious to the dizzying height, he flew across the catwalk at the top of the tower. His hand found the knife in his pocket and shot out before him, striking at the branch that was tightening around Tuava-Li. The thing uncoiled and she was free. She flapped her wings and sailed up over the creature's head, watching for the tendrils that could bring her down again.

Matt found himself staring into the enormous green face. It was no more than a few feet from him now, and he could smell its dark vegetable odor, a rank perfume of earth and mold. The Green Man was focused on Matt, and his heavily lidded eyes, blanketed with leaves, blinked. Matt stared into the eyes of the beast and felt himself growing weak with fear. In one hand he held his knife, and with the other he clutched the railing for support. He felt his fingers loosen their grip. The creature's mouth opened and for a moment Matt thought the Green Man was going to speak. But suddenly his tongue, like the slippery root of a tree buried in the soil, shot out of the mouth and came for Matt. He screamed and leapt back, just catching himself on the edge of the catwalk. His knife fell from his hand and bounced off the railing. It spun in the air and was gone. The Green Man's tongue coiled around one of the steel beams, then uncurled and went for Matt's arm.

Get back in the drum, Tuava-Li called. *Close the door behind you.*

"He's not going to go away," Matt yelled, backing away from the vines and branches that seemed to come at him from everywhere. "He's not going to stop until he's killed both of us!"

On the ground, Tomtar watched helplessly. There was absolutely nothing he could do to save his friends. He had witnessed the Green Man scaling the tower like it was a step-ladder. His calls had been lost in the wind. Now he saw movement at the top, but in the darkness there he could only imagine the fate that awaited Matt and Tuava-Li. Tomtar wondered—could his uncle Vollyar have known about the Green Man? He realized that his uncle must have been in such a sorry state that he forgot to warn them of the danger. He shuddered and stamped the ground, his mind flooded with terror.

Tuava-Li flapped closer to the Green Man's face, screeching in his ears, trying to distract him so that Matt could climb to safety. In desperation she decided to focus her mind and shoot a burst of energy into the creature's brain. This was a matter of life and death. If she had stunned an Elf and killed a Human, perhaps she could slow down this monster enough that she and Matt could escape. *In the name of the Mother and her Cord*, she said to herself, and felt the energy contract like a ball of fire inside her.

She breathed her own awareness out into the space where the Green Man hung from the steel lattice, and as soon as she felt that he was enveloped in her consciousness, she closed her eyes. Imagining the words to the ancient spell, she forced the ball of energy out of herself and into the dark space behind the Green Man's eyes. The exertion of what she had done sent Tuava-Li spiraling down. Her body struck one of the girders and she grasped for it with her claws. Meanwhile, the creature shook his head, raining down a shower of leaves. Then he reached once again for Matt, who leapt into the aluminum drum and slammed the circular door behind him.

The Green Man flung himself at the drum and Matt felt the bolts along the wall groan. Above him, the roof bent down from the impact in a razor-sharp crease of metal. Moonlight spilled through the crack and suddenly Matt could see. He stumbled as the floor shifted beneath him. He had to find the maps now, before the whole thing came loose and plummeted to the ground. In his imagination he'd thought that the Clan treasure would be spread out in a glorious display of riches. But instead there were stacks of cardboard boxes along one wall, the metal workings of the antenna, and nothing more. Matt pried open the first box and jammed his hand inside. It felt like it was full of seashells or pebbles that rattled as his fingers sifted among them. Perhaps it was Jewels, perhaps not. It didn't matter. He tossed the box aside and reached inside the next one. More of the same. He threw box after box out of his way as his fingers sought something like paper or parchment, anything that felt like it might be a map.

Outside on a high railing, Tuava-Li let her consciousness move once again toward the Green Man. The crude burst of energy she'd shot into it before was little more than a light going off in comparison to what she was about to do. She forced herself into the Green Man's mind and a kaleidoscope of images rushed toward her. She felt his soul brush against her, like she'd felt the souls of the dead outside the schoolhouse where so many Trolls had perished. And then in an instant she saw the Green Man's brother, and she saw Orin, and she knew.

Matt tossed away statues and relics, coins and jewels and untold treasures before his hand closed on a soft paper folio. In the moonlight he unfolded the document on top and saw that it was a map of Argant. With shaking hands he pulled off his pack and shoved the papers inside. Then he crept for the doorway. "I found them!" he cried as he pushed the door open, just a little. If the Green Man was waiting for him, he wanted to stay out of his reach. "I found the maps!"

The giant drum shifted again. Matt heard the bolts pop beneath him and realized that it was about to break loose from the tower. He shoved open the door and reached for the railing above, but his hands slipped and suddenly he saw the ground looming up at him. "Tuava-Li!" he cried.

The drum broke free and bounced once off the steel girders. The roof of the structure tore completely open. Matt clung to the antenna rod and felt the boxes of treasure bump against his legs as they spilled out into the night. The drum banged against one of the tower legs again and Matt lost his grip. He was a skydiver without a parachute. He felt as if his spine would snap as he spun around and around in the open air, and the roaring wind rushed up at him. His pack flew away from his back and suddenly he couldn't breathe. He wasn't flying, he was falling, and he knew he was going to die.

Then he hit. The force blew the air from his lungs, and a light seemed to explode in his brain. He expected his body to burst into a million pieces. Instead he felt the leafy fingers of the Green Man close around him, breaking his fall. The creature held Matt safely, firmly in his grip. He climbed down to the base of the tower and placed Matt on the ground. The boy stood on shaky legs for just a moment, and then dropped to his knees. He clutched at the thin grass on the hillside, and felt the dirt beneath his fingers. Glorious, filthy, incomparable, dusty, dirty dirt. He felt the brush of Tuava-Li's wings as she came to rest beside him. Tomtar, too, rushed to his side. Matt glanced up and saw the luminous eyes of Khidr staring down at him. Twinkling stars and constellations, sweeping across the endless void of space, framed his massive, shaggy head. If he'd been standing up straight, the Green Man would have been three stories tall. "What's going on?" Matt cried.

He heard Tuava-Li's voice in his mind. *The Green Man's brother is the creature we saw in the basement of St. Elmo's Firehouse. Orin was holding him captive there. I saw it all, in his mind. I told the Green Man that we'd show him where his brother is, in exchange for our lives. I'm not sure how well he understands, but at least he's given up trying to kill us. Are you all right, Matthew?*

Matt nodded. "I'm fine, but I've got to find my pack. All of Vollyar's maps are in it."

Tuava-Li soared over the hillside as Matt and Tomtar searched below. When she saw Matt's backpack in the grass, she swooped down and changed to her Elfin form. She got down on her knees and scanned the aged parchments that Matt had shoved into the pack. There were maps of all the regions of the world, seen from the perspective of the Faerie realm, as well as Human maps of the oceans and continents. Her heart raced with excitement when she found the map of the top of the Faerie world. Then she found a map that showed the roads from Argant to all the other major Faerie capitals. *Helfratheim,* she said to herself. She took the map by its corners and carefully tore it to pieces. With predator's eyes she pored over the others, took out any that made reference to Helfratheim, and tore them up as well, letting the breeze carry them away. She shoved what remained of the maps into the pack and shouted over the hillside. "I found your pack, Matthew!"

"And I found my knife," Matt yelled. "Bring it over here!"

At the foot of the tower Matt unfolded all the maps on the ground and flipped them over, one by one. "Something's wrong," he mumbled, turning them over and rifling through them again. "There's nothing here!" His chest tightened as he felt his hope drain away, and the truth slowly dawned on him. He was never going to find Helfratheim; he was never going to get the chance to save his parents. Tomtar watched helplessly as Matt crumpled the maps and tossed them aside. "No," Matt cried, "no, it can't be, after all this, there's not a single map with Helfratheim on it. Nothing, nothing, nothing!"

He kicked the papers and was about to stomp them into the dirt. "Please, Matt," Tomtar said, gathering them up. Matt felt a sob rising in his throat and he turned away, his face buried in his hands.

"We must go," Tuava-Li said, looking up at Khidr. "I promised that we'd take him to his brother."

Sorrowfully Matt climbed into the Green Man's outstretched palm. He hoisted his companions up beside him. With Tuava-Li pointing the way, the leafy giant passed the funicular and skidded down the hill to West Carson Street, holding the boy, the Elf, and the Troll in one fist. Footsteps thundering, he made his way toward St. Elmo's Firehouse. Traffic lights swayed on their cables and windows rattled. It was late enough that no cars approached to see the monster loping down the middle of the road. When he reached his destination, the Green Man knelt so that Tomtar, Tuava-Li, and Matt could climb down onto the street. Then he turned, gripped the roof of the building with both hands, and tore a chunk of it away. The front door of the club banged open as the customers inside hurried out into the moonlight. Tomtar pointed. "There goes Stefan!"

The juggler and his friends scattered like cockroaches caught in the glare of a kitchen light as the Green Man held a piece of the crumbling roof in one hand, picking it apart with clumsy fingers. He tossed the wreckage onto the road, and used his fists to smash the facade of the building into a ruined heap of glass, brick, and stone. Matt led his friends into an alley as a black cloud of dust and debris swept down the street. Car alarms up and down the block began to sound. Lights flicked on in apartment windows, shouts of dismay and terrified screams rent the night air. The Green Man went on with his search, oblivious to the chaos he had caused. When he came to the worn oak boards of the first floor he punched through them and reached down into the darkness, pulling away the timbers like a gardener plucking weeds from a bed of flowers. He did the same to the floor of the first basement, and then the second.

Fire trucks and police sirens wailed, slowly awakening to what was happening.

The Green Man roared as he peered down at his brother, pale and leafless, slumped in a pool of dark liquid. He thumped into the deep basement and ripped away the chains that bound his brother to the floor. Then he took the limp figure in his arms. Matt saw him climbing from the ruins of the club, struggling with the weight he carried. "He wants us to come with him," Tuava-Li shouted. "I can read it in his mind. He wants to show us something."

Matt helped his companions scale one of the arms of the Green Man. They worked their way among the vines and branches that made up his bicep and shoulder, and came to rest in the shadow of his enormous head. Matt looked down at the pale, flaccid figure in the Green Man's arms, and could hardly believe that these two beings were related. In the cold moonlight the creature that had languished in the basement of St. Elmo's was a nightmare image of a man, misshapen and crude, all broken angles and twisted shapes. Its flesh looked like the gnarled tangle of roots ripped out of the ground when a storm brings down a mighty tree. It was still alive, though; Matt could see its chest heaving, and its clouded eyes gaze with gratitude at the leafy figure that had saved its life.

The sun was coming up, streaking the city skyline with purple. The Green Man bounded down the street, across a bridge, past warehouses and boarded-up buildings toward the old rail yards that had once served the vast steel mills of Pittsburgh. When they came to an abandoned railroad tunnel the Green Man stooped low to go inside. "What's he doing?" Matt cried.

Branches on the creature's head scraped the roof of the high tunnel, knocking loose a few of the bricks from the arch over the entrance. It was a tight squeeze for the enormous Green Man. His brother's limp legs banged against the wall and a shower of mortar and dust fell on all their heads. Tuava-Li sent a message into Khidr's mind. *Be careful! The tunnel isn't safe!*

A groan echoed down into the depths of the earth as the entrance started to collapse. The Green Man lunged ahead. Behind him, the last glimmer of daylight vanished in a cloud of rubble, brick, and dirt. Matt was in shock. He opened his mouth to cry out, but his trembling lips made no sound. He had never seen darkness so complete. The air was thick and damp, and he labored to breathe as the Green Man stomped onward. After a few minutes he felt the cords of the creature's neck straighten and stretch, as if he was standing taller, so he knew that the tunnel must have widened somehow. "What's he doing?" he croaked. "How are we going to get out of here?"

"I don't know," Tuava-Li whispered. "I can sense his desire, his drive to share something with us. His mind isn't like yours or mine, you know, it's simpler, purer, somehow, like a —"

A light came out of nowhere. Then another, and another, like stars shifting in the sky, or a swarm of fireflies. Matt blinked, unsure what his eyes were seeing. The lights grew brighter as they came closer. "Fire Sprites," Tuava-Li said. "They must live down here, along with the Green Men. I think they're welcoming them home!"

The Sprites circled in a crackling cloud of flame, then turned back down the tunnel. "The Green Man's going to follow them!"

The roof and walls of the tunnel were blackened with age, and mold, and decay. Iron tracks along the floor gleamed dully as the Green Man trailed the swarm of Fire Sprites down, and down and down. The bricks and cement walls slowly gave way to rough-packed dirt. Finally the Fire Sprites settled along the top of a boulder that lay across the path. Gently, the Green Man laid his brother on the ground. The pale creature sat up slowly and rubbed his arms where tiny buds were beginning to grow. Matt, Tuava-Li, and Tomtar climbed down the Green Man's shoulder, and stood facing a niche in the crumbling earthen wall. A pool of black water was all that separated them from the shallow recess. Matt gasped as he realized what was on the other side of the pool. In the flickering light he saw cardboard boxes spilled over with glistening jewels. Enormous urns in broken crates overflowed with strands of pearls as big as robin's eggs, and medallions dangled from heavy silver chains. Daggers encrusted with precious gems jutted from mounds of glittering coins. "It must be the rest of Vollyar's treasure," Tomtar breathed.

Matt looked at the untold riches that spread out before him

and shook his head. "We've already got plenty of jewels. There aren't any maps here. This means nothing to us. Do you think the Green Man wants us to have these, or to bring them up to Vollyar's Clan, since so much of his treasure is strewn all over the top of Mount Washington?"

He pulled a twig from his hair and tossed it carelessly into the pool. Immediately a black, slippery shape shot out of the water, snapped up the twig in a mouth rimmed with hideous pointed teeth, and disappeared beneath the surface. "What was that?" he cried in surprise and disgust.

"I think this part of the treasure is protected, too," Tomtar ventured.

"Then why are we here?" Matt asked. "What are we supposed to do?"

"I think I know," said Tuava-Li.

Matt turned to see the Elf walking past the boulder into the damp, suffocating darkness farther down the tunnel. "Come and look."

At first Matt did not recognize the Cord. Its surface was not unlike the rough earthen wall around it, but it seemed to breathe, moving slowly in and out. "My God," he said, stepping back. "It's a Cord! It's enormous, as big as the entire wall!"

Tuava-Li nodded excitedly. "Khidr brought us here because of the Cord. When I read his mind, he must have been able to read mine, too. He's trying to tell us something." Tuava-Li looked at the Green Man's face. "Does this Cord go North?"

Khidr nodded his heavy head. Then he stalked across the tunnel to where his brother lay, and offered him one massive hand. Slowly the pale and sickly Green Man got to his feet. Together they lumbered away, the one leaning on the other, down one of the dark and endless corridors.

Matt, Tomtar, and Tuava-Li glanced nervously at one another as the Fire Sprites formed a glowing orange line, and nudged the three of them toward the Cord. "The Green Men are leaving," Matt said, "and these fire sprites obviously want us to go, too. We have to decide what to do now. Do we follow the Green Men? Try to go back above ground? Or do we slit this Cord open and go for a ride?"

"There's only one thing to do," Tomtar said.

Matt took his knife from his pocket and held it up. "Who wants to do the honors?"

"You do it," Tuava-Li said.

Matt placed the tip of the blade against the Cord and gently gave it a push. A rush of air blew into his face, like a punctured tire, and the odor of it was strong with a vegetable smell. He drew the knife sideways. "We've hardly got any supplies," he said, "except for what's in these packs. We've got nothing, except one another, I guess. Oh, and a couple of sacks of jewels. You guys are my only friends. I wouldn't be able to do this if it wasn't for you."

Tomtar and Tuava-Li said nothing, but they felt Matt's love like a glow in their hearts. The sensation made Tuava-Li feel

Ill, and she thought of the maps she had destroyed up on the hill. She thought of their destination, and what Matt was going to sacrifice when they got there. She grabbed one edge of the leathery skin of the Cord and pulled it down. Matt pocketed his knife and pulled the upper edge as high as it would go. He peeked into the Cord and listened to the dull rush of air. "All clear," he said. "Let's go."

END OF BOOK TWO

ACKNOWLEDGMENTS

THE TITLES of the books in my *Elf Realm* trilogy—*The Low Road*, *The High Road*, and *The Road's End*—were inspired by several things. One is the old song "The Bonnie Bonnie Banks of Loch Lomond," the lyrics of which concern a dying soldier. Far from home, he tells his friend that his spirit will return to its homeland via the low road, which some scholars believe is meant to be an underground passage where faeries travel. I was also inspired by the quest of the mythic hero, a literary tradition going back at least as far as *The Odyssey*. Finally, the road is a metaphor for everyone's personal journey of discovery. In these troubled times when we must address the consequences of global warming, nuclear proliferation, economic meltdown, and worldwide pandemics, it's important to remember that we're all on a perilous quest, and the road we choose will define not only who we will become but what becomes of the world we live in.

I am inspired by the quest of all those who choose to do the right thing, even when it is the difficult choice.

My heartfelt thanks and appreciation go out to the Amulet team, whose work and dedication remind me that the strongest books are a group effort. Editor Howard Reeves keeps his eye on the big picture while finessing the details, art director Chad W. Beckerman applies ingenuity and style to the virtue of consistency, and marketing director Jason Wells applies light so that people will not fail to see there are jewels glimmering off the beaten path.

For help with research during the writing process, thanks go to my uncle Jesse Porch and my cousin Kent Porch, avid hunters who provided me with knowledge about the tools of their avocation.

Thanks also to the models for my illustrations, Miranda, Paul, Thea, Greg, Jack, Jane, Fred, Allison, Ivy, Raleigh, and Russell, none of whom are Elves or Trolls!

ABOUT THE AUTHOR

DANIEL KIRK has written and illustrated a number of bestselling picture books for children. He lives in Glen Ridge, New Jersey, with his wife, three children, and a rabbit. For more information about him, visit his Web site: www.danielkirk.com.

THIS BOOK WAS ART DIRECTED

and designed by Chad W. Beckerman. The text is set in Cochin, a typeface designed by Georges Peignot and named for the eighteenth-century French engraver Nicolas Cochin. The font incorporates a mix of style elements and could be considered part of the Neorenaissance movement in typography. It was popular at the beginning of the twentieth century.

The illustrations in this book were made with charcoal pencil on Arches watercolor paper.